About the author

Nina de la Mer was born in Scotland and
now lives in Brighton with her husband
and daughter. *4 a.m.* is her first novel.

4 a.m.

NINA DE LA MER

Myriad Editions

First published in 2011 by

Myriad Editions
59 Lansdowne Place
Brighton BN3 1FL

www.MyriadEditions.com

1 3 5 7 9 10 8 6 4 2

A CIP catalogue record for this book is available from the
British Library.

ISBN: 978-0-9565599-5-1

Printed on FSC-accredited paper by
Cox & Wyman Limited, Reading, UK

For Roly, with love

'The Army Catering Corps course is the hardest in the Army – no one has ever passed it.'

Old Army saying

Chapter One

Cal

I nick tae the block and check on Manny. Are my eyes playing tricks or what? Forty-eight hours later and he's still buzzing – sprawled on his pit, throwing out shapes wi his hands in the air, music blasting fae his stereo. Still, the vital signs are there, so I fling him a 'Back in a bit' and march across the parade square tae the cookhouse.

Ye've got tae be kidding me.

The kitchen thermometer's only went up a degree in the few minutes I've been gone. Insult tae injury, it's an Indian summer and the fans are on the blink. One degree higher and that'll be me, melted away tae a greasy spot. But there's bugger-all use complaining, so I get tae work, my hands shaking as I dice the onions and mince the beef, my eyes watering as I add the sweating bulk tae a vat of oil. *Hisssss*. The air clags thick wi bogging, fatty smoke. Oh, Christ, I think, my mouth swimming wi liquid, I'm never?

I am.

I'm gonnae boak. I'm defin-ately gonnae boak.

Deep breath in... deep breath out... and the danger's over, just in time tae add the garlic before the mince mixture burns. From the other side of the kitchens Corporal Clarke throws me daggers. I wince.

'Wilson!' That's him, Clarkey, his temples swelling in irritation as he shouts over, 'Look lively! That food's going out on the hot plates in half an hour… and counting!' he adds wi a fake smile.

'Yes, boss,' I reply wi mair enthusiasm than I feel, a shower of sweat pouring fae underneath my chef's hat. I wipe it away, my hand wilting in the heat. Whoops! A few beady drops splash intae the spag bol. I grin.

'Slop jockeys', the other squaddies call us. A slagging I wouldnae contest, the night.

Today's going fae bad tae shagging worse.

Nine hours I've been here working like a daftie, huvin as much fun as an ice cube in a sauna. Manny's only got himself a sick chit, and guess who he buttered up tae cover fur him? Aye, right. Muggins here.

But hang on, before yous take me fur some kind of misery bucket, chill out – it's no my usual style tae pish and moan. In fact the other lads call me Happy, after wan a they seven dwarves. They'd say that's 'cause I'm 'happy-go-lucky'; I'd say they're taking the urine, 'cause I'm only five foot five in my bare feet.

Anyway. Truth be told, the reason I'm on a downer is on account of all the dirties Manny and me done this weekend. Dirties? Dirty rugs. Drugs, yeah? Which reminds me. He's needing something tae bring him back down. I know! Orange juice. Manny's always on at me: 'Vitamin C's a bender-mender; it sorts you right out.' I huvnae a clue if he's right. But who knows? Mibbe it'll huv wan a they – what d'ye call it? Placebo effects.

C'moan, Cal, concentrate! 'Scuse me a minute while I deal wi the spag bol – a bit of seasoning here, a stir there. Nope. Still looks and smells like shite. Whoah! Here comes the boakiness again. If Clarkey doesnae let me vamoose soon, my liquid brekkie's gonnae end up in the lads' dinner. I do a recce tae see how the land lies fur a quick exit. Nae chance. The others on duty the night are just the type of cunt tae land you in it, if ye let on ye've been out on the randan.

'I'm watching you, Wilson,' Clarkey bellows over the din of ten lads and lassies scuttling like ants across the cookhouse.

My face becomes a mask of pure hard graft.

That Clarkey, he's an arse-wipe, so he is; loves a whinge mair than he loves himself. Just. I'll gie yous a fur instance. Say he parked on double yellas and the man gied him a ticket, he'd make a fuss, get violent even mibbe, even if he was in the wrong. Or say I made a mistake in the cookhouse, that'd be me in the *merde*, even if I apologised my cock off and all that malarkey. That's just the kind of cunt he is.

Och, c'moan! I'm gonnae fuckin burst if I don't get out of here, right now, this minute! There's nothing fur it but tae raid the fridge and shove an OJ carton under my whites, telling the other lads, 'I'm away fur a pish.'

Clarkey watches me, eagle-eyed, but what can he do? If ye've gotta go, ye've gotta go, eh?

Still, I cannae be too long, so once again I bolt back tae the lines and find Manny Bert-alert, eyes hanging out his heid, continuing his manual re-enactment of the raver's favourite dance move – big box, little box, big box, little box.

No change there, then.

I decide it's time fur action. 'C'moan, pal,' I say, 'yer no gonnae come down if ye carry on like that!' and, offering him the juice, 'Here, get this down yer neck.'

He doesnae move a muscle, but. I fling the OJ carton at him in frustration. Tae my shock and surprise, he catches it. No flies on him, even if he is in fuckin la-la land. Not that he drinks it, mind, just tosses it fae hand tae hand as if it was a ball or something.

Is he acting it, or what?

'C'moan. I huvnae got all day. Gonnae just make an effort…?'

Silence.

'For me?' Fuck me, he's almost got me begging now. 'Please?'

Then, out of nowhere, he gives up, opens his gub, and knocks back the OJ carton in a wanner. Watching him gulp it

3

down, my own comedown smacks me in the face, as if tae say, *I'm here, ye stupit bastard, did you really think ye'd got away wi it?*

Away tae fuck – I'm no huvin that!

I check the coast is clear and rack up a quick line of speed, putting two fingers up tae the comedown, as well as the regiment. Aw, c'moan! Yous can hardly blame me. Only a wee wan tae get me through the arse end of my shift. The minute the bitter white stuff hits the back of my nose and throat, my heid clears and I waken up. Right. I can do it – a wee while mair and I'll be in my pit and in the land of the big zeds. Besides, going back tae the cookhouse doesnae seem so bad wi a wee bit of billy up my nostrils.

Och, no. What now? Manny's only back at the happy-clapping, grinning at me, making zero effort tae come back tae the land of the living.

I am beelin now, so I am.

'Nae bother!' I spit out sarcily as I turn on my heel tae leave. I mean! He husnae thanked me fur risking my backside tae bring him the juice *or* fur covering his arse again. Double whammy! I storm out, imagining masel like wan a they comic book characters, smoke blowing out my ears, clouds of dust following behind.

Back in the kitchens I take a pure maddy, banging the pots and pans and accidentally on purpose smashing a few plates. My anger doesnae last long, but. I mean, Manny's my best pal here. We've pallied about thegither since haufway through the basic training, even though he's a soft southerner. Aye, he tried tae pull the Big Man act when we first met, was up himself 'cause he'd started his Army career training fur the infantry. Still, the rest of us chefs soon twigged how hard he is – about as hard as a bag of marshmallows, if yous want tae know the truth. It was mibbe when he put his Take That calendar up in the kitchens that we finally hud him sussed. The numpty.

If ye forget the boy bands, we've a lot in common, me and Manny, so we huv. Both scored the same on wur Army

4

entry tests. That is, no very highly. Not that I came up the Clyde in a banana boat, as my granda used tae say. I mean tae say, I'm no stupit. Manny neither. The main thing we huv in common, though, is wur love of the rave. Kept us sane back at the training down Aldershot. Okay, yous've got me. Insane's probably mair like it – going tae the dancing Saturday nights, getting zebedeed fur days on end.

Anyway. Ye know how an Eccy buzz makes you pally up wi folk, even if yer just after meeting them? That's how it was wi Manny and me. Pure bezzie pals after wan all-nighter at the Rhythm Station. There we was, hammering the dance flair tae the sounds of DJ Slipmatt when we clocked wan another across the smoky room. Buzzed off each other all night, then broke back intae camp, tunnelling through a piece of broken fence. And that was that – bezzie pals fur life.

Talking of the rave, it's often misunderstood, if yous want my opinion. Folk that aren't on the scene, they think raving's all about drugs, forgetting that it's the music that sends most ravers mental. Och, okay, scratch that, it's the combination of the two that's magic: like bacon and eggs, beer and fags, Kylie and Jason... Alright, alright, I'm kidding yous wi that last wan. But tae get back tae my point. If yous huvnae a Scooby what I'm on about, yous'll huv tae take my word fur it: there's nothing beats hardcore rave music on this Earth. The banging bass lines, the breakbeats, the speedy-up vocals.

Sorted!

Oh, and while I'm on the subject, I was forgetting another reason the lads call me Happy. I'm intae 'happy hardcore': it's got mair BPMs than your common-or-garden hardcore, it's mair euphoric and uplifting, working harder tae get yer heart racing and yer blood pumping. Problem is, Manny and me huv seen mair of the above than a fitba fan at an Auld Firm game, so we thought we'd knock it on the heid fur a bit. Ye know? Go straight; sort the heids?

Aye, right. The other day wur pal Taff turned up wi some Eccies we'd asked fur a while back, and Manny had the bright idea tae arse the whole lot in the wan go. Nice wan, pal! You see, I'm no intae double dropping so it was a mathematical certainty he'd end up in a worse two-and-eight than me.

So, he starts off on Thursday wi two tablets – snowballs they were, the wans that fuck you right up. Aye, I know I said he was soft, but when it comes tae the dirties he's harder than a fuckin brick wall. I took just the wan tae start. I'm no being funny but I like the dancing too much, so if I'm on Eccy and we're no at a rave I hold back, otherwise my mind can go off on a ramble. Sometimes I even think of the bad stuff, like my da dying, my ma's love of the cheeky water, and how the Army's no lived up tae expectations. Aw, c'moan, yous can put yer hankies away. Plenty of time tae use them by the time wur stories are finished.

Anyway. Where was I? It's Thursday, Manny's double-dropped, I'm on the wan, we're both trying tae act casual, waiting fur the Eccy tae work its magic, when he says tae me, 'I'm thinking of jacking it all in, mate, going back to Southend. Fuck the consequences.'

Kick in the baws, or what? I mean, I know he isnae huvin the best crack ever, but leaving? So I goes, 'C'moan. Who'll I pally about wi if you go AWOL on us?'

His answer? 'You'll always be alright, you will.'

And I was thinking, *What's he mean by that?* but I didnae huv time tae mull it over 'cause my fingers were tingling and my heid was birlin, which could only mean wan thing – coming up – so I made my way tae the lavvies fur a dump. Job done, I took a look at masel in the mirror. I get obsessed by my reflection when I'm coming up 'cause the size of my pupils tell me whether the gear's working and how far gone I am.

That night they wernae saucers, they were fuckin flying saucers. I was defin-ately buzzing.

Thing is, the rushes were coming on so thick and fast that my eyes went skelly. Took me a pure hauf-hour tae feel my way along the corridor tae wur pit, me and the wall being best of pals by the time I'd finished. And obviously I avoided the eyes of any square pegs walking past me in the block – nothing worse than huvin a serious blether when the dirties are kicking in. But would yous believe, by the time I got back, Manny hud only gone and dropped his third E?

Houston, I thought, *we huv a problem.*

Little did I know he'd wind up doing four by 4 a.m.

Which reminds me. Best check on him again. I glance at the clock, willing it tae be heading towards six. Wicked! Five to!

'Come on, you mongs!' Clarkey bellows, and the whole kitchen becomes a hive of activity: tomato soup, kedgeree, spag bol, raspberry bombe and baked Alaska all on the menu, the night.

My part of the menu's ready, so I lug this culinary delight tae the hot plates in the mess hall, and wi a, 'Night, Clarkey,' I lug my ugly self back tae the accommodation; my eyes going thegither now, I'm that shaggin tired.

Ah, here I am at wur block, my pit and my pillow just beyond the door, which judders as I open it, my body screaming fur some –

C'moan tae fuck! Yous willnae believe what Manny's up tae now, the crazy bastard?

'Manny! Oy, Manny, get down fae yer pit!'

He's standing on his bed, wearing nothing but his boxers, by the way.

'Aooooouuuuuuuh!'

Who's he think he is? Tarzan, King of the Jungle?

'Hoy, Manny.' I go. 'Keep the heid.'

Aye, yous are right, it's a losing battle – he's away wi the fairies this time, mibbe all the way tae Neverland, and without a return ticket. My throat closes up and my palms start sweating – somebody's sure tae come in and clock what's going down.

'Come on, ye tube, pull yersel thegither!' I say. I've lost all patience with his antics now.

'I am invincible.'

What's that? He's mumbling something at me, through a spittle mouth.

7

'Manny, pal, gonnae speak – "
'I AM INVINCIBLE!'

Alright, alright! Nae chance of missing that yin: he's pure hollering now.

But no sooner has he opened his gub than he buttons it and falls back ontae his pit, launching intae some major zeds. There's nothing else fur it. I lay him in the recovery position and bunch down next tae him, in case he takes a baddie.

Aye, I could leave him there tae choke on his own boak, but – as yous huv mibbe already guessed – that just wouldnae be me.

Pte C. Wilson
231042189
BFPO 179
4 Sept 1993

Dear auntie Edie

Its bean a while so I thought id drop you a line and let you know how im getting along. Lifes treeting me not so bad but I do still spend too much time board out my brains. Sometimes youd think we serve up shite with sugar on top seeing the looks on the other lads faces! As you would say, so I don't feel bad for swaring. I cant wait for my next leave when Ill cook a rare feast for you and uncle Bob.

Im looking forward to a wee hug as well as I do get lonely sometimes. Ive got my pals around me. Remember Manny and Iain? There good pals and make life bareable and we all go to the dancing when we can which just about gets us through the boardom. Though Ive been trying to take it easy and consintrate on my work the last couple of weeks. I hope uncle Bob is okay and helping with the messages and that while your legs bad. Sometimes I think hes so lazy he wouldn't get out of bed if he won the Pools. I hope your getting on and not missing me too much.

Please write soon and tell my cousins to stop being so lazy and write to me. There letters put a smile on my face.

Love from Cal

Fallingbostel British Army Base

Manny

I'm sweating worse than a paedo in a playground, so I shake the gorgeous girl lying next to me awake. *Babe, open the window, will ya?* Phwoar! While she does as she's told – good girl – the towel wrapped round her slim, tanned body slips to the floor to expose her massive... (Manny!) She pouts, her fuck-me eyes pleading, like some grot-mag slapper. *She really wants it, she does*, I think, as her hand slips towards my... (Manny!)

What the fuck? It's Amy! My ex! Nause! How did I...?

'Manny! Wake up, ye lazy cunt. It's seven o'clock.'

Seven o'clock? Fuck about. Must be a PT morning. Physical training. No chance of me making that – ten hours' kip and I still feel like a bag of shite. Then I remember, nah, it's Sunday, on duty but no PT, and I slouch back into the comforting filth of my bedclothes and the filthy comfort of my woody... Cal's bang out of order cutting my dream short just when things were getting interesting, even if I was fooling around with my ex. Can't be arsed to go into that messy little story right now.

'Aw, mate, give us five,' I say. 'I'm well sketchy.'

'Now there's a surprise after what you pulled this weekend. C'moan. I'm no kidding. Up. Shower. On duty.'

'Oy, oy!'

The fucker's only dragged off my sheet, exposing my naked body – crown jewels and all! Alright, alright, I know sleeping naked in a shared room's weird, but if you had to sleep in a feckin' sauna, you'd have yer kit off and all. Anyway. There's no effing way I'm getting up: my head's pounding, my mouth tastes like a badger's arse and my comedown's probably gonna

9

cling to me all day like a bad fart. I screw my eyes shut, trying to drift back into the sexy mood of my dream.

Not if Cal has anything to do with it. 'Your fuckin funeral, pal, if you want tae end up on ROPs again, and no weekend passes.'

Shut the fuck up, you big girl's blouse! That, I'm screaming on the inside. Out loud, I just go, 'Yeah, yeah, whatever.'

'Laters,' our other roommate, Jonesy, says, flobbing out the window on the way out.

'Oy, oy!' I shout – meaning at the spitting. Christ, that lad gets on my tits with his filthy habits. Been following us about like a lapdog recently and all, trying to get in with us and that. Trust our luck to land only three in a six-man room, but end up with Jonesy as the spare prick.

Anyway. Cal really lets rip now he's out of the picture. 'Cheers, pal – what happens then about wur trip tae Hamburg this weekend? I'm no being funny but yer no just fucking things up fur yersel, are ye?'

Fair dos. Stay in bed now and there's no way I – or anyone else – is getting battered at the Tunnel Club in Hamburg, Saturday night. The thing is, no other fucker's prepared to drive, so if I land up in the punt they've had it.

'Alright, alright, keep yer knickers on,' I say. 'Give us a minute.'

Fuck all this 'going straight' malarkey. Couldn't take another weekend without a healthy dose of my medicine, if you catch my drift. I mean, I ain't being funny, but the only thing's gonna get rid of this comedown is coming up again. Specially when OJ's done nothing for me this time, apart from leave a ton weight on my pelvis.

I am fucking aching for a slash!

Pissing in my pit's not an option – I get enough shit from this lot as it is – so with maximo effort I kick off my sheets, scowling at Cal as I make my way to the bogs.

'Good doggy, off you trot,' Cal goes, flicking me on the arse with a towel – the wind-up merchant.

A toxic stench swamps the late summer air, overpowering me as I get nearer to the bogs. Yup, that's it – the unmistakable reek of *eau de crap*. I cough up a glob of sick and wipe it away with the back of my hand. I guess one of the lads has only gone and staged another dirty protest. Would you believe some joker finds it funny as fuck to smear his own shit over the cubicle walls and graffiti in it with his finger?

Here we go: *You are fuckin dead meat.*

Whoah! That's well suspect. My eyes dart about; that ain't aimed at me, is it? Wouldn't fucking surprise me. I'm not exactly Mr Popular round here.

Not surprised the graffiti shit artist has lost it either, mind you, living in this fucking dump. Still, don't give him the right to fuck up the bogs for the rest of us, does it?

Lucky I only need a slash for now, so I head for the urinals… pull out my dick as I go… steady myself against the wall with both hands as I empty… try to control my breathing. It's difficult, 'cause when I think of the amount of gear I done over the last forty-eight hours, my chest squeezes in and out like one of them accordions. I close my eyes for a second, try and blot the anxiety out. Wish I hadn't bothered.

Behind my eyelids my own guilt and dread gang up to chew me out:

Only got yourself to blame, intya, ya gob shite?

Better to open my eyes and deal with looking and feeling like shit in the cold light of day. Fuck, no, that ain't much better! There's still a load of negative thoughts twittering through my brain.

I feel like kicking something, like blubbing, disappearing into a black hole. It's as if everyone hates me, and I hate them; or something bad has happened or is about to happen; as if something's not right with the world but I'm fucked if I know what.

In short, my chums, I'm consumed by The Fear, that nagging post-drugs-binge worry that you did something majorly not big or clever the night before.

Right now, I have got The Fear big time.

I mean, did I say summit to Cal last night that I shouldn't have? Did I fess up to what's doing my nut in? Nah, couldn't have done, wouldn't have done. He's been a blinding mate to me. Still, there are some things – some things you don't even tell yer mates.

Got to watch each other's backs in this game though, innit? Especially 'cause Corp Clarke's been breathing down my neck more than usual recently. He's always had me down as a loser, a fucking nobody, 'cause he knows the truth about me leaving the infantry training. Now though, he seems to really have it in for me. Went and reported me to the troop sergeant for having an 'incomplete kit' the other week, and I copped a beasting – had me marching around the football pitch carrying a sack of spuds on each shoulder. Yeah, yeah. Doesn't sound that bad, does it? But it was twenty-five degrees in the shade that day; he's lucky I didn't get heatstroke.

Still, could have been worse. Corp Clarke's got form for dicking me about.

Yeah, and we all know why that is, don't we?

Fuck about! Things have gone pretty tits-up when even yer own thoughts have turned against ya, eh?

I try and block them out by humming a favourite tune as I slope over to the block.

I'll take you up to the highest heights,
Let's spread our wings and fly away...

By the time I get back the dorm's empty. Cal must have fucked off to the cookhouse without me. Oy, oy! I know what you lot are thinking, but get back in your prams. Yeah, he's been good to me. Being late for once in his life wouldn't fucking kill him, though, would it? Fuck's sake, where's my fucking gear – my whites? Could have sworn I had my kit out ready before we started our session the other night. What a top buzz, though. A shiver of pleasure runs through me. Worth

12

the agony I'm going through now. That's what it's all about, people: the agony and ecstasy. What I'm all about.

Course Clarkey's waiting for me when I finally rock up to the kitchens. Two minutes late. It might as well be two years.

'Oy. You. Manning!'

He's striding towards me as if I've told him I fucked his mother. In the arse. Here it comes. The Payback.

'SNCO kitchens – and you're lucky that's all I'm dishing out to you, you woeful little cretin.'

He's got to be kidding me. I don't mind rustling up the scran for the lads – quite enjoy the banter as it happens. Cooking for the officers, that's a different story. Fucking complaining wankers, they are. Everything has to be 'just so'.

And this, he's having a laugh, ain't he?

Got to make two hundred marzipan rosebuds to go on some Rupert's wedding cake! A cunt of a job at the best of times, never mind when my arse is hanging out my elbow.

I glance sideways at the other lads. Yeah, course. They've only gone and jiffed me up, 'cause I'm late again. Nothing like sticking up for your mates. I throw out evils to anyone who catches my eye. Cal don't have the guts to look at me, of course, making himself busy chucking potatoes in the chipping machine. Still, at least I'll be flying solo, can get lost in my own thoughts, not have to speak to any fucker.

Like they want to talk to you – loser!

Fuck about! There's them negative thoughts again. I try and shake them off as I walk over to the counter.

'Right, mate,' Clarkey goes, a token gesture of friendliness 'cause he knows he's landed me in the *merde*. 'Made these before?'

'Um, yeah. I guess you just have to, um, make sure the marzipan's thin enough to, um – '

'Come on, speak up, son.'

What I wouldn't do to punch his lights out.

'Yeah, you have to make sure the marzipan isn't sticky, and it's thin enough to shagging roll out – '

13

Death stare from full-screw Clarke.

'Corporal,' I add in the nick of the time – best to be formal with Clarkey when you're in the shit.

Seems to do the trick 'cause he goes, 'Okay, fill yer boots,' and stomps off, leaving me to roll out the marzipan. Fuck about! What a mare. Make it too thin and it breaks, too thick and it won't look right. I settle on my third attempt – I mean, who gives a flying one if the Rupert's wedding cake looks like it came from Tesco?

Always cutting corners, eh, you useless slacker?

Fucking hell, mate, concentrate, I tell myself, *ignore your constant self-loathing and self-pity!*

I try and do just that, and start again from scratch, laying down the marzipan and rolling it into a soft smooth ball. 'Perfectly pink', they want the roses, so in goes one tiny drop of red food colouring. Looks more pukey pink than perfect. Whatever. It'll have to do. Next, I lay out the wax paper, starting to roll out very fine layers of the pink gunk between each sheet – the thinner each layer the better, to make sure the roses are delicate. Then, as precisely as possible, I cut out three circles for each rosebud petal, overlapping each one to roll it up into a cylinder. Whoah! My fingers surprise me with a massive tremble as I try to roll up the first petal. This is hardly the job for someone with the shakes, I tell ya.

I'll take you up to the highest heights,
Let's spread our wings and fly away,
Surround you with love that's pure delight,
Release your spirits, set you free.

There's that tune again. Baby D, 'Let Me Be Your Fantasy'. Wicked!

And as it continues to rumble around my head, I rack my brains to remember the last time I heard it out at a rave. Fuck, yeah! It's that last time me and Amy went to Dreamscape, with my crew back home. She and I had a stonking row, over –

14

Hold up. I don't want to think about that. Why did that little nugget pop up? Always freaks me out, that. How thoughts steal their way into your mind, as if some evil ghost-fuck had whispered them in your ear. So now I'm thinking about thinking. Where do our thoughts come from? And that one too. Where did that last one come from? And that, why that? Fuck about! A fella could go fucking mental if he went on like this all day.

I tune in to the *tick, tick* of the big clock on the wall instead, trying to blot out all this other shit chasing about. Don't want to look at the time, mind you – I've probably only been at it for half an hour. But yeah, you guessed it: now the 'what time is it?' seed has been planted I can't help myself. I steal a quick look. Harsh! Over an hour to go till lunch, or, put it another way – another fifty sodding rosebuds.

It's not like me to be a clock-watcher, as it goes. Hate them, in fact. I was brought up to work hard. Had to. My mum's a teacher, my dad's a copper, always pushing, pushing, pushing me to make the best of myself. Yeah, yeah, Cal's started on his life story, now you're getting mine. What did you expect – one of them books where the characters appear out of thin air?

Anyway. Right now I can't stop myself looking at the clock. I think: if I can just follow the second hand round for one tour of the clock-face without chucking up, throwing a whitey or screaming, *That's it, you got me, I'm a fucking druggie*, then I'll be alright till the end of the shift.

One. I button my lips and clench my arse cheeks together, to stop myself fainting like a girl. *Ten.* I take a few deep breaths to stop my heart from going like the clappers. In out, in out, in out. *Twenty.* The last, tiny frail rose I've made rebels, gluing to my hands. *Forty.* What's stopping me from doing one? Holding my hands up, handing myself in for drugs and fucking off back to Blighty? Fastest fucking way of signing yer papers, so they say. Answer? Fear, most probably. Don't want to leave Cal in the shit, neither. *Sixty*! Right. Times that last minute by what – seventy? – and I'll be out of here faster than a virgin jizzing over a porno.

15

Cal

I'm feeling brand new in my civvies, happy tae huv ditched my whites fur the last time this week. At last! A weekend off! I'm wearing my Firetrap DayGlo waistcoat, white gloves stashed in the pocket fur the dancing later. Mibbe I'll even lumber a lassie in the Tunnel Club, the night. Ye never know. As my granny used tae say, 'What's for ye will no go by ye.'

The sweet smell of blow kisses the air as I walk up the short path tae Iain's. A group of pad brats are playing fitba in the street, making the most of the weekend. 'Goal!' wan a them shouts and they do an OTT celebration, their smiley wee faces depressing the fuck out of me fur some reason. So do the rows of pad houses, the accommodation fur the married squaddies: two-up, two-down, all the fuckin same, a red-brick monster sprawling over this area of camp.

Anyway. I guess I huvnae tellt yous about Iain yet? He's aulder than the rest of wur crew, pure thirty-wan, a Tankie lance jack living here in Fally wi his wife Kelly. Manny thinks Iain's the bees' knees, even if he is a grave-nudger. I'm a bit more – what d'ye call it? Cynical. He gets on my nerves, always moaning about something tae do wi his house. What's he want, the place tae burst out in fairy lights? At least he's got his own bit and the love of a good woman.

Speaking of her, Kelly's a nice lassie, even if I think her heid does button up the back. I mean, she comes over like she and Iain are pure loved-up, while he's off visiting the Pink House every chance he gets. That's wur local hoor house in case yous are lacking in imagination. But Iain, honest tae God, I never met anybody so randy. Never mind wearing his heart on his sleeve, he wears his cock and baws an aw! Kelly's alright, but: doesnae have an eppy when us neds hang about her house all day, smoking. Well, tae be fair she's a huge toker herself, especially after working all day down that gift shop on camp. And if yous must know, she's a right wee stunner...

Aye, Iain doesnae know he's born where Kelly's concerned, right enough.

Aw, c'moan man, gonnae answer the door!

I'm like a wean waiting fur Christmas, pure bursting fur the weekend, 'cause I've hud a nightmare week by the way. Clarkey had Manny and me pan-bashing – that's tae say helping the LECs, the civvies, wi the washing-up – as a punishment fur 'not pulling our weight' after wur bender. Tars me wi the same brush as Manny even though I worked that double shift. Take this afternoon. We're just after finishing the pot-washing fae lunch when Clarkey goes, 'Right, Jock the Cock and Manning you little shit bag, you can get scrubbing them pans again.'

Aye, gie us a brush, I'll shove it up my arse and sweep the flair an aw.

That, of course, I didnae say out loud. Instead, I plunged my arms intae the grimy water and gied him a, 'Yes, boss,' and a winning smile. As I huv mibbe already indicated – I. Hate. That. Cunt. Thinks he's funny as fuck wi that insult: 'Jock the Cock'. Stupit bastard cannae think of a better slag word than a wean in a playground.

Where *is* that sex pest Iain?

Och, I know. Likely he's up the stairs poking Kelly. Why? 'Cause there's bugger all chance of Manny and me going hooring wi him the night, that's why. I turn up the volume on my CD Walkman, tapping my feet, shivering in anticipation of wur night out. But that doesnae help.

'Embdy haim?' I shout through the letterbox, and see Iain, at last, bouncing down the stairs like a loon. He opens the door wi a dirty great grin on his coupon, his hand outstretched.

'Alright, son.'

What he's doing wi that 'son' is trying tae make out he's a pure hard ticket, by the way.

'Alright,' I go back, shaking his hand, as if we were bastartin businessmen or gangsters or something.

I shuffle intae the house after him, my nerves jangling. 'Kelly no about, then?'

'Just freshening up, son.'

There's that 'son' again, accompanied by a big, sleazy wink this time.

I feel like saying, *Aye, got the message loud and clear, SON, ye've been doing the hot and nasty*. But, me being me, I crap it, and sit down on his flash white leather couch, which farts as I plank my arsehole on it. I quickly change the subject.

'So, the others no here yet?'

'Nah,' Iain mumbles, hand down his trousers, adjusting his crown jewels, 'Tommo ain't coming out; 'spect Jonesy and Jay'll be here in a mo. Fuck knows what time Manny'll rock up.'

In the background, BFBS, the forces' radio station, is droning a cruddy pop tune before the rave show comes on. Otherwise, there's an embarrassing silence while Iain fishes about fur Rizlas, burns a lump of hash, and starts tae build a reefer. I drum my fingers on the arm of the couch... yawn... try tae think of something tae fill the quiet.

I settle on Iain's second favourite subject. 'We – um – sorted, the night, then?'

'Too right, mate,' he replies, rubbing his hands thegither.

I shift about on the couch, getting mair embarrassed and uncomfortable by the minute. I mean, 'son' is bad enough, but 'mate'?

'Me and Taff went down the Dam last week,' he continues. 'Mate, you should – '

Ding dong!

Thank fuck fur that, saved by the bell – the cavalry huv arrived. Well, I think, recognising the voices coming fae the hallway, as long as the haemorrhoids crawling out of Iain's anus, they wee hangers-on Jonesy and Jay, can be called 'the cavalry'.

'All set for a big night, then?' Jonesy says to the room in general as he sashays in. But hold on, Manny's right behind them. I catch his eye, and we share a 'what a tosser' kind of look. I mean, big night? What's Jonesy know? It's his and Jay's first time up Hamburg.

Iain, perking up now he's got an audience, replies on everyone's behalf. 'Too right, a big night. Was just telling Cal. Me and Taff drove down to the Dam this week, got hold of some new pills. Fucking blinding, they are.'

Oh, go on, lay it on thick as per usual, I think.

'Tried them out the other night,' he says. 'Doves. Make you well loved-up.'

Jonesy and Jay's coupons light up as Iain reaches under the couch and fishes out a bag filled wi small round wans, Manny turning his back on the three of them as they huddle over it, making a 'wanker' gesture wi his fist.

I snort out a laugh and Iain whips back around. 'Finish making that doobie, will ya?' he snaps, handing me the – what's it? paraphernalia – and, turning back tae the others, 'Go on, lick 'em, they're the real deal.'

We do as we're told, me getting tae work on the spliff, Jonesy and Jay mumbling the expected oohs and aahs of appreciation: Tweedle Dum and Tweedle fuckin Dumber. Manny, meanwhile, makes himself busy rifling through Iain's CD and tape collections. Iain's no wrong, mind. Ye can tell a good quality Eccy if it tastes bogging when ye sample it. Not like aspirin or paracetamol which have a chalky flavour, Eccy has a weird, bitter edge tae it, that gies you the boak. Now there's a tip if yous ever need tae buy some Eccy off a dodgy-looking cunt – just gie it a lick.

Anyway. Not satisfied by Jonesy and Jay's brown-nosing, Iain hands me an Eccy – just fur quality control purposes, yous understand; we're saving the main event fur later.

I lick it, and nod. 'Ya dancer! This is good stuff.' And I mean it, I'm no just kissing the brown ring like the others.

Another thing I'll say fur Iain is that he does get the best gear: Eccies, blow, acid – the lot. Not that I'm intae marijuana. I'm no even intae ciggies if yous want the truth. Aye, yous've got me, I'm skinning up as I say this, but when a cunt like Iain hands you the gear, ye do as yer told. Ye don't want tae look like a prick, do ye?

Only no sooner huv I put the finishing touches tae my artwork than Manny grabs the spliff and takes a humungous toke. I'm about tae gie him what fur when Kelly appears in the doorway, her long wet hair hanging limp at her side, a big fluffy white towel covering up her tiny body, showing off her pretty shoulders and neck. Whoops! The towel's slipping; looks like that's not all she's gonnae show off... I look away quickly and stammer, 'First dibs, pal,' at Manny, thieving back the doobie. Okay, so I'm no a fan of the wacky baccy but I don't want tae look like a cunt in front of her, do I? Och, alright, I know, I know. But that's how it is in front of mates, eh? Always trying tae save face.

I give Kelly twos-up on the spliff before she goes off tae get dressed, and then we lads sit and smoke in silence fur a bit, nodding wur heids tae the sounds of the DJ Ramos. Till, all of a sudden, Manny leaps up, and jokes, 'C'mon lads. Get your coats. You've pulled.'

His words kill the spell of the breakbeats and the blow, and we tumble out the house, full of giggles. I'm haufway down the path when I wonder if Kelly's coming along and turn back tae see her, standing on the front porch, the lights and music sorry-seeming in the house behind her.

I mosey back up the path. 'No coming out, the night?' Kel's always good fur a laugh on a night out, so she is.

'Nah, didn't fancy it,' she mutters, her eyes resting on Iain fur a second as he slips past her out the house.

'Oy, leave old twiglet legs alone,' he says, 'girls' night in, eh, Kel?' Her only reply is a limp wave. Nothing limp about the way she slams the door shut after him, but. *Bang!* I jump, and wonder fur a second if the noise might shatter her tiny frame intae a thousand pieces.

I soon forget about her, though, 'cause outside, on the way tae the motor, the air's biting and brisk, and I flashback tae going intae the school gates fur a new year. I used tae like that feeling, that things might change and everything was new, always promising masel that this year I'd make an effort.

Aye, right.

By the end of the day I was always back tae my auld tricks, ignoring the teacher, flicking the lassies' bra straps, and generally being a ned. But I put these thoughts out my mind the minute we pass the camp gates, as Iain sticks on a new mix tape, Manny puts his foot on the accelerator, and we wheech towards the A7 and Hamburg.

Manny

The sentries on the front gate give me a thumbs-up as we leave camp. Good bunch of lads stagging on this evening. Result! No third degree when we come back KFC'd later. KFC'd? Deep-fried, get it?

My hands slacken their grip on the steering wheel. I was well on edge then, back at Iain's. Don't get me wrong, Iain's sound as a pound. That gear he gets, though – blows your fucking mind. Had to exit sharpish before the lads sussed I was spinning out. Feel better now. It's like the minute that security barrier at the gates lifts you can forget all the Army bollocks, be yourself again.

Whoah! I swerve back into lane. Gotta concentrate!

Tonight's gonna be a good 'un, I reckon. Still, I ain't feeling quite right; there's a crowd of noises in my head: Jonesy and Jay chuntering on, the sounds of Iain's mix tape, the whirr of white noise in my own brain. They're doing my nut in, as it goes.

I check my rear-view mirror. Fuck about! There's only a police car racing towards us... I take the speed down a notch. Not that them German rozzers give a fuck if you give it some welly; there's no speed limit here on the *Autobahn*. Still. Can't be too careful, what with all the medicine we're holding.

'... so I said to the sarge: I dunno, sarn't, am I looking at it?' Jonesy's saying, the punchline to some dick-weed story, exaggerating as per usual. An 'Elevenerifer' we call him. You know: you say you've been to Tenerife, he'll tell you he's been to Elevenerife. Christ, that nasal whine of his. It's pissing me right off. I zone in on the bass of the car stereo instead, an electronic distraction from Jonesy and my jitters:

Here's another chance for you to dance with me...

Oh yes, oh yes! I fucking love this tune. 'Sound of Eden'. It's the dog's bollocks.

'*Every time I see the gi-irl,*' Jonesy and Jay go in unison with the voices on the tape, high-fiving. Fucking sissies.

'Oy, Manny. Ye remember they played this wan out that last time we went tae the Rhythm Factory wi Amy?' That's Cal, doing his best to wind me up even more. 'We fuckin run to that dance flair, mind?'

'Oh, yeah, Cal, wasn't that the time *blah, blah, blah,*' Jonesy's going, saying something or other of fuck-all note, always wanting to join in with whatever we're taking about.

Cal ignores him. Not surprised. Jonesy couldn't have been there that night – he wasn't in Aldershot at the time! He's such a little scrote. Can't even be arsed to describe him and Jay properly to you lot. I mean, no point; you wouldn't remember them if I did. And it's not like he means much to our story. Not yet, anyway... The thing is, every now and then a few new lads hang about with us. 'Cling-ons,' Iain calls them. Then, after a couple of months of partying hard, they can't take the pace and go back to being wallpaper with all the other straight heads.

Meanwhile, for my own reasons, I'm ignoring Cal. I'm not being funny, but Amy's the last person I want to think about before a heavy night out.

He don't take the hint, though.

'You remember!' he continues. 'That time we drapt they rhubarb and custards. Amy was massaging the fuck out of us all night.'

Fucking Cal. He's a good lad but he can be a right nause when he gets on the gear; not giving the yapping a rest like the rest of us.

'C'moan!' Cal goes on, leaning through the gap in the seats to slap me on the back. 'Ye was stripping down tae yer boxers, and the bouncers come over. Amy was laughing so hard she wet her knickers…?'

I keep stumm, but I'm thinking, *Of course I fucking remember*. On top form, Amy was that night. Got a letter from her the other day, as it goes. Banging on that 'a different time and place we'd have done alright', that she's worried about me being sent down to Bos (as if!), and how she hated dumping me, but she couldn't hack the months of being apart.

Yeah, right.

I feel about for my ciggies. Fuck about – somebody's had them! They was definitely in the top pocket of my puffa jacket back at Iain's.

'Alright then, what joker's had me fags?' I say, relieved to change the subject.

'Not me,' Jonesy pipes up, right away.

In the mirror I notice Cal shrugging his shoulders – yeah, course, he don't smoke ciggies unless he's battered.

'Are you sure they was in your pocket?' Jay goes.

'Yeah, yeah,' Jonesy says, wide-eyed, one of them blokes who hates being accused of anything, 'didn't you leave – '

'Sorry mate,' Iain interrupts, smirking as he pulls a fag packet from his jacket pocket. 'Must've picked them up by mistake.'

He flicks the bottom of the pack with one finger and a ciggie pops out. I take it, keeping my eyes on the road, sparking it up as we pass the first road sign for Hamburg.

'Right. Listen up, you lot.' I go. 'Do you think I can get five minutes' peace, so I can concentrate on me fucking driving? Alright for you, just sat there yapping.'

'Ooh,' Iain goes, holding up his hands as if to say, 'handbags!'

But they button it, all the same. At last. Just the tunes, the hum of the engine, and the sounds in my head that, like the beat, go on and on and on.

Cal

We screech tae a stop in the car park at the edge of St Pauli, spilling out the motor in a fankle of limbs. It's wet in Hamburg, the night, the backdrop of the bars and sex shows almost pretty-looking fur a change, the reflection of their neon signs wobbling like jelly in the puddles.

Iain, cock-swinging as usual, drops his first tablet as we walk past the polis station. He assumes, I guess, that the German polis huvnae a Scooby what he's popping in his mouth. That's just like him tae take risks. Tae take another recent example: if wan a they mooching Monkeys, the military police, hud walked past his gaff this afternoon and hud caught a whiff of blow, that'd've been him – locked up or on ROPs. It's all the same tae Iain, but. He doesnae huv the same boundaries as other folk.

It's gonnae be rare, the night. Been feeling like something amazing's gonnae happen all day. In my baws, no less. At the same time they're aching with a kind of sickness, mind, as if the Kiez is tugging at them, trying tae infect us wi its sleaziness.

St Pauli, or the Kiez, as the locals call it, is Hamburg's red light district, by the way. Aye, I know yous might think, *Squaddie, you pure love it*. The truth is, I cannae bring masel tae window-shop in they sex supermarkets on the main drag, the Reeperbahn, never mind go in. Aye, honest! They plastic dildos and blow-up dollies turn my stomach. But it's like the Kiez is way too powerful – ye breathe in and ye cannae help but sook up its sweaty, nasty air. And ye wouldnae huv tae be a dirty auld man to spot all the prossies provoking on every street corner.

I suppose it mibbe being raised in a God-fearing house, but I would never pay a lassie fur sex. Not that I'm wan a they folk who carries his religion like some lads carry johnnies. I mean, something tae huv at your disposal in a time of need – it's deeper than that.

24

Sploosh! Away and fuck – a giant puddle. Aw this thinking and I've no been looking where I'm going. My trainers are soaking!

'C'moan, let's crack on,' I say tae nobody in particular, and we pace it, turning down a back street, past a huddle of prossies outside Burger King on the corner.

'Wait up,' Jonesy says as him and Jay hang behind, eyeing up the talent. The numpties. First rule of the Kiez is no eye contact wi the tarts or they'll be on ye like a seagull after a chip.

But Tweedle Dum and Dee soon catch us up – probably remembered they don't know the way – as we turn ontae Friedrichstrasse, a creepy street at the back of the Reeperbahn. Aye, creepier even than the Reeperbahn itself, where at least there's some honesty about the sleaziness. Here, the windaes of the knocking shops are blacked out so ye can only guess what goes on behind them. Tonight a sheen of rain on the black makes the street even seedier. I shiver. Lower my eyes as some tarts mince past... still, it's got tae be done, 'cause among the sleaze of Friedrichstrasse is Purgatory. The bar, no the place of sin-cleansing and repentance, by the way. Its wur usual stomping ground before a night out.

Three guesses why.

Aye, right first time. The bar's an Aladdin's cave fur drugs, so it is.

The place is decorated like an Aladdin's cave an aw, flashing lights twinkling over the bar, the bar itself sparkling wi glitter. Anyways, description over.

I will say this, though: if yous are ever in Hamburg and yous are needing fixed up, just head here tae Purgatory. There's a wee guy, props up the bar, Welsh accent, coupon like a joiner's nailbag, he'll soon sort yous out. That's wur pal, Taff. An ex-Army lad whose girlfriend binned him as soon he got his exit papers. Come straight back here after, saw a business opportunity wi the hordes of squaddie ravers, and has been dealing ever since.

There he's now, pattering away wi the locals in fluent Kraut. Fair play tae him – about all I can manage is '*Tschüss*', '*Dankeschön*', and '*Ein Döner bitte*'.

I elbow my way through the throng and get Taff in a hauf-Nelson. Not in a homo way or nothing. I'm just happy tae see his wee rat face after a few weeks away fae the fun of the Kiez.

'Happy, my main man,' he chuckles, patting my back. 'Iain, Manny,' he nods at the others. Iain and Taff huv got what ye'd call a business relationship. No love lost between him and Manny neither.

'Jonesy, Jay, this here is Taff,' Manny goes.

Taff gives them a once-over and has them sussed in a second, turning back tae his drink without even bothering his backside wi a hello.

'Drink, anyone?' Iain asks, breaking the habit of a lifetime.

He loves that German lager and orders a *Grosses*, his coupon deadly serious. C'moan tae fuck! Face tripping him even when he's drapt an E!

'Yeah, mate, I'll 'ave a *Weissbier*,' Jonesy says, showing his true colours as yer typical beer-swilling kind of squaddie.

'Me too,' says Jay. 'Ckin copycat!

Manny and me keep it real, sticking to Cokes, saving wursels fur the Class As later.

I am loving it now, so I am. Nine fuckin weeks of working like a daftie, of Army shite, will soon be zapped intae space by an evening of fun, drugs and techno.

We're gonnae be on wan soon!

Aye, too right we are, I think, tapping my waistcoat pocket tae check on the tablets Iain sold me earlier. At the same time he turns his back tae the bar, handing over a bag of goodies tae Taff in a covert operation – the weekend supply. Seems we've all got the same thing on wur minds...

A few swallies later, and we steam intae the night, loaded wi E, booze and plain auld excitement. I drop back so Manny

26

and me can walk thegither and we march like that, two-by-two, towards the Tunnel Club, six shining examples of Her Majesty's finest.

Manny's no saying much this evening. If yous want the truth, I'm fuming that he slung me a deafie in the motor earlier. I dunno what's got intae him recently. Nothing's gonnae spoil my mood, but, so I'm happy tae advance in silence, dropping my first tablet as we slop along the rain-soaked Reeperbahn... past the slot machine rip-off joints... past the tacky souvenir shops... past the gay lads and their fag hags... past the young ravers, like us, out fur a night of excess.

My heart does a flip as we turn the corner intae Grosse Freiheit. I hear the beats dancing out of the bars and clubs and I feel like laughing out loud.

Yes, yes, yes! We're gonnae get right fucked-up!

Above us, the neon signs of Grosse Freiheit's bars and discos act like a magnet fur Hamburg's partygoers, tempting the punters in. We keep going till the biggest temptation of all is smack bang in front of us – Tunnel Club. Not much of a queue, the night. Wicked! 'Cause of the rain mibbe? Outside, the bouncers are a wall between us and party-heaven. We shuffle past them, baseball caps pulled low, avoiding eye contact...

...and we're in!

No way, man. It's mobbed inside. Everyone must huv come early 'cause of the rain, or tae make sure they got in; that famous DJ Sven Väth's playing, I just noticed. He's no bad. I mean, it's no like there's a hardcore vibe here. Still, the German trance does the job when I'm on wan.

I'm on my way back fae a quick trip tae the lavvy when the DJ drops a classic, 'Marmion', and that's me: tingling, buzzing, coming up on my tablet... and the strings at the beginning of the tune are swallowing me whole... I'm rushing all over, my E has taken hold: my face, fingers, ears, heart, lungs, kidneys, cock, liver, every vital organ pure eaten up wi pleasure. I give in, a slave now tae the rhythm and the E.

I'm a pneumatic drill on the dance flair, pounding my life out tae the bass. I check my watch. C'moan tae fuck: 2 a.m… *doosh doosh doosh doosh*… I wipe the sweat from my brow… whoah! another euphoric rush… this is too much, man… *doosh doosh doosh doosh*… I'm gonnae huv tae chill fur a bit… I slide down the wall; push the air out my lungs in big 'oohs'; think about a wee sit-down. The DJ has other plans fur me, but. Another booming and blinding trance classic, 'Vernon's Wonderland'
hands in air, touch the sky
Manny and me high-five
buzz off each other
T-shirts peeled off
a warm E'd-up hug
sweat dewing wur chests
gluing us thegither
'Yer alright mate, yer alright,' Manny's going. 'I love ye, pal, you're the fuckin dog's baws,' I gush back. And we slap backs, pump fists, share another E'd-up hug. But we're in tune wi wan another… wi wan another and the music… we don't want tae miss out on wur chance tae dance like mental
so we break apart again
reach up high fur the stars
make patterns in the air
kick wur feet, jump wildly
do whatever the fuck we like
'Whoop, whoop, whoop,' I yell
gotta keep bubbling, moving
gotta keep up wi the tempo
And the smoke machine pumps out… and I wheeze as it blows over… and there's Jonesy and Jay, good lads, they are, good lads, and Iain's handing out fags… och, he's a good pal too, so he is… just misunderstood is all… and he hugs me, his mouth stretched out in a gurn, and I'm pulsing, throbbing, rushing, riding the E… until the beat breaks down… and I swoon… comedown… it's as if I'm treading water as I melt slowly, slowly back tae normal as the DJ's mixing in the first rhythms of the next tune.

Then, as the whispers of smoke are drifting away, and I'm still coming back tae the land of the living, I notice two lassies pointing mine and Manny's way, smiling.

No way, man! They're coming over.

'*Blar blar*...' This wan tall, skinny lassie's leaning in Manny's ear. She's the wan wi all the patter.

Her pal, though. Wow. Her pal. She is gorgeous, by the way. Long blonde hair, wearing a tiny dress – a real arse-freezer.

doosh doosh doosh doosh

'*Blar*, Hamburg, *blar*...' the skinny wan's continuing.

doosh doosh doosh

What's she on about? They tunes are too fuckin loud. I lean in closer.

'So, what's it you said, *blar, blar*, in Germany?' she's saying.

No way, man! They're speaking English!

We're driving back tae Fally. I'm in the front wi Manny, keeping him company as he drives; the others are giving it some zeds in the back of the motor. Manny and me huv got the verbals, cannae stop talking. 'She said this', 'they pills were that', 'Jonesy and Jay pulled it off – they're no such straight pegs, after all'; wur coupons pure fizzing wi pleasure, just one thing on wur minds – what a night.

Pure. Dead. Brulliant.

Chapter Two

Cal

Feeding time at the zoo.

That's how my ma used tae shout me in fur my dinner. Until she stopped bothering her puff tae cook anything worth eating, that is. Which was about the same time she took tae the Bell's like a duck tae water. Aye, no coincidence there, then. Up till that point she'd been a rare wee cook. Pies, flans – anything wi pastry, they were her speciality. I lick my lips and wipe away a trail of drool as I bring tae mind her mutton pies. Out of this world and better than they wans fae the butcher's. Saturdays we used tae have them, wi a pile of baked beans and a bottle of ginger, sat huddled round the box watching *Starsky and Hutch* or *Wonder Woman* or whatever new American show was on. It was magic.

Then the love affair wi the cheeky water began.

I mean, she'd always been a drinker. After my da died, though, the bottle swallowed her whole and didnae have the good grace tae spit her back out. Now, if she hud tae give out prizes fur her favourite things, the winners would be – like they say – in reverse order: 3. her weans; 2. God; 1. the bottle. I'm no surprised they social workers decided I should live with my auntie Edie and uncle Bob back in the day. I cannae mind when exactly. Mibbe I was ten? What I do remember is when the tasty smell of good home-cooked food in wur house made way fur the reek of whisky and stale fags, that when ye fished at the back of cupboards fur sweetie treats – Tunnock's, Creamola Foam an that – hauf-empty whisky bottles clunked out instead. This wan time a full bottle of Bell's flew out and smashed tae smithereens on the flair, cutting my feet tae fuck. Would yous believe my ma gave me a row for that? As if it was my fault! So even though I was greetin like a babbie the day my auntie Edie came tae take me away, and my ma was – what's it? incon-soul-able – I think it was the best thing fur wur family.

Alright, alright, I'm mibbe getting a wee bit like wan a my gran's Catherine Cooksons here, so I'll gie yous a rest fae all that shite fur now. Why was I thinking about it, anyway? Oh, aye.

Feeding time at the zoo.

Exactly what I see as the illuminated hot plates cast a murky spotlight on the animals burping and fighting and slurping in the mess hall. Behind them a row of miserable-as-fuck chefs getting ready tae plate up. C'moan tae fuck! This is the best bit of being a chef if yous ask me: seeing the grateful faces of the lads as they come through the hot plates. But honest tae God, they other chefs. Thick fucks. Hauf of them couldnae run a flag up a pole; the other hauf wouldnae be arsed to try. Me, I just get on wi it. I'm happy tae huv a chance tae hang out wi the other lads: the Tankies, the REMEs, all of them. Best thing is tae laugh along if they dish out the slaggings as ye dish up the scran. Mibbe I'm too laid-back but I like it: like hard work, running about stupit; don't even mind being barked at by the screws and hauf-screws. Apart from Corporal Clarke. I reserve the right tae despise being given a roasting by him. Lucky he's on leave at the moment.

Hope he takes a long walk off a very short pier, wherever he may be.

I whistle softly as I heave a huge saucepan over fae the hot plates, shuffling to and from the kitchen tae refill the metal trays wi this and that shite. Aha! Yous see. Whistling while I work like wan a they stupit dwarves I mentioned before.

Right, here comes the second sitting, a line of lads preparing themselves tae expect the unexpected: elbows jostling, eyes peering over the glass counter, nostrils flaring.

Aw, cool, first in line is Davie, wan a Manny's pals fae the infantry training.

'Awright, Davie boy, what can I get you?'

He looks at the hot plates slanty-eyed as if they were the fuckin enemy. 'Where've you had your grubby mitts?'

'Beef stew, pal,' I say, knowing what's coming next.

'Kedgeree for me then, chum,' he says wi a twinkle in his eye. I plate it up wi no bad feelings – Davie's a good lad, really.

'I hear you had a good time up Hamburg Friday,' he then says. 'Bit of success with the ladies?'

Well. He was a good lad till he come out wi that. I take a pure reddie and fuss about wi a plate of stew fur the next in line. Man, ye need fuckin octopus arms tae do this job!

Davie doesnae get the hint, though. 'So, come on then, spill it – you gonna see them again?'

Now I'm getting evils as a bottleneck of hungry soldiers builds up behind Davie.

'Anything else, mate? Veg?' I say, tetchily. Davie points at wan a the metal trays and I dollop a suspect-looking pile of green gloop ontae his plate. Wur eyes meet over the UFO (Unidentified Fried Object) and we both chuckle, breaking the tension.

'Na, I huvnae a Scooby either,' I say.

And he comes back, as he plonks his plate on his metal tray, wi, 'Fitters and turners, mate.'

That's another slag word the lads huv fur us cooks, by the way: 'fitters and turners'. Somebody tellt me this is 'cause we 'fit food intae saucepans and turn it intae shite'. Doesnae bother me. I get on wi the fitting and turning and if the result tastes worse than a poofter's bum crack, so what? There's always Maccy D's in Fally if yer that hungry. Besides, mostly the lads don't insult the scran tae wur faces. Fear of the legendary chef's 'special sauce' puts a stop tae that. Davie can get away wi it 'cause we're pals.

Should have told him really, what's going on wi they lassies. I mean, it's no like he's wan tae take the pish. If yous want tae know, Manny called them, the day. The first surprise is they didnae gie us a fake number; the second is we're gonnae meet them the morra in the Tunnel Club again. Thinking of a lumber's making me high as a kite, and work less of a nause, tae use wan a Manny's favourite expressions.

Hold on. Who have we here?

'Alright, mate?'

Iain, fully suited and booted in his regimental gear, is at the back of the line. What's the fucker doing in the singlies' mess? I mean, I know he says Kelly cannae boil an egg, but still.

Fuckin bean-stealer.

He points at the beef stew, mashed potatoes and the green stuff. No 'please', no 'thank you'.

'Brand new, thanks. How's about you?' I answer after a pause, spooning out a ladleful of the mysterious greenness. 'Kelly no around, then?'

'Mrs H. senior has only gone and broke her leg. The missus has gone back to Blighty to help her out.'

'That's a shame, pal.'

'Shame? Too right. Wrong time of the month for her to be off.'

'Eh?'

'Wanted my bad boy swimmers to 'ave a go.'

I drop my eyes tae the mashed potatoes.

'You know,' he goes in a hushed voice, 'at her eggs.'

Stunned silence from yours truly.

'Oh, come on,' he bangs on. 'Facts of life? Babies?'

'Och, aye,' I say, 'Nice one,' thinking, *Yeah, yeah, I got it, big mouth*: trust him tae be after the two-point-four kids tae add tae the trophy collection!

'Anyway, you know what her being offski means, don't ya?' he says, changing the subject, thank Christ.

'Well, don't ya?'

Eyes twinkling.

'While the cat's away...'

Wink, wink.

I shrug.

Which makes me wonder if I've described Iain tae yous yet? Aye, I know I've tellt yous he's a skirt-chaser wi a vengeance and slimier than a bucket of jizz but huv I described him tae yous? Looks-wise, I mean? Well. All I'll say is, he could defin-ately pass fur the good-looking wan in a boy band. And no the wee cutesy wan like Mark or Stephen, mair the classic babe-magnet like Howard or Ronan. Och, hang on there just a mo – don't get the wrong idea. I'm no a shirt-lifter. But, unlike some lads would claim, I do know a good-looking fizzog fae a Hallowe'en mask.

'Happy, you listening, son? I was saying why don't you and Manny come over tonight, play some cards, and that?' The 'and that' emphasised, so I know he's meaning something dodgy. Davie, who's sorted out his pudding, gives me the thumbs-up, glares at Iain, and walks off in a huff.

When he's out of earshot, I blurt, 'Could ye no have invited Davie? He's sound, pal, I can vouch fur him.' By sound, I mean that he isnae likely tae grass us up tae the SIB. I mean, he's as big a toker as anyone.

'Nah, mate, Taff's shouted me an ounce of weed for my birthday; don't fancy sharing it with that no-mark.'

Fuckin Iain. He's good-looking, right enough, but as I've mibbe mentioned, he's that shagging tight, he wouldnae gie you the itch. 'Suit yersel,' I say tae his drab olive-green back. Aye, he's already marched off, no even waiting tae hear whether we'll be there tonight. He knows we will. Same auld story – Iain says jump, we ask how high.

Finally, my shift's ended and I plonk masel down next tae Davie, who's identified the green gloop fae before as creamed spinach. I didnae eat earlier, and despite being hungry like the wolf I'm way too excited tae get anything down.

We're gonnae meet up wi they lassies!

Their names are Steffi and Emma, by the way. The wan I fancied, the wee feisty wan, she's Steffi, and the tall, leggy wan, that's Emma. Steffi, she's German, studying at the university, and Emma's English, but at uni as well, on some sortae exchange thingummy.

We didnae speak fur long but that Steffi, there's something about her. Ye know, when ye meet somebody and it's like an electric shock? C'moan, yous must know what I mean? It's as though yer body's been hit wi a thousand volts… yer alive, buzzing… turned on wan hundred per cent tae life? Och, I know, it sounds mental but I'd swear there's an energy in the air, that sparks are flying, even as I think about her and the night tae come. Not that I can remember her face exactly; all I can picture is a hazy parade of blue: indigo eyes, dark blue dress, bright blue eye make-up.

The soundtrack tae this daydream is a tune I love which drifts lightly like smoke at the back of my mind while I eat.

Just close your eyes and dream with me, you'll hear the sound of music,
Just close your eyes and dream with me, I'll take you to a place of wonder.

And I do just that, close my eyes, the words echoing lazily in my heid, till the screeching of Davie's chair pulls me back tae reality, and he's saying, 'Nice one, chum, thanks for that.'

See that's what I like about Davie – he's polite and thoughtful.

So the next time yous assume squaddies are all uncivilised and uncouth, remember that in the Army, same as on civvy street, there's the kind, gentle folk and there's the obnoxious cunts.

Manny

'Leave it out, mate, you'll be there tomorrow night. I'd bet me next month's wages on it.'

I scowl at Tommo as I lay down the ace of clubs on top of the ten of hearts.

'Twenty-one!' The others stare in wide-eyed disbelief – it's ace high and I'm on a winning streak. 'Thank you very much, gents,' I say, and make a big show of opening my arms up wide to sweep up my winnings: a *Zehner*, a half-empty packet of ciggies and a blimsworth of hash. But still, winnings all the same.

'Nah, mate, seriously,' I say in reply to Tommo. 'If you're gonna drive I don't need to come. Gotta calm it down a bit or the CO's gonna shit a fuckin baby.'

Would you lot believe, I'm in seven degrees of *Scheisse* again 'cause me and Cal's been going at it like billyo since our supposed 'break from drugs', caning it more than ever before? Hardcore till we die, we are. The thing is – and I don't want to sound like a pussy – but I don't want to fuck up my Christmas leave by irritating the Master Chef even more, turning up late, or in a state, or what have you. So, I've made a little pact with myself to rein it in a bit; you know: go straight for a while?

'Oh, leave it out,' Tommo goes again, as he flicks open the ring-pull on his, like, gazillionth beer.

'Yeah, serious. Ain't gonna happen.'

Cal's sort of like staring at me in disbelief. Probably 'cause he's so fanny-struck with that German bird, he thinks he needs me as a wingman. In the cold light of day, I'm not that interested in that Emma, though. I mean, how could anyone compare to my Amy?

'Think I'm gonna call it a night.'

That's Iain, kicking at the riot of debris – lager bottles, Rizlas, coffee cups and that – covering his fluffy white rug. Talk about putting a downer on things! We look from one to another. Surely he's not hitting the hay 'cause he's lost at cards?

Does he want us to fuck off? Not like him to be the first to bang out.

'It's alright, lads, you can hang on,' Iain says. Reading our minds or what? 'Got a big day tomorrow and want to be fighting fit. Just tidy up before you leave, will ya?'

Course, I forgot Iain's motto: 'work hard, play hard'. That's how he gets away with so much. But before he heads upstairs he surprises me from the doorway, by saying, 'Manny, a word in your shell-like?'

For cunt's sake. Why's he singling me out? I follow him into the kitchen, fearing the worst. An accusation of cheating? Chewing me out for not coming out tomorrow? I rack my brains for something I might have said or done to piss him off.

He runs the tap, fills a glass of water, then leans back against the kitchen counter, grinning from ear to ear.

'So, matey, don't you want to know what you've won?'

'Won?' I repeat dumbly.

'Yeah, man, you won overall tonight, didn't ya? And your prize,' he says, tapping his hands on the counter in a makeshift drum-roll, 'is a trip to the Dam with me.'

'Oh, yeah?' I say, secretly pleased, but trying to stay cool. 'When's that, then?'

'A few weeks' time? Thought we could drive down there, get baked, meet a few ladies...'

I groan at this, but actually I'm dead chuffed he picked me, if you lot want to know the truth. Yeah, it's a small thing maybe, but what you don't realise is that it's not like I've ever been part of anything before. Didn't do well, or fit in, at school. No fucking point, what with my mum and dad going ape 'cause I didn't get into the boys' grammar. All that stuff my mum and dad spouted's a load of bollocks anyway: 'Anyone can go to university these days, son; work hard and you can go anywhere, that's what Mrs T says.'

Thanks, Mrs T, thanks, Mum, but if you mean I can work hard to become one of them loadsamoney dickheads, then forget it. Would you believe the old dear wanted me to become one of them red-braced City boys, flashing the cash, all out for themselves? I don't think so. But YTS wasn't exactly my cup of tea either. Supposedly being trained to be a joiner, but getting all the shit jobs with fuck-all money to show for it. Fucking liberty, man! Not that I'm greedy, but still I can't deny I like getting kitted out in the right clobber, wearing the right trainers and that.

'Manny, mate. You on for it, then?'

'Yeah, yeah, man, sorry, lost in thought…'

And as Iain goes to bed, shouting, 'Laters, lads,' into the other room, I spark up a fag in his kitchen, thinking about my parents a bit more. Had to get out of their place in the end. It was like they'd read a textbook on how to wind up your kid: *You treat this house like a hotel*; *What time do you call this?* All them clichés churning out like one bad joke after another. In the end it wasn't my decision to go anyway, 'cause our house was repossessed. Mum landed in court bawling her eyes out, practically begging them for more time to pay the mortgage. Soon shut her up about England being the land of opportunity when her and my dad had to move back to my nan's. So the dream I'd always had of joining up came true. And just in the nick of time. No room at Nana's for a fucking layabout. My dad's words. And, well, in spite of everything, I'm kind of glad I did join up. Being a chef's class, if only the Army didn't expect us to be feckin' soldiers first, chefs second. That's where it don't feel right, where I don't fit in.

Probably just as well things went tits-up during the infantry training. Me not liking the soldiering bit, I mean.

Anyway. That feeling of not belonging, that's probably why I love the raving so much. With that, it's like Cal and me, we're free, but part of something at the same time. The all-nighters, the pills, the smoky dance floors, the lasers, the bubbling and moving, the banging tunes, the smiley faces, the blissful highs – all them things bring us ravers together like one big happy family. Fuck the bond you're supposed to get in the Army; it's nothing like the bond you get when you're hugging

38

your mate on a crowded dance floor – nothing. Yeah, too right. I tell ya, I would fucking die if I didn't have my raving. That's it! Go straight? Forget that fucking shit.

I put my fag out with a new resolve, and stroll back into the living room, where Cal, Tommo and Jonesy have started another game of Twenty-one. I chuck a bit of loose change on the now beer-stained rug, and go, 'I'm in.'

'Good man, good man,' Cal says. 'And tomorrow? Come on, pal, you know you want to…'

'Oh, yeah. Course. I'm in. I was always in,' I go, half thinking I've made the right decision, half thinking things might go totally Pete Tong.

Hamburg – Kiez

Cal

We take a short cut through Ten-Mark Alley, 'cause Steffi's desperate for a pish. It's a mistake. Ten-Mark Alley (called that fur obvious reasons by the way) is wan a Hamburg's 'men-only' streets. One time we come down here and this lassie got covered in a bucket of pish that was chucked out wan a the windaes. Ye see, the tarts don't like girls walking down here – think they're bad fur business or some shite.

'*Na, du Arschloch!*'

Bugger. We've been seen. An Asian girl stood in a dingy doorway further up the *Strasse* continues the slagging, calling out some more stuff in German, then firing a glob of spit fae her brightly painted mouth. It whistles like a bullet through the air and lands at Steffi's feet, missing her trainers by a millimetre. I pull her towards me, brushing up against her soft skin as the scabby-minged creature continues tae whistle and catcall.

They're out in force the night, the tarts, a pure battalion of them determined tae drag legions of sex-starved males off the streets: bald married men not getting any; young lads out tae impress their mates; nervous-looking teenagers getting their first times over with, their skin erupting in acne volcanoes; everyday men, desperate men, ugly men and good-looking men, randy men and men who cannae get it up. Aye, it's a wonder there are the other kind of men, right enough – the 'not interested' wans like me. Not that Hamburg gives up. Poking and prodding at ye every time ye walk its streets – tits in yer face, pussy flowing freely as lager, it's all fur the taking.

If ye want it, that is.

Anyway. Mibbe the hoors out the night are harvesting it like squirrels, 'cause it willnae be long before the days get shorter, and there'll be less folk about tae hassle; business will be harder once they're intae their winter uniforms.

'Cal, let us hurry,' Steffi says, as a small gaggle of women join the pink-lipped hoor tae give us a piece of their minds.

'Okay, gotcha,' I say, using the excuse tae link arms, flexing my muscles as I do – well, if ye've got it, flaunt it, isn't that what they say? I mean. What wi my Mr Potato Head, my muscles are about all I've got.

But I see yous are wondering what I mean by the tarts' uniforms. I shouldnae laugh. I mean, if it was wan a my female relatives sucking off some auld codger tae pay fur food or rent, my sides wouldnae be splitting. Still, their 'uniforms' are funny as fuck. In summer, they wear the Jane Fonda look – leotards over leggings or tights tae show off their figures. In winter, they go fur full padded ski-suits. And come rain or shine, the make-up and hair's the same – '80s poodle perms, the slap pasted on wi a trowel. Look like they've stepped off the set of a Gloria fuckin Estefan video. Anyway. What I'm leading up tae is, I always wonder how they get down tae business wearing all they fuckin layers? Something I should mibbe ask somebody who's an authority on such things.

Aye. No prizes fur guessing who.

'At last,' Steffi says as we dip back ontae the main Reeperbahn. 'That was a near one.'

'Aye, right enough,' I laugh. 'Now let's get ye to the lavvy before you huv an accident.'

'An accident?' Steffi asks, her brow furrowing in a cute way. 'Oh! An accident. *Ein kleines Malheur*, as we would say.' And she throws back her heid and laughs. Always laughing, that yin.

We're pure loved-up now, by the way. I've seen her a couple times in the Tunnel Club and we're just after another brulliant night there. I huvnae kissed her or anything yet but we've hud loads of E'd-up cuddles. And the best thing – get this – the best thing is, we're gonnae be boyfriend and girlfriend!

Aye, too right!

It all happened tonight when we were stood at the bar in the Tunnel, chilling out fur five, glugging back water, when I says tae her, 'I like you, Steffi.'

And she says, hugging me, 'I like you too, Cal.'

'No, I really like you,' I'd went, making masel clear.

And she was like, 'I really like you too.'

'So, we're like, um, we can be – '

'*Ja, ja*, we're friends, Cal, no problem.'

'So, like you mean, we can, go out and that? I mean, just us two?'

'Yes, we can see us as – '

Then Iain, who'd been stood at the bar gawping at us, the nosy fuck, come up and dragged us back tae the dance flair, holding Steffi's hand, the cheeky cunt. Still, that was defin-ately an affirmative, don't yous think?

I huv got me a fuckin girlfriend!

She's forever telling me how she thinks I'm 'super'. Or sometimes she says in German that I'm '*soopi*'. Och, I could go on all day about what a wee cracker she is. And it's not about looks, before yous think I'm shallow as fuck. She's brainy too! Studying German and science and wanting tae be some kind of researcher when she leaves college.

That lassie's doing weird things to my body, though; I'm gonnae huv tae clear the custard soon… Oh, aye, yous mibbe think it's easy – just gie the duvet a dusting back in my pit at Fally. It's no that simple, but. What I wouldnae give fur some privacy, some space away fae prying eyes. And yous can wash yer filthy minds out. I'm no blethering about my need tae wank in peace. Well, no just that, anyway. I'm meaning I'd love time alone tae think about my lovely Steffi, and tae thank God fur making me the happiest man this side of heaven!

Hamburg – Grindelhochhäuser

Manny

That Steffi, she's out of order. Bang out of order! A prick tease, as Iain would say.

There she goes again, batting her eyelashes at Cal, but keeping him at arm's length. Not that he'd do anything about it even if she lay gagging for it, begging him for some. I don't think he's had anyone since… What is it…? A year ago? Still, I'll be chuffed for him if they finally do it; he's well loved-up. And she's a quality bird, I suppose. For a Box Head – a German – anyway. Yeah, a bit loopy what with the weird barnet and the make-up and all that malarkey. Quality all the same.

Emma, though. Can't figure her out. I mean, Iain would tell you that birds usually fall into four categories:

1. The gorgeous girls you'd like for a girlfriend.
2. The NBRs – No Beers Required to give them a right going-over (and who might later become girlfriends, depending how they was in the sack).
3. The slags who you just fuck and chuck.
4. The munters you wouldn't touch with a bargepole.

Yeah, yeah, alright, you lot, pipe down. I'm saying that's what Iain says; they're not my rules, so don't get your knickers in a twist. Besides, I know I'm nothing special myself. (Apart from being tall: the birds love that.) Still, a bloke's got to have his standards. As to Emma, she's sorted and that, but I still can't decide if the lads would have her down as a 1, 2, 3 or 4.

I mean, she's a bit la-di-da for my liking, so you wouldn't exactly want her for a girlfriend. Then again, she's too nice to fuck and chuck. Not that I'd kick her out of bed given half the chance, know what I mean? It's been fucking months since I've had my nasties, since that time on leave I tried with Amy…

'Right, you lot, time to take your medicine!'

We've been here at Emma's place at least half an hour and nobody's mentioned the goodies burning a hole in my pocket.

'Bloody hell, Manny, you're an eager beaver.' That's Emma, piping up her two-penneth. 'We don't need to go out for another hour or two,' she goes. But her eyes are sparkling.

'Okay, kiddies, special treat tonight. We're gonna do some boilers.' I head to the kitchen to boil the kettle and fetch a spoon while Cal throws me a look.

I say kitchen but Emma's place is pretty basic. No better than a squat, really. There's only one room, with a loo in one cupboard and a cooker in another – no fridge. The dozy mare keeps her milk and that cold on a window ledge. Still, lucky cow don't know she's born to have her own gaff.

Talk of the devil.

'What are boilers?' she's asking, suddenly beside me, a whiff of perfume floating alongside as she sidles up. She does look foxy tonight, to be fair.

'Boilers, my dear,' I reply, putting on my poshest accent, 'are a fine method of getting the Ecstasy pill into your bloodstream quicker by mixing your E with boiled water and drinking it from a spoon.' Then, normally, 'In other words: the quickest way down the happy road to lost-it land.'

She pulls a face and glances over at Steffi, who shrugs as if she don't give a fuck. Always up for a crack, is Steffi, I'll give her that. Or maybe it's one of them language barrier things.

'Sorted!' I say drawing out the *rrrrr*, rubbing my hands together as I get to work with the raw materials.

Simple as, really – boil the kettle, let the boiled up water cool down till it's drinkable and mash it together with the E in a teaspoon. Tastes rank but it's worth it – end of the day, the results

43

speak for themselves. I gulp the first one down and the others come in one-by-one for a dose of medicine, Manny-style!

Then the waiting starts. If you've done loads of pills, you'll know what I mean. That time when everyone's pretending to be cool, joking about. You know, nonchalant. In reality, they're waiting for that first hit, that first sign they've not been sold a dud.

To pass the time, Emma sticks on some music, bloody student dirge, that Massive Attack, and her and Steffi start chatting about some German book that Emma's got to read for uni, that she can't get to grips with. Steffi's saying that the reader should have known that it's obvious the main character was gonna kill himself 'cause the 'storm and stress' writers always climaxed with big romantic gestures. That she needs to re-read the book and check out the obvious signs of the tragedy to come. And I think how I hate them kind of books, where the writer drops heavy hints about what's going to happen. Fucking halfwits don't think most people can read between the lines.

I turn my attention to Cal, who's listening, nodding his head, as if he agrees. Like he knows what she's banging on about. Is that really fair, though? I mean Cal, he's one of them people who's well clever but who didn't get the chance for a proper education. Yeah, yeah, another squaddie character from a sink estate. Ask yourself why that is, if you've got a problem with it.

Back to the present, and the girls' chatter is soon chased away by the first vibrations of the pill. Me, I try and ignore them, still wondering about that expression 'storm and stress'. I think it's quite a good one. Cyclone and bloody stress would be a better expression for my life, though. Hold up, think we've got a problem – Steffi looks seasick; her boat race is well green. Don't tell me she's throwing a whitey? Fuck, maybe we shouldn't have gone this far with them boilers. I mean, they're decent girls, not fucking hardcore nutters like me and Happy boy over there.

'Steffi, *was ist los*?' Emma's grabbing her arm and they head off for the bog. Twatted don't even begin to describe it.

This is going majorly tits-up, I think, as the first rush comes on, harsh as a fucking left hook. I try to settle into the familiar buzz but it's attacking hard and strong as a boxer. There's no dodging this little beauty! I purse my lips as the gurning and the eye-rolling takes hold, looking over at Cal to check out how he's doing. Same as, really – pacing up and down, riding out the initial overwhelming onslaught by looking out the window across Hamburg.

'Flash the ash, pal,' he says, and we both spark up a fag, sitting smoking quietly to give us something to do with our hands. *Twitch, twitch, twitch*, my fingers are going; *rush, rush, rush*, my blood courses through my veins; *tick, tick, tick*, Cal's left eye is flickering, something it does when he's stressed.

'Ye think they're okay?' he asks after a bit.

But he's way too spastic with E to continue that line of conversation. Instead he pats my back. 'Gie's another fag, will ye?'

By the time the girls reappear we've done the whole packet, and look at them; yeah, they're cool, and they're smiling. Thank fuck for that! I exhale slowly. They can handle it. Steffi puts this into words.

'I'm zo high!'

I think she means in good way, even if her and Emma do look like they belong on a ghost train.

'Let's go dancing now!' Steffi blurts, fidgeting about. 'I don't like this atmosvier.'

'Yeah, yeah,' Emma goes. 'It's claustrophobic in here.'

'But the club don't open for ages,' I say, and look at my watch. 'Ckin hell! We've been bugging out for an hour. 'Alright then, ladies, let's have it! The loved-up mobile's parked outside.'

'If you think we're driving with you in that state, you're off your head!' Emma twitters, and then, realising what she's said, throws me a big E-grin. 'No, really, we'll get a taxi.'

'Furry muff,' I say.

Cal seconds that. 'Aye, makes sense, we'll see yous there.'

Aw, mate! Could he look any more infatuated? But Steffi's gawping at him just as doey-eyed. Maybe she likes him after all?

We head downstairs in the piss-smelling lift, past the winos huddled in the entrance, the fresh air outside kissing new life into our pills, and the girls run like maniacs to the roadside, flagging down a cab in seconds. Good. I'm not hanging about, no matter how much Cal wants to spend every waking second with Steffi; I cannot fucking wait to get on that dance floor! Soon as the girls have vamoosed, Cal and I leg it to the car, swallowing another tab as I switch on the engine.

'Hey pal, stick on BFBS,' Cal says and I nod in agreement.

'Yeah, yeah, it's the rave show on a Friday night.'

I put the pedal to the metal, and we're halfway into town in minutes, the second pill kicking in early, as we approach the traffic lights at the edge of the Alster.

'Oy, oy, check it out,' I say, spotting the girls out the corner of my eye, 'there's the girls' taxi.'

Cal looks round and throws his hand out the passenger window at the same time as Steffi does from the taxi and they're pissing themselves laughing holding hands across the middle of the road and then the light turns red or is it green...? My eyes roll as a tsunami of Ecstasy surges through me and a jumble of colours appears before me never mind amber red or green...

don't panic

don't panic

deep breath

... Cal pulls his hand back, taps me on the arm, shouting, 'It's green, pal. Go!' and I manage somehow to get my foot on the accelerator and we're driving around the ring road at the edge of Lake Alster towards the Kiez at least I think we are 'cause whooooooah, I am well and truly caned.

Fucking wicked!

Cal's like, 'Follow the taxi. Y'alright?' but he's not worried, he's laughing his bonce off thumping up and down on his seat, cranking up the volume on the car stereo as Ultra-Sonic blasts out, *'Wind it up! We're gonna get some energy! Wind it up!'* and then that fucking killer tune comes in, 'Annihilating Rhythm', and we're both bouncing up and down now punching our fists and I have to swerve to avoid a lamppost with some Kraut bird shouting at me something like *'Spinnst doo?'* from the pavement.

This is the best rush I've had in ages, man.

There's no stopping it.

These birds, what a laugh, never met birds so up for a crack before.

I'm going to have to tell that Emma when we get to town, what a fucking excellent bird she is. And Steffi. Top birds! Top buzz! Forget giving up the pills. I ain't ever gonna give this buzz up! Fuck, another traffic light but this one's definitely green so I go, go, go and keep going overtaking the taxi and speeding up till we reach the car park at St Pauli, stopping as soon as we get there, parking up on the nearest spot and the girls' taxi pulls up too and I can see they're trying to look straight while they pay the taxi driver, only they end up handing him a note, any old note, and running over to us.

It's a cool evening but I'm sweating like a cunt already and finally the girls have catched us up so I say, 'Oy, Emma, love, over here,' and whisper, 'You look aston-aston-astonishingly beautiful tonight,' and she fucking does, her tight red dress contrasting with her green eyes which are nearly black now, chocka with E, and she replies, 'You don't look so bad yourself,' and I think that maybe something might happen between us, you never know.

We huddle together, lowering our eyes as we walk past any strangers; it's all about us tonight, our crew and everyone else can fuck right off as we walk arm-in-arm down the road, joking that we're defending the pavement against enemy invasion. We make it into the Tunnel no trouble. Too right.

Got a fucking bird on your arm, nobody says jack shit, no questions asked. It's fucking heaving so we head straight for pride of place to 'our spot', the balcony overlooking the main dance floor where all the fucking losers wave their arms about like a bunch of epileptics.

With our bird's-eye view over the ravers below, we fucking own the place!

I'm still flying but the effect of the boiler and tab's not as fierce now, so I do a quick line in the bogs, dancing all the while, even in the cubicle, my trainers hardly touching the floor. Back on the dance floor, I'm a jack-in-the-box, up down, up down, a spinning wheel, swirling and turning. Wheeeeeeeeeeee!

I just want to dance my socks off, want to feel this fucking high forever!

Cal hands me the water bottle for a sip – I'm always forgetting to drink it – and pulls me close to say, 'Nice wan tae se ye back on form,' and I think I've been a bit cuntish to him recently, got to be a better mate. And for a second we all hold hands as we jump about: our mate Taff who's dropped by, then Steffi, then Cal, then Emma, then me, and we're all raving like that in a line when the DJ drops our favourite trance tune, that corker, 'Eternity', and as I whoosh up to the highest heights of fuckedness I clutch Emma to me shouting, 'What a tune,' and she leans in and before I know what the fuck's happening we're kissing and oh yes! oh yes! it's like that saying 'sparks flew', which is scary... and when I close my eyes fireworks are going off... and when I open them again I think I'm melting, literally melting, into a puddle of sweat and E'd-up love, and I think maybe this new lot of pills are a bit trippy so I focus on the lasers flying about and slash my hands through them back and forth watching the trail that follows, mesmerised.

We're back where we started at Emma's place and yeah, them pills were well trippy. It's alright, though, we got sorted with some doves later and we was well loved-up again. Back where we started, like I say, at Emma's, as she plays it cool with me and me with her and Steffi's back to stroking Cal's ego. Not stroking anything else, though, is she? Like I also said – prick-tease.

But in some ways we're not back where we started, 'cause Emma catches my eye and smiles and yeah, I meant it too. She is really fucking pretty. I look up at her wall at a poster of Nirvana, Kurt Cobain staring down at me.

Not that you'd let her get close, his look says.

Here it comes. The revenge of the comedown. Out to get me for having a great time for once in my life.

For once in yer life? That's the only thing you're good at, eh, the pills, the fucking about, acting the hero of the dance floor?

Maybe Kurt's right. I mean, my one dream, the infantry, was taken away from me. The one girl I loved, too. And them memories are so heavy, heavy as fucking concrete, in fact, that I know the comedown's gonna be a bad one again, so what can I do but say to Cal, 'Get us a beer, will ya?' And to young Steffi, 'Two's-up on that doobie, love.'

Fallingbostel British Army Base

Cal

I'm sat on the end of my pit, bulling my boots ready fur kit inspection, one eye on the fitba. It's Sunday, the first day I've hud in ages tae do my admin – that is, tae sort my kit, and prepare fur any of the other shagging Army nonsense that goes on. Rarely huv kit inspections these days, but, still, the NCOs pure rip ye a new arsehole if yer boots arnae scrubbed up right, so ye make sure ye *do* do it right if yous see what I mean: melting the polish before applying it in several layers, using the right amount of pressure and never, ever using spit is the way tae go.

Rat-a-tat-tat.

Typical – an interruption, just as the second layer of polish is coming on a treat. I sigh and drag my eyes away fae the game tae answer the door.

'Wotcha. Where's yer bum chum?'

Och, could be worse – it's Davie. 'Aye, very funny,' I snort back, as he breezes in the room. 'If yer meaning Manny, he's away tae the pool wi Jonesy and the others.'

Sundays, some of the lads hang around the outdoor pool we huv here in Fally, sneaking in a few beers, getting lashed up. But today I fancied a dose of peace and quiet, some time tae think about Steffi, and mibbe even do a wee prayer or two. Aye, I could visit the chaplain tae do the last yin, go tae confession even mibbe. And I would, if it wasnae that wur resident padre is a gobshite, providing spiritual discomfort fur any poor fucker who happens tae pass his way.

Davie planks his arsehole on a chair, and says, 'Surprised he's out his pit, what with you lot being up Hamburg again Friday.'

Now, from what yous've heard so far, yous've probably assumed we're all at it, getting pilled up at weekends, raving and misbehaving. And ye'd be hauf right. See, it's like ye've got two Armies living side by side. There's the 'Army Barmy' lads. They pure love the Army life, the routine and the discipline; they've probably wanted tae join up since they played sodgers as weans. Then ye've the lads like us – the ravers and the tokers – fogging up the dorms wi clouds of weed that no amount of Lynx will cover up...

Aw, c'moan!

Yous think we shouldnae be doing it? How no? Every other fucker in the UK is. It's the fuckin '90s! Besides, 'sno like the lads who are getting fucked up arnae good sodgers. It's just that, fur us, the Army isnae the be-all and end-all.

Davie's a weird wan, but. He doesnae fit intae any box. He isnae a square peg – I mean, he has a smoke – but he isnae exactly Army Barmy or a raver neither. Used tae be a skinhead. No the bald, glue-sniffing, racist type, he's way too chilled out fur that. I suppose what I'm trying tae say is he's the kind of person to get on wi anyone. Still, I cannae help wondering why he keeps asking about wur nights out. Och, I know, tinfoil hat time. But it wouldnae be the first time a so-called pal hud grassed up his mates tae the SIB.

Would be surprised if it was the last...

So all I say is, 'Aye, went up that Tunnel Club,' and, nodding towards the telly, 'So, who d'ye think's gonnae win the league, then?'

'What, the proper league? Or that SFL bollocks?'

'Aye, very funny. I mean that Premier League. Doesnae look like your lot are huvin much luck.' Actually I huvnae a clue if his side, West Ham, are doing okay, but that doesnae stop me taking the urine.

'Oy, oy, kings of the claret and blue we are, doing alright since we was promoted.'

'Aye, and ye know the claret and blue came fae Scotland.'

'Eh, what's that?' he says. 'Leave it out, you Rodney.'

'Aye, the maroon's fae Hearts, the blue's fae Rangers.'

'Oh, be'ave,' he goes, aggy seeming now, 'everyone knows nothing good ever come from Scottish football.'

It's that kind of banter that's always going on here, that kind of banter that exhausts me, that I was trying tae escape, the day. It's almost a relief, then, when Davie gets back tae his original point.

'Anyway, I was wondering. Do you think it's a good idea, mate, you and Manny going up Hamburg so often, when he's in enough of the *merde* as it is?'

So that's it. I look at my feet. C'moan, Cal, wind yer neck in, thinking Davie might be a grass. Should huv known he's worried about Manny, them being pals since way back. All the same, convince Manny tae go straight? I'd rather stick my heid in a deep-fat fryer.

So I try batting him off. 'Ye'll huv tae ask him yersel, pal.'

He gets more huffy then. 'Oh, be'ave. You know he's in the shit, that things are going to get worse if he doesn't get his act together. Can't you give him the daddy talk, get him to calm it down a bit?' Then he puts the final screw in. 'You're his best mate, ain't you?'

Fair play. Then again, asking Manny to calm down would be like asking a wean to give up the sweeties – not gonnae happen without a fight. I want tae get back tae my boots and the fitba and my own private thoughts, though, so I say, 'Yeah, nice wan, pal. You're probably right.'

We hang out fur a bit then: Davie telling me about his Tankie mates who've been sent down Bosnia wi the UN peacekeeping mission, me opening up about Steffi, glad tae huv somebody's ear tae bend about her, all the while the fitba blaring in the background – until Davie gets the message and bangs out when I dip my cloth in the water and start on the third layer of polish.

Och, yous are right, as usual.

Davie's spot on. I mean, Manny, he's got bags of potential, and mibbe the pill-swallowing, the late nights and the comedowns are keeping him back.

The thing is, ye wouldnae huv tae be a genius tae recognise that I'd be a hundred per cent legit hypocrite tae ask a pill-monster like Manny tae stop, when I'm as fierce intae the scene masel.

Chapter Three

Manny

Iain's slipperier than an eel on an ice rink as he squirms and slides about in his seat. I try to catch his eye. Fail! S'pose he's avoiding eye contact 'cause he's trying not to split his sides. Split his sides, now that would be feckin' funny! I stifle another guffaw and oh, man, was that a trickle of piss running down my leg?

I can't tell wet from dry, 'cause, folks, I am tripping my nuts off!

The gyrating half-naked girls on the giant video screen shake their things. I look away. One more jiggle and that'll be it – a dead cert that I piss myself laughing.

I mean, I don't want to show us up; we're getting some well filthy looks from the other punters as it is. Why'd they have to show them lame nudey films during the interval, anyway? Ey up, it don't matter, the banging euro-dance music's started up; it's time for the live show again. Here come the girls, mincing it back on stage. Zany feathery outfits this time, their minges showing through lacy crotchless knickers. Hold up, here comes the gorgeous blonde bird, the one with the massive tits. Whoah! She's coming right over to our side of the audience. Iain hoots with laughter as she shakes her bazookas in our direction.

I nudge him, say, 'Fucking big blancmanges she's got,' and we both double up – spastic with the giggles now.

She gives us a V-sign and stomps off in her thigh-high boots – what's she up to? Never mind. Now there's a trio of talent shaking their bits in our general direction: a black girl, one white, one Asian. The United feckin' Colors of Benetton! Oy, oy, here comes Mrs Big Tits again. Nause – she's only got the bouncer in tow.

'Alright, ladsh, fun's offer, time to moff on.'

He's got one of them funny-as-fuck Dutch accents. Comedy gold, it is! I cling to Iain like a limpet, trying to hold back the titters. 'Now!' Mr Bouncer shouts, doing a not half-bad impression of our RSM.

I try and get out my seat but nothing doing, my legs are rooted to the spot. 'I can't move me legs, I can't move me legs,' I explain, between giggles. 'They're stuck.'

He's not having that. 'I help you, then,' he says, and he's lifting me out my seat in one go, booting me in the arse in the general direction of the door. I fall over. Iain goes ape-shit. And meanwhile the increasingly aggy doorman takes a swing at us. Oh, mate! You want to see Iain now. Winding his arms around like a windmill, flailing at the bouncer. I choke back more laughter, putting my hand to my face in case I'm lamped. Mr Bouncer pushes us further into the street – he's determined to get rid.

Iain don't give up, though. 'We want our money back,' he's wailing. 'Give us our moolah.'

I drag him down the street, saying, 'Mate, mate, let's just go, forget the argy-bargy for once in yer puff.'

It don't matter. The bouncer doesn't follow us as we stumble arse-over-tit along the pavement – he got what he wanted, the tosser. And so we stop… catch our breaths… stood outside yet another titty bar, and I'm laughing like a drain.

Only Iain ain't the same, is he? Instead he's got his back to me, leaning against the wall, gasping in fresh air, spluttering, 'Fuck me, they were some bad vibes.'

So much for a feckin' nudey show being 'the best place ever to trip in'.

Let's try plan B.

'How about we find a park, then, somewhere we can trip our nuts off in peace?'

Not exactly the evening we had in mind. The mood Iain's in, though, it might just sort him out.

'Yeah, nice one. Good idea,' he says, pushing ahead.

Can't believe I'm gonna have to hold his hand through this. Hard nut like Iain, having a bad time on trip!

If only my legs were connected to me, I think, *I'd be able to direct us towards some better place. Some place quieter, with no fucking bouncers.* They ain't, though. My legs, I mean. The reverse in fact. Feels like they're made of elastic, stretching out in front of me as I walk. Tee hee! I'm taking giant steps, like I'm moon-walking or something.

'Oy, Iain, look at my legs. Turn round, will ya? They're like Inspector Gadget legs.'

He swivels slowly towards me and… Fuck about! His boat race is well fucked-up, blood and shit spilling from above his right eye. *Change the subject, change the subject*, I tell myself; don't want him to notice.

'Come on, let's find that park, then – you got the map?'

He pulls it out his pocket, turning it this way and that. 'Is this the right way up?'

Like I'd know any better. All I can see are squiggles and lines smiling at me.

Alright, Manny, they're saying, *know your arse from your elbow, do ya?*

Them squiggles have got a point. I mean, the treetops of the park are in plain sight, like a hundred metres away. Fucked if I know how our legs are meant to get us there, though.

'Think we'll have to give up on that one, mate,' I say to Iain. 'C'mon, let's try this way.'

There's nothing for it then but to wander aimlessly… tittering whenever anyone walks past… getting the occasional nod from sussed-looking types. The freaky moment you get on every trip seems to have passed, thank fuck, 'cause Iain was in bits. Better to be safe than sorry, though, so we head away from the red light district, away from Amsterdam centre with its kaleidoscope of clichés – canals, bikes and prossies – which are spinning me out.

Oh, behave. What's going on now? The pavement is rising and falling, falling and rising, in waves. Eugh... and what's that? There's something like sweat oozing out of it.

That'll be the LSD, then, the pavement says, taking the piss out of my confusion.

Fuck about! Not the old talking bloody objects again. And I realise there's no going back – the trip's reaching its peak – as the whole scene suddenly goes pear-shaped... everything bright and cartoon-like, as if someone had taken a paintbrush to the canals and streets, splashing on splodges of colour. I try and blink them away, but then it's like the place is wallpapered with trippy '60s patterns, an invasion of geometrics and flowers and colours stabbing me in the eyes. Holy fuck – what's that? I run my fingers along the glass panel of a bus stop. No, no. I was imagining it. It's not bubbling up or on fire. Still, can't be too careful, eh?

After we've been bumbling about in acid land for what might have been ages or possibly only five minutes, we come across a group of musicians jamming on a street corner, right in the middle of nowhere. The music has got to be the sweetest shit I ever heard. This one guy, the one on the guitar, he's got a voice like an angel. I'm thinking, *This is great, sort our bonces out, lift us out of the intensity of the trip*, when Iain nudges me.

'Oy, stop staring at them, yer freaking them out.'

''Ckin hell, Iain, cheers for that,' I go, 'cause now the musical spell's been broken. And so I drag myself away from the sweet melody and we continue our hallucinogenic journey.

'Amsterdam. It's the real city that never sleeps, ain't it, when you think about it?' Iain says after another while of acid-related fuckwittery. Hmm. Quite a sensible comment from someone so twatted on a tab, innit? Especially from someone whose face is melting. Ignoring that little reminder of my two-and-eight, I'm sort of like awestruck by this comment. I mean, Iain's bang on when you think about it, ain't he? When you're asleep in your bed at night, Amsterdam is open. Like, all the brothels and sex shows, the cafés and nightclubs, the coffee shops and sex supermarkets, they don't ever close. Or say you're at work, doing your laundry, chucking one off – whatever, all these places are still open. Yeah, just think about it, will ya? Any time of day or night, whatever your location, whatever your activity, the prossies are being yarpsed to death, nine bars of weed being sold, old dancing Big Tits and them lot waving their bits. All day and all night long. Amazing!

'Fucking too right, mate,' I say. 'Like, any time day or night, you could come to Amsterdam and do like the most depraved, disgusting – ' I froth at the mouth with enthusiasm but ain't quite sure how to finish my sentence.

Iain waggles his head like one of them nodding dogs, and I think, *How mental is this? We're on the same wavelength. Our brains, they're connected somehow by the trip. We're like the same person. It's… what is it? It's cosmic, that's what it is.*

Cosmic now, is it, ye fucking acid head. What are you? A fucking hip –

But my voices are interrupted by Iain. 'Oy, Manny, no way! Check out that café over there!'

I look over at the window of one of the Dam's many coffee shops and I get it right away. Three words standing out as if they was lit up from behind with giant spotlights.

'Open 24/7'.

And the words shine out, it's as if they was placed there just for us and I think, *Everything has a pattern, it's all related.* Me and Iain, we're linked to the rest of the universe by the force of a magical paper-clip chain, and man, the acid's making this force stronger than ever. Could we even be better mates now than him and Taff, me and Cal? Dunno, mate, but one thing's for sure. Amsterdam. It never sleeps. Never fucking sleeps.

I grip my knuckles tight.

Just let me sleep, let me get some fucking kip.

Fucking micro-dots, fucking Iain. He fell asleep hours ago, or was it minutes? I don't know 'cause I'm in a wormhole and time has stopped and I can't get out and maybe I'll be trapped in here forever. I watch Iain sleeping, bollock-naked, the white light of early morning drilling holes into the curtains. Must be about 4 a.m., then? Don't know how long I've been sat here. Don't remember Iain getting undressed. Or getting back to the boatel. Can't remember the last five minutes, even.

This whole world is fucked to its core, man, when no fucker will let me sleep and the wormhole won't spit me out so I can get some fucking shut-eye. Got a bloody late shift to work tomorrow and all – got to be on good form. Can't think about that now, though, 'cause Iain… Is he? Is he laughing at me while he sleeps? I shut my peepers, willing the trip to stop. Like that's gonna help, what with the dwarves and witches and trolls in my head, who're like – what? Having a what? Having a disco?

Come on Manny, they tease me, *thought you liked to party hardy. Bring your dancing shoes!*

Stop it stop it stop it stop it stop it.

I can control this. I'm not being funny but I've done hundreds of trips so get away to fuck, you dancing troll fucks.

I. Can. Control. This.

I line them up in a row, and tell them, 'Right – you are headed for the land of the big zeds which is where I want to go so roll over and get your heads down.'

They stick their tongues out at me. Nothing doing. *We can keep this going all night. Just watch us, ya big pussy.*

Out of the corner of my eye I notice the telly. I know – maybe there'll be an old film on or something, something to distract me from the things which surely don't even exist.

Fuck, no. Fifty channels of static and a dozen of hardcore porn. I settle on that for a bit but the greased-up dildos, the 69s, the butt plugs, they make me want to puke. Forget it. I stumble over Iain's snoring hulk as I switch the telly off and try lying on my pit, closing my eyes again.

Here comes the blankness, the darkness, the nothingness.

No no no no no. One of those fucking trolls, the one with the spandex trousers and platform boots, is still in the mood for dancing and I tell him again, 'Go to fucking sleep.'

And gradually I can close my eyes for longer before the demons start acting up again, until finally total darkness comes, and I think this time, I can sleep, I can sleep and, even as fractals explode in front of my eyes, and trolls and goblins still rattle around taking the piss, poking and prodding at my sanity, I drift slowly off to...

Hamburg – Grindelhochhäuser

Cal

Steffi and Emma are away tae college and I'm in so much trouble. I was that off my tree last night, I didnae drive back tae Fally wi the others. Now I've missed getting back fur my shift and didnae even bother tae ring anybody tae explain. I know, I know, I'm stupit as fuck. But ye know how it is – sometimes E just drains the life fae ye; a fuckin – what's it? parasite – on yer energy an that.

I've got a plan, but. I'll wait fur Steffi tae show me the way tae the train station later, and Manny can pick us up the other end at Fally. Then there's sure to be a beasting and a charge the morra, mibbe even a day or two in the punt.

As if I could give a rat's arse.

I mean, spending all this time wi Steffi, it's been amazing. It's like the more I get tae know her, the deeper I want tae dig intae who she is. Never met anybody like her. We can talk about anything. Not like wi they mongs on base, even me and Manny.

We wur blethering about all sorts last night. Like I was telling her how I believe that God sees everything and that's why I try tae do good and she was like, 'I'm a scientist, how you can you expect me to believe in God? Everything can be explained by science,' and I almost thought that I'd become wan a they atheists right then. So I could get intae her knickers, like.

It's funny. The last lassie I went wi, fae Australia, she wasnae a believer either. Why do I always end up wi birds who'd give my ma the screaming abdabs? Not that she lasted. Cheeky tart tellt me she liked mair experience in a lad. What did she expect? It's no usual fur a ned fae the east end of Glesga tae huv an intimate knowledge of the *Kama Sutra*.

Steffi, she's different. No some margarine hoor who puts out right away. Och, okay, yous are right. If she wanted tae go the *whole* way, I wouldnae exactly come over all religious. Not that I've a Scooby if she does, though. Do the do wi me, I mean. When we finally decided tae get some zeds this morning, we laid down thegither on Emma's camp bed but there wasnae exactly any action tae speak of.

Just thinking about lying next tae her hot wee body's making me hornier than a rhino wi a hard-on, so I rifle through Emma's videos fur possible wank material. Piles of fuckin *Brookside* somebody fae home must've taped. What is it wi birds and soap operas? Och, c'moan, yous cannae accuse me of being sexist. I'm all fur – what's it, women's lib? Still, yous cannae deny that birds and blokes are different, that women coo over aw that lovey-dovey stuff and men love something wi a harder edge on telly – sport and aw that. Fact.

Anyway, back tae mair important matters. Am I gonnae unearth anything worth spanking the monkey over in they *Brookside* tapes? Hmm. That Anna Friel's a bit of alright, as Manny'd say, but I cannae bother my arse tae go through the tapes tae find a scene wi her in. My woody pokes at my boxers, urging me tae continue my search. Next video's *Star Trek: The Next Generation*. Good choice, Emma. But I'm no that desperate that I'll thrap wan off over alien life forms. Yet.

Hold on. What's this? *Cindy Crawford's Next Workout Challenge.* A curvy supermodel in a tight wee aerobics outfit? That'll do! I stick it on and find Cindy doing her exercises in skintight Lycra, right enough. Mostly she's in a gym doing weights an that, followed by these daft intervals where she's standing on top of a mountain, looking glaikit, chilling out tae stupit ambient background music. But what do ye know, even though it's all a bit silly, the Lycra's huvin the desired effect, so I slip my right hand in my boxers, keeping the remote in my left.

I fast forward tae an exercise where Cindy's doing weights, bending over tae reveal her cleavage, her huffing and puffing sounding like sex.

Och, c'moan!

Just as I'm getting somewhere, a baldy instructor – who's the spit of Mr Magoo – appears tae help Cindy wi her weights. I windy it back again tae the good part, the part wi the cleavage, and keep that going fur a bit. C'moan tae fuck! Here's Mr Magoo again.

Once mair wi the rewind, and I freeze-frame on Cindy's bosom, freeing up my left hand tae fondle my baws. I cannae hold back now... I'm thinking of me and Cindy – no, me and Steffi, her bent over and me doing her from behind as she huffs and puffs, puffs and huffs, moaning, 'Yes, yes, yes,' and that's it, that's it, that's it! I'm...

... what the... what's that noise? It's never...?

Aye, it is, but it's too late. 'Cause at the same time as a cough sounds out fae the doorway, a river of jism splatters fae the end of the bed across the telly.

My prick is a bouncy sausage outside my boxers, my eyes making best pals wi the flair while I scrabble tae pull up my kecks. Then, suddenly, I'm aware of a movement beside me, a glimpse of feet, and Emma's saying in a hushed voice, 'Just came back to pick up a book,' and, as she shuffles away and the front door reopens, she calls out, 'Don't worry, Cal, your secret's safe with me; I've seen it all before.'

Manny

It don't seem right Cal being on rippers, not allowed off camp, and here's me and Iain out with his bird, fucked on whizz. Still, I'm well excited. It's been ages since I've been to the cinema. I fucking love movies. Go and see horrors mostly. Anything with mass-murdering psychos, busty teens getting slashed up, zombies feasting on each other's half-dead flesh – I can't get enough of all that blood and gore. Not that I'm into violence in real life after everything that's happened.

Fuck about! Don't want to think about that. Better to focus on my next line or how I'm gonna feel Emma up when the lights go down. She reading my mind or what? She's taking off her hoodie, revealing her skinny arms and big tits underneath. What I wouldn't give for a feel of them bubbies! She better not be wearing one of them body things with the poppers underneath. Person designed them obviously wasn't worried about getting his nasties, that's for sure. Feckin' hell, this billy's making me randy – and stupid – as fuck.

As if a nice girl like Emma's gonna let me touch her up in the back row of the cinema!

'Oy, Manny, what you staring at?'

Shit. She's caught me perving her up. I garble something vague in reply. Hold up, saved by the Box Head; here comes Steffi, carrying a load of beers.

'How'd you get them in here, then?' I say and Iain clunks me on the head.

'It's allowed here, you retard. This is Germany. Drink more *Bier* here than *Wasser*, ain't that right, Steffi?'

Steffi shrugs her shoulders – her response to loads of things, as it goes. Iain, being Iain, don't give up.

'Give babies lager here instead of milk, don't they, Steffi?'

Steffi sighs, but I catch her winking at him. Winking? Hold up. That don't seem right; glad Cal weren't here to clock that. That Iain's a cheeky fucker. Told me just now outside the cinema, when I asked him where the whizz was from, 'You should know.'

And I'm like, 'Eh?'

So he tells me it was hidden among a load of pornos in the back of the car when we come back from Amsterdam. That's why he wanted to go there; only made out he wanted me to come 'cause he didn't want to drive on his tod. Feckin' liberty!

Then he was like, 'Remember when you was having a kip? Thought I was away having it large with some prossie? I was seeing the Pharmacist, my main supplier in the Dam.'

So I told him, 'Cheers, chum. If we'd been caught, we'd've been banged up for life.'

And he'd told me to leave it out, ruffling my hair. 'You told me before you wanted in, pal; thought you needed the cash.'

And then I'd replied hastily that of course I wanted in. I mean. Better in than out, eh?

The thing is, Iain don't see what he's becoming. Back in the day he just sorted us lot out with what we needed for the weekend. Now him and Taff are getting into something major. Course it's good to have whatever we want on tap, but you lot can see what's coming, I can see what's coming, but it's like Iain's got a blind spot about his future.

Anyway, talking about having stuff on tap, it's about time for another line; I don't want to keep getting up during the film. I jump out my seat and peg it towards the bogs.

'Hurry up, film's about to start, you'll miss the best bit,' Emma says. 'Scoot.'

Lovely girl, Emma, but she don't half sound like my mum at times.

Anyway. What's wicked is that today is a 'Sneak Preview'. Basically they could be showing any of the latest releases. Like a sort of movie pot-luck thing. And in English too! Hope it is a horror, get the ladies excited; young Emma might even have to put her head in my lap. There I go again. Jesus. I need help. Yeah. Another line – that oughta do the trick!

I race across the foyer to the bogs, and lock myself in the cubicle, leaning over the cistern, fumbling to unfold the wrap. No way – somehow the speed's got wet and sticky, so it's gonna be tricky to chop out a line. Oh, fuck it. There's not much left, and plenty more where that come from. I roll the sticky mass up in a Rizla and bomb it down in one.

My mouth is drier than the Sahara and I'm chewing my cheek to fuck as I walk back across the foyer – the after-effects of the whizz – best buy some chewing gum to sort myself out. I disturb an old dear on the counter, reading a magazine. My German isn't all that, so I try it in English.

'Erm, got any gum, *bitte*?'

'*Gummi Bärchen*?'

'Yeah, yeah, gum, and four *Warsteiner*.' I hold up four fingers, muttering, 'Um. *Vier Bier*?'

The woman behind the till grabs the lagers, and then only goes and hands me a packet of chewy sweets. Oh, fuck it. The girls will probably like them, think I've bought them specially. I open the door to screen five and the lights have already been lowered. Film's about to start. I stumble past Iain, then Steffi, spilling beer as I go along, and take my place next to Emma. It's fucking hot in here, man, and someone's trainers are honking in the mugginess. Probably Iain's. He might be a ladies' man, but he ain't got much idea about personal hygiene, let me tell ya. I hand out the beers and throw the bears on Emma's lap, and yeah, get the reaction I expected.

'Aw, Manny, that's sweet of you. Steffi, look, gummy bears!'

I think, shit, yeah, *Gummi Bärchen*, but no time to think about that 'cause the whizz is making me feel rather pleasant now if you must know and the curtain's rising. Emma grips my hand, chirping, 'I'm so excited.' I don't say so out loud, but I'm excited too. The curtains are near the top now, and a collective cheer goes up as the Sneak Preview of the day's revealed.

Aladdin. A fucking kids' film!

'*Geil!*' shouts Steffi, while Emma takes one look at me and claps her hands together, eyeing me up with a sarky look. Oh, go on, laugh, you lot. Been looking forward to this all day and now I've got to sit through some Disney bollocks with a mega-stiffy, grinding my teeth to dust in a cinema that's hotter than hell.

Fuck. Don't know how much speed was left in that wrap but I am flying! Ha! Flying like Aladdin and Jasmine on their magic carpet. Them beers have gone down a treat. And the whizz. *Wheeeeeeeee heeeeeee!* I am off my fucking tits. This film, man, it's funny as fuck; that genie, he's cracking me up. Ah, now Aladdin and Jasmine are kissing as they soar through the clouds; they're well loved-up. I start chuntering on in Emma's ear, want to tell her how much I like the film, how glad I am we've come here.

'Shh,' she says, giggling, giving it the old librarian-over-the-glasses-look.

Hmm. Might be a good time to try and sneak a clammy hand across her shoulders instead. You know how birds get turned on by all this sentimental bollocks. And yeah, she don't seem to mind as the old arm goes round, my hand brushing the edge of her vest top. The warmth in the room, the closeness to all that flesh, it's making my chubby close to bursting out my trousers – I'm in a fug of lust.

She wouldn't mind, would she? I mean, it's not like we ain't snogged each other's faces off once already. Oh, fuck it, nothing ventured and all that malarkey. I slip my hand further down and feel my way inside the vest towards all that lovely softness. Emma squirms in her seat and grabs my hand. But instead of pushing it off like I expected, she draws it further inside her vest. I'm almost insane, I want to touch her so bad. Let's see how much further she'll let me take it. Never know your luck, eh?

I take my hand out the vest and run my fingers along the top of her jeans... make to undo the top button... bummer, the squirming's different now. She takes my hand off and puts it back around her shoulders and says softly in my ear, 'Later,'

65

the warmth of her breath making me damn near cum in my trousers.

When the film finishes we all clap and cheer. I'm glad it weren't no sick-flick now. It's one of them life-affirming movies, and we're all high on it. Or maybe on the whizz and beer? Whatever. Haven't had this much fun in a long time. We link arms laughing and taking the piss as we leave the *Kino*, them stuck-up Krauts eyeballing us as we dance and sing and run out the foyer on to the street.

It's like five degrees outside, but I've got my beer and billy coat on, an invisible layer of warmth to help me on the way. Emma and Steffi don't bother with theirs, piling them into Iain's arms, so they can skip down the street, holding hands, singing that 'Whole New World' song over and over. Iain's acting the goat, chasing after them, dropping the coats on the ground, doing a cartwheel, catching quizzical looks from the passers-by. He roars with laughter at something Steffi says, and they all link arms and continue the horseplay.

I catch them up and slip my arm through Emma's, whispering, 'Come on, let's ditch these two, go back to yours.' She's making my eyes melt, she looks so fucking hot.

She don't hesitate, saying, 'Yeah, yeah, good idea. Let me just tell Steff.'

And I wonder, but just for a moment, if it's a good idea to leave Steffi alone with the minge-magnet Iain. But of course I'm too fucked to know what I'm doing really and besides she can look after herself. So Steffi and Iain walk off down the street linking arms, and I watch Emma as if she was a fucking supermodel or something on the catwalk as she comes up and goes, 'Show me the way to go home, I'm not tired and I want to go to bed.'

'No, it's I'm tired,' I say, and she goes, 'Duh,' and I think, *Oh, I get it, I'm in there!*

There you go, mate, if you ever needed any advice on pulling. Easiest way into a bird's knickers apparently: gummy bears, whizz and Disney all the way.

Cal

My palms are sweating as me and Steffi walk arm-in-arm along the Reeperbahn. The sun's coming up, turning a weak spotlight on the carnage of the night before. Food wrappers, beer cans and fag ends blow around wur ankles and the streets heave a sigh of relief tae bid good riddance tae the hoors, the dealers and the sleaze fur another day.

Steffi has never looked mair beautiful. She clutches my arm, kicking at the rubbish in her new Adidas, her pupils still dancing with E.

And after a while she takes my hand and asks, 'Do you have anything more?'

Her eyes are big and bright and lovely.

What can I say? I root around in my pocket, knowing full well there are two small but perfectly formed yins left. I hesitate. Should I hand wan over? I mean, it's getting harder than ever tae cover fur wan another in the cookhouse; I need a clear heid fur work the morra. Aye, yous are right: mair tae the point, what about Steffi? When we met she was a clean-living student. Pretty much. And now? Now she's madder fur it than any of us.

'How many ye've hud?'

I'm sure Iain's already sorted her mair than once, the night.

'Um – Iain, he gave me two. One and two halves.' She uses her fingers to tot that up. '*Ja total zwei* – two.'

I know she's got college the morra but I cannae say no tae they Bambi eyes. Besides, I wouldnae want her tae think I'm a tight-arse.

'Aye sure, doll. There are two. Here ye go.'

I groan. Why the 'doll'? And here's me trying tae play up my sensitive side. But she doesnae seem bothered as she puts out her palm, takes a glug of water tae drap the E, and kisses us on the cheek as if tae say thanks. I lean in fur a hug, sooking up some of the girlish smell of her hair, and something in me stirs.

'Come on, Cal,' she says, interrupting this none too unpleasant – what's it? Sensation.

'What? Come on what?'

'You must do one too. You said there was two zingies – two pills.'

I groan. I was melting intae that snugly comedowny feeling, imagining masel going back tae Emmas's, blethering till we fell asleep, huvin a wee smoke, mibbe getting up close and personal at last.

On the other hand, part of me's still buzzing, still high enough tae be tempted, still high enough tae blurt, 'Only fur a kiss.'

Oh, fuck! She's looking at me. What's that look? Angry? Hurt? I feel like running very far and very fast, till she pushes my arm gently and simply says, 'Cal!' in a bossy sort of teachery way, and I know it's alright. And then she does it – kisses me fur at least five seconds on the lips.

I am zombied tae the spot.

She looks at me weirdly. Taps my pocket. Oh, right. The tablet. She's wanting me tae take the tablet. As wan a they MCs would say, *Here we go again.*

The third E is never the same as the first or second yins. Yer buzz has already peaked, so the vibe isnae as climactic. Not that it's completely pointless either, 'cause in another way it takes ye to a whole new level of fleeing – yer mibbe not as loved-up as on the first two but now all common sense, all yer world experience goes out the windae as yer brain goes intae meltdown.

If yous huv never taken three tablets, or even the wan, I'll try tae describe what I mean. By way of example, let's compare it tae going Banzai over yer favourite food – a pie or what huv ye. As ye bite intae the first wan ye experience a whoosh of pleasure, of satisfying a hunger deep inside. But sometimes the crust is that melt-in-the-mouth good, the filling that succulent that yer insides gnaw at ye, begging fur mair, and so ye think, fuck it, and huv a second. Now, even if that second wasnae as

68

tasty as the first, there's sometimes enough pleasure in it tae think, I'll gorge masel on another. Now this yin, this third wan, ye know ye defin-ately shouldnae be eating, but its like yer addicted now, ye want tae take it as far as ye can till yer belly is full tae overflowing. And that, my friends, is what it's like getting cunted on yer third pill... Only mair psychedelic and euphoric, evidently.

Anyway. Enough of this blethering. The E has dropped its bomb of happiness and ecstasy and blissed-outness on me, and I am rushing like a good 'un. I hug Steffi tight and she returns the favour, and we walk along hugging... past the sex and booze shops wi their shutters down... past the overflowing bins and littered pavements.

Then, suddenly, Steffi does a cartwheel just as a street sweeper is slouching past.

'*Guten Morgen*,' Steffi says to him as she topples upright again, and he nods at us and smiles.

Everything is good with the world.

'Aah, lovely, lovely Cal!' is the next thing Steffi says, squeezing my arm.

'Och, behave!' I say, pleased as punch.

'You see, that's why I love you, you're zo modest, but you should know you are *einfach fantastisch*!'

'Fanta-what?' I ask, hauf sure of what she's on about. 'See, I tellt ye I was stupit.'

But my heart is pounding as if a herd of elephants was running through it. *That's why I love you!* She's just after saying that, right? I'm no imagining it?

'That's my meaning, there you go again, you are not stupid. *Du bist einfach* fantastic.'

And I can see the E has really taken hold now 'cause she's skeltering down the street like a mad yin, shouting, '*Cal ist einfach supppiiiiiiiiiiiii!*' I run after her, as rubbered as I've ever been, and we tear towards the U-Bahn, like that, two energetic rays of sunshine, helping Hamburg wake up tae another day of drug deals, sex shows and everything else that's unholy.

Manny

I swallow back hot, salty tears, my heart pounding. *Don't lose it, man, don't lose it!*

Dozzer goes, 'Walkman? Nah, mate, haven't seen one. You lads?'

He turns to his two goons, that mentalist Brian and his sidekick Jock. They punch each other's fists in a jokey way, and Jock says, 'Two second rule, pal,' leaving me in no doubt whatsoever that they lifted my CD Walkman when I went to the bog. Trust them to abuse the unwritten rule that anyone's entitled to swipe whatever ain't nailed down in this shit-hole. Brand new Ministry of Sound CD mixed by Tony Humphries in my Walkman too. And the CD Walkman itself. It cost a fucking packet!

I blink back a new emotion – anger. They've no right. All I've done is come to the pool room for a few practice shots and they're fucking starting on me. Rage flashes through me, only to disappear again quick as lightning – the last thing I need is to provoke this lot, so I pick up a pool cue and take a shot, smothering my irritation.

After a couple of shots Brian leans on the table, following me round it each time I move to ready the cue. Jock meanwhile backs off to close the door, heaving all his weight in front of it. There's a lot of weight – he's built like a fucking brick shit-house. Shit! Do they want more with me than just the Walkman? My throat and chest close up, and I'm thirsty for air.

I force myself to breathe out.

Come on, Manny, act normal! But, what with Brian blocking my every move, there's no point trying to take shots. So then we all stand motionless for a bit, a recurring thought sprinting through my head – it's Saturday, someone's bound to come in, want to shoot some pool.

And Dozzer, what's he doing all this time? He's stood still, like some sort of monstrous stone statue, with this evil fucking grin on his grid. Oh, that's right, you lot, give it the 'there's no such thing as evil, got to feel sorry for him, must have been beaten as a kid or something'. Even Cal with all his fucking God-bothering cuts Dozzer too much slack. Worst he says about him is, 'That bampot could start a fight wi himself in a phone box.' Still, Cal don't know the half of it, to be fair. He don't know why this lot are out to get me, about the real reason I left the infantry training, when I came up against Dozzer's mate, one Sergeant Blake.

Hold up. Dozzer's making for the door.

'Not worth the bother, is he, lads?' he says, like he's doing me a favour, and my shoulders come down, the sweat tipping down my back all the while.

Then, stepping towards me again, he shouts in my face, 'It's a wind-up, you plonker!'

And I feel smaller than if it had been for real.

Seems like a good time to leave, but as I head for the door Dozzer goes back on his word and he's on me quick as a panther. Grabs me by the throat. Turns me round. Pushes me hard against the vending machine. Punches me, *oof!* in the gut. Then raises his fist again, saying, 'This is for Blakey and your little Chinese meals with the RMP,' and I'm steeling myself for more when we hear shouting from the corridor: '*Ole, ole, ole, ole,*' a singsong which takes the piss out of the menace of the moment.

It's now or never.

Now!

I raise my knee to Dozzer's crotch and slam it with as much force as I can into his bollocks. He falls to the ground with a thud, clutches his nads, lets out a gut-wrenching, 'Ugggggggh.' There's a hammering at the door, which Brian and Jock are leaning against. I make for it anyway. Dozzer kicks his foot out to trip me up. I'm too quick for that. I barge into a forest of arms, legs and fists and in the scrum the door flings open and a group of lads I don't know walk in. They take one look at me, another at Brian, Jock and Dozzer, and a question from one of them hangs heavy as a rain cloud in the air.

'What the fuck?'

I push past the lot of them, and run through the block, bumping past people, objects – anything in my way – going at it like the clappers, running, panting, retching, till I'm out the main doors. I embrace the open air and peg it across the parade square – course we're meant to march across it and salute the effing flag, but it's not like I can get in any deeper shit. My legs don't even feel heavy, like they do in nightmares, they fly me all the way to the pad houses, the adrenalin urging me on, till I arrive, spitting up bile, at Iain's front door.

My legs have given up the ghost and I'm a sack of spuds on the floor when, after a second lot of knocking, Iain finally answers.

'Oy, oy, what brings you here?' he asks, irritated. 'Just in the middle of something…'

It's a good question. But what with Cal up Hamburg with Steffi, and Davie and his lot acting weird around me recently, it's not like I had anyone better to turn to. It's another question left unanswered for the day, though, as Kelly comes up behind him, twigging right away that something's up.

'Forget the fucking racing for a second, Iain, and help your mate.'

She crouches down to help me, leading me into the house like I was a wounded animal or something, her small frame weirdly strong-seeming as she guides me on to the sofa. Meantime, Iain plonks himself down in an armchair, looking over at the telly. I lie there, heart thumping, sweat gluing me to the white leather, concentrating on the rhythmic pounding of the horses. *Clippety-clop-clippety-clop-clippety-clop*. My heart pounds in time to the beat of the galloping. *Thuddedy-thud-thuddedy-thud-thuddedy-thud.*

I can't take it! The telly's up way too loud. It's as if them horses was racing right here next to me, I can almost smell them in the room. I want to shout, *Shut those fuckers up!* but I throttle my desire to yell, squeeze my buttocks tight, and dig my fingernails into the fist I've made.

Nobody says a word till Kelly comes back into the room with a brew. 'There you go, pet,' she says, 'something hot and sweet, sort you out.'

Not that I need it; I'm still cooking up. Kelly gives Iain a sharp nudge in the ribs.

'So, what gives, fella?' he finally asks, still fixated on the telly, his legs dangling over the side of the armchair. My silence and a glare from Kelly from the doorway force him out his seat, and he switches it off. 'Come on, chum, don't bottle it up.'

It's all the encouragement I need.

I spew out all about Dozzer and about how he's had it in for me since I got on the wrong side of his mate Blakey in the basic training, how he's told me he's gonna make my life a world of shit since he got his stripes. Even tell Iain I'm thinking of jacking it in. I stop short telling him the worst that Blakey done way back when, though. Could guess his reaction. How we can get Dozzer back; Iain'll have a word with his mate, the sergeant provost who runs the regimental jail, they come from the same home town. It'd all be *blah, blah, blah*, though, eh? Iain wouldn't bend over backwards to suck his own dick. Besides, tea and sympathy aren't exactly his forte, so it's no surprise when he changes the conversation to something more to his liking.

'How did it go with you and Emma the other week, then, big fella?' he asks, doing a crude gesture with his hands and tongue as if parting a girl's legs. Kelly raises her eyebrows skywards.

I suck in the lie and say, 'Yeah mate, yarking it up her all night, weren't I? Right dirty cow.'

Kelly dead-arms me. 'Sorry, Kel.'

'Oh, mate, mate! What, she take it up the hoop and everything?'

With that Kelly flounces out the room.

'And you, mate? What about you and Steffi?' I ask in a low voice, with a feeling of dread. I mean, there's Cal up Hamburg with Steffi now, thinking he's in loved-up land, when Christ knows what went on with Iain and Steffi the other week.

Iain puts his fingers to his lips, and says in a stage whisper, 'Shh, a gentleman don't tell, does he?'

As for me and Emma, course it weren't like that, was it? What with all the billy and beers, couldn't come, could I? So yeah, we was rutting all night, but it weren't exactly porno-standard. Some impression I made on her. She's far too good for me anyway. Not surprised she rolled over after a while, said we should try again in the morning, that she needed her kip. What would she want with a loser like me?

Briny self-pity makes its way up my throat again, so it's a relief when Iain says with a grin, 'Fancy a toot of Charlie, then? Cheer you up?'

I'm just nodding a quick yes – too quick maybe – when Kel comes back in the room.

'Fancy a line, love?' Iain goes.

'Yeah, right – some of us have got work today,' she says, leaning over the coffee table and picking up a set of keys.

'Do what? Work?' Iain goes, as if she'd just told him the moon was on fire.

'Told you, the gift shop need me to do an extra hour or two today.' And I think she might be welling up as she goes, 'Do you ever listen?'

And then he's grabbing her by the wrist and they're having words, but I don't see or hear what goes on 'cause I'm putting all my effort into bending down over the coffee table to hoover up a fat line.

And yeah, you've sussed me, I'm that shagging predictable. Didn't come here 'cause I hoped Kel wouldn't be at work, that, true to form, she'd put on a brew, or 'cause I thought that Iain would have any advice worth hearing. Come here 'cause I knew what might be on offer from Iain's medical chest... Dr Iain and his medicine, taking away the pain of another fucking day in the Army. Another fucking messed-up encounter with a bird. Another fucking day in the life of a dyed-in-the-wool loser.

Chapter Four

Cal

Think what yous like, there's no way she's given me a dizzie.
No my Steffi. It just wouldnae be her tae stand me up, and no
page Iain tae let us know if she wasnae coming. I elbow my
way tae the bar, trying no tae throw a blue flakie in front of
Emma and the rest of the crew.

I turn tae the throng behind me. 'Another, embdy?'

Manny squeezes past the others, puts his hand on my
back. 'Mate, mate, slow down,' he says. 'You don't want to be
bladdered time she gets here. You know what you're like on
that big wheel, best of times.'

Fair play. Last time we come to the shows, I honked up my
currywurst all over my Reeboks. And he's right, she's an hour
late just, but the waiting's doing my nut. Tae make matters
worse the pub's speakers are blasting out Irish music. Aw that
phoney Celtic worshipping ye get fur the Irish abroad drives
me up the wall. Kiss the Blarney stone. Kiss my fuckin arse.
The Irish huv got that Celtic thing sewn up, though, right
enough. Folks go inside pubs like this yin, the Shamrock,
planning a merry auld time, hoping some of that Irish charm
will be – what's it? Contagious. Step inside a pub filled wi
Jocks on the randan, on the other hand, and ever fucker's feart
they're gonnae get glassed. Neds of the Celts, so we are.

I decide it's time tae live up to wur reputation.

'Pint a Guinness, *bitte*,' I shout over tae the barman, waggling a *Zehner* over the bar.

'Oy, oy, what have we here. Happy boy on the sherberts? Don't tell me the little Box Head's gone and given you a knock-back?'

That's Iain, by the way, paying no mind whatever tae a fellow human being's suffering, as per usual. He turns tae the others, sniffing, 'Come on, let's do one; silly tart knows where to find us if she wants us.'

The sniffing a sure sign he's back on the Colombian marching powder again, by the way. The numpty. Surprise, surprise, then, wan by wan, the rest of them – Emma, her pal fae uni Sarah, Manny, Taff, Jay and Jonesy – follow the big man like he's the Pied Piper of fuckin Hamburg. Fucked if I'm going with.

'I'm hanging on here for another swally,' I say. But of course I'm talking tae smoky, jig-filled air – they've already left. I knock back my fourth pint in a wanner, and order a fifth; this Steffi business is making me thirstier than a jakey waiting on his Giro.

Och, I know I'm always saying I cannae stand it when folk get jarred up. It's like an unwritten rule for us ravers. If yer gonnae be a bona fide hardcore nutter, Es and speed are what it's all about; aw they other substances that take the edge off life, they're fur losers. Take the bevvy, fur instance. It's fur straight-heads who want tae keep a grip on reality, knuckle-swingers who go intae town Saturday nights – sole purpose tae get drunk and intae fisticuffs; or paint-stripper-drinking alkies who've reached rock bottom like my ma. Cocaine, it's rich man's speed fur loads-a-money lads showing off, or folk poncing about in house music clubs – doesnae make ye feel the love like E. Weed, weed'll do ye on a comedown, right enough, but regular smokers – kiffers we call them – they're just wannabe rastas, or lads who are feart of moving ontae the Big Boy drugs. Aye. Fuck aw that lame shite.

Still, end of the day, I'm no stupit. I know nothing beats getting posit-ive-ly steamboats drunk when ye think ye've been given the heave. Worse than any drugs comedown, so it is, thinking ye've met yer soulmate and she doesnae even show up fur a date.

Och, away yous go. Huv ye never felt like this, become so obsessed wi somebody that ye blank out everything else? It's the mixed signals I cannae take. Yous remember, the other day, she was full of it? Happy tae give me kisses and cuddles, right? Aw, c'moan, I'm only just after telling yous about it. So don't yous tell *me* she's no interested. I know she's fuckin interested.

I need a sit-down. My legs are pure concrete, my heart sagging at the bottom of my trainers. I find a space away fae the speakers, squeezing masel intae the corner of a table filled wi jolly Americans. Space. Ha! That's a joke, the place is fuckin mobbed. I stumble, splooshing drink on the table, as I plank my arsehole on the edge of a bench. The women on the table look through me.

'I'm sorry, hen,' I mumble tae wan a them, as I take on the human form of the Leaning Tower of Pisa, and she looks back at me, anxiously.

Then again, mibbe it wasnae an anxious look, 'cause she's saying, 'Oh, are you a real Irish?' As if she was a wee lassie meeting the real Snow White in Disneyland, by the way.

'A real Irish what?' I mutter under my breath, then, 'That's right, hen, aw the way fae the Gorbals.'

The dozy mare's turning tae her pals then, telling them the wondrous news. I sit back on my bench, hoping my body language will speak for itself. Nae chance. They're still eyeing me up, as if I was an exhibit in the National Museum of Irish Folk. There's nothing else fur it – I start greetin, wiping away big bubbles of snot wi my sleeve. Ha! I've space now, right enough. The space saved for beer-swamped mentalists in pubs fae here to Timbuktu, that is.

I'm sorry for that just now, accusing yous of no being on my side about Steffi. It's the swally talking. I know it's my fault

77

tae think a lassie like her would want tae go wi me. And I'm forgetting I need yous on side if yer gonnae stick by me, by the time wur story's finished.

C'moan tae fuck, what now? The barman's eyeballing me as I lie jaked out on the table, spreading my worries over it like a bad hand of cards. He's never coming over? He is! That does it fur me. I've got tae get out of here...

away fae Irish jigs

away fae they stupit Americans

away fae the spot reminding me I've been thrown a dizzie...

I elbow my way out the pub, and trip out the door, a blast of cold air propelling me further into pishdom. Where's it? The Dom? I can hear the yells and shrieks fae the other side of the road. But where's it? The entrance?

I stand haufway in the road without a Scooby where I'm going... away tae fuck! A car wheechs by me as I launch masel further across the carriageway, horns blasting, German sweary words firing at me fae all angles. There's a bench the other side of the road. Mibbe a wee sit-down... get some zeds... make it all go away? I try tae get cosy... lie there... pull my jaiket over my face. But the heid-whirling and ground-spinning soon put a stop tae that. I grope masel upright... stagger... fair entrance cannae be far now. There it's, over there... the smell of meat and candy floss and mibbe vomit cling tae the air and guide me forwards... a final burst of energy... a marathon effort...

...that's me, walking again.

Mibbe find the others... get a ride back tae camp... find out if Steffi paged Iain, after all? C'moan, Cal, one foot, then the other...

I walk round the Dom till eventually the blur of lights and sounds and smells of the sideshows, rides and tents come intae focus; the heid is cleared. Even manage a go on wan a they coconut shies, try and win a teddy fur Steffi, show her no hard feelings that she's no made it, the night. I keep going, taking in the atmosphere of folk out fur a night of putting their troubles tae wan side. Och, I'm almost enjoying masel now, so I am. Ah, there's the entrance tae the big wheel. Manny's favourite. Mibbe I'll find him and...

What the – ?

There's that fuckin scunner Iain. And yous're no gonnae believe what he's up tae. Well, I'll tell yous. He's only all over my Steffi like a rash. Putting a heart-shaped biscuit round her neck, like he's gie'ing her a fuckin winner's medal! I'm on him like a shot.

'See you. Are you noising me up?'

'Eh, what you on about? Noising what?'

'Och aye, jus' make out like ye cannae understand me. I'll make it clear – Are. You. Trying. Tae. Wind. Me. Up?'

Iain just stands there, smirking like a naughty schoolboy. I look sideyways at the others: Steffi frowning, Sarah shrugging her shoulders, Davie making wanker gestures. Meanwhile, Emma and Manny are nowhere tae be seen.

The night air tenses and we all stand fur a bit in silence, till Steffi pipes up, 'Cal, *was ist los* – vot's wrong?'

I bump past the others towards her, taking a beamer, my cheeks the colour of toffee apples. Got tae try and keep it thegither – for her sake. She hugs me awkwardly.

'Vere have you been? I was here for hours waiting. Iain boot me the *Lebkuchen*, the cake thingy, to say sorry, that he did not ask you to call me when I sent him the thingy – the page.'

It's Iain's turn tae blush now. 'Yeah, sorry about that, mate. Seems she tried to page me, but I... uh... I had the thing switched off in case Kelly got in touch.'

That rat-bastard, that baw-bag, that fuckin slimy bucket of jizz. I swear he done it on purpose, I swear he knew she was here and left me in the pub tae beel masel intae a frenzy.

'C'moan, Steffi,' I say, Dutch, Irish and German courage all swilling about inside my belly as I drag her away fae the others.

'*Au*, Cal, you're hurting me.'

I'm trying not tae break down, not tae cry with relief, too wrapped up in masel tae realise that I'm gripping her arm too hard. She was here. She was waiting. I wasnae imagining it. She was here, and that's aw that matters, I think, as Steffi gives me a squeeze.

That's what fuckin drinking does to ye, man. Makes ye paranoid, takes away yer natural happiness and confidence. I'm no gonnae make that mistake again, I think, as me and Steffi link arms, headed fur the waltzers.

Gonnae get back tae basics.

Too right.

It's Es and speed aw the way fur me again from now on. Es and speed, and plenty of them.

Fallingbostel British Army Base – Regimental Jail

Manny

The duty officer and duty SNCO enter the cell. My shoulders brace, heels come together, and I recite the lines, as instructed last night.

'Sir! I am 23619754 Private Manning, 9 Platoon, Charlie Company, of the Royal Logistics Corps. Awarded seven days' military detention for bringing the Army into disrepute, under Section 69 Alpha of the Army Act 1955. Awarded by the Commanding Officer of the Second Royal Tank Regiment. I have no requests and no complaints… SIR!'

The duty officer raises his eyebrows and bellows, 'At. Ease!'

I don't fucking believe this: I recognise him now. He's only some bloke I used to pal about with. That explains the eyebrows. Just what I need. He's one of them blokes who's turned 'Army Barmy'; it's no wonder he became an RP. The jumped-up little prick. He stares me out, making me feel ye big, and the walls close in on me, making me gag for air. I steel

80

myself for a bollocking. I mean, my kit's laid out ready, and my bed block's in order for inspection – but I am crapping it, all the same.

While I'm 'at ease' the SNCO pokes about my bed layout, checking the blankets and sheets in my bed block are folded with 'hospital corners', and that my boots have been polished within an inch of their lives. My neck and shoulders are a tangle of knots from a bad night's kip as it is, and holding my arms straight behind me is a further strain. As for keeping my head high and my chin raised, it's like some sort of sick joke. I mean, only in the Army could 'at ease' mean the shagging polar opposite.

Fuck about! Now the SNCO's grid is a squashed orange as he inspects my boot polish tin, and he starts banging on: was it cleaned with wire wool as instructed? Only for about ten fucking hours before lights out, I want to shout in his mush. But of course my reply is much more in line with Army rules and regulations.

Why did I have to go and chuck that fucking brick?

Seven days of this!

Still, I'm off the hook for now: the dynamic duo are leaving the room, their distinctive white plastic belts, RP armbands and canes whizzing past me. I sink back on to my pit, my stomach churning. Nerves maybe? Or maybe a reminder I've eaten nothing since yesterday morning. In too much of a two-and-eight last night, I was, to be marched over to the cookhouse for dinner.

Anyway. I suppose you lot are wondering how I got into this mess. Well, it's like this. Ever had a bad day? Woke up late for work, burnt the toast, stepped in dog shit in yer new trainers, maybe? Sure you have. But even if you did once get your spanking new Nikes caked in dog's mess, burnt yer brekkie or slept in, it's swings and roundabouts, innit? Probably later that day you got a phone call from an old mate inviting you out for a beer, yer girlfriend gave you a blowie, or you found a tenner in your back pocket. So, let me tell you about my bad day yesterday. Not some half-arsed one that starts with the toast landing butter-side down. A proper shit day which begins in humiliation and ends with you marching double time to the cells.

Started with a 'willy wakeup'. Just what it sounds like, really. You wake from six or seven hours of blanking out all the Army shite, dreaming about fanny if you're lucky, only to open your eyes to find a group of lads in your bed space rubbing their cocks on your head, shouting, 'Willy wakeup!' Funny as fuck, right? Yeah, right. Funny as fuck if yer a halfwit squaddie.

You see, what the lads don't realise is that any kind of aggro opens the floodgates for all them bad memories. The memories of Sergeant Blake and the infantry training, I mean. It's like everything bad that happens now reminds me that I wasn't cut out for this bullshit from day one. And yeah, I know you lot are dying to know what happened back then, and believe me, I'd like to unload. But it's like I've got an outline of what happened for you, but I'm not quite ready to colour in the detail, if you know what I mean.

That's it.

I've got to get out of here, get away, forget all the crap that's gone on. Away from shit like last week's fun with Dozzer and that lot. Where to, though? Well, that's the million-dollar question. Mum and Dad are still at my nan's. Still not many jobs around back home, so Amy said in her last letter. Suppose I could get a job in kitchens somewhere, even if it's down the pier for – what, two quid fifty an hour tops? – beg my nan to kip on her sofa for a bit. The knots in my neck tie tighter at that thought. I lie back on my pit, trying to stretch out the tendons, looking up at the cell ceiling. A jigsaw of broken plaster in the ceiling leers at me.

Ain't got the energy to fart, though, mate, have ya, never mind go AWOL?

Too right. Can't even face going back home for the traditional turkey blowout and family blow-up at Christmas. Probably spend it with Cal up his place. Get a load of that

82

Hangar 13 rave action. This feeling like I've nowhere to go, though – that's another reason I snapped this morning. Why I did what I did and ended up in the punt.

Basically, if you want to know, after the willy wakeup, I thought, fuck it, pure and simple – I'm not turning up on duty. Fuck the lot of them. Wanged on a pair of my favourite Adidas tracky bottoms, and lay on my pit, waiting for the shit to hit the fan. Cal went off to the kitchens with Jonesy in a right old pissy mood. He was hoping I'd drive him up Hamburg again Friday, go down the Tunnel Club. Second time in a week he'd asked me to do it. 'Ckin liberty. He can get the train if he's that desperate to see the little Kraut. She don't even like him that much. Told me so herself, Thursday at the Dom. We had a little conversation before Cal turned up and did his Jock-on-the-rampage act. Asked her if she thought they'd be together and she told me straight, she wouldn't see anyone who believed in God. And I was like, 'What really, you'd dump someone 'cause they believe in sky pixies?' And she was like, 'Sky pixies. Ha ha ha. Ferry funny.'

Can you believe her?

I don't even know if Emma believes in God. Don't care really. We've been seeing a bit of each other too when we can, as it happens. Suppose you could even call us an item. As for God and me, we're not exactly on speaking terms. Maybe on my deathbed I'll get to know him better. That's a long way off, though, innit?

But I'm getting sidetracked. It's just to show what I was thinking when I didn't show up for my shift this morning, only to get invited by the Master Chef for a little 'career brief'. Meaning a proper bollocking, in case you lot aren't familiar with the old Army lingo.

Some fucking invitation. That was enough for me, and I naffed off. Headed into Fally to look for some liquid refreshment. Didn't even try a flanker, to dream up some excuse or plan to get out of the mess I'd got myself into. Strutted straight out of camp in my DayGlo tracky bottoms.

About the most exciting thing that had happened to the lads on duty at the gate since Iain stagged on off his tits on acid.

Anyway. You'd have thought the walk into Fally would've helped clear the red mist, made me rush back to face the music and do some damage limitation. Not that simple, though, is it, when you've hit the self-destruct button? So, all the walk done was increase my agitation. Paced a twenty-minute walk in ten, taking my mood out on little heaps of November leaves piled up on the side of the road. By the time I reached the first pub in town my trainers were swamped in the mulch. Anyway. Where I went was one of them traditional German *Kneipe*: fat, round and red-faced blokes stood at the bar. No women. Course we're advised not to drink in these kinds of locals. Didn't have my thinking cap on, though, did I?

Them fellas were alright in the beginning. End of the day, any wanker drinking at 11 a.m.'s got his own problems. Enjoyed a couple of hours' heavy boozing, one eye on a football match on a telly in the corner. But then one of them Box Heads started up on how crap English food is 'cause he'd been to Manchester once. Yeah, mate, and fucking *Sauerkraut*'s *haute cuisine*, I thought. But I left it, shouted another round, and carried on drinking. Only he wouldn't give up: the food's shit, the coffee's shit, the girls are fucking ugly... he went on and on and on and – you see what's coming – I flipped.

Flipped and done what any self-respecting Englishman would do. I gave his mush some five-knuckle attention, pegged it outside, grabbed a brick, and wanged it through the *Kneipe* window. Sort of beautiful, it was – razor-sharp splinters of glass swimming through the air, twinkling like a pretty tune. Scene that followed weren't pretty, mind you. Got myself arrested, didn't I? Soon as them German *Polizei* find out I'm Army, they're on the blower, and the RPs arrive to cart me back to the jail, with a blast of, 'Soldier and Escort, by the right, quick march!'

And that was me in a world of shite. Again. Oy, oy, there you lot go, leaping to conclusions and out yer prams; on the

Army's side. Like, I know my Bad Day's my own making. Think about it, though. What would you do? Abide by their rules, stick to their version of what's right and wrong, or throw a mental and end up on a charge: fined a week's wages ('hit 'em where it hurts' is the Army's way of thinking) and a week in the punt. Play it safe, would you? Well done, you lot! The Army would love you, a bunch of round pegs to fit into their round holes. Me, I'm the square peg all the way.

I fling my boot polish tin across the cell and it bounces off the metal door with a clatter.

Fuck my parents for pushing me into all that grammar school application crap and for being all snidey when I failed, and again when I flunked my CSEs. Fuck Cal for drooling over that little tart all the time, no time left for his mates. Fuck Blakey for getting me sent out the infantry. Yeah, mainly fuck him and fuck the Army, and its five-year trap for stupid young lads – stupid young lads like the sixteen-year-old me.

Got to be a way out of this, surely?

Hamburg – by the Alster

Manny

'Fuck about, woman!' I can't bear it when birds whine to get their own way. 'If I want to have a little toot, I'll have one.'

Emma's face is like thunder. Thunder – ha! The perfect match to the lightning strikes of the fireworks exploding above our heads.

'Can't we do something straight for once?' she's asking. 'I mean, you're only a day out of jail; shouldn't you be taking it easy? I dunno. Maybe have a beer or something instead of the chemicals for a change? You know, like a normal...' She trails off.

'Like a normal what exactly?' I ask, my voice raised, my eyes boring into hers. Bloody nause. All day Emma's been banging on at me to 'sort yourself the fuck out', worried about last week's little incident in the nick. Doesn't get it that a week in the old regimental jail is like water off a duck's back.

Yeah, too right, having a bird's alright but why do they think they can interfere in every bit of yer life? People are checking us out now, our voices rising over the commotion of the crowd, even. I grab Emma's wrist and pull her away from the main viewing area at the edge of the lake, towards some bushes. Never know when them Monkeys, the military police, might be lurking about, listening in to our conversations, trying to catch us out when we're in our civvies.

'Look, love. It's alright for you, eh? You can relax all fucking week, smoking puff with Steffi, doing what the fuck you want while I'm stuck on that base getting cunted about from dawn till dusk. Been banged up for a week, got to let my hair down, innit?'

Her grid softens. 'Yeah, yeah, you're right. It's only – well,' she says, blushing. 'Well, 'cause I'm worried about you. It's not like it's puff we're talking about here. You know how I feel about Charlie. It's more, um, more – '

'Oh, come on, live a little,' I butt in. 'Long time dead, intya?' I crack one of my killer cheesy grins that the birds love and squeeze her close. 'Besides, it ain't like you'll be complaining later...'

Emma's well into me getting coked up when we're getting our nasties. Things are more than working out in that department now, as it goes.

'Oh, alright, then. Only if you promise we'll go on, like, a date or something – do something normal together soon?'

'Course, love, anything you say,' I hear myself saying, but my mind's already wandering onto more important matters. Like where can I rack up a line among all these crowds?

We've come to watch the fireworks at the Alster, you see. Happens three times a year, a fireworks display to mark the end of the Dom. Bit sissy to come along I suppose, but, still, it's free. Hold up. Over there – I can sort myself out in them bushes.

'You hang back there a second, will ya?' I say to Em. 'Unless you fancy a line, of course.'

Don't know why I said it, really; I know full well the response. Yup, there it is – the classic Emma stare of death.

'Got the message,' I say, heading on my tod into the bushes, thinking, I'll snort it straight out the wrap, rub some on my gums, to save time and effort. Only I'm confronted by a right old messy scene among the gorse and the leaves and the dogshit – two lads having at it right in the middle of a small clearing.

'*Hau ab du Arsch,*' one of them yells.

Fuck about! They've spotted me, looking well aggy that I've interrupted. I don't need to be told twice – they're big fellas – and I scarper, catching my tracky top on the sharp spines of the gorse as I run by. I take my glove off and try and unpick the Adidas, and ow! – 'ckin hell, my fingers are ripped to shreds. I ignore the paper cut-type pain, and, fumblingly, manage to open the wrap, a drop of blood splashing down staining the powder.

It looks well dramatic, the red against the white. And I'm reminded of something... Fuck. Maybe it's a sort of warning or something?

Oh, behave! I tell myself. Not like I'm in one of them books with fucking omens and that flying about. Bollocks to that.

I scrape up a nailful of coke and snort it back.

When I first come here that would have been a right head-fuck – them boys in the bushes, I mean. You would have thought: Christ, better not get close, they've probably got AIDS or some shit. But you get used to it. Have to, amount of gays larging it in the clubs over here. Even feel a bit dumb now for thinking about AIDS and that. Anyway, those lads remind me of the first time me and Cal went down to Camelot after the Unit club. There we was, all wide-eyed and innocent after, like, our third pill, when somebody suggests we carry on partying at this after-hours bar. Get there and it's well fucking seedy, real spit-and-sawdust place owned by the Turkish mafia. So there's, like, our crew lounging on the benches, bugging out to fuck, 'cause, well, at the beginning three pills was a mental amount to take, when in walked these German queers. Then it was as if we was watching a movie from the '70s – *Saturday Night Fever* or what have you – 'cause they all start busting a move to the trance music the barman's laid down: limbs making shapes at right angles, shirts off, skin glistening with sweat. I didn't fucking believe what I was seeing after a while. I was thinking, *Am I that far gone? Am I hallucinating?* when two of them started going at it like fucking animals, grunting and all that on the floor. And I mean really going at it. Cocks out, blow jobs – everything.

Like I said, head-fuck.

Now you realise it's part of the Hamburg scene. I mean, it's sort of like you could do anything here, and nobody'd bat an eyelid. Or, say Hamburg was a person, it'd be the lowest of the low – a kiddy-fiddler or some revolting shit. Alright, alright, keep your shirts on. I'm not comparing gays to paedos. I mean, I've got nothing against gays; one of my oldest mates back home is a bum bandit. Just saying: in this place, anything goes.

Anyway, by the time I've thought this, I've picked my way through the mass of bodies and I'm snuggled back with Emma, feeling pretty tasty as the white stuff works its magic. The crowd's going ballistic as the sounds and colours explode above our heads. I've got to admit – they're pretty shit-hot fireworks. I nuzzle Em, who's looking well cute in her hat and mittens, to warm up.

Meanwhile, this dippy woman in front of us is well into the display, saying, '*Erstmal rot, dann blau, dann grün. Geil!*' and Emma's sort of like taking the piss, translating for me in a low voice. 'First red, then blue, then green. Wow!' and we giggle like naughty schoolkids.

She's alright is Emma when it comes to having a laugh. Yeah, she might be posh but she's always up for a giggle. Talking of posh, did I mention that she's minted? Parents send her an allowance to pay her rent, all her food and that. And she still moans that she can't afford to go out. Not that she gets up off her backside and does anything about it – get a job or anything. She's too busy watching *Star Trek: TNG* on video, smoking puff all day while we work our cocks off at the cookhouse.

Fucking students!

She's generous, though, I'll give her that. Shouted me this last gram of Charlie as it happens. Hang on a sec, you lot, don't get the wrong idea. I can look after myself, can't I? We do alright out of the Army, especially being BAOR and getting topped up with local allowances. And, well, more times than not I've been the one shouting the medicine.

The problem is, being fined that week's wages has put me right in the shit this month, what with Christmas around the corner. And, besides, blow's, like, way more expensive than pills: not sure I can cough up the cash for the amount I've been doing. Having a little toot here and there before work, maybe a bit during. And, well, got to let your hair down after, too, intya? Even you lot would allow a fella that, surely?

Chapter Five

Cal

Bile rises up my throat in a corkscrew; been bumping along in a truck fur over an hour. Nae good letting on ye get car-sick tae this bunch: never hear the end of it. Then, suddenly, the four-tonner lurches sideways, and I bounce out my seat, my Bergan swinging intae Clarkey who's sat next tae us. Whoops! Nearly took his shagging eye out. I catch Manny's lips curling in a smile at the edges, and I think, fuckin amazing: his first smile since we got back fae Christmas leave.

Meantime Clarkey's face is slapped fish, so I mumble, 'Sorry, Corporal,' minding tae address him by rank; he likes us tae do that when we're on exercise. The baw-bag.

We've been deployed fae Fally tae a mystery location in the boonies this morning fur a weekend testing wur soldier and catering skills: using a cook set in the field, patrolling, and doing guards and all that malarkey. Manny's been giving it the big sulks since we was tellt by the Master Chef last week. Cheesed off 'cause – what wi being in the jail and Christmas – he husnae been down the Kiez fur weeks. Even complained tae Clarkey about it, who tellt him straight up, 'What? You'd rather get sent out to Bos with no preparation?'

And there's me thinking, *No way, man – the unit's about tae be deployed?* While all that's on Manny's mind is missing a weekend up Hamburg. Okay, okay, I wouldnae huv minded the chance tae see Steffi. Only hung out wi her the once before the holidays. Lucky she forgave me fur acting like a total bampot that night at the Dom. Met up in HH, and gave her a Christmas pressie. Spent hours choosing some earrings fur her down the jewellers in Fally.

Might as well have wrapped up a fart.

I mean, wes've still no – what's it? consummated – wur relationship. She did get me a bar of chocolate, I suppose. Probably bought at the last minute at –

'RIGHT, YOU LOT!'

I jump, yanked away fae the usual 'does she like me or no' worries, 'cause Clarkey's come over all wannabe sergeant major, coupon puckered in his 'cruising for a bruising' expression. Six lads in olive-green working dress – woolly pullies, denim trousers and berets – stop picking their noses or acting the goat and bolt upright, chins raised, eyes straight ahead.

'Great. Got your attention, sitting there like a bunch of wee fannies. Not being funny but you lot know we need to pull it out the bag today in front of the major and the other units.'

Bums shift about on seats.

'You know what I'm talking about.'

Eyes boring into ours.

'What am I talking about?'

More bum shifting and floor gazing.

'You. Paddy.'

Paddy, a good lad fae Belfast who's recently been made a lance jack, says, 'You're talking about the last inter-unit cookery competition judged by her.' Pause. 'Where we didn't exactly cover ourselves in glory.'

'Yes, dear,' Clarkey goes. 'No more Towering Infernos involving a mishap with a petrol tank and a No. 5 burner.'

The whole truck breaks down intae snickers then. Shame. Paddy's a nice lad. Well, nice when he keeps his trap shut, that is, but mair often than not he's suffering fae an overdose of verbal diarrhoea.

Clarkey lets the piss-taking die down and then he says, 'Alright, this isn't a competition, but I want to show the major that we can work well as a team, that we know what we're doing.' Then, he's practically frothing at the mouth as he goes, 'I want you banging out the food on them stoves as if your lives fucking depended on it. GOT IT?'

And wi that the truck comes tae a standstill and we pile out intae the middle of some woods, rain fuckin tipping down, wind rushing through the trees like in some horror film. Another group of lads are already lined up in a clearing – think there's about five units fae across North Germany as well as ours on exercise the day – and we join them waiting fur the major organising this little party tae belt out the orders. Ah, here she's now: built like an oversized gorilla, face like a melted welly: yer typical lumpy-jumpered SNCO.

Then it's all the – what's it? formalities – and that and she's going, 'For those of you who don't know me, I'm Major Lauren Tredegar in charge of the exercise this weekend. Today is all about cooking with limited rations in the field. You've got one hour to get your kitchens up, and then we need three meals for twenty lads squared away in six hours. Limited rations, but use of a minimal larder.'

And she points tae an area which is already under canvas, packed wi the usual probably: herbs, flour, salt and pepper an that.

'Remember you could be cooking up a mountain, in a jungle, under canvas. So use your imaginations and improvise, improvise, improvise.'

The fuckin numpty.

Then it's all the rules and regulations and we split off intae groups, five of us on our team: Clarkey, Paddy, Manny and me, and a lieutenant who's usually holed away in an office. Manny's away fur a skive of course as soon as we huv tae lug the cook set out the back of the truck, but Clarkey's bang into it, asking fur menu suggestions, putting his back behind it: a man on a mission. *A man looking tae rise up the ranks, mair like*, I think, and snigger.

'So how was your leave, then, pal?'

That's Paddy, me and him wresting over lugging the mark 5 cook set fae the truck, and I holler over the clanging and the banging about seeing Steffi and, once we've got a flame going under the tea urn, I continue, more quietly… 'then back tae Glesga fur Christmas. My auntie cooked us a rare Christmas dinner. Delicious alcohol-free trifle, would ye believe. Nice tae see someone else behind the stove fur a change,' I blether on.

But of course Detective Maguire latches on tae the 'alcohol-free'. Knows about my ma's little problem, but screws up his forehead and says, 'Alcohol-free trifle? That's like a brothel without the whores, eh right?'

'Och – you know, alcohol-free 'cause my ma was supposed tae come and join us.' He shrugs. 'You know, she likes a drink?' He nods a quick yes. 'Of course, she didnae make it.'

Don't tell him what else my auntie Edie told me. That my ma's back on the bottle. Big time. So I made fuck-all effort tae see her when I was on my leave. Anyway, my family was waiting for me in Ayr. Went down tae the Hangar 13 to a Hogmanay rave there wi my cousins Gordon and Malcy.

But lucky Paddy doesnae dig any deeper, 'cause Manny's rejoined us, actually breaking intae a sweat as he gets tae grips wi putting the stove thegither.

'And Manny, how was your Crimbo?' Paddy asks.

'Yeah, blinding,' he scowls. 'Getting it in the neck from me dad. Mum not sticking up for herself as usual. Wish I'd come up to Jock Land with Cal…'

And then a thought springs tae mind and I go, 'What about Amy…' feel bad fur no asking him since we got back '… did ye visit her?'

Manny starts hammering away at the metal then, slinging me wan a his deafies. But I cannae push him any further, 'cause Clarkey's on top of us, Lieutenant Grainger looking on.

'Come on, ladies, mothers' meeting can wait till yer back on camp.'

And as the rain beats down on canvas, I forget everything else fur a bit: just think of teamwork and rabbit stew and – fur once in my puff – wanting tae do Clarkey proud.

I nestle down intae my maggot bag, woolly pully on 'cause it's fuckin Baltic, the night – no exactly camping weather. Ouch! Something's scratching my toes. I pull out a pine needle – must be left over fae wur last exercise out in Canada – then chuck off my beret and try tae settle down, listening to the quiet of the night. But my brain's buzzing; I'm way too tired fur sleep.

'Oy, Manny,' I say tae his curled-up back, 'what do ye reckon the command task will be, the morra? Mind that time we had tae get all that stuff over that fake electric fence? You pole-vaulted right through the middle?'

'Oh, yeah, and that time you jumped out your skin at a banger, even though it was a mock minefield we was patrolling.'

'Ooh, touchy, touchy!' I say.

And I think he's rolling over tae catch some zeds but then, tae my astonishment, he pulls a book out his Bergan. I gulp back a snigger when I see the title: *Trainspotting*.

'What the f – ' I splutter. 'Reading a book about trainspotters, ye weirdo?'

'Oh, it can read, can it?' Clarkey goes as he enters the tent.

Just our luck. A three-man tent and we drew the short straw. Manny ignores him, turns to me instead. 'Nah, mate. Got it all wrong. Me aunt, the one who works in a bookshop, give it me for Christmas. 'Bout some Scottish pricks from Edinburgh, into skag and all of that. You might like it, as it happens.'

Squeaky bum time or what? I mean, what's he like wi his rubber gub about the dirties in front of Clarkey? Anyway. 1. I'm fae Glesga; 2. I'd never touch the brown; and 3. I know fuck-all about trainspotting, so I'm Scoobied why he thinks I'd like his book.

94

'Nah, yer alright. I'll stick to my vampire stories, thanks,' I answer back, nodding at Clarkey as he unrolls his maggot bag.

Aye, don't laugh, but when it comes tae reading it's vampires all the way fur me. I read this series, *Vampire-Ville*, these funny-as-fuck stories about an American town where the vampires try and live normal lives alongside the everyday folk. Only of course they cannae live thegither 'cause the vampires huv tae suck the ordinary folks' blood in order tae survive.

Actually, a raver's life is kind of like a vampire's, if yous must know. Aye, really, think about it! First, there's the way we look – peely-wally skin 'cause we shy away fae daylight, only going out after the sun goes down. Second, we like infecting virgin ravers wi a tablet, getting them hooked on E and increasing the size of wur posse. Mostly, though, to my mind, we're like vampires 'cause we're outsiders, the black sheep of society. I mean, it's like we're sticking two fingers up tae the never-ending pish flow of everyday life: living fur yer job an that. Why bother when ye can live for the weekend instead; when ye can lose it tae the hardcore and the dirties, concentrating on fuck aw else but the moment of being on that dance flair? Och, I dunno. Mibbe I'm just a good Catholic boy looking tae justify my way of life.

Anyway. Mibbe I will give that *Trainspotting* a shot. Manny's right stuck intae it, so it must be a good story, right enough.

'Come on, lads, let's turn those torches off. Got to give those Celle boys a run for their money tomorrow.'

'Alright, chief,' I say, and Manny just grunts.

Och, I dunno. Sometimes when we've had a good day 'at the office' it makes me think I should give up the pills, after all. I mean, mibbe it's time tae turn over a new leaf? New year, new me. Think about quitting the pill-swallowing, the fleeing and the dancing.

Aye, yous are right. I know I'm – what's it? contradicting masel. But look, I didnae get bumped by the stupit tree on the way down; I know this way of life cannae last forever. So, while we can get away wi it, fuck it. Aye, fuck it: while we can dodge the pish stain of real life, I'm gonnae enjoy these best of times. Don't worry, though. I'm no gonnae bore yous, go on and on about us raving and misbehaving, I see yous've got the picture. So now I guess it's time tae see what happens when the best of times blow over, and look at the worst of times tae come.

Hamburg – Purgatory Bar

Manny

Iain's like, 'Keep a lid on it, eh, chum?'

How can I? What he's just done, it's out of order – bang out of order!

I want to say something, want to pummel his pretty-boy face to a deepest, darkest black and blue, if you want the truth. Only I ain't got the nerve, have I? Besides, he can be a fucking mentalist if you start on him. Or even if you don't. Take this one time when we was out on the lash in Fally – he beat some GI's head in, the yank had to have nine stitches, all 'cause he'd accidentally spilt Kelly's drink in some cheesy bar. Not sure I'm ready for the same treatment.

So I just say, 'Sure, boss, my lips are sealed,' and smile, weakly, turning back to my *Grosses* on the bar.

But, I'm thinking, *Oh, come on, Manny, have a word with yourself. I should get revenge for Cal, shouldn't I? He's done nothing, nothing whatsoever, to Iain to deserve this.* Typical Iain to pull a fast one while Cal's stuck on camp and all. Yet another reason I should give him some five-knuckle attention. Maybe another line in the bogs and I'll have the bottle? Second thoughts, Steffi's still down there and the shoulder-to-cry-on bit's a nause at the best of times.

What Iain's done ain't exactly a bolt from the blue, though. I mean, he's one of them blokes who likes nothing better than to chase the tail of the one bird that you fancy. Better still, cop off with her. You know, because he can? So, if we're out in some sticky-carpet place on the pull, you have to be a bit clever and pretend you don't fancy the bird you're after.

Yeah, I know – warped.

Not as warped as what he's just gone and fucking done. Eh? Oh, yeah, you lot don't know. He only went and slipped Steffi a Mickey Finn, put a pill in her drink, and she'd only just dropped one herself. Think about it. Her pretty new to the scene and double-dropping without realising. The fucking bell end. That's not the worst of it, though. He's just told me he's been giving her the fun finger in the bogs. 'Making the most of it while she was coming up,' is how he put it. Fingering her in the fucking bogs of Purgatory! I mean, he could have at least taken her outside to the motor.

Yeah, yeah, I know, more to the point, what about Cal? Not the first time Iain's gone behind his back. Cal was seeing this Australian bird on the Hamburg scene before. She was a pig in knickers as it happens, but Cal, well, you know... beggars can't be choosers. Then Iain steps in. Starts flirting with this bird in front of Cal. Just with little comments at first, like, 'You look sweet today,' or, 'You're well pretty, you don't need to wear make-up.' Cal was cool about it, turned a deaf ear – I mean, you have to or you look a cunt, don't ya? And when we was all out high on pills, Iain was sort of like first in there with – Mandy, I think her name was – when it was time for them E'd-up hugs. Sure, that's in the rules, it's a proper loved-up free-for-all when yer pilled-up. Weren't exactly fair on Cal, though. I mean, I'm not being funny, but if you had to choose between Iain's rippling deep brown six-pack and Cal's short-arse white Scottish bod, I think I know which way you'd go. Anyway, I think maybe something else happened between Mandy and Iain in the end, something serious, 'cause suddenly she goes right off Cal and we never saw her again.

I actually think Iain's jealous of Cal in a way. Yeah, serious! Cal's one of them happy-go-lucky blokes, popular with all the lads in the cookhouse, on the block, even with the SNCOs. Iain, well, not sure why, 'cause I've always thought he was diamond, but – mates aside – he's about as popular as a dose of herpes on honeymoon.

So, I'm thinking, *Come on, Manny, give him a smack in the chops for Cal, get him back double for what he's done* –

But hold up, Steffi's back on the scene. Man, she does not look good.

'We're leaving,' she's saying gruffly to nobody in particular, as Emma comes up behind her. 'Ciao.' She don't look over in our direction.

Iain's grid is a deflated balloon. Yeah, he's that warped, he probably thought Steffi'd hang out with him tonight, even after what he's done. 'What? What? You not coming clubbing?' he says, his eyes bulging in disbelief. 'Come on, ladies, if yer skint, we'll sort you out, eh, Manny?'

Yeah, mate, I think. *Depends what you mean by 'sort you out'.*

I shrug. I don't give a stuff one way or the other.

'I want to stay,' Emma says, stamping her foot, 'but for some reason her ladyship here's out of it, wants me to take her home.'

She's not wrong. Steffi's gripping a table, as if, without its help, she'd fall off the edge of the world.

Anyway. 'Ckin hell, seems Steffi's not told Emma. What's all that about, then? Does Steffi even realise she was spiked? I'm mulling this over as Emma starts picking among our coats piled up in one of the booths, which has been commandeered by a few gay lads while all this has been going on.

Emma pulls out her green puffa jacket and starts saying, 'Sorry, hon, but I'll make it up – ' but she stops short, 'cause –

What the fuck?

Steffi's falling down in a dead faint, heading arse-first for the filth and cigarette butts and beer puddles on the bar floor. She lands *smack*! with a bump, her beer bottle flying out her hand, sailing through the air – *wheeeeeeeeeee!* – and bouncing across the floor, splashing showers of lager over Iain's new white Reeboks.

A helluva commotion follows.

Emma starts crying.

Taff shouts, 'Call an ambulance.' And then, '*Achtung! Krankenwagen.*'

Iain goes, 'My fucking brand new trainers.'

What. The. Fuck? I take a swipe at him. I want to punch that fucker's fucking lights out. Taff grips my arm. Holds me back. Looks at Steffi. Is he putting two and two together? Come on, Manny, think of Steffi now! So, I'm like, 'Don't fucking crowd her.' And to Iain, 'Do one!'

One of the gay lads rushes over to the bar, while me and Emma crouch down over Steffi. Lucky her arm has twisted above her head, cushioning the blow. Still, it don't look good. Her eyes are closed tight and her face is a full white moon.

'Get me some water,' Emma says, not crying now, very serious.

The lads in the booth are flapping and fussing like girls, and one of them hands Emma a water bottle, which Em splashes on Steffi's face till, just as suddenly as she went down, she blinks twice. She's coming round.

I say quickly to Taff, 'No fucking ambulance, right?' 'cause no way I want to have to deal with rozzers or whatever again. That would be me, up shit creek without the proverbial. And he heads to the bar to tell them the bad scene's over.

Steffi sort of leans up then, only to flop back down right away as she says, '*Geht schon... geht schon*, I'm fine, I'm fine,' followed by, 'I don't know why this happened.' But her wide-eyed gaze is now fixed on Iain, who's fidgeting, hopping on one foot, behind Taff.

What? He hasn't left?

'You still here?' I shout at him, and he glares at me, but, with deliberate slowness, finds his Tacchini tracksuit top from among our now messed-up pile of coats, moseying towards the door like nothing's happened.

The lads in the booth make way, and we lay Steffi down across the seats, unzip her hoodie, giving her little sips of water, till she's like, 'It's okay, it's okay, I can sit.'

We're not gonna bother with the Tunnel Club tonight. Nice one, Iain. Fucked it up for everyone. First weekend off the leash in '94, and it ends up like this. Means I don't get to kip over at Emma's neither.

Last thing she done, Steffi, before her and Emma left, was, like, pull me away from the others and squeeze my hand, saying, '*Bitte*, don't tell Cal. Please don't tell Cal.' And I'm thinking, *Does she mean about being spiked or fingered or fainting or about all three?*

'Right shiner she'll have on her backside – Steffi,' Taff says, interrupting my train of thought.

'Ouch!' I say, and then, feeling awkward 'cause I realise me and him have been left on our tods, I go, 'Fancy a bevvy?'

'Sure, I'll get them in. *Grosses*?'

I give him a thumbs-up.

And while he's at the bar, I think of the bruise that's gonna spread over Steffi's backside in the days that come, and I can't shake this thought of a giant black, blue and purple shadow spreading over me and the rest of the crew. I mean, what's with us? A mouldy fruit cocktail of drink-spikers, pill-munchers and girlfriend-stealers, coke-heads, fuck-ups and prick-teases. It's like, if you put us under a microscope, you'd see a slimy crawling black stain that's getting out of hand, and you'd want to crush it with your thumb, just like that; take it out completely before it spreads any bigger.

'What was all that about anyway?'

Hold up – here's Taff, joining me in the booth, plonking the *Grosses* on a soggy beer mat in front of me, his eyebrows raised.

Hang on. What's he staring at? I look down to grab my drink and realise that in the time he's been gone I've crushed a fag packet with my hands – a shagging full one and all. I chuck it quickly in the ashtray, as if I done it on purpose, and answer his question.

'Dunno mate, everything and nothing, I guess.'

Thinking, *Why the fuck am I covering for Iain, again?*

Fallingbostel British Army Base

Cal

The kitchens are a stainless steel monster today. The chipping machine could be its belly, gobbling up endless potatoes, the electric whisks its motorised hands, the noise of the whirring, stirring, dicing and slicing, its terrifying growl. No wonder the lads and lassies are swarming over the place trying tae look busy – otherwise the monster'll get them.

Burp! There it goes, belching out yet mair chip fat and grease. And there's the evil controller of the machine, LC Patrick Maguire, who's helping run the shop floor, the day. Och, he's never? He is. He's coming over. Hold on, though, he looks angry. Don't tell me somebody's peed in the soup. Again.

'Was it you, then, Happy, boy?' he asks, his eyes darting about madly over my work space.

I continue wi my work – gutting a sardine – and say simply, 'Sorry?'

'Me best paring knife has gone walkies, and I wondered if it had found his way to you,' he says.

'Um, not me, boss,' I go, wi a tight smile on my coupon.

'Hmm,' is all he says.

I flinch. I mean, c'moan tae fuck! I'm a lot of things, but I'm never a thief.

And he just stands there, watching me fur a bit, as I score the underside of the next sardine. Gonnae just do wan, I think, but he's obviously in wan a his chatty moods, 'cause after a long conversation about the ins and outs of sardine bones he asks, 'Did ye hear the latest about Bos, then?'

'Oh, aye?' I ask, curious. 'What's that, then?' I put down the knife and wipe fish guts on my whites.

'I heard 1 RTR are coming back from their six-month rotation with the UN peacekeeping mission. Seems the unit may be deployed there soon.'

Christ. Looks like that exercise down Sennelager was prep for Bos, then...

'Och, right – ' I blather, boggling at the thought, but also minding that there's a long list of dos and don'ts in the Army – mainly don'ts, right enough. Number one being letting on ye'd rather mop the flair of a peep show cubicle than see active service.

'Well, there you go, the time has come,' is the best thing I can think of saying.

There you go, the time has come? Did I really just say that?

And then I ask him, 'Look, d'ya mind, this is a fiddly job,' and he mooches off tae hassle somebody else wi his prattle.

C'moan tae fuck – Bosnia!

Aye, yous are right, 'sno exactly a shock tae learn I've tae go on tour. Sure as night follows day, death follows life, heaven (hopefully) follows death, you join up and you'll see active service at some point. But this? One lad said he knew a cookie monster who went out on patrol and got shot at by a sniper.

Och, whatever, you never know, it might be us, it might be another unit that gets their three months' notice, I think, and I finish up my work, no giving it much mair thought fur now...

The dorm's a morgue when I get back after my shift. I'm working the weekends fae now on till the start of February 'cause I used up all my leave on Christmas and New Year. Can still go down Hamburg but mibbe not as often. As if I care. Steffi always seems busy wi her studies at the minute.

I lie on my pit, first on my back, then on my side. Mibbe try the front too? I know – read something, that'll take the edge off. I pick up a copy of my latest book, *Dead and Buried*, the last wan in they *Vampire-Ville* stories I was telling yous about. I read a line... my mind drifts... reread it. Sigh! Makes you almost *want* tae go on tour, some days are such a fuckin drag here.

Hold on – what's that on Jonesy's bedside locker? Aye, it is, it's a copy of *The Face* magazine. Fuckin ponce! I pick it up, though; huv a flick through. And there, slap bang in front of me, is a weird advert illustrated wi blue toy sodgers resembling the UN peacekeeping force.

Talk about rubbing it in!

I flick straight past that, past the trendy pictures, past the millions of adverts and the stupit captions wi words like 'buzz' and 'cool'. Ah, that's mair like it: an article on Bobby Gillespie! 'A skinny white boy from Glasgow?' it says. We've a lot in common, then, so we huv. But, actually, I don't fancy reading. My mind is now being prodded and poked wi thoughts of Muslims and Croats, booby traps and snipers.

I chuck the mag tae wan side. Lie back on my pit. Pick my nose. Wipe it in the snot farm I'm – what's it? cultivating – on the wall behind my bed space.

Christ, I huvnae been this fed-up since the basic training – bored out my box, cooped up on that fuckin training centre down Aldershot, where the only combat any sodger saw was the hand-tae-gland variety. No wonder we gave in tae the lure of the dirties and the dancing down the Rhythm Station.

Fur most of the lads, it was the booze that got them through the nut-numbing dullness of the place. I was fuckin gobsmacked when I arrived tae see mair cheeky water down that training centre than round my scheme in Glesga. 'Nothing to do here but drink,' wan a the lads tellt me when I arrived. What's that expression? Frying pan intae the fire? Well, as yous know, me no being intae the swally is how come I ended up doing my first tablet. This wee guy who never made it through phase one of the training brought some tablets in wan night – cannae mind his name now. Kenny? Anyway. Proper crack we hud thegither, screaming down the corridors of the block after the mid-week NAAFI disco, singing show songs, would yous believe, higher than I've ever been since.

Anyway, the basic training. Aye, it was dull, but it was hard as hell an aw. Phase one lasts ten weeks just, and ye cannae even drink in the first two. The toughest ten weeks of my puff – ten weeks running about stupit, doing all the physical shite, fuckin learning drill parades, how tae handle a weapon an that. Or, in other words, ten weeks of them doing their best tae turn ye intae a sodger, intae a fuckin yes-man. The rest of the two years there we learnt wur trade, which was okay, and even the final two weeks of guard duty wasnae bad. And, tae be fair, when Manny joined us, during the first year of the trade training, life became sweet.

And what was all this leading up tae, and the two years since? A tour! Bosnia!

I thrust out a sigh fae deep in my belly. Close my eyes. Think about having some zeds. Lie on my back, turn on my front, scratch my heid. Bash the life out of the pillow. Och, c'moan! Cannae get fuckin comfy.

But then there's a knock at the door. I leap up. It's Tommo and Davie. Result! Cal 1, Boredom 0.

'Alright, chum, we're off down the NAAFI – fancy a lager?' That's Tommo, dressed in his usual civvy gear – Fred Perry and skin-tight jeans.

'Aye, think I'm needing wan. Paddy tells us we cookie monsters mibbe headed fur Bos soon. Help out the UN peacekeeping mission.'

They fall about laughing. 'You won't last five minutes,' Tommo chuckles, slapping his thigh. 'Last time I checked, there weren't no bloody raves in Bosnia.'

Och, aye, very funny.

Still, I'm no surprised at his attitude. He's always taking the urine about my raving. And that's him wi a fuckin addiction tae prescription drugs, mind. Not his fault, I suppose. He's a tank man alongside Davie, and worked like a daftie till wan time he got injured out on exercise in Canada. Wan a the tanks ploughed intae him and that was it, his legs were fucked. Since then he's been on permanent light duties – and permanently on fuckin heavy prescription painkillers.

'You can always buzz off lighter fuel or neck anti-nerve agents. That's what the lads done in the Gulf to get high.' That's Davie's contribution.

Things are looking better by the minute, I think sarcastically. No Steffi, no E – and buzzing off chemical weapons.

Then Tommo butts in my thoughts. 'No Manny around?' he asks – which makes me think of another problem.

'He's away up HH wi Iain,' I say, my mind already drifting.

Manny. Shite. It's wan thing me getting sent down Bosnia, but him? *Way he's going recently*, I think, *it'd be the death of him*. In the expression way, I mean, checking my own thoughts. Sure, Manny's as well-trained as the rest of us, but right now his heid is that far up his arse, it's a wonder he can get out of bed in the mornings, never mind do the sodger thing fur real.

Hamburg – Kiez/Hafen

Manny

'Leg it,' Iain says, and I don't need to be told twice, pegging it down Friedrichstrasse, away from the police station – what the fuck, why'd he have to rob someone so close to the bloody cop shop? – my feet not stopping as I bump past the prossies who ogle and crane their necks as we fly past. I can hear the *thump, thump, thump* of Iain's feet behind me over the sound of the pounding rain, and he's overtaking me now as we turn the corner, further away into that seedy street, the one that women can't even walk –

I have to stop… gulp in a few breaths of air… bend over double, hands pressing into a wall. If I could only rest…

… but Iain's yanking my jacket, pulling me forward, and I can't believe how fit he is, how fast he can run, how unfit I am compared to him; and we're going at it hammer and tongs, my feet bashing and slipping on the cobbles, the colourful reflections from the knocking shop windows making weirdly beautiful patterns on the wet ground. No thinking about that now, though, as Iain grabs my arm again, saying, 'Come on this way,' directing me away from the Kiez...

... and we bundle past the Irish pub, the one in that little square off the Reeperbahn... think he must be headed for the port round the corner, which is fine by me 'cause my legs are giving up the ghost. What the fuck? That's not a posse of them Green Berets from Hohne camp coming out the pub, is it? Can they see us? Do they recognise us? But no time to take them in, 'cause we're whizzing past them like rockets... not far now, I tell myself, the adrenaline keeping me going, the fear of getting caught not doing a bad job neither.

We arrive about the same time, panting, at the water's edge by the *Hafen*, the port, and Iain sifts through the wallet, before lumping it in the river. His chest's heaving up and down and he's bent over, holding on to me.

What the fuck. Is he blubbing?

Course not. The mentalist's laughing like a drain.

'Y'alright, son?' he asks.

'Yeah, boss, sweet,' I manage to get out between deep spurts of heavy breathing and gobs of phlegm.

It's dank and dark here by the water and the smell of fish makes me want to chuck. Iain, of course, is cool as a cucumber, dwarfing the skyline and the giant ship docked behind him with his heaving bulk. Gotta get my act together, like he has, I think; I don't want to lose face. So I shake myself about looking silently at the black water as Iain goes and sits on a rain-drenched wall to count out the wads of cash.

'Sweet indeed. Three hundred smackers from the machine, ten in the wallet. Here you go,' and he hands me two soggy fifty DM notes.

'Oy, oy, we agreed halvesies, what about the other fifty?' I go – in a half-arsed way, 'cause it was his idea: he was the one what punched that bloke at the cashpoint to the ground.

'Just think of it as half of what you owe me,' he goes, the light from the ships behind him making his face look well sinister. 'We can settle the rest later, yeah?'

Fair dos. Not that I'm sure I want any of the moolah anyways; feeling a bit gutted about what we done, as it goes. Bile rises up in my throat when I think about that old guy lying on the floor. That's Iain for you. Wheedle you into anything, he can; makes you feel well small if you're not up for it.

'Come on, Beluga Bar's round the corner. We can lie low for a while,' he says when we've got our breath back.

Lie low? Thinks he's in a chuffing gangster movie!

But I don't argue – can't believe with all them one-and-a-half-mile runs we have to put up with, that I'm this out of puff – a sit-down, a *Grosses*, maybe a line, will do just the job.

'Yeah, okay, your round, chief,' I say, more in hope than expectation.

Fair play to him, soon as we're in, Iain heads barwards, and I settle myself in a corner out the way, getting swallowed up by an enormous shaggy sofa, hugging myself into it with a sigh. In some ways you could say Iain's only looking out for me, I suppose. In others you could say he's a slippery cunt.

Anyway, what happened was, we was headed to Camelot for some 'big time' deal Iain had up his sleeve. And – yeah, yeah, I know after what he done to Steffi I should be avoiding him like the plague. Emma's well put out with me for even speaking to him, since she found out. But it's sort of like, I don't know anyone else to get my coke from, got to keep him sweet. Talking of which, he's got a batch of this shit-hot new Colombian stuff in. Plan was to come to HH to sell half of it to a dodgy Turkish geezer he knows down the Camelot. But we was bang out of luck – the geezer didn't show, I'm out of pocket till pay day and Iain had no cash or cards on him, expecting the Turkish guy to sort him. So, a few bevvys and lines later and my wallet's empty and it's Iain who's dreamt up this plan: that we could whack some poor fucker at the cashpoint, use that for our evening spends.

And I was sort of groaning when I said, 'Aw come on, mate, you know the RSM'll have me on a charge if I cross the line again.'

Iain went dead quiet then. 'So, what, you got that hundred you owe me on you?'

I didn't think he was fucking about. But one of these days, I tell ya, I'm gonna put him straight. Tell him what liberties he's fucking taking. I mean, I like the bloke, he's a mate, the best even, but he don't half get you into all sorts of scrapes.

Like this one.

First things first, we stashed the Charlie in the motor – give or take a gram or two. The idea was to head out on the Reeperbahn, do the first fucker over we could at one of the cash machines. Only the place was like a morgue, weren't it? It had been chucking it down in razor blades all day. So it seemed like we'd been sheltering under this one tree for, like, forever, when finally a straggly-haired soap-dodger came out one of the titty bars and headed for the cash machine.

And then the actual mugging happened, like this:

Iain gave me the nod, mooched over to the bloke, dropped a *Zehner* on the floor – deliberately, like. I come over, point out the *Zehner* to the guy, bloke stoops to pick it up. Then, as planned, Iain grabs the cash churning out the machine. Then, not as planned, Iain lamps the now stunned geezer on the chin, flooring him in one punch. And we leg it. But not before looking back to see the guy, a curled turd on the floor, cradling his face with his hands. And Iain goes back then, don't he? Gives the guy a kicking and snatches his wallet and all. And, I'm thinking, *Fuck about, talk about sticking the boot in*, and that's when you joined us, legging it down Friedrichstrasse towards the *Hafen* and this trendy bar.

'There you go son. Pint of wobbly and a whisky chaser, settle your nerves,' Iain says, dragging me away from them thoughts. Wobbly being this tasty beer you get over here, *Warsteiner*, incidentally. No prizes for guessing why the lads call it 'wobbly'.

'Thanks, man,' I go, then, 'Ciggie?' Iain shakes his head, pulls out a Red from his own packet. Yeah. I was forgetting. Iain thinks Lights are for pussies. Unless he runs out, of course, then he's suddenly thieving yours.

'So, then, what'd ye think of that little adventure?' he goes, taking a swig from his beer bottle.

'Yeah, man. Um... wicked?' I say, but that meekly, even he can't be convinced.

'Good to hear that, good to hear, 'cause there's something I've been meaning to ask you...'

So, that's it. Iain's idea of some sort of initiation ceremony, is it? His way of seeing if I'm 'man enough' like him and Taff to do the Big Boy stuff? And yeah, you lot might think I'm a fucking pinhead, I know I done some stupid things, acted like a twat. Do you know what, though? I'm not interested in what he's got to say, in that 'Big Boy stuff' he's telling me about. Still, I know him, know he don't take no for an answer, so I look him square in the eye, answering his question with a quick nod, saying, 'Yeah, mate, sound.'

But my hands are trembly as I pay the barman for the next round, my temples beating out a deafening march which drowns out the background hubbub of music and laughter and happiness in the bar.

Hannover – Hanomag

Cal

The first thing we clock on arriving at the rave's an ambulance parked up outside, a young lassie laid out on a stretcher beside it – her eyes going thegither, her mouth frothing wi spew. The paramedics belt out instructions to wan another while the lassies' pals flap about, adding tae the general commotion.

That's got tae be some kind of warning, right?

'Silly tart,' Iain says. 'Caning it before she even got here, probably.'

'Leave it out,' Jonesy squeaks, 'she's only young.'

'*Leave it out, she's only young,*' Iain mimics, and Jonesy laughs, not seeming to notice that Iain's noising him up.

Or maybe he does, 'cause he coughs up a greenie, ejects it on the ground, trying tae – what's it? reassert – his manhood probably. Kelly, who Iain's let off the leash fur once fur some reason, thumps Jonesy on the arm.

Some night this is gonnae be.

Even the journey up here was a downer: Kelly and Iain tearing strips off wan another up front in the motor, her chain-smoking filling the car up wi fumes, Jonesy sat next tae us in the back, giving us the silent treatment the whole way.

Meanwhile, Manny's no even out the night, huvin come down wi a severe case of 'cannae-be-arsed-itis'. That lad. When he's no hanging like a limp dishcloth over the stove in the cookhouse, either he's on the sniff, out wi Emma or lying on his pit, overdosing on the auld Egyptian PT. Och, okay, yous are right, I didnae huv tae come out like I just said, exactly, but there's a chance – just a chance, mind – that Steffi's out, the night.

Fingers crossed: huvnae seen her fur nearly two months.

Och, even if she's no out the night, mibbe an evening of hardcore heaven's what I need: a night of my feet sticking tae the dance flair, the air thick wi whoops and smoke, the BPMs rupturing my eardrums. Besides, wi Kelly in tow mibbe Iain will forget about getting lumbered, and wes can all huv a crack like the auld days.

'C'moan, then,' I say, 'let's go in,' and I tug on Iain and Jonesy's arms as they rubberneck at the lassie while the paramedics put her in the back of the ambulance.

The auld red Hanomag building looms in front of us. Been down tae a few raves here in the past, each as bad as the other. Still, it's all we've got – Tunnel Club's closed the night – better than nothing. Besides, I think, as Iain hands me a tablet, ye get a good enough tablet and ye could be anywhere.

But then I notice the E.

'What's this?' I ask, my eyes popping. It's brown and flecky, doesnae look like E at all.

'Elephants,' Iain says, all bright and breezy. 'Pill's alright, but maybe a bit mongy,' his voice rising at the end of his sentence, as if he was asking a question.

I keep staring at it.

'Well, do you want it or – ' he goes, making to grab the thing back off me.

'Alright, alright,' I cut in, 'let's not be hasty,' and I bang it back wi a glug of water.

As I'm swallowing it down, Kelly's paw dives intae Iain's pocket and pulls out a tablet. He grabs her wrist. Too late! She's gulped it down wi no water. Look on his fizzog. Priceless!

And then he's banging on at her. How does she expect tae get up the duff if she keeps munching pills like sweeties? I turn away, embarrassed, but no before I catch her spitting out something about no wanting a baby hanging off her tit all day. C'moan tae fuck! This is getting out of hand! So I say 'C'moan, let's go,' chivvying the others along again, and we start the long walk through the different rooms of the Hanomag towards the main arena, taking in the scene.

'Sno pretty.

Seems like everyone's pure glaikit wi drugs, the night, there's that many weirdos and sad fucks about: E casualties shivering and vomming in the draughty corridors; crusties wi acid house bandanas shrieking like banshees on the dance flair; square-peg teenaged Germans gawping at the freak show. The soundtrack tae this sorry sight is the worst kind of ear-bleeding techno an aw – heavy, dirgy, and – what's it? Monotonous. We're taking this all in, and, for once, me, Jonesy and Iain are a trio of perfect agreement – the night's gonnae be a bag of shite.

And then a row starts.

Jonesy wants tae head tae the house music room; I'm all fur staying in the main arena – mibbe the next DJ'll be better, I tell them (aye, right, mair chance of Steffi turning up here). And Iain, well, he doesnae give a rat's arse what music we hear.

As yous know, he's only intae this scene fur the dirties and the lassies. So, it's a surprise when he pipes up, 'Stay here it is, then.' Then, scruffling Jonesy's carrot top, 'Two against one, mate. Sorry.'

Kelly's opinion doesnae count, then? I glance at her as she mooches a few feet away fae us, sparking up yet another fag.

'Aw, suit yourselves,' Jonesy says, 'I'm off for a bit of bouncy housey.'

Bouncy housey? The baw-bag.

Second time the night he's been on my side, though – Iain. In fact, he's sooking up tae me no end at the minute. If I hud my tinfoil hat on I'd say something was up.

Och, forget that. Must be the dirties giving me the heebie-jeebies again. *Speaking of which, we dropped they tablets a hauf-hour ago, and I'm no exactly rushing*, I'm thinking, as the MC shouts out, 'Move yer arses, move yer arses harder.'

C'moan tae fuck! Even the MC's on a bad yin, the night.

'Oy, Cal,' Iain shouts over the industrial techno, 'how about a game of freak or unique?'

A topless German dude, his body painted in swirly fluorescent colours, floats psychedelically past us.

I nod towards the guy, want tae tell Iain, definitely freak, but it's as if my lips were superglued thegither, my tongue rolling slack and heavy around the words which eventually crawl out my mouth. 'Def---in---ate---ly fr---ea---k.'

And just before my brain switches off completely, I think, *Away tae fuck, mongy tablets*, but then there's no thoughts whatsoever 'cause

I'm a lead balloon, plunging
down
    down
        down
            down

sucked intae a bottomless pit of spaced-outness. I try and float along wi the feeling – 'sno exactly unpleasant, 'sno exactly nice either – but it's all I can do tae keep my body upright. I lean back against a clammy wall. Breathe out. Submerge under the ton weight of the pill, drowning in a sea of sledging which shuts out the outside world.

'F-u--------ckin-----g mo------n------gy pills,' I loll – as if drunk – lost in a bubble of dreaminess fur Christ knows how long: body floating... bobbing along... girl touching my arm... Steffi?... then, finally calm... feeling at peace...

And by the time I'm next sort of aware of things around about me, I vaguely notice the first rolling drums kicking in as a jungle DJ takes over the decks.

Could things get any worse?

I eyeball the person slumped next tae us against the wall, the one who touched my arm, I think, and realise that it's Kelly, that Iain's no about. I manage tae drawl over the increasing racket, 'Oy, fancy banging out? I'm no that intae this scene.'

'Yeah, alright, pet,' Kelly says, and then I cannae believe my ears when she goes on, 'Iain promised we'd be home before two.'

'Oh, aye?'

'Yeah, it's our wedding anniversary,' she says, looking away.

Aye, ye wouldnae huv tae be an agony aunt to see what that says about their marriage. But instead of saying anything useful, I just nod, 'Alright, then, let's go find him,' and I grab her skinnier-than-ever wrist tae help her up off the ground.

We find him before long, chatting tae some German birds we know, Kelly hiding behind me as we approach him. What is she? Embarrassed fur him? So, I break up the mothers' meeting and put forward wur plan tae bang out. And he's like 'Fair dos, let's go,' but then I'm suddenly hit by another huge wave of Ecstasy, so I ask, 'You alright tae drive, pal?' I know I wouldnae be – even if I hud my licence – my eyes are fuckin ping pong balls, zig-zagging all over the shop.

And he's like, 'Oh, yeah, I knew them elephants were duds, so I didn't do one.'

I'm way too fucked tae even care what a cunt that makes him.

'What about Jonesy?' I bellow over the rampaging drum and bass.

'Oh, yeah. We'll have to go and get him…'

'Sfine by me. A walk around this bad dream of a rave'll mibbe sort the heid. Aye, right again! There's also some miserable, rotten, stupit wee part of me thinking we might still find Steffi an aw.

But there's no Jonesy in the bogs, no Jonesy in the house room, no Jonesy at any of the bars we look in.

And no Steffi anywhere neither.

But by the time we've swedged wur way through the car park, I've almost forgotten tae care, 'cause me and Kel are arm-in-arm, buddied up 'cause we're on the same wavelength, in a different place tae Iain. He doesnae seem that bothered.

He's got a doozy of a new motor, by the way, Iain. Loves tae flash the cash these days, does that yin. I share this wi him as I'm sinking back intae the cotton wool comfort of the back seat, Kelly by my side.

'Class, innit? Always wanted a Beamer.'

And, as he twists back around tae turn the key in the engine, Kelly pokes her tongue in her chin, as if tae say: 'what a mong'. I chuckle.

Course, if he kept the heid, he'd no splash the cash, no give the RMP a Scooby that he's earning over the odds fur a lance jack. I mean, sure, loads of the lads huv nice motors an that, but a BMW? And a K reg at that. Might as well get a T-shirt printed saying 'I'm a dealer'. So I say, 'Aye, but you don't wannae give the game away, do ya, pal?'

He turns on me, cheeks flaming, then. 'Oh, behave! Them Monkeys haven't got a freaking clue.'

Your funeral, pal, I think. C'moan tae fuck! Funeral, death, my da. Now they words are cycling through my brain, bringing me down further.

But the drive back tae camp perks me up. Kelly's blethering away, wanting tae find out what's going on wi me, asking me tons of questions about Steffi, about her family, about her being a 'bloody student' as she puts it. Only it isnae long before Iain sticks his oar in, spoiling things by asking, 'So, you boned 'er yet?'

The heat coming off Kelly's cheeks at that yin could light a shagging bonfire.

Och, not another row the whole way back! I try and make a joke of things, tae lighten the mood, and say, 'Mind your own beeswax.' But inside I'm seething, want tae blurt out, *Who're you tae talk about my bird like that?*

Sure, my ma used to say 'Tell the truth and shame the Devil'. *But how can you shame the Devil,* I think, catching sight of Iain's demonic dark eyes in the car mirror, *when he's sat right in front of you – and he plainly doesnae give a fuck?*

Hamburg – Kiez

Manny

We step out of Frühclub after a marathon session, rabbits in the headlights as a mishmash of random colours and sounds and the dazzling cold light of day smack us in the face. What the…? The Reeperbahn is usually dead in the daytime but right now the place is feckin' mobbed. Crowds of people: adults, kids, samba drummers and other musicians; a load of them carrying yellow banners with bright red sun logos on them and the slogan *'Atomkraft. Nein Danke!'*.

Am I hallucinating or what?

Emma throws her head back, laughing, and answers that unasked question. 'Jesus H. Christ. Think it's some kind of anti-nuclear protest. How we gonna cross the street to the U-Bahn?'

Don't ask me – my heart's hammering, prickles of sweat breaking out on my skin. The chanting and the clanging of the steel drums, the herds of people shouting and yelling – they're doing my nut.

Gotta get away from here, and fast!

We huddle together, the usual crew – Me, Cal, Emma, Iain and Taff, trying as best we can to hatch a plan. Which is tricky when you've been caning it for twelve hours solid. Finally we agree to battle it through the scrum, followed by a smoke back at Em's place. Yeah – and it takes us ten minutes to make that earth-shattering decision. But Emma's having none of it.

She catches my eye and pulls me back out of earshot of the others, hissing, 'I'm not having that nearly rapist at my place.'

'That's a bit harsh, innit?'

'Fucking hell, Manny, he spiked Steffi's drink and tried to fuck her in the loos of Purgatory. He's a fuckin thug, a – a – a – ' she says, searching for the word.

'A what – come on, then, out with it!' I say, my hackles rising, as we're swept along with the throng.

'A yob, that's what he is,' Emma says, twisting her neck back to face me 'cause she's been pushed on further ahead. 'A fucking yobbo.'

I splutter sarkily, hissing in her ear now we're pinned together again, sandwiched between a young family and two punky lezzers, 'You've been reading too many newspapers, love. They call anyone that these days. Besides, a yob's small beer compared to what Iain gets up to.' My voice, temperature, they're all rising now, and I shout in her grid. 'He ain't a yob, he's a – '

'Oh, really – a what?' she says, and even over the shrill sound of the whistles and the chanting I can tell her voice is as sarky as mine was before.

I button it, catching my breath as the march comes to a standstill.

'Well, that's that, then – even you can't defend him,' Em says. 'My mind's made up: he's never coming to my flat again.'

'Oh, leave it out, Em. He ain't that bad,' I say, and in the back of my mind I'm thinking of the gram nestling in his wallet.

'Fuck you, Manny. Jump off a cliff if he did, wouldn't you?' Her face is tight with anger now. Then there's a pause as we both squirm our way through another wave of protesters and manage to get to the barrier at the side of the road. But she's not done yet. 'And don't think I'm clueless about all that coke business you two are messing about with.'

I try and make a joke of it. 'Oh, stop your nagging. He's a mate, ain't he? Can't have everyone else back and not him.'

Joking don't get me anywhere, though, and she presses back into the crowd again, sending some poor kid's red sunflower windmill flying.

'*Entschuldigung!*' she blurts, and I follow her, trying not to lose it as elbows pinch into me, the air shrinks, and I'm blinded by corkscrews of red and yellow streamers. I bat them away only to realise – as I'm confronted by a sea of faces – cunting fuck, I've lost her!

You'd think I'd spot her no probs, what with her being tall and the red hair and all. My eyes become binoculars, swivelling this way and that, till I spot her. Yeah, mate! There she is, trapped among the blaring instruments and uniformed musicians of a brass band, her shoulders heaving up and down. I spin her round to face me and realise her eyes are swimming with tears, and I watch in sort of like amazement as one dances on to her cheek. I've never seen her cry before.

And suddenly I get it.

She's not nagging me about Iain for the sake of it – she's nagging 'cause she cares about me, don't want to see me get in trouble. I want to say, *Emma love, I need you, please help me, I'm not coping with all this shite flying at me; Iain's getting me into all sorts, and I'm afraid.* I want to say, *I'm worried about the coke, I want to leave the Army, can't even think of doing the year of my five I've left to do – can't see a future for myself back home, anyway.*

But instead of saying that, I stick to the habit of a lifetime, of fucking things up for myself, and growl, 'Get a grip, you uptight little bitch.'

With that she's off again. She weaves athletically through the throng, ducking under the barrier over the other side on to the pavement. The march is moving faster now, the sounds and the colours whirling about, the twirls and swirls of kids' windmills and balloons dizzying and giddying me.

She's over there, they say; *no, over there*!

Shurrup, shurrup, shurrup, I tell the fucking voices disorientating me. Gotta catch her up, tell her she's the best thing that ever happened to me! There she is! There! I duck under the barrier and on to the street, my cheeks on fire as I approach her, sat on a bench outside of Burger King, her make-up smudged in blotches on her cheeks.

I don't care if anybody hears; I manage it now, what I wanted to say all along. I take her hand in mine, and say, 'Emma, please don't give up on me. I need you... you... you... make me happy. I'm sorry I called you a b-b-bitch,' my eyes welling up. 'I know Iain's a cunt, but I dunno... he helps me out too. It ain't like I've got anyone else apart from him and Cal... and you. In fact, there's only you really... only you right now...'

And now the tears are puddling my cheeks and all, and Emma opens her arms, and she's blubbing again too, as she says, 'I think that's the most I ever heard you say.'

Chapter Six

Cal

I grip the edge of the lavvy and my stomach heave-hos, belching out an ocean of spume. *Huuurrrrrrrl.* No way, man. Don't let me die the night, choking on my own boak, from wan bad tablet. And in the fuckin bogs in McDonald's, by the way. Some headstone that would be:

> *He lived. He raved.*
> *He died vomming under the Golden Arches.*

Fuck, here comes another wan. *Speeeewwww.* Now a painful cramp grips my stomach, but I've nothing left tae give but bile; after that, it'll be the dry heaves.

Aye, yous are right, play Russian roulette taking Class As and what should I expect? Fair dos, as Manny says. But, still, c'moan! Meeting my maker in Maccy Ds? What would my auntie Edie say?

We got tae Hamburg late, the night. Manny's on dirty jobs again; they hud him polishing weapons in the guardroom all day, didnae let him off till late. I hud nothing better tae do, so I skulked about outside waiting fur him, Walkman on, counting down the hours and minutes tae hardcore heaven. Could've cadged a lift tae the Kiez wi Iain earlier, right enough, but he

119

was headed fur the delights of the Reeperbahn first. (I'll pass, thanks, was my way of thinking.)

'Scuse me a minute. *Heeeeeeeave.* That's got to be the last wan, surely? This is some way tae lose weight – I'm spouting mair liquid than a fuckin SodaStream.

Anyway. As I was saying, 'cause we were late we didnae get sorted by Iain before coming up HH, thinking we'd score later on. Turns out all Taff could get us were these tablets fae a local Turkish dealer.

Tellt us straight up, 'Not a good batch, pal. Worse than Elephants. Mong you right out.' He didnae mention they'd also produce mair vomit than a bulimics' convention.

Not that Manny and me would huv listened, I think, as I cough up another dry heave – *better shite pills than no pills.*

Right, that's me all heaved-out, so I head back tae Manny at wur corner table in the window, looking out on the Reeperbahn in all its seedy night-time glory. But as I cross the brightly lit restaurant another cramp tears through my stomach. I hesitate. Should I go back tae the lavvies? The doughnuts behind the counter eyeball me as I decide. Look on their coupons, ye'd think I was a fuckin jakey. I've paid fur that Big Mac Meal I huvnae touched, ya nyaffs! I eyeball them back, stagger a few paces, sidling across Manny tae take the window seat.

Yous should see the state of him. Could be taken fur a jakey, right enough. The eejit's straggled over the table top, ketchup and other shite pure mussing up his jaiket, baseball cap pulled down. I flit it up and he smiles at me wonkily, his eyes spinning around in their sockets. I think fur a second mibbe he's acting it, then I recall my spastic jittery reflection in the mirrors in the bogs just now. Coupon white as fuckin death. I'm looking in the windae to check my face fur any sign of improvement, when I notice Steffi, Emma and that rat-faced German lassie Tamara walking past, arms linked – headed towards the Tunnel Club, probably. I duck down – no way Steffi's seeing us like this, even if I huvnae seen her in ages.

Too late. They've clocked us; they're coming in, pushing open the double doors in a flurry of trainers, perfume and girly excitement.

'Hello,' says Emma, cheerily. 'What you two doing in here? Don't they let you eat in your own kitchens?'

'Alright, love,' Manny says. And he tries tae get out his chair, only tae slump back down instantly, heavy as a sack of spuds. 'Too many pills. Ain't got the *Bock* for dancing, so we come – ' but before he can finish he hurls out a gassy belch.

Emma's face tenses in pure disgust. 'Oh, right, another night of Manny too fucked to do anything, and me dancing round my handbag.'

'Bag of shite in there tonight, anyway,' he says in a small voice.

Ow! Manny's kicked us under the table. I take the hint. 'Aye, he's no wrong, Emma. The music's fuckin shite, the night.'

'But, Cal, I thought you said you never do a pill without dancing. That you love to dance?' Steffi says.

'Aye, not tae fuckin D:Ream.' Then, thinking that come out wrong, I add quickly, 'But sure I do, I love the dancing, right as usual, Steffi.'

Right as usual, Steffi. Even I know that sounded creepy!

'Come on,' Tamara says, '*gehen uns, blar blar* in German, Iain, *blar blar Spinners,*' and they all laugh.

I frown questioningly. Did she say Iain? What's '*Spinners*' mean? 'Ckin bitches, speaking German on purpose.

That Tamara gies me the willies, I think, reaching tae scratch an itch on my back. Iain tellt us some of the lads fae Hohne camp caught scabies after a chill-out at her place last month. Fuckin minger. Cannae be a coincidence that she's out, the night. I mean, it's like they scabies are a sign of how bad the scene's become; as if there's been an infestation of the wee buggers scuttling over everything that was good about the raving over here.

We used tae huv a laugh, loved that German trance, always got good pills.

Not any more – now the music's shite, the pills are shite, the atmosphere is shite.

Then, there's the troops – like Emma said, 'sno like Manny, Iain and Taff even dance these days. Pure sit there flopping about gurning, fleeing out their boxes, the main objective being tae neck as many dirties as they can. If yer no dancing, yer no a hardcore raver, as far as I'm concerned.

'Right then, Manny, I'll see you later. If you wanna stay at mine you've got till one to come and find me,' Emma says. And to me, 'See you down there, Cal, yeah?'

'Aye, mibbe.'

But I'm talking pish; they tablets huv me zombied tae my chair. And, I dunno, it's like the bright white lights, the squeaky-cleanness of Maccy D's seems appealing compared tae the infested folk and the sweat oozing fae the walls in the Tunnel Club. Besides, I think, as the nausea swirls in my belly like a turd in a toilet, got tae keep near a lavvy.

So we sit, me and Manny, sometimes in silence, sometimes pishing and moaning about the tablets, daring the doughnuts fae Maccy D's tae boot us out wi wur eyes, till the double doors swing open and a draught of cold air comes in wi the next customer. Och, away tae fuck, it's only Iain. I need tae see him like I need a second anus.

'Oy oy!' he says, mooching over, legs cowboy-wide, 'just saw T and that lot – told me I'd find you in here, you bunch of losers.' Then, ruffling Manny's hair, 'Look like you belong in the rehab.'

Oh, aye, keep them coming, I'll write them down and send them tae Harry Enfield, I think. And I'm also thinking, *Don't sit down, don't sit down; say yer piece, then bang the fuck out and annoy the lassies at the club*. But he's been on the powder, hasn't he? and his mouth's a fuckin sewage pipe, spilling out endless rivers of shite: where he's been the night (hooring, of course), how good the powder is, how nae bird can resist him... yada yada yada. *They're fuckin hoors, ya cunt, of course they cannae resist ye!*

Then he turns on Manny. 'Anyway, what you doing in here? Thought you was meant to get rid of that stuff for me.'

That's a wake-up call fae the sledging.

'What do ye mean, get rid of the stuff?' I ask, looking fae wan tae the other, and back again.

Iain puts his fingers tae his lips, mumbles, 'Shh,' while Manny stirs more than he has done in an hour. What's he doing? The right arm reaches in his pocket, scrabbles about fur a bit, finally fishes out a humungous bag of pills.

'Sorry, chief,' he falters. 'Fuckin monged off me trotters, ain't I?'

C'moan tae fuck! There's fuckin hunners of them, I think, as they scatter over the table top like sprinkles on a fairy cake.

But before me or Iain can put him bang tae rights about getting they pills out in full public view, Manny's bolt upright, knocking his chair over, clawing at his stomach...

No way, man. He's never?... Aye, he is...

And the next thing we know Manny's leaning over the table, regurgitating strawberry milkshake, and me and Iain watch, boggle-eyed, as it rains down in undigested splatters over the Eccies and my untouched Big Mac Meal.

Hamburg – Blankenese

Cal

The train chugs intae Hamburg Hauptbahnhof and I'm the first off, barely waiting fur it tae stop before I open the door and jump ontae the platform. Steffi's phoned the kitchens last night, got the lads tae pass on a message and huv me meet her here, suggested we spend the day thegither. Aye, really! And Emma's said we can kip over at her bit while she goes back tae England fur a wedding. Imagine! A whole day and night wi my Steffi! I couldnae ask fur anything mair. I'm gonnae surprise her wi some baked beans fae the NAAFI – she's always on at me how funny it is we Brits eat beans in tomato sauce.

There she's now! In the auld DMs and Army coat she wore when we first met, before she got intae all the raving gear.

'Steffi! Steffi!' I go, rushing over, breaking my golden rule about showing yer feelings in public.

'Oh, hello, Cal. How was the journey?' she asks, very polite.

'Brand new, thanks,' I say, kissing her on the cheek.

And we chat fur a bit, about what she's been up tae, and then she says, 'Zo, would you like to go to this place, Blankenese, see the river? There's a little beach there too?'

Sounds magic, so it does.

'Aye, hing on, I'll get us some supplies,' I say, putting my arm through hers.

We wander through the food hall in the station, buy some picnic stuff, even though it's dreich the day, and jump on the S-Bahn for this Blankywotsit place that Steffi wants tae show me. And she's telling me how pretty it is, it's where all the posh folk in Hamburg live, that it's very 'impressionive' (I think she means impressive) and will hopefully 'chill me out'.

Chill me out? Everything's the dog's baws, as far as I'm concerned.

Only, on the journey Steffi's a bag of nerves, fidgeting about, picking at her fingernails, telling me about her studying, how she's worrying about her exams coming up. Always fuckin worrying about her studies, that girl. I try and put her mind at rest but, nothing doing, so I give up after a while, studying the folk in the carriage, who gradually disappear as we come tae Blankenese, the end of the line.

Steffi seems tae brighten as we come out of the steps of the station, and she grabs my hand, leading me through the streets, pointing out this and that church, telling me the history of the place.

She wasnae wrong, by the way. Picture-postcard pretty here, so it is. Wee cobbled streets wi pastel-coloured houses, set on a hill. Reminds me of the village in this telly programme *The Prisoner* my da was intae – he almost shit a brick wi excitement when it come back tae Channel Four in the '80s. Been missing him like blazes recently. And my ma. Thinking it was a mistake, mibbe, not tae visit her when I was on leave at Christmas. Och, mibbe the weather's just reminding me of haim – pure soggy and overcast like Glesga. But I try and shelve these thoughts. I mean, c'moan, I should be living up tae my nickname, seeing as I've got all this time with my girl.

Speaking of her, she's steaming ahead. Best run and catch her up.

'Oy, wait up!' I shout, and catch her by the arm, relinking it wi mine, as we zig-zag down the windy hill till we reach the river.

At the bottom we stand on the shoreline fur a bit, taking it all in, looking up at the hoity-toity houses on the hill through a thick blanket of fog.

'Imagine living in wan a they houses!' I say after a bit. 'I bet they have lovely Christmases.' And I blush as soon as I've said it.

'Oh, Cal, *du bist so suss!*' Steffi says, turning to look me in the eye. 'You *are* so sweet.'

And she turns back again tae look up at the houses. It's weird, but. They're near but they're out of focus, smudged round the edges, 'cause of the fog. Same goes fur me. Blurry round the edges, or what huv ye. Still no recovered fae they tablets the other night. Must be getting auld.

But this, the fresh air, the view, it's doing me good. In fact, the vibe is that calm and peaceful here, it's almost spooky if yous know what I mean. Think about it – I'm no used tae this fresh air and normal day-out type stuff. I mean, apart from when wes went on exercise, the past few months I've spent every waking hour zebedeed in dingy clubs or working like a Trojan in the cookhouse. Here, it's like yer joining the land of the living – I can see why Steffi brung me. Still, I've hud a funny feeling since she arrived at the station: she's acting weird the day – first chatty, then quiet. There she goes, off again, searching fur a good spot.

Eventually we find a dry, rocky stretch on the beach and Steffi pulls out a picnic blanket fae her rucksack, spreads it on the rocks. As she does, another waft of dank air hits me and I'm minded of my ma and da again, of being a boy: wee runs in the motor up the M8 tae Lochgoilhead, sandwiches and a flask packed in the boot, getting tae a beauty spot and eating wur picnic in the car, it was that chilly outside.

'Zo, Cal,' Steffi says after we've feasted on paprika crisps and Rittersport. 'I did want to talk to you on something.'

'Oh, aye – what's that, then?'

'It's about us, how we be with one another.'

In my belly, dread.

She picks at the tassels of the blanket.

This is pure torture, so it is. 'Go on, then,' I say, 'spit it out.'

And she starts tae speak. Slowly at first. But she soon gets intae it, the words flowing fast like the river in front of us. I tune in and out of her speech, in time tae the waves lapping at the shore.

Tune in.

'… and you see there was no way, with my studies, I could continue…'

Tune out.

Tune in.

'… these drugs you do all the time…'

Tune out.

Tune in.

'… think you did not understand rightly when I said…'

Tune out.

Tune in.

'… and I never could be your girlfriend since…'

Tune out.

Tune in.

'… so vot do you say, Cal. We can still be friends, *oder*?'

My brain's screaming fur me to hold it thegither, not tae show the pain of her dagger-words stabbing at me. There was me, thinking she'd brung me here fur a romantic day. And guess what? She's only brung me tae give me the heave!

Aye, yous are right, she's pure sensitive as a fuckin claw-hammer.

Flummoxed, I go, 'Aye right. Never thought we were anything more. 'Sfine by me.'

Fine in so far as I've gone fae hope and joy tae misery and despair in the time it takes tae huv a pish. I fumble at the rosary beads under my jumper.

'Truly, Cal. I was thinking you belief it could be more. So that's – ah – cool, then. We can be the same as before.'

'So – um – you brung me here to talk about that? Might have just called the kitchens.'

'Vell, I suppose. But I also wanted you to have a fun time, you know without the – um – *Drogen* – the drugs, you know. Show you they are not the be-everything and end-everything. *Quatsch*. I mean, be-all and end-all. You know, just have a chocolate drink, go to the river...'

Huv a fun time? Forget claw-hammer, she's the whole fuckin tool box!

We mooch about fur a bit after that, Steffi doing most of the talking, blethering away now that she's unloaded. As if I want tae hear about her fuckin essay now, on 'the science of the enlightenment' – whatever the fuck that is.

As the afternoon wears on the fog rolls away fae the river, the sun peeks out, lighting up the view and making it prettier than ever.

Funny. It's the opposite fur me. Nothing's clear.

Did she lead me on?

Was I imagining it?

I mean, what do yous think? Was I that brainless I couldnae see what was what?

Och, as if I care. Plenty mair lassies out there fur me. That wee Tamara fur wan. Mibbe I'll gie her a go, see how Steffi likes that.

'Cal, you are shivering. Shall we go for warm chocolate?'

127

'It's hot chocolate. And no. Think I'll be getting back now. Should huv mentioned before, I was fine fur the day pass but no the evening an aw…'

'*Alles klar,*' she says, scooping up the blanket, I take you to the *Hauptbahnhof.*'

And even though I know I should say I'll make it on my own, I nod.

'Aye, okay, then.'

The S-Bahn journey's like huvin a tooth pulled. On the outside, I'm like, everything's fine, there isnae any pain; on the inside I'm sewing my feelings in tight, gritting my jaw thegither. And then I do what I always do in a crisis – blether. Tell Steffi about mibbe going tae Bosnia, how I'm thinking about trying tae get some leave, go and visit my ma, and she's all serious and encouraging.

'Oh, yes, you must visit your mother,' she says, her coupon wrinkling like a torn pocket.

Lighten up, love, I want tae say, *'sno your business any mair, is it?* when I hear, '*Nächste Haltestelle, St Pauli.*'

My ears prick up. St Pauli. The stop fur the Kiez.

And I'm no kidding yous, it's as if the Reeperbahn was calling fur me, grabbing fur me with long, scarlet-painted fingernails. I grab my overnight bag, the can of baked beans clunking against my thigh as I scoop it up, and dive for the doors.

'Cal! Cal! Vere are you going?'

'Nipping down Purgatory, see if Taff's around…' and the doors slide shut before I manage, 'I'll see ye about…'

I look back and see Steffi's face, frowning, and I go at it like greased lightning along the platform, headed fur the only comfort I can think of.

Purgatory.

Funny as fuck, isn't it? A place meaning mental anguish and suffering being my only hope of comfort. There you go. That's life.

I only hope Taff's no breaking the habit of a lifetime, keeping the bar stool warm, waiting for some old sad fuck tae come in, needing a dose of his medicine.

Fallingbostel British Army Base

Cal

Wheeeeee! I'm zooming round the drill square in a shopping trolley we've hauf-inched fae the NAAFI. Ye should see the coupons of the lads as we whizz past. Fuckin wicked! I am pure dead bladdered, so I am. Five pints in the NAAFI bar, two shots of sambuca.

I am posi-tive-ly steamboats!

Who needs lassies like Steffi when ye can get mortalled wi yer pals? Manny, he's been my rock since I got given the heave. Probably 'cause Emma's in England but who cares why he's here, he's here and that's enough fur me. And here we are, rat-arsed on the swally again, ready tae do some damage fur the third night in a row. Aye, I know, I've blethered on about how alcohol's fur losers mair times than wan. But if yous've been paying attention ye'd also know there isnae any other option but tae get steamin mortal bastartin drunk when ye've been given the heave.

Talking of heaving, Manny and me are just after honking wur guts up down the alley at the back of the NAAFI.

Manny excuses wur behaviour. 'Tactical puking,' he calls it.

'Synchronised spewing,' I say, and we pish wursels laughing as we head back tae the NAAFI bar fur round two.

It's still early so the bar is pretty empty. A couple of lads playing darts, a telly on in the corner showing football wi the sound down. The fruit machines are free but I'm no thinking about sports or games – I've a wan-track mind, the night.

'Hoy, Manny, what about wan a they snakebite-and-blacks?'

'Yeah, whatever, rack them up,' Manny says, as he heads off tae the bogs fur the hundredth time – has he got some kind of bladder problem? I get the drinks in and plank my arsehole at a table out of sight of the only other lads sat down in here. Typical! It's only a load of cookie monsters. Cannae be arsed tae make small talk after another nightmare day in the cookhouse, my hands covered in blue plasters fae losing my concentration, my heid hammering fae hours of trying not tae think about... Ah, here's Manny back. Time tae reignite the party spirit.

'Hoy, Manny, what's that song, that wan we used tae sing doon Aldershot?'

'What, that drinking one?

'Aye, *Show me the way to go home*,' I start up.

'*I'm tired and I wanna go to bed*,' Manny joins in, pure steamboats now an aw. The barmaid's heid swivels around, like that lassie in *The Exorcist*, as wur voices drown out the only other noise in here – the electronic song of the one-armed bandit. That barmaid is the wife of some Rupert who's got it in for us. Manny snogged the face off their daughter once at an officers' function we catered fur – she's been looking fur an excuse tae get back at us since.

I sing louder, hoping she'll baw me out and wes can get in a row. '*I had a little drink about an hour ago...*'

But wait, here's Davie. 'Hoy, Davie, Davie. Over here, pal!' Huvnae seen Davie fur donkeys. 'Hoy, c'moan, join us fur a Fally schwally.'

Manny

Fuck about! Why's that no-mark Davie always have to show up, put a spanner in the works? Cal and me, we've been having such a crack on our tod. Course I'm handling the booze better than Cal, with a little help from my old mate Charles.

Just look at Davie! He reckons himself, he does, wagging his finger at us. What's he, my mum? I skulk to the side, leaving Cal to do the talking.

I fidget about, my long legs uncomfortable under the table as he drones on to Davie about the little Box Head, how much he loves her, she was the best thing that ever happened to him. Blah, blah, blah. He's giving that little cow way too much air time. Besides, he should know the golden rule of being dumped: dry yer eyes, pick up yer teddy, move on.

And then I have a lightbulb moment. I mean, he didn't even get to bone her, did he? I reckon it's about time Cal got himself laid. At least I get my end away with Emma, even if she is a nag. Cal, though – never mind a dry patch, his sex life's drier than the chuffing Kalahari.

What do you reck', you lot? Trip to the Pink House? Sort him out good and proper? Oh, behave! Not like we're gonna fucking murder someone. A bit of hooring'll do him good, shag his way out of his feckin' misery and pain.

'Oy, Cal, Davie, what about a trip to the Pink House, then? Bit of the old carnal gymnastics?'

No reply.

Where's Iain when you need him? Know what he'd say: 'Go for it, lads, but watch out for the Jacuzzi.' Never did know what the other lads meant about the Jacuzzi. Now's the chance to find out.

'Oh, come on, let's go, have a currywurst, watch the show – don't have to go upstairs. What say you?'

Fuck all, apparently.

'My shout,' I add, flashing the DMs which have been burning a hole in my pocket since my last little job for Iain.

'Fucking go on me tod, then, won't I?'

Losers!

And so I flounce out the bar, kicking the one-armed bandit machine on my way out.

Fucking Cal. Gets on my wick he does sometimes, what with all his religion and fucking goody-two-shoes stuff. Where's being 'Happy' and a 'nice guy' fucking got him? A bird that's given him the right runaround, that's where. Me, I'm on top form. No one to answer to. No parents, no God, a girlfriend who does what she's told. Pretty much. Yeah, fuck trying to be a nice guy – act like a pansy, cunts will treat

131

you like one. 'Cause, let's face it, you've got two choices as a modern bloke. You can become a whatsit they're always on about in them magazines – a 'new man', a fucking pansy who panders to his mum, his wife, his boss. Or you can fly solo – look after number one, not think about any fucker else.

That's right, people. From now on, it's all about me.

The lads on the gates nod as I walk past but I don't even bother with an 'evening' as I huff along, thinking I can make it to the Pink House by foot in ten minutes. Then, two minutes down the road to town, I look on the horizon for traffic, duck about, and dab a blob of the white stuff off my finger. There we go. Better already!

I pick up the pace, and the gravel crunches satisfyingly beneath my feet as I strut my stuff.

Too right, I tell myself, *forget every fucker else, look after number one, don't owe nobody nothing...* Oy, oy, what's that? I can hear more crunches in the gravel, and Cal's voice, panting behind me.

'Oy, Manny, wait up.'

Good lad! Not such a pansy, after all.

Cal

I'm dragging a hauf-ton weight as I lug masel along the path tae catch up Manny... got tae hunt him down... tell him what I think of him... thinks he's the fuckin Big Man... flashing the cash... making out he's intae hoors... about time he was made tae see sense!

Come on, legs! I think, lurching forward as I attempt tae chase him.

'Sno right... 'sno right... aw this bother he's been getting us intae; I've hud enough of carrying the can... ah, there he's... stood there waiting fur us, on the roadside, smug fuckin look on his coupon. Thinks I've caved in, does he, gonnae go down the Pink House after all?

That's me, beelin!

I bend my right arm in a hook and make a fist alive wi all the thundering anger and annoyance I've felt at Manny fur the last few months – his laziness, the Charlie, his selfishness...

Pow!

'What the...? Leave it out!' Manny goes, dodging his gangly frame out of the way, and my knuckles scrape nothing but air. I lunge towards him, *grrrrrrrr*, both hands forward now, legs lashing out, fists flying. Whoah! He dodges me again and I'm carried forward by my own weight. I stumble. Topple. Fall on the gravel, cutting my hands tae fuck.

Manny dances around on the grass, his arms flailing wildly as he tries tae avoid falling in the ditch at the side of the road. And then we laugh. Both of us ejecting hearty fuckin laughs fae way down in wur bellies.

He crouches down next tae us fur a – what's it? Reconciliation. 'Mate, mate. Come on. Only trying to do you a favour, ain't I? No point us falling out too. See what that bitch has done? We was best of mates before she came on the scene.'

He leans over, puts an arm round us. Weird. His hands are trembling.

'Come on,' he goes. 'We don't want a bad scene, do we?' Then, 'Go on, come down the Pink House. Might be a laugh.'

The road's quiet, but he's right – if Manny gets in any mair bother, he'll likely be getting the bump. I lie spread-eagled on the flair fur a bit, picking wee slivers of gravel out my hand, weighing things up. No sense making a bad scene, I suppose. Besides, don't fancy going back tae the NAAFI tae Mrs Chumbley-Warner or whatever the Rupert's wife's name is, wi my tail between my legs. 'Och, alright,' I say, 'you win. Again. I'll come wi ye. But like you said, currywurst and the show. I'm no going up the stairs wi wan a they scabby-minged creatures.'

Manny

'Ckin hell. I don't believe that – Cal lamping me one. I'm a bloody pansy, after all. Didn't have the nerve to hit back...

It's bad enough with Dozzer and that lot reminding me what a loser I am. Now even Cal thinks I'm an easy target.

Things have got to change round here, show people what's what! Even them bouncers gave us aggro on the way in; Cal had to convince them we wasn't blootered. Oh, man. Can't think of that now, 'cause the antics on the stage are well foul.

You should see it. There's this bird, Asian girl, half-naked, gyrating and shaking, thrashing about like a madwoman, half the punters not even watching, the other half jeering and clapping. A few local geezers, but mostly boys from the base. Cal's watching alright, though. You should see the look on his grid. Priceless! The music's well funny and all, soft rock and power ballads that went out in the '80s. I get in another *Grosses*; Cal's that bladdered now, bet I can even convince him to take the trip upstairs... not that he'll probably be able to get it up.

Cal

This is too fuckin much, man! I take a pure reddie as the woman on stage slinks towards us. C'moan tae fuck! Now her fanny's within spitting distance. I close my eyes... what's that? She's saying something like, '*Na, junger Mann*,' taking my hand, and I'm like, 'What the – ?' but she's got me in a vice-like grip, pulling us on stage. I lumber on in a daze... everything suddenly fuzzy... a swelling of excitement in the crowd... faces perving and leering... music throbbing... beer glasses raised and swilling about...

... but then suddenly the world comes intae focus again, 'cause the woman's pushing me ontae a chair, pulling at my belt, and – what the fuck? – she's taking out a whip!

Manny

No fuckin way! Cal's lost it big style, hollering at the dancer. Can't understand a word he's fuckin saying – always speaks the old Jockanese when he's had a few sherberts. What the fuck?

He's never... I can't look.

I cover my eyes, but in half-arsed way, so I can peek out. Oh, mate! You lot ain't gonna believe it – he's only grabbed hold of the dancer's nipple, twisted it right round. Fuck about! Now the bouncer's on his way over, grabbing a big glass ashtray off the bar... the crowd parting to let him leap on the stage... He's never! He is. Wallop! He's banjoed Cal right on the –

Cal

'Awwwwwwww, my heid!'

Manny

I drag Cal by the scruff of his neck, out the bar, all the while him lashing out and cursing like a good 'un. I don't believe this. Now he's fucking blubbing.

Cal

Fuckin Manny... sniff... brung me here... sniff... all I wanted tae think about was her... about... 'Steffiiiiiiiiiiiiiiiiiii!' I howl her name intae the night.

Manny

Fucking Cal. Prick probably done that on purpose, so we'd get chucked out. What's he – some kind of benny?

Cal

Last time I fuckin hang about wi him.

Manny

Next time I'm coming here with Iain.

Cal

Cunt.

Manny

Cunt.

Fallingbostel British Army Base

Manny

'Oy, Manny, fag break?'

I am fucking aching for a fag, as it goes. I skim the room to see if Clarkey's about. Sick and tired of his gob-shitedness. No, no cunt's looking. I give my old mate Paddy the nod.

Paddy was made a lance jack a couple of months back. Bit of a bent-head, loves the sound of his own voice, and he's the last bloke on camp I'd share a secret with. But he's a good lad, all the same. Anyway. Fair play to him, if he's determined to rise up the ranks. Just so long as he keeps his nose out of my business.

I ask the lad next to me to keep an eye on my potatoes boiling away, and me and Paddy nip outside, huddling together upwind of the bins, the cold air and rain taking our breath away compared to the heat of the cookhouse.

Christ, Fally's bleak on days like this.

'Got a light, then, pal?' Paddy goes. I pat myself down but nothing doing. 'Never mind,' he says, producing a Zippo. 'There you go,' and we each spark up, sheltering under the tin roof to stop our ciggies getting soggy, listening to the rain battering down.

'Where's your bosom bud, then?' Paddy asks after a bit, as he dusts off a spot on the ground for us to park our arses on.

'Got a bump on his head, didn't he?' I laugh, fakely. 'The MO's given 'im a sick chit for concussion,' and I tell him all about the Pink House and our fight. Don't tell him that we've

136

not made up yet, though, that Cal's sent me to Coventry – don't want Paddy sticking his oar in.

'You two always on the craic,' Paddy says, chuckling. 'Thought he'd gone back home to Jock Land.'

'Nah, haggis-hunting season ain't till next month,' I say, making a joke of things.

'No, no, seriously,' Paddy continues. 'He's been telling me about his ma, how he's missing her and that.'

Bloody hell, when did Cal tell Paddy that? That time down Sennelager on exercise? Anyway. Might as well have gone round camp with a loudspeaker.

Then, as if I wasn't freaked out enough, Paddy kebabs me with a real shocker, going, 'Did you hear about them lads down Osnabrück, then?'

'Eh, no, what?' Osnabrück, incidentally, is another Army camp near here, where Taff was posted till he jacked it all in. We've still got a few mates down there.

'The Monkeys have had the Green Jackets on video surveillance – about two dozen have been busted for drugs, so they have.'

I feel the colour bleeding from my grid. Why the fuck's he telling me? What's he trying to say?

I stub out my fag and lean over from the support of the wall to fiddle with my bootlace, thinking how to act. 'Bloody boots, been giving me grief all day,' I blurt, stalling, my heart in my mouth. Then, when the bootlaces have been loosened, I ask, casually, 'Anyway, what was you saying?'

'I was saying,' Paddy replies, inhaling his ciggie in quick puffs between talking, 'I visited a pal down Osnabrück Wednesday. Saw a bunch of their jocks wandering around the parade square in overalls. I was like, *What the fuck?* and me pal told me a load of lads are being done for pills, that they're awaiting trial; doing dogsbody stuff for the GD platoon in the meantime.' Pauses. 'RGJ 1 battalion have had a real problem with drugs recently, apparently.' Looks at me, eyeball to eyeball. 'There's going to be a big crackdown everywhere.'

Then he jumps up as if he'd said fuck-all, flicks his cigarette butt and it loops through the air before landing on my left boot. My jaw gapes but not 'cause of the cigarette-butt acrobatics. Didn't dare ask him about my mates Stevie and JC. (Manny!) Are they okay? Was they busted? And, more to the point, I'm remembering that I've gone down Osnabrück for a smoke a few times in the last year. Was I caught on camera? (Manny!). Fuck about, wish I hadn't done that line before work today.

I have got The Fear big time.

'Manny, going in, pal…'

I realise Paddy's been trying to get my attention for a minute or two, so I go, 'I'll – ah – hang out here, spark up another.'

'You'll be needing this,' he goes, getting out his lighter again and sparking up my fag. Then whispers, his breath hot in my ear, 'Chill out, chum – think you'd have heard by now, if it was biting you on the arse.'

And with a wink he goes indoors.

That Paddy, he's a cheeky fuck. One of them chameleon kind of lads – in with everyone from the brass down. You can tell this from the kind of smoker he is. *How come?* you lot might well be asking. Well, the way I see it, you can suss a bloke out from his smoking habits. Take lads like Paddy, only smoke when they're getting blootered, or when someone else is smoking – one of them lightweight – what do you call them? – 'social smokers'. You just can't trust them.

I mean, it's like them bisexuals, don't you think? Neither Arthur or Martha. 'Ckin hell: make your mind up!

Me, I'm one of them who sparks up before breakfast. Remember them ads when you was a kid? The 'Natural Born Smoker'. That's me. Oh, come on, you lot, do me a favour! Isn't it better to be an honest chain-smoker, to give in to it with your heart, soul and lungs, rather than just doing it to fit in? As for non-smokers, they're the worst of the shagging lot. I mean, when did you ever meet a non-smoker you could trust one hundred per cent? There you go. Never. Like Corp Clarke.

A one-man advert for why not to be a health nazi. He don't drink, don't smoke. Like the song goes, what does he do?

'Oy, Manny, they'll be sending out a search party for you, if you don't come back in a mo.'

Paddy again.

I leap up, dust off my whites, pick up the ciggie butts and wang them in the bins, and shout over as lightly as I can, 'Coming, boss,' before heading back to the kitchens.

Back in the cookhouse, I shiver despite the heat. Fuck about, man. First Cal tells me we might be headed for Bos; now this! I try and concentrate on the job. Bangers and mash tonight. Good old British grub, mangled good and proper by yours truly. I drain the potatoes (which have turned to mush in the time I've been gone), and go at the mash as if it was the face of one of them RMPs who busted the Osnabrück lads. I get well into it – violent almost. Well. At least it helps pass the time till the end of my shift.

Clarkey comes up after. 'Lovely mash. Redeemed yourself for once in your life.'

'Cheers, boss,' I go, and start tidying my work space, noticing that Paddy's sharing a joke with Clarkey now. See what I mean? Chameleon. Time to do one, I think, and I put all my weight into the kitchen doors on the way to the mess hall with my tray.

I traipse back to the block, shift over, my nerves in tatters, if you must know. Forget that film *The Hills Have Eyes*, the fucking barracks have eyes, more like. I look about. Has word got round about Osnabrück? Am I first in the firing line? I swear people are pointing the finger at me. I put my head down and pace it back, trying not to picture them Green Jackets, all being pushed about on GDs. Fuck me, they'll lose their pensions, the lot, if they get done when it comes to the trial.

Not fair, is it, when you think about it? I mean, your typical squaddie is a piss-head – goes out swamping himself in as much voddie or wifebeater as possible as soon as he's on downtime;

some even turn up on duty still pissed after a night out. But of course the brass think that's alright, don't they, 'cause alcohol's legal? So, even if some mentalist goes out and bangs a few heads together, the consequences aren't that bad – a few dirty jobs, a fine, or a day in the punt. Deep down the NCOs are probably thinking, 'just one of the lads'.

But Ecstasy. It's illegal. So it's got to be Bad and Wrong. No scientist has ever come out and said weed or pills was any worse than alcohol but the Army's gotta play by what the law says. But so long as them lads wasn't on duty, or handling a weapon or whatever, what's the problem? *Yeah, too right*, I think, convincing myself, as the first lightning bolts of a mega-headache flash through my bonce. *Fucked-up fucking laws we've got in this country*. I shove open the door to the dorm, but then notice Cal's laid out on his pit, dead to the world, so I tiptoe quietly across to my bed space.

Desperate for a kip myself actually, so I tear off my whites, grab some painkillers from my wash bag, being careful not to wake Cal as I close my locker, and gulp down four ibuprofen with the dregs of a can of flat Coke I find laying about. Next, I pull out my comfiest tracky bottoms from a neatly folded pile in the cupboard, noticing at the same time that Jonesy hasn't bothered his arse to sort his bed space as per usual.

That fucking waste of space, he's such a messy bastard. Drives me up the wall how his kit's never squared away, his bed space always looks like it's been gone at by a pack of wild dogs. Then there's the Newcastle scarves pinned above his bed and on his locker, splattered with beer and mud. Not to mention the soiled grot-mag calendars scattered about. I'm tempted to tear the lot down, bin the gash-shot pictures, drown the beer-infested scarves in disinfectant.

But hold up.

Jonesy don't ever get in trouble for being an admin vortex – somehow stays on the right side of the brass. I edge closer to his bed space. What if? What if he's already in with them – they've promised him a rise up the ranks, if he dobs us in? That why he's decided to come up Hamburg with us recently? He's spying on us for the RMP?

And that's that.

It's as if my mind has freeze-framed on this one idea, that Jonesy's a grass, and I can't find a remote to wind the image on. And, as that idea gets brighter and louder, so does the headache swelling in my temples.

Bang, bang, bang; throb, throb, throb.

Come on, Nurofen – do yer job!

I jump off the bed and grab a cassette out my locker and wang it on my old Walkman – still haven't had a chance to get myself a new CD one yet. Stone Roses. 'Sally Cinnamon'. And as soon as the smooth tones of Ian Brown start up, I zone out, turn up the volume, and hope the jingle-jangle of the indie guitars will strangle my worries, sort my headache, and, most of all, let loose the strangling grip of The Fear.

Chapter Seven

Manny

Ruff, ruff, ruff.

It's true, they're coming. They're fucking coming! I try to catch Cal's eye from the opposite pit but he's laid out flat reading one of them vampire books.

Ruff, ruff, ruff, the dogs go again.

Cal lifts his head and mouths at me, 'Keep the heid.'

Meanwhile, Jonesy sits on his bed, oblivious, flicking through his latest grot-mag. That lad is so fucking thick. Clueless as a clueless thing on National Clueless Day, as Blackadder would say. The barking gets louder, rising above the sound of The Clash. 'Clash City Rockers'.

We've only had to go and hide all our mix tapes and listen to their dirge. In other words, we've had to hide anything to do with dance music, or they'll have us down as fucking druggies, even if they don't find nothing. 'They' being the RMPs and the RAF dog-handlers.

The footsteps reach our door. I can't help myself – a loud whiff of nerves escapes and fills the room.

'Oy, oy, trying to break the sound barrier, are ya?'

That's Jonesy, unfunny as ever.

Then it comes – a sharp *rat-a-tat-tat* at the door.

Cal answers.

142

The dogs and RMPs enter with our RSM, who's a whirlwind of regimental colours, clomping feet and testosterone.

'Okay, lads, block inspection. Stand by your beds!'

We play it well shocked, but that *No, sir, we don't mind if you have a nose about, fill yer boots...*

The thing is we got word yesterday from our mate – who's a dog-handler – that this would be going down. The RSM told us that there was gonna be a block inspection but we knew better: that is, that the RAF dog squad have been called in to search the accommodation for drugs – in the whole of fucking Fally! Here in the lines, the pad houses – everywhere. Me and Cal was straight round to Iain's as soon as we got wind; loaded up the car and that was it, ten minutes later and we was up the A7 to Hamburg and round at Taff's, a nine bar of weed, an ounce of coke, two hundred pills rattling around in the boot. Then back here at 3 a.m., and to work this morning looking like butter wouldn't melt. I'm fucking knackered now, as it goes.

'Got to search your lockers now, lads.'

The Clash continues above the noise of the dogs and the boots and the general mayhem.

'And turn that fucking noise off, will ya?'

They ain't messing about. The dogs have got their noses into everything, the dog-handlers staring on blank-faced, the RMPs ripping the place apart, no stone left unturned. Mind you, Jonesy's bed space don't look much different to usual. The messy little prick.

'Oy, oy, easy!' I go as they pull apart my old Walkman.

I instantly regret what I've said when they start shouting me down.

Jonesy's taking it all in his stride. Still don't trust that little fucker. Alright, he's a toker like the rest of us, had to get rid of an eighth of solids himself last night. Still, I can't look at him the same way any more – I'm sure he's up to something. Fuck about! Now they're into our wash bags. Got to take away any medicine for testing, they're saying, make sure it's not the illegal kind of medicine – if you catch my drift. Fucking

Zehners' worth of painkillers in there. What if I get one of my headaches?

Oh, what?

Now they're pulling out all my tapes – only a few of them left; the hardcore ones are stashed up Taff's. Into Jonesy's locker now and the dogs start going at the yapping like crazy. No way! This RMP guy's emptied out Jonesy's tracky bottom pockets, and you lot aren't gonna believe this. They've only found a blim-sized lump of fucking hash. What a Joey! And that's it. They go at the rest of the room like a hash-seeking missile: drawers emptied, books and magazines flicked through, bedclothes and duvets rifled.

Minutes pass.

Half an hour.

They don't find nothing else. Jonesy's whisked away for a chat with the RMP and Cal and I stand there, gob-smacked – we've only got away with it.

Fallingbostel Town – Blau Bar

Cal

'Fur a Thursday night in Fally the place is fuckin mobbed, eh, right?' I say tae the lad next tae us, trying tae make conversation.

He doesnae reply.

The butterflies in my tummy flit about even mair then. How's he no answering? Does he hate squaddies? I mean, it's no like the locals arnae used tae squaddies here – it's where all the Army Barmy lads hang out tae get blootered.

So, I try again. 'So we's've come down for my pal's birthday. Manny. Twenty-wan, the day. Fell out wi him the other week, but, well, we've been bezzie pals fur years so…' and I continue my flow of verbal diarrhoea fur a bit, but still he says nothing so I change the subject '… I mean is the place always like this? Full of young lassies wearing too much make-up?'

Again, no reply. I lean over and tap the lad on the... oh, right, I think, as I take off my shades. It's a pillar. I've only been trying tae make conversation wi a fuckin pillar. I shake my heid, try and shake of the effects of the –

'Are yous all on drugs?'

Hold on a mo. I've got company.

I swivel round tae look at the young Jock stood next tae me – a real wan this time, I think, or else he wouldnae be talking, would he?

'Eh, leave it out, will ye?' I say, and turn back again tae look out on the dance flair. Nothing, I repeat, nothing, is gonnae make me move fae this spot. I mean, the world's gonnae burst intae flames, isn't it, if I don't stand here and keep an eye on things?

But the lad's no fur giving up. 'I said,' he shouts, grabbing me by the shoulders and swinging me back around, 'are yous all on drugs?'

I fixate on the lads on the dance flair again: Manny's still as a fart in a trance, apart fae his heid, which he's nodding in time tae the music (the music is very hard and very fast, by the way); Jonesy and Jay are whizzing around like aeroplanes, pulling on wan another's shirt sleeves; and Taff and Iain appear tae be doing impressions of various zoo animals.

But I repeat, 'No way, man, we're no on drugs. Away and bother sumbdy else.'

And I put my shades back on tae try and disguise the effect of the micro-dots – the LSD – on my pupils. I could murder Taff, so I could – only bringing blotters wi him tae Manny's birthday bash, paranoid that the dog-handlers would be still be about after three days and sniff out anything else.

'I fuckin hope not, pal,' the little hard nut is continuing, ''cause it's dicks like yous who are letting down the unit. I mean, they Green Berets, it's cunts like them who give the Army a –'

'Hold on a minute,' I interrupt him, as I'm suddenly aware of something hairy brushing against my leg, 'who let that cat in

145

here?' And my hand goes down tae flick the thing away. 'I'm fuckin allergic.'

'What the – ?' the lad goes, looking down, incredulous like. 'It's the fur on my fuckin parka.' He screws up his face, looks over at his pals stood at the bar and stabs me in the chest wi his index finger. 'Yous *are* all on fuckin drugs, aren't ye?'

I don't waste any time. I put my beer bottle next tae the pillar tae guard the spot and brave the dance flair, pushing past the forest of gyrating townies, their arms branches waving in the wind, their legs tree trunks rooted tae the spot.

Fuck that, I think, blinking the hallucination away, and say tae the others. 'Lads, lads, wes're gonnae huv tae bang out.'

'Too right,' Manny pipes up, the first words he's coughed up in fuckin ages. 'Fucking SIB are in here, scoping us out. Look.' And he points towards a Turkish lad and a young German lassie. She looks about twelve, by the way.

But before I can say, no way the SIB, the special branch of the military police, are here, Iain's waded in wi, 'Nah, nearly time to feed the penguins,' and him and Taff fall about laughing, drink swilling out over the top of their glasses as they waddle about wi their backsides sticking out.

'Pick up a pick up a p-p-p-penguin,' Taff goes.

Fan-fuckin-tastic. They've reached their final destination down the crazy-paved path tae lost-it land.

'Sort it out, pal,' I say, looking nervously over my shoulder at they lads again. 'I'm no kidding, that lad's after us.'

And I'm right, so I am, 'cause him and his pals are beating a path towards us, pushing past the dancers and the drinkers on the dance flair in a threatening cluster formation – chests puffed out, arms swinging by their sides.

'Fight!' Taff and Iain say in unison, in that way acid can make ye think of things at the same time. And I think, *Is Taff gonnae do himself an injury?* 'cause he's doubled-up, laughing.

I shrug my shoulders. 'Your funeral, lads,' I say and – as the young Jock and his pals square up tae Iain and Taff, and Iain's

146

stance changes fae fucked-up nutter tae full-blown psycho – I add quickly tae the others, 'C'moan. Let's leave them to it.'

We're ten feet away when the first fists start tae fly.

Outside the bar, I cannae believe it's dark. We must huv been tripping wur tits off in there fur hours. Lucky the streets of Fallingbostel are deserted 'cause a right motley crew we must look: Jonesy and Jay still zooming about; Manny grappling wi the zip of his puffa jacket; me looking back shiftily the whole time tae check we're no being followed.

'Hold on,' Manny says, as we turn the corner past Lidl towards the taxi rank, 'if I put on my coat it'll make us invisible.'

'Aye, right,' I say, sarkily. Then I have huv a wee argument wi masel whether that's possible – I decide, aye, it probably is.

There are taxis galore at the stand, thank Christ, and I wave at the driver of the wan in front till he notices us, chucks down his paper, and revs up his engine while we scramble tae jump in. I reach fur a passenger door.

'Oy, oy.' This, I'm saying tae Jay who's pushing me out the way. Looks like the others huv the same idea as me – nobody wanting tae sit up front wi the driver – 'cause we've ended up the four of us squidged up in the back. Manny tells the driver where to, and then there's a deafening silence as we sit jittering and fidgeting, afraid of letting on how fucked-up we's are.

I cannae take this, got tae say something – this silence, it's doing my nut!

I lean across tae the cab driver, trying my best tae seem normal as I ask, 'Busy, the night?'

Ow! Somebody's kicked me in the leg. Aye, I guess chuntering on at the cab driver's no the best plan – that's if he even speaks English – so I start a conversation wi the others about whatever pops up in my box – the weather, Scooby-Doo, whether they'll use that Channel Tunnel that's opening soon. Only in my mind it's like we're in a film, playing wursels. I mean, it's like I know it's Manny's coupon and Jonesy's body and Jay's voice but it's as if they're in the skins of actors. And we're like saying lines that someone's wrote for us already. But it seems like the writer's changed the script tae spy thriller, and the script looks something like this:

MANNY (in a hushed tone): I'm sure the driver's SIB. Look, his jeans have got creases down the front. No other fucker irons the front of their jeans.

CAL (whispering back): Aye. But if I put my shades on, he willnae recognise us.

The driver picks up speed, chasing an amber light. Manny is hurled across the seats.

MANNY: (alarmed) Fuck about. I reckon he's after us. On some sort of mission fur the SIB to kill us.

The lads are then possessed with the same thought: that the driver is on a suicide mission and he wants to take them with him. Jay is the first to express this.

JAY: Yeah, he's SIB and he's on a suicide mission: been told to get rid of all the druggies. To get rid of us.

JONESY (panicking): Shh. Don't want him to know we're on to him.

CAL: Yeah, keep it down, you lot.

Whoah! Only then the script ends and we're back tae reality, 'cause the driver has taken a corner way too fast and is skeltering towards death, and I think, *Forgive me Father for all my sins*, as *wham!* my shades fall off, I'm jabbed in the eye wi an elbow, and dug in the leg by a trainer.

'I want my mum!' someone shouts.

'Don't kill us, don't kill us!' says another.

'Open the door!' I yell, and pull at the handle, only tae find it locked.

After that there's nothing but sobs fae the back of the taxi while the driver swerves back intae lane and we pull up at another set of traffic lights.

'*Ein Fuchs*,' he says, turning around after the light hits red. 'It vas an – um – fox. I try not to run him over.'

And at last me and the others see sense, and the group gets a fit of the giggles just as we're pulling up, safe and sound, tae the front gates at Fally.

Hamburg

Manny

The washing machines grumble, the dryers drone, the radio's buzzing like a bee in the background, and all the while Emma's chuntering on. I can't barely make her out what with all them other noises swarming about. Wish that I could get a hold of them, grab on to them somehow, smother the fuckers with my bare hands. I put my fingers to my temples, rub them a bit, screw up my eyes and try and get back into Em's drift. Something about the latest *Brookside* tape she got sent from home.

Fuck about, woman!

She told me she wanted to see me to chat about us, not some feckin' girlie soap opera. Got to get out of this place. Nothing more depressing than sitting in a launderette, best of times. And that smell! Starch, detergent, other people's laundry. My eyes blur over, my mouth fills with spit. Emma looks at me, moves an empty washbasket off the bench we're sat on, and sidles up.

'Your eyes are particularly cheeky and blue today,' she goes, and moves closer. 'I've got a little belated birthday something for you.'

'Thanks, love,' I go, touched by the gesture, grinning as she presses something into my hand. Oy, oy, that's a touch! Looks like an eighth of bud. I hold the cling-filmed weed close and breathe in the sweet smell.

'Come on, love, let's do one.' I smile, giving it the old twinkling blue-eyed boy bit that the ladies love. 'Can't stick it in here.'

'Okay, we can collect my stuff later. But I'm starving. Fancy a *Gyros*, then back to mine?'

'Yeah, alright.'

We step into the sunlight. At last spring's here, green shoots popping up everywhere, leaves sprogging on trees. We trudge two shops along to the Turkish place. It's a little row of shops, like you'd get at home. No fish and chips, no corner shop, no post office, though. Fuck about! Don't tell me I'm homesick? Got a letter from my mum this morning, as it happens. Told me a few new shops have opened up down Victoria Circus way, a couple of new caffs and restaurants where I could maybe find work. Mum and Dad have even moved out of my nan's. Rented a two-bedroom place and all. Maybe room for me? I wonder.

Only this thought is soon replaced by hunger as we step into the *Imbiss*. I dribble as I inhale the sweatiness of *Gyros*, hopping from foot to foot while we wait in the queue. Would you believe the radio's blaring out that same song that was in the launderette? Somebody sort out the volume! My head is fucking swamped with sounds now. I hang back as we reach the front of the queue and leave the talking to Emma.

'*Zwei Döner und zwei Cola bitte.*'

'*Mit Pommes?*'

'Manny,' Emma turns to me. 'Do you want chips?'

But I'm already out the door, pulling up a pew at a plastic table on the street outside. What's with me? My head is fucking pounding. The radio in there, the guys' booming voices, it's as if they was coming out a loudspeaker. I dust a heap of crumbs from the last meal off the table top, trying to get a grip. Sit there monged out, pressing my hands to my ears till Emma comes out, plonks my change down on the table, puts my *Gyros* in my hand.

'You alright? You look like boiled shite.'

'Aw, thanks a lot,' I say, pulling another chair over for Em. 'Ravenous, that's all.'

And so we munch away for a bit, enjoying the *Gyros* and cans of ice-cold Coke. Sitting outside's sorting me right out.

Fresh air, blue skies, silence. It's like I can breathe again. Then, after a while, Emma turns and looks at me expectantly.

'So, um – what do you think then, about what I was saying in the launderette?' She picks a piece of lettuce from between her teeth, blushes, and continues, 'I mean, about us. You'll give it some thought?'

I am truly gob-smacked. All I could hear was *Brookside*, washing machines, and 4 fucking Non Blondes.

'Yeah, sure. Course,' I go.

Emma flings her arms round my neck. 'Oh, Manny, that's fantastic. So you'll stop hanging about with Iain, go easy on the sniff, yeah?'

Do what? No wonder I was blanking her out.

I weigh it up. The sniff. Well, it's not like she'll know if I go easy one way or the other; to be fair, she's still a bit fucking clueless when it comes to the dirties. I mean, how's she gonna know what I'm up to most of the time? Problem one, solved.

Problem two – Iain. That's a whole different kettle of crap. Been hanging out at his place more than ever. Nerves are too jangly in singlies' quarters to smoke weed. Iain don't give a fuck, though. Reckons the Monkeys will steer well clear of the pad houses, concentrate their efforts on finding druggies in the lines. And, alright, I know that he's a mentalist, that his middle name's trouble. Fuck, that'd he even do Cal over for the sake of a possible shag. Not got many options left, though, have I? I owe him cash for my sniff and the only way I'm gonna pay him back is through the dealing. I know, simple as – I'll make out to Em that I'm not hanging about him, but not change anything. Not like she'll ever know, is it?

'Alright. Done,' I go and hold her close, whispering, 'Let's go back to yours and seal the deal.'

We lie in a nest of tangled sheets, smoking and laughing, stoned as you like, our bodies sweating out sex. Beat my record – three shags in a row! Emma's place don't even have a shower, so I'm gonna have to rock up back on duty reeking. Worth it, though. She's a stunner, is my bird. I snuggle in as she erupts into another scream of laughter.

She's got the giggles big time.

'So, like, football and sex, they're the same, aren't they, when you think about it?'

She's also feckin' confused.

'Erm, what are you on about, love?'

'It's just, I can't figure it out. If I score a goal, will I get pregnant?'

I ruffle her hair. 'Leave it out, you mong.'

Emma plays football at uni. She's going back home soon to try out for next year's team. Too right, it's a head-fuck, innit – a girl playing footie? But she's not lezzerish-looking, if that's what you think. Like I said, she's fucking lush.

'Oooh!' She's rubbing her eyes now, stretching out like a contented cat on the mattress. 'I am so confused! Think I need a kip.'

I hitch myself up on my elbow, tickling her tit with my fingertip. 'Not before round four, you don't.'

'Hmm,' she goes. Not unenthusiastically. 'It'll have to be a lazy one, I'm not moving.'

This turns me on more than if she'd been up for it.

And she lives up to her word. Don't move, that is; lets me move my fingers over her sticky pubes, her tits, her gluey cunt. I wet my finger and root around her arsehole. Worth a try, eh? What's that? She's making a noise. I don't think it's 'no', so I poke about the opening for a bit, until my index finger stutters gradually in. After a few minutes of this, of anal fingering, we're both grunting and gasping. And I have got the horn big time. I try finger number two...

'Oy, Emma,' I whisper the lie, 'we're out of condoms. Can I...?' but she stops me before I can finish, arches her back, grabs my cock and grapples with it, twisting and turning, guiding it in till she's comfy. I do not fucking believe this. It's only going in!

I am doing anal!

I go at it slowly at first, don't want to hurt her, but I'm way too horny, so I pick up the pace... *hung, hung, hung...* oh, my God, amazing feeling... *thrust, thrust thrust...* melting into Emma... *ram, ram, ram...* I hope it lasts for –

'Urghhhhhhhhhhhhhh.'

No such luck. It's over in less than a minute.

She pulls me out, grabs my hand and squeezes it, and I spoon her, stroking her hair, watching as she falls asleep. I close my eyes and all, and picture me and Emma, naked. I don't mean doing the hot and nasty. I mean, naked in a wholesome way, kneeling opposite one another, our palms face out and touching, and it's like we're in a bubble of trust.

Alright, alright, leave it out! I know I sound like a fucking sissy, but, well, I'd hate for you lot to think that I've got no feelings. I'm human too, ain't I? Despite what you might think.

Hamburg – Hafen (Port)

Cal

I put on my sunglasses, pure dazzled by the bright spring sun. At last! Summer's around the corner: Sundays hanging out down the pool at Fally; lassies' bare arms and legs on show; and all-day raves like this yin, down the port in Hamburg. There's nothing like it, bouncing around zebedeed in the daytime – a big fingers-up tae the nine-tae-five rats, the square pegs, and the Army.

There's a big bunch of us lads fae camp come down tae this party, the day. Ye've got yer usual ravers: Manny, me, Iain, Taff, as well as Jonesy and Davie who are getting mair intae the scene now an aw. It's four in the afternoon but the music's already pouring out the speakers in a mad rush of breakbeats and hardcore bass lines. The other lads are all stood on a wall, looming over the crowds, throwing out shapes, making a general nuisance of themselves.

All apart fae me and Iain, that is, who are loitering at the gates of this closed-off area of the port close to the river, a gentle breeze blowing over us, taking the heat out of the last of the day's sun. I sit on the kerb midway between the gate and the party, watching him slyly from behind my sunnies. He pulls out his Ray-Bans. Smoothes down his hair. Flexes his muscles.

Poser!

He's winding me up mair than ever, that yin. Way he's always brown-nosing Manny. And Manny himself – ye wouldnae huv tae be a – what's it? psychiatrist – tae see he wants his heid examining, the amount of dirties he's consuming.

Och, I know, I'm no exactly living up tae my name, 'Happy', am I? If yous must know, I'm trying tae go straight again. They micro-dots – the acid – have fucked my box up big time, messing wi my vision, fucking up my concentration. Besides, Steffi's coming down later. Want tae make the right impression. Manny tellt me that Emma tellt him that Steffi willnae do Class As any mair, not till her exams are over. So mibbe if I stop kicking the arse out of the dirties, she'll gie us another shot? What do yous reckon? Should I go straight? Feel right as rain fur wur shift the morra? Mibbe get some brownie points fae Steffi?

The thing is, I think as a loud whoop swells up fae the crowd, *my feet are pure slaves tae they beats! Then again*, I reconsider, as I squirm intae a better position on the pavement tae catch sight of Steffi when she arrives, *life's no just about fun, is it?*

Aye, right.

I turn tae look at the crowd again, wistful-like, and notice Manny approaching.

'Oy, Cal, mate, next DJ's jungle,' he's saying as he gets closer. 'Emma's up for one of them boat tours round the port while we wait for the next hardcore set.' He planks his arsehole on the kerb next tae us, water spilling fae his plastic water bottle. 'Fancy it?'

Yippee fuckin doo, a boat trip. What are we, ten?

154

'Um mibbe later, pal. I'm just – '

'Waiting for Steffi. Say no more.' And he nods over at the gates, saying, 'There she is,' and I swivel round tae catch a look, my heart lurching upwards, strangling my collarbone, eventually finding its way tae my throat. First time I've seen her since wur 'chat'. She looks beautiful, so she does, like a perfect wee china doll. No make-up, the day, her long blonde hair in plaits, wee vest top.

I think I'm gonnae fuckin greet.

'Ciao, everybody. How's it going?' she says, her plaits swinging about her face.

Her and Iain swap air kisses, and she hugs Manny. I hang back, making a show of wiping clean my sunnies. Does she look over my way though, anyway? Does she fuck!

'Just talking about doing one of them boat tours, Steffi. Fancy it?' Manny says.

'Oy, oy, boat tour?' Iain butts in. 'Let's have at it then.'

'Ja, sooper, I have not done *Hafenrundfahrt* for years,' Steffi says, linking arms wi the sleazy prick.

This boat tour's taking a fuckin age, man! Some fuckin crack it is an aw. My trousers are damp fae the spray splashing in, Manny and Emma are canoodling, ignoring me, and Steffi and Iain are hanging over the side of the rails, thick as thieves.

I pick up the headphones and switch on the taped guided tour, tae break the – what's it? Monotony. The tour guide on the tape's piffling on about how this area used tae be run-down. Now they've pumped money in: 'built a stunning array of new waterside apartments'. C'moan tae fuck! As if building a bunch of posh show-haims fur yuppies is gonnae fix the sleaze lodged in Hamburg's gut. Sits there like a slab of undigested meat, so it does – porn and drugs, hoors and crime, it has them fur fuckin breakfast, lunch and dinner. Before we got posted to this arsehole of the world, Manny and me, our raving was fuckin innocent. Then Hamburg got its teeth in and we were on a helter-skelter ride tae hell.

Besides, take away the cracks, the crack and the crackpots, ye take away a city's soul, far as I'm concerned. Look at Glesga. Poshing up areas like the Gorbals. My auntie Edie tellt me they knocked down they Queen Elizabeth Square flats last year tae make way fur new housing. That's right, move the yobs out fae the city centre, bring the yuppies in. How no just go all the way? Cart aw the poor cunts away in buses, bury them six feet under?

Ah, hold that thought – at last, we're out on the open sea, chugging past aw they container ships, 'laden wi goods from all four corners of the globe', the tape says.

But I'm no interested in that; I'm on a roll now, thinking about that fuckin class stuff. I mean, if it wasnae fur the working classes there'd be no fuckin culture, no community in some towns. Aye, really! I mean, c'moan. Name one pure dead brulliant band who didnae come fae some arsehole inner city, or fae the concrete culture void of wan a they new towns like East Kilbride. Och, okay. The Rolling Stones. I'll gie yous that wan. How's about the Jesus and Mary Chain, the Stone Roses, or the Happy Mondays? Cannae imagine they'd huv got it thegither if they'd been brung up in some la-di-da place where ye went tae a 'nice' school and yer mammy had yer dinner on the table at five o'clock. Nope, that's me convinced. There's no better inspiration than tae come fae some pish-smelling, soul-destroying – what's it? monotone – fuckin hellhole.

And if yous don't believe me, take it from Morrissey instead. What's it he said? 'Time that the ordinary folk of the world showed their faces.' Too fuckin right, pal. I'll never forget that. Same goes fur books an aw. Enough of aw that middle class shite. 'Should we get a divorce 'cause ye fucked the nanny over the Aga?'

C'moan tae fuck! It's real life we're talking about here.

Fuck me. Rant over. I cannae take these negative thoughts – it just isnae me. Still, two minutes I huvnae mooned over Steffi's got tae be a Brucey bonus! Then, like some fuckin weird love tick, just thinking of her makes me cast about, tae check her latest move, the expression on her face. That fuckin Iain, there he's again, trying tae chat her up. Can imagine what a slime bucket of patter's vomming fae his mouth.

A splash of dirty water spills over the side of the boat, messing up my trousers, bringing my mood down further.

It's time fur a change. Time tae be happy. Time tae be me again.

I nudge Manny, who's been sat touching up Emma next tae us, so fanny-struck that he's ignoring aw the container ships he was banging on about seeing. 'Medicine time,' I say.

'Knew you'd come round…' he goes, digging in his pocket.

He hands me a crumbly white tablet.

I gie him a look.

He hands us another.

Pure doves like the auld days. Magic! And I bang back both pills as the boat pulls back in tae the harbour, double-dropping my way tae a temporary time warp of blissed-out not remembering.

Fallingbostel British Army Base

Manny

Emma's sat in the block glued to BFBS, forces' telly, 'cause her idol, that Kurt Cobain, has only gone and blasted his brains out with a shotgun. Nause. I wanted her to come down the shower room with me, have at it, while most of the other lads are up the outdoor pool. (No chance of any interruptions, if you see what I mean.) But she's goggling at the telly, transfixed. Cal's no better. Look at the pair of them, will ya? They're welling up!

The TV reporter drones on, '… those who idolised him and those who didn't understand what the fuss was about.'

'Too right,' I say irritably, flinging myself on to my pit. 'Some junkie who played shit music tops himself, and you two are in bits.'

Cal spins around. 'C'moan tae fuck. What about the stupit teenagers who might copy him, did you think of that?'

'Yeah, have a heart,' Emma says, throwing a random empty fag packet at me. 'Not exactly the easy way out, is it?'

And I'm thinking, *Well, yeah, actually that's exactly what it is*, but I can't be arsed to argue, what with them two ganging up on me. Besides, grunge music ain't exactly my thing, is it? So, I'm bored out my skull as we watch a conveyor belt of arseholes churned out to talk about the 'sad loss to the music industry'.

'Oh, look, they're going to interview John Peel,' Emma chirps.

Big fucking hairy deal!

Thought Em coming up here to camp would be a laugh; didn't realise she'd get wrapped up in English telly. I root around in my pocket for a wrap. I know, I know, should be careful at the mo, what with all the hoo-ha about them lads in Osnabrück. But we've heard naff-all about it since Jonesy got busted.

Except from Jonesy, that is.

Thinks he's The Man 'cause he got caught; it's made him more of a gob-shite than ever. There he goes again, on his other favourite subject, screeching that he's just given his duvet the fifth dusting of the day. And with Emma in the room and all. Not that she's noticed. Like I said, she's sitting worshipping at the altar of telly. Not like Jonesy's got much to shout about anyway. All he got charged with was three nights in the punt and a week's wages. I mean, even the feckin' Monkeys could spot that a blim's worth of hash don't make him a professional toker.

Now the TV's going on about how Nirvana touched the lives of millions of kids; how they 'embody the slacker generation'.

I've had about all I can take of this. 'Emma, love,' I say, 'you be alright? I'm nipping to the lav?'

She don't move a muscle, the light from the telly shining on her, like a halo.

'We'll look after her, won't we, lads?' Jonesy pipes up in his nasal whine, thrusting his hips out suggestively to Tommo.

Very funny. They'll be lucky. Not like she's even going to do me, by the looks of things. Besides, she's not one of them groundsheets who come back here to screw anyone who'll have her. Groundsheets? Easy to lay, of course. No, not my Em. She's a class bird. Not like some of them who come back here and get up to all sorts of filth.

Take last week. Christ only knows how, but Jonesy and Tommo had three German girls back here for a right old messy time. A gangbang, if you must know. Cal and me had to escape to Davie's room. Don't know what's worse, mind you: three hours of ska music and Davie trying to convince me to go easy on the dirties, or watching Jonesy in the throes of his carnal gymnastics. Nause! Still, wish Emma was up for some kind of action today. Managed to persuade her to come back here 'cause she'd banged back three pills, but that Nirvana dude's made her go all limp-dicked – or whatever the fucking female equivalent is.

Ah, finally – the bogs at last!

I nip straight past a lad stood in the urinals and bolt the cubicle door, pulling out my wrap in a flurry of excitement. About half a gram left. That would probably do six lines for most cunts. For me, I'm thinking, maybe three? One for now, one for back at Emma's after I've driven her home, one for the journey back to Fally. I cut the stuff up with my Sparkasse bank card, chopping out the biggest line for now. Take a rolled-up fifty DM note from my wallet. Snort to clear my nostrils. Hoover up a line. *Bang bang bang bang!* Oy, oy. What's that? Some idiot's hammering on the door. I swing it open gracefully for him, feeling rather lovely now, as it goes.

'Alright,' I say to the lad, sniffing.

He throws me daggers and closes the door in my grid.

Whatever. Don't care what anyone thinks of me no more. I wipe my nose and sniff again, sucking up the white powder through my sinuses, down my throat until it fires up in my belly. Hold up. Here come the 'video vegetables' – a couple of the infantry lads who like nothing better than to trip their nuts off to some video nasty on a Sunday afternoon.

'Boo!' I shout, snarling, to shit them well up. They sidle past me, bug-eyed, their backs to the wall.

Ha and fucking double ha. I am the fucking man!

I swagger full of coke and confidence along the corridor, only as I'm approaching our room I hear raised voices. Hang about... I think it's Emma's and... I crane my neck... hold up... some bloke's? Sounds like an argument. It's not *him*, is it? I swing the door open, my heart doing Wacky Races as I enter.

Yeah, it is, it's Iain.

And, what the fuck? You lot aren't gonna believe this!

The cunt's stood squaring up to Emma, whose face is well puffy and red; Cal's in the middle of them, hopping from foot to foot, his right eye ticking.

Emma marches straight across to me, grabs me by the elbow and drags me out of earshot of the others. 'That's it. It's over. I can't be doing with your lying any more.' Snivelling, as she continues, 'Is that – that *yob* really more important to you than me?'

And them tears which were flowing so freely in front of the telly just now don't seem to want to come any more. That's so like her. Brave, not wanting to lose face. I gulp. Looks like she's going to fucking burst if she don't cry again in a minute, I think, as she wipes away a snail trail of snot with her sleeve. And she fills me in – Iain's only gone and told her that there was no way I wasn't gonna hang about with him, that I've been dealing bits and bobs of Charlie and pills and that. Just my fucking luck he's come over to borrow my new Ministry CD.

Oh, pipe down, you lot, with your 'told you so'. So, I've hurt her, so what? What's that stuff? Karma? Amy hurt me, I hurt Emma, she hurts me back, Steffi hurts Cal. But hold up, who does he hurt? Well, who gives a shit? This is why you don't let people come close, break that fucking chain of pain. The funny thing is, where there should be pain, all I can feel is a gaping black hole. And all I can think of to say is, 'Your loss, love,' while I puzzle over how I'm gonna get rid of Emma off camp without causing a scene.

I pull the car round to the front of the barracks. Last thing I need is for her to get spotted. I bib the horn and Emma provokes me by walking slowly to the car. I open the door and gesture to her to hurry up, and she does, sliding into the passenger seat, ducking down low.

'Put on that radio station you get – um, BF whatever – I want to see if they've got more about Cobain.'

I'm like, no way, 'cause my head's done in now, mashed by the commotion of our argument: by Cal and Iain bitching at each other; by the lads all mouthing off in the background. I need quiet. And I need a line.

'My car. Radio's not going on. You want a lift, just belt up, will ya?'

'Oh, fuck you very much,' Emma goes, and pulls her hooded top up over her head. Then, 'Hold on a sec,' and she jumps out the car, rattles the back door open, slams the other one shut. *Bang!* 'I'm going to sit up back.'

The A7's empty and I do the journey in no time, putting my foot down and accelerating to ninety. In the rear-view mirror, I watch Emma's knuckles turn white as she grips the door handle so I speed up even more. But she don't say nothing, even as I go yet faster, the trees lining the road and other cars blurring into a background smudge, making the outline of her pretty face more alive than ever.

A face you're not gonna kiss again, eh, you fuck-up?

Don't think about that, what a stunner she is, what a fucking rock she's been, don't think about it, don't think about it. I close my eyes to try and blot it out.

'Oy, Manny, wakey wakey,' Emma goes, and I focus, swerving back into lane.

Forty minutes later – record time – and I'm pulling up to the first U-Bahn stop we come to in the suburbs of HH.

161

What? And you lot think I should drive her to her front door after she's binned me? This will do her. She opens the car door clumsily – think she's been asleep; her eyes are red – then blushes as she raps on the driver's window. I wind it down.

'And to think,' she goes, 'I let you... let you... do *that* to me!'

I laugh like a drain at that. But inside I'm not laughing, am I? Didn't know it meant that much to her – as much as it did to me, I mean. I just don't chuffing believe this. The best thing that ever happened to me, walking out my life.

And as if she was reading my mind, she says the last words I ever hear her say. 'I hope I never see you again.'

And do you know what? She doesn't.

'Cause now, ladies and gents, that's it for me, and there's a shit-storm brewing that you lot have probably been expecting since you first met me in black and white on page nine.

Hannover – Hanomag

Cal

The camera sweeps the dance flair, and Manny waves, his pork pie hat cemented tae his heid wi sweat. They're only filming this rave fur RTL! Some of the other squaddie ravers put their hands across their coupons. I mean, c'moan – last thing we need is the RSM to spot us fleeing out wur boxes on German telly.

'Oy, Manny, use yer brains, let's bang out,' I say, grabbing his hand, pulling him away fae the cameras.

'Nah, mate, I'm staying put,' he goes, throwing himself in front of the cameraman again. 'Fame at last.' The numpty.

I catch a hold of his T-shirt, and drag him kicking and screaming deeper intae the heart of the rave. Aw, magic! The vibe is fuckin electric down here! I sook up the atmosphere and chill out right away, can even laugh as I say tae Manny, 'Fuck, that was a close wan.'

But he just goes, 'Oy, mate. I'm spinning out, help me stand up, will ya?'

So I grab hold of him, tap him up fur a fag, and we lean against a speaker fur a bit, its vibrations deep and overpowering. But I ignore the lure of they speakers 'cause I'm still coming up, too spacey tae dance, lighting the fag instead, inhaling deeply fur a change, blowing the smoke out my nostrils.

They cameras remind me of way back at the start of the rave scene when the *Daily Record* ran a scare story about Es. The centrefold was some lad at Rezerection, gurning his tits off with a big yellow 'E' painted on his chest, clutching a Vicks inhaler. And guess what this lad did fur a job? Aye. Right again! Turned out he was a serving sodger wi some Scottish battalion based out of Edinburgh. A pal of mine tellt me that the raver's RSM almost had a baby over that photo. The lad was hauled in front of the CO and the RMP, but they couldn't do him for just being at an event. Nowadays, though... they've wised up about the dirties; we'll be dead meat if we're caught...

Fuck that fur now, though, I think, 'cause Manny's off tae find the others, and I quickly follow, energised by the dance flair – a human circuitboard packed wi high-voltage ravers. I stub out the fag and squeeze further through the crowds tae find wur crew, shoving thoughts of work out my box, blissed-out as I'm missiled by the love bombs dropped by the tablet. Now where are they? I wonder, as I reach the heaving sea of ravers down the front near the stage. There they are – there! Manny, Taff, Davie, Tommo, Iain, and –

No way, man, Steffi. Didnae know she was coming out.

Will she bang out now she's seen me?

But no, she's spied me, and oh, yes! oh, yes! she's smiling – a beautiful E'd-up grin – and she's saying, 'Cal, come here, Cal!' and I start dancing next tae her, holding her hand, and a rush like the auld days goes through me, and we pure go fur it, fleeing tae fuck, buzzing off wan another...

... and I think, *Mibbe Manny's right – mibbe Steffi'll come round, huv me back* – and fur the first time in ages wur crew are in sweet harmony, no fucker sledging on his own in a corner, no wan wankered on coke, and as I peak on my tablet I become hung up on just one thought – what a night, what a buzz, what a crew.

One Love, One Family.

My family.

The BPMs huv picked up, mair tablets dropped. Force multipliers in action on the dance flair. I am higher than the fuckin sun – mission accomplished!

Now the DJ's dropping a blinder, my favourite hardcore tune – '4 a.m.' by Orca. I check my watch. Aye, true tae form, he's spun it at four in the morning. Cheesy, mibbe. But who gives a fuck? 'Tune!' I yell, my heart doing a drum roll as the beats come in:

> Electric flashes fae the strobe strike out in blinks and
> winks across the dance flair *FLASH* dry ice pumps
> in gush after gush *FLASH* I reach fur the stars,
> the blood rushing tae my heid *FLASH*
> ravers' arms and legs stutter in the strobe,
> their eyes closed against its dazzle

> Steffi *FLASH* dances *FLASH* hands chop the air
> *FLASH* Iain *FLASH* top off *FLASH* gold chain
> bangs against his chest *FLASH* Iain kisses Steffi
> *FLASH* she kisses him back *FLASH*
> breakbeats make way fur blissful piano highs
> *FLASH*
> crowd go fuckin primeval

The strobe cuts out.

We're in the hazy clublight again.

I can see fuck-all.

Where are they? Where the fuck are they? I wipe a patch of sweat fae my eyes and brow. Where've they gone? Where've they cunting gone? We stay blinded till the clouds of dry ice lift, and then I clock them – her arms straddling his oily naked back, his tongue darting snake-like in her mouth.

I am stone cold fuckin sober.

I sit on the front steps of this monster of a building, watching the first pinks and oranges of the new morning. Looks of things, it's gonnae be a clear day. Wan or two clouds in the sky just, butting up tae the fuzzy colours of the dawn. I crumple intae the red brick steps of the Hanomag.

Steffi and Iain. Iain and Steffi?

Steffi and Iain?

One Love? One Family? That's a joke!

Aye, I should've seen it coming. Aye, I could see the prick chatting her up, playing the Big Man act. I cannae believe she got sucked in, but. I mean, c'moan, a girl at university, wi a brain like that? What's she see in that fuckin brain-dead airbag? Och, okay, there's the smarmy Robert De Niro grin an that, but he's as much else going fur him as a shagging soggy lettuce.

And yous, what about yous? Oh, aye, yous seen it coming. Shame yous couldnae huv jumped on the page and warned us. But would yous huv? That's how it is wi pals, eh? Never huvin the baws tae tell things like it is. It's no right, though, is it, when ye think about it? Ye should be able tae tell a real pal anything. Or else what's the point? So, there ye go, if yous are gonnae take anything away fae this story, make it this – when a pal's being shat on, gonnae just tell them straight, no messing?

I hug masel intae the concrete steps again, shivering. Just realised I left my coat back at the rave. My T-shirt, my favourite – the wan wi the Dready logo – is clamming to my skin an aw, damp fae the night's adventures. I shiver again. This time not fae the cold, though, but fae an attack of trembles at the thought of what they two were up tae behind my back.

This fuckin car-crash of a lumber could huv only happened at 4 a.m., by the way. Strangest time of the day, so it is – isnae night, isnae day yet either; a heavy in-betweeny time; a time fur decisions and change. I mean, say yer at a rave at 4 a.m., it's the time when the men are sorted fae the boys – either yer fucking off haim wi the drinkers and the square pegs, or yer necking mair pills wi the hardcore lost-it crew, dancing yer way tae dawn. And if yer awake at haim at 4 a.m., it likely means wan a two things – either yer laying there sweating in a stew of sleeplessness, trying tae say goodbye tae the shite of the day before, or yer wakeful 'cause yer counting down the minutes tae the rise of the sun, excited about some event in the day tae come.

I mind my gran – who was a nurse – tellt me that folk who die in their sleep often pass on at 4 a.m. Aye, that's it, I think, 4 a.m.'s a crossroads. A fork in the road between life and death, between day and night an aw. And mibbe that's what this is about. I mean, what my story is all about – that I'm at a crossroads, changing fae a boy tae a man.

I snort at my own stupidity.

Boy to man? Some man I am, no standing up tae they traitors, no telling them what I felt, pure running away wi a mumbled, 'See yous later,' no looking back, afraid of what I'd see.

Which makes me picture that snake-tongue probing Steffi again, and I feel poisoned to my stomach. I want tae scratch out the eyes that seen her kissing him, that seen her in the first place; tae rip out the tongue that couldnae stop saying her name; tae claw at the fingers that held her hands. I sigh. I mean, I would never, not in a million years, huv put her down as wan a they lassies who'd like the 'treat them mean, keep them keen' kind of lads. And what about Kelly? Poor cow doesnae even know she's being treated mean. Fuckin Iain!

Another tremor of cold rips through me. Mibbe I should go back in? Fetch my coat? But no, there's only wan thing fur it.

Back tae camp.

I breathe a sigh of pain and giving-in, and pick masel up fae the steps. I hope the trains are running, that I can get back tae the block and sleep in peace, no Jonesy about, playing the wind-up merchant as per usual.

'*Vorsicht!*' A group of lads and lassies are bundling past me on the steps and I take the chance tae follow them through the maze of cars in the car park towards the exit.

Outside the main gates of the Hanomag the streets are empty as the city rests. Only the nutters and the street cleaners and the early risers about, leaving a blank canvas, pretty much, fur the new day. In the distance I spot the clock tower at the station and I work my way towards it, walking quickly down a steep hill, a typical German street, packed wi bakeries and tanning salons and coffee shops, trams chugging past every now and then, only wan or two dour faces in each.

After a time a click of heels breaks the silence of the morning as a young couple come towards me, arm-in-arm, and I cannae help it. I imagine Steffi's lips on Iain's again, and my teeth start chattering uncontrollably, my legs trembling. But even so, I manage tae break intae a sprint, new sweat melding wi the auld, tae speed up my escape...

fae that fuckin Hanomag

fae Steffi

fae the emotional excrement of life.

Mibbe I'll gie the padre a wee visit when I'm back in camp, I think, as I take a second tae lean against a lamppost, panting. *Own up. Tell him I'm needing help tae get me off the drugs, tae start afresh.* Aye, right. Like I can trust that cunt. I heave up a glob of bile. Spit. Watch it slide down the side of the lamppost. Besides, it's hard tae love your God when he's shat on you fae a great height yet again. I sigh, another deep and sad wan, and think, *Who else tae turn to, though? Auntie Edie? My ma – ha, that's a laugh* – and I'm left cold by they choices, cold by the nip in the morning air an aw, so I hurry along, down, down, down till I'm at the bottom of the hill, where the city centre and the station cannae be far off.

Chapter Eight

Manny

As the cosy numbness of the pill and my E-goggles melt away, I open my eyes to a comedown of epic proportions in Iain and Kelly's front room.

It ain't a pretty sight.

An orgy, in fact, by the looks of things.

Them German birds Tamara and Bruni lie snogging, a heap of sweat-soaked sports clothes and twisted limbs on the floor, while Jonesy and Tommo ogle, leching to the max. The carpet's a boggy, beer-soaked mess and – oh, mate, you lot ain't gonna believe this – now Tommo's getting his knob out, letting it worm there in a semi, not even bothering to do nothing with it.

But that's not the worst of it. Bobbing back and forth on the leather sofa is a cratered full moon, in other words Iain's round, white – and spotty – arse. How long's that been going on? I've been too monged-out to take it all in, laying on the other sofa cosied up in a maggot bag trying to avoid that minger Tamara. She's been after me all night, the slapper.

Whoah, fuck about! The bobbing action is getting more intense. I look on, transfixed. Not in a pervy way or nothing, I'm way too freaked out for that. I mean, couldn't they have used the bedroom? Surprised at Kel doing it in her own front room – not like her to put on a show.

Fuck. About.

It ain't Kel, is it?

She's gone back to Blighty to visit her sister, so Iain says. Anyway. You lot saw it coming, I saw it coming, but now it's staring at me in all its spotty-arsed and panting glory I can't quite believe it. The unlucky receiver of the bobbing moon-fuck is none other than young Steffi. As if it couldn't get any worse, the soundtrack to this head-fuck is Tommo's Gabber tape, the distorted kick sounds multiplying my head-fuckedness and anxiety.

Get me fucking outta here!

Carefully, quietly, I unzip the maggot bag, picking my way across the debris of empty beer bottles, Rizlas and fag packets towards the door. Each bottle's chocka with fag ends, the carpet littered with Rizlas – Christ, I must have been monged out for hours. The door handle squeaks as I turn it and Tamara flicks her eyes towards me... stops for a sec, only to continue the lezzer action when I flash her a V sign. Outside in the hallway, things are a right state and all. I mean, they've even used Kelly's china ornaments as ash trays. And – oh, mate! if you could only see this – that's taking the piss, that is: her porcelain poodle's been used as a dumping ground for a condom; dollops of spunk dripping over the pink bow around its doggy neck.

'Ckin hell! I can't take this – it's twisted.

And *bang*! Insult to injury, one of them headaches is starting up.

I yank open the kitchen door but the powerful strip lighting blinds me, making my head pound even more. I know! Kel's bound to have some painkillers. I open cupboard door after cupboard door until I find what I'm after.

And just as I'm knocking back four of the Nurofen with a glass of water *bang*! another explosion tears through my skull with all the subtlety of a machine gun.

See, this is why you need Charlie – doesn't give you a headache like E. Bad luck for me, there's a drought on cocaine at the mo. Iain's off to visit the Pharmacist in the Dam soon.

Looks like he wants me to schlepp along with him. Too right, I will – make sure I'm first in line for a toot on my old friend Charles.

Still, I've got to admit them pills last night were blinding – caned the arse out of them, we did. It was almost like the old days down the Hanomag – giving it large up the front near the stage, pumping our bodies, minds and souls in time to the four-four beats.

That was then, though; this is now.

Then, we had a right old laugh, no birds in on the act nausing everything up. Now, it's come to this – me dumped, Cal shat on by Steffi, and a feckin' orgy.

Then, we went Banzai for the dirties and managed to get through the day at work. Now, each new day in that cookhouse is a living hell.

Then, me and Cal was top mates – nothing could come between us. Now... I dunno – I turn it over in my mind – we've made up since that fight but still... fuck, what I wouldn't do for a line.

Missing him right now, as it happens. He's always a top lad on a comedown, is Cal – knows how to lighten the mood. He'd know what to say to make me feel better about Emma and all. I'm missing her like crazy if you lot want to know.

That's it.

No way I'm hanging around with this lot for the rest of the day. I'll put the kettle on, have a brew, one last fag, head back to the block, see if Cal's okay. Can't even remember seeing him leave last night... Well, at least he's not here to see this going down.

I'm mulling this over, about how I'm gonna tell him, and finishing my cuppa when there's another bolt of pain, tearing, ripping, searing. I rub my temples, willing the painkillers to do their job. Hang on a mo, door's opening – bloody hell, not that Tamara?

No, it's Steffi, a towel wrapped around her, her legs moist. She jumps when she clocks me.

'Oh… hello, Manny. I just – um – come to get a glass of – '

'Steffi, what you up to? Thought you was gonna come upstairs?' And here's Iain, towel round his waist and all, slung so low that his six-pack is showing.

'No, Iain, I have to go now, I'm working in the ice cream place today – I told you so.'

Iain stiffens. 'Aw, come on, love, pull a sickie, why don't you?' he says, his mouth tight as he inches towards her.

She backs off, and I turn to the sink, making out like the teacup is in dire need of a scrubbing.

'Zo, um, Manny,' Steffi's saying. I turn reluctantly to face them again, noticing that she's biting her lip as she continues, 'You leaving? Could you drive me to the train station?'

Iain throws me daggers. But I stand there, defiant. 'Yeah, but hurry up, love, I want to get back to Cal,' and I search out her eyes as I'm saying his name. She don't meet them but at least she's got the good grace to blush.

Someone's meeting my eyes, though, alright. In fact, if they was doing a competition for filthy looks, Iain'd win first prize, no dramas. He bangs down his glass of water, then flounces out the room without a word.

Time for another fag, I think, as I wait for Steffi to fetch her stuff. I fumble around in my pocket, spark the found fag up, taking the smoke deep down in my lungs. The nicotine hit's bittersweet, though. I mean, Charlie and fags, they're perfect partners, don't you think? So now I'm prey to the thought of whether I've got a bump of coke somewhere or other, back in the lines.

'Come on, Steffi, hurry up,' I yell, chucking the half-finished fag in the sink, *hiss.*

From the hallway I hear raised voices, something like, 'No, Iain, never again, it was just the drugs…' and I spy a photo on the wall of Iain and Kelly on their wedding day, a pair of perfect Hollywood smiles on their grids. I turn it over so Kel's facing the wall just as Steffi joins me, and I go to close the door, gently, not wanting to provoke my headache. But just before it comes to, I hear another raised voice – Iain's, this time – saying, 'Come on, Tamara, you little sexpot, let's have at it, then.'

And I'm sure, from the look on Steffi's face, she must have heard him and all.

Hamburg

Cal

A row of grey faces eyeball me fae the seats opposite, and I'm minded of they gargoyles that peer down at ye fae churches and cathedrals an that.

Twisted, leering, judging.

The tube train's rattling along like a bastard, and, hauf-asleep, I judder intae the woman sitting next tae us. Whoops. She's been making a bodge job of putting on her lipstick; now a red stripe slashes across her cheek, and she curses, '*Scheisse*.' Turns around as if she wants tae gie us a doing. Takes wan look and decides the better of it.

I cannae look that fucked-up, surely? Aye, I've been up all night, look like I've gone ten rounds wi a bowling ball in a sock. *Still, I'm holding it thegither, pretty much*, I think, as I gurn-smile at the lipstick woman. She smiles nervously back and looks away, just in time tae miss me slurping back a dollop of dribble.

Like I say, I'm holding it thegither – pretty much.

It's Wednesday morning. Most folk are thinking about the start tae a day of work. A day of sooking the boss's baws, of being the office joker, or worse still, the office fall-guy, the butt of everybody's jokes. Me, I'm on a mission. A mission me and Taff put thegither last night during an all-night session at his place – a mission tae find Steffi at that ice cream place she works in, so that I can say goodbye.

Aye, goodbye.

Too right. There was me fannying about trying tae decide my future when suddenly wur RSM is telling us the regiment is being sent through tae Bos, tae take part in Operation Grapple. And he's asking if any of us cookie monsters want tae head out wi the advance party, that there's money and opportunities fur thems who do. So there was me still hauf off my tits fae that night at the Hanomag and I thought, *There you are, there's my escape hatch…* and that was me walking intae his office and signing on the dotted line.

Aye, ye wouldnae huv tae be a brain surgeon tae guess that I'm huvin second thoughts about that, the day…

Manny's escaped this particular pleasure fur now, the jammy dodger; he'll be coming out wi the rest of the lads in a couple of months. Still, he's been a real bezzie after everything that's happened. And I mean after 'everything'. Aye, it's okay, yous can be spared the suspense, Manny tellt me all about back at Iain's bit last week, about Steffi getting on wi that slime bag after the Hanomag. Not that he's got much more advice than the usual Army lads' response for a knock-back: dry your eyes, pick up your teddy, move on.

Anyway, it's all wrong, isn't it? Manny and me getting close again when I'll be off without him fur at least two months. He's promised he'll give Iain the cold shoulder when I'm off, that he's realised what a cunt he is. Meanwhile Davie's promised tae keep an eye on Manny, tae keep him out of trouble. And I believe him. Manny, I mean. After everything that's went on, I've faith in him. Mair faith than I've in my God right now, if yous want tae know the truth.

But I see yous are wondering how comes I didnae go haim, visit my family before going on Ops. Well, fur wan, I wasnae allowed a free flight back tae Blighty on my embarkation leave – and anyway, what family? Huvnae heard fae my ma or my auntie Edie in months. As fur my cousins – probably the last time they put pen tae paper was writing tae *Jim'll* fuckin *Fix It*.

Och, okay, yous've got me, I huvnae even tellt the family I'm headed fur Bos yet; it was my decision to spend my embarkation leave up here in HH, sleeping on Taff's sofa, hoping I'd run intae Steffi. But I've been bang out of luck, so

I huv – no Steffi in Purgatory, no Steffi in the Tunnel Club, no Steffi in the Unit. So here I am on the U-Bahn headed fur her ice cream place in Kiwittsmoor – a last ditch attempt at a – what's it? Reconciliation.

And yet, there's a wee voice nagging at me. Some teeny part of me wondering is she worth it anyways? I mean, we're no exactly two peas in a pod, are we? Mibbe I'd be better off…

Don't think about that, don't think about that, I order masel, and as I comb through my brain for a different subject, along comes a song in my heid – something about misery and happiness. You know, like it does when yer brain's switching off?

What *is* that song? I cannae mind who that's…

Och, now I remember – the fuckin Proclaimers. Last thing I need is an ear worm fae they two speccy gits. They've a lot tae answer fur, the Proclaimers, so they huv. I mean, c'moan. Ask anybody fae south of the border tae name a Scottish band, and they'll soon be taking the urine, naming the worst possible musical outfits they can think of: Run Rig, Deacon Blue or, worse yet, Wet, Wet, Wet. Aye, too right. Think they're hitting an easy target, the English, when it comes tae music.

I slump back in my seat. Narrow my eyes. Punch my hand on the armrest. Fuckin English.

Fuckin bunch of baw-bags.

Aye, yous are right, it's no the English I hate, it's wan Englishman in particular. I close my eyes, try and sleep, let my mind go blank. And by the time I arrive at the right stop I've calmed down – and I've made a decision. Fuck this blimmin cake-and-arse party. 'Cause, what's the point? No like Steffi wants anything tae do wi me. Bad boys, that's what she likes. A little prick tease, like Manny said – loving the attention, leading me on, no brave enough tae tell it like is.

Besides, it's no her I should be thinking about. It's Iain. Iain's fault. All this mess he's caused.

And a flame of anger sparks alight in my box, bold, red and bright. I want tae burst that cunting-fuck Iain's arse. Tae get him back fur the pain he's caused me. Fur turning Manny ontae the sniff. Fur sleazing his way intae Steffi's knickers. Most of all though, fur doing the dirty on Kelly. Imagine! Pulling a fast wan on a cracking bird like her.

Then it hits me. A lightbulb moment.

I know a way I can get him back, I think. And I'm stalked by that one thought as I jump off the train, run across the platform tae take another back intae town. *Aye, too right*, I convince masel, chewing it over, *I know exactly what I should do tae get that fucker back*.

And I grin as I settle back intae my seat, thinking that fur once everything is clear; that, fur once, the answer has been staring me in the face all along.

Hamburg – Kiez

Manny

Snnnnnnnnnort.

I hoover up the last of the Charlie off the cistern. A nice fat line to balance the monginess of the pills. Just spark up another fag and I'll be sorted. Whoah! Only trying to make my way out the bogs is a right nause. I try one step... two... hoping to get my balance; take the stairs one at a time, holding on to the wall as I head for the main bar upstairs. Here we go, last step and... fuck about!... the bar door swings open and I'm smacked around the head by the sounds, smells and lights of Friday night in Purgatory.

Deep breath and I enter the fray, swaggering over to the booth where our crew are squashed up – Tommo, Jonesy, Davie, Tamara and her mate Bruni. Cal's back in the lines, sorting his stuff out, wanting to keep straight before he heads to Bos.

I know, can you lot believe that? Head-fuck, innit? Him to be off like that.

'Come on, then, who's for a shot?' I ask, keen to blot out any thoughts of Cal being offksi. 'Oy, Tamara, what about you?' I say, sliding into the booth next to her, slipping my arm across her back.

Only she don't answer, but recoils, saying, '*Oh, Mensch*,' pointing at me, nudging her mate Bruni in the arm.

'*Igitt! Der hat nasenbluten*,' Bruni says, or words to that effect.

What she shagging on about? I think, searching out the others' eyes for an answer. Tommo looks over at me, and hands me a piece of bog roll from his pocket. Jonesy wipes his finger across his nose like a moustache. Then I feel it – my nostrils warming and clotting; see it – the blood spurting on to the table. Fuck about – another nosebleed! Been having a ton of them recently.

A shower of fresh blood follows soon after, collecting in a mini-puddle on the Formica table top.

And it's sort of like I'm in a trance, spun out by them colours: the vivid red of the blood; the yellow lights in the bar; the blue neon across the DJ booth; the strong pink of Tamara's top – they're taking me in a trippy flashback to a different time and place, back to that final beasting during the basic training, back to…

No, no, no! No way I want to think about that. Like I said before, I'll tell you about it some time, I'll tell you when I'm good and –

only it's like them colours are bullying me into it, telling me, *It's now or never, you've got to let it all out, you ain't got long to get them on your side…*

and I'm in a bubble of my own memories, then, vaguely hearing the blur of Tamara saying, '*Wir hauen ab*.' Then, 'Manny, we're going. You coming?'

and Tommo saying, 'We'll hang on for a bit. See you down there.'

Him and Jonesy start yabbering away then, about who they're gonna pair off with later – a right pair of nauses – and I huddle up in one corner of the booth, cradling my beer, weighted down by them memories.

Oh, for Chrissakes, just tell them, my voices badger me, *lighten the load. Besides we're on chapter eight already – you ain't got long to let it all out.*

Okay, okay, I give up, I'll tell you about it.

But I need to go back to the beginning.

I take a big glug of Wobbly, of *Warsteiner*. Gulp. So, this is how it was.

Well, at the start, there was the basic training. Like I mentioned, I started out training for the infantry. Every Friday our unit did our mile-and-a-half run. I'm not blowing my own trumpet or nothing, but I was always well ahead of the others, sprinting off from the main group like a greyhound. Usually came first, believe it or not, out of the three hundred or so soldiers taking part. Only I did the run in my DayGlo tracky bottoms and a Stone Roses T-shirt, bouncing around like Tigger, didn't I? That seriously pissed off the senior ranks, as well as some of the other lads. They thought I wasn't taking the training serious, that I was letting myself down – as well as the unit.

Especially Sergeant Blake, the PT in charge of our troop. After the first week it was clear he had one ambition in life – to tear me a new arsehole. 'An admin vortex,' he called me, 'cause, despite my physical fitness, I never quite managed to get my shit together, was always turning up late and in the wrong dress kit and that. Should have known from the start he'd be a headache. I mean, take his first words to us, when he was put in charge of our troop. Think it went something – give or take a 'cunt' or two – like this:

'Morning, cunts. PTI Sergeant Blake in case you didn't know. From this day on, your backsides belong to me, and it's my one aim to cunt you about till your feet bleed, to spend fourteen weeks nagging, niggling and needling you, so you want to run home to yer mammies. If you let me down, I'll make mincemeat of you, so help me God.'

To which none of us spotty oiks replied, so he yelled full in our faces, 'Got that, you cunting fucks?'

This was the beginning of us getting fucked around by him from dusk till dawn. Never met a bigger head-case in the Army since. Yeah, you lot might think there's a load of bullying goes on, but you'd be missing the point that the Army needs its soldiers to bond – you know, for when you have to look out for each other's lives and that. Blake, though, he seemed to have forgot this simple fact. Yeah, he'd be nice enough if your kit was squared away, if you were on time for parade – generally being a good boy – but then if you fucked about, gave it a load of backchat, he'd introduce you to his twin brother 'Ron'. 'Ron' being a figment of his imagination, evidently. Tried to break me down with the twin brother thing, he did, with 'Ron', sending me on cake-and-arse parties – pointless errands – just to make me look a prick; making me push out a hundred or so press-ups in the rain and mud; or if I cracked a smile on parade he'd hold back my block leave, so I was left alone in that shithole of a camp at weekends...

'Manny, Earth to Manny.'

Hold up, it's Tommo.

'You coming or what, mate? We're off down the Unit before the queue gets too long.'

'Nah, you're alright. I'll finish my *Grosses*, catch you up,'

'Suit yourself,' he says, and they bang out, leaving me in peace.

So, where was I? Oh, yeah. How could I forget? Blakey. And the Incident, we'll call it. I'd just passed phase one of the training by the skin of my teeth – spurred on by the thought of having to go home to Mum and Dad with my tail between my legs – and we was a week into phase two, when Blakey lost it completely.

I take another big swallow of lager. Stick my finger in my pocket. Scoop up a nailful of coke and snort it up discreetly. Wait for the white stuff to hit.

Okay, I'm ready.

Then *it* happened – the Incident. And I can picture it right now, as if it was playing out directly in front of me:

Me wearing the wrong dress kit for parade... Sergeant Blake reading me the riot act... ordering me to hold my mess tin in my teeth... telling me, 'Don't you fucking dare drop that.' And then the inevitable – the mess tin clattering to the floor... being forced to pick it up... putting it in my mouth again... Blakey picking up a boot... slamming it across the mess tin... the mess tin breaking my face.

Teeth everywhere. And the blood. Fucking shed-load of blood, there was.

Fuck about! My nose has come out in sympathy. I tip my head back, cushioning my neck against the top of the red leather booth, pinching the bridge of my nose, waiting for the flow of blood to stem.

Waiting for the clamour of the memory to fade.

Waiting for this fucking nightmare to end.

So there you are, you lot. Now you know. Yeah, yeah, it weren't male rape, I wasn't beaten within an inch of my life. But I was humiliated. My nose broken, my teeth needing three months of dental work.

At the time, I thought the world was falling out my arsehole. I was only sixteen years old, remember? Immediately afterwards I mulled it over, bleeding like a stuffed pig in Maccy D's down Aldershot, thinking about going AWOL. But somehow my gut told me to go back to camp. And I was right, 'cause as soon as I was back in the dorm I was knocked up by the RMPs. Seems like they'd had an eye on Blakey for some time. They took me out for a Chinese meal, told me if I gave evidence against him, they could transfer me anywhere I liked for phase two of the training – the ACC, I decided; that they'd put in a good word for me, tell the new unit I was a model soldier. A week of this, of being buttered up, of sweeties and fags and daddy talks, and I done it – bubbled Blakey to the RMPs.

Mine and another lad's evidence saw him court-martialled, busted to a private and RTU'd (returned to unit), sent straight back to the RHF in West Belfast. Last I heard, he eventually discharged a full magazine into the wall of his room 'whilst having a bad dream', and was certified a full-blown fruit loop.

It's no wonder Dozzer and them lot tried to get me back that time in the pool room; that they wanted more than just my Walkman. They were part of the same unit as Blakey back in the day. All that Army camaraderie don't pass cunts by, you know.

Yeah, too right, I think, my cheeks burning, *it's no wonder that I'm a fuck-up.*

I'm the lowest of the low – a grass.

A tell-tale tit, that's what you are, my voices jeer in agreement.

That's it. I can't take this!

I push past the crowd of drinkers in the bar and catapult myself out the door of Purgatory, tripping over my own feet as I'm drawn to the magnetic sleaziness of the Kiez. 'Sorry, mate, sorry,' I say as I barge into the bouncer on the steps. He scowls but lets me go on, and I skulk along Friedrichstrasse waging war on the road with my Reeboks, turning on to the Reeperbahn and pounding its filthy pavements... past the dreary shop fronts... past the countless prossies... past the dingy sex shops doing a roaring trade this Saturday night.

I'm cocky, aggy, fighty.

I want to argue, burst out, rip things apart; I want to punch a hole in the world.

I want to shout, *Fuck you, world! Fuck you, Emma, with your pissing and moaning! Fuck you, Tamara, you scabby bitch! Fuck you, Iain and the Big Man bollocks! Fuck you, Blakey!* But I stagger on in silence, with nothing going on upstairs; it's all about my body – my muscles, my bones, my limbs, my skin alive with coke.

The streets are teeming with whores as usual, scattered like exotic bugs in their multicoloured Lycra. They hit on me as I strut past, full of it in the disguise of their make-up and clothes, and I mull it over, eventually deciding, *You know what? Why the fuck not?* and I beckon a beautiful Asian girl in red hot pants towards me. She's been stood in a doorway, watching me approach, indifferent to the rivers of piss streaming past her white plastic high heels on the steps.

Looking closer, I notice the dark circles under her eyes but she smiles at me brightly as I say, 'Hand job,' making the action with my wrist. 'How much?'

She holds up both hands, palms turned in, and pushes them out twice. Twenty DM. Sounds like she's stitching me up but – whatever. I need to do something physical, to have at it with my body before my brain kicks into gear again, before them memories...

I nod quickly and she entices me across the way with a wiggle of her hips, pointing towards the car park at the edge of St Pauli. I trail a few steps behind her, like a kid after his mum – don't want to be seen with her, don't want to lose sight of her neither, soon catching her up at the busy crossroads.

What now?

She's looking at me with sort of like disgust as we wait with all the other weaklings and wankers of the Kiez at the kerb, watching the evening traffic whizz by.

Oh. Right. My T-shirt's freckled with blood from before. I wipe my nose and notice the blood spouting again. Fuck about! Think my brains are spilling out!

And I think, *I can back out now*, but then the Green Men – two of them in Germany, you get – flash and we cross the road.

Go on son, they're goading me, *forget about the hand job, go for the whole shebang, fuck that little madam till she's sore.*

I hesitate, resisting the voices. But it's too late to back out now, 'cause we're entering the car park, greeted by the solidness of concrete, the manliness of petrol fumes and metal boxes, going against my need for everything human, flesh and skin right now. The petrol smell burrows up my nose. I snort, tasting my own blood at the back of my tonsils; my eyes searching out the *Ausgang*, the exit, as I pray for a way out.

Oh, go on, you fucking wimp, my voices tease me, *do one, then, if you can't even get it up.*

Only it's too late – the girl's posing against a post, reaching out her long painted fingernails, slipping the cash in her bra before I can leg it. She minces towards me, her red hot pants like a second skin on her thin, bony hips.

And I'm gone again.

The vivid red.

I'm living it one more time: the blood, the mess tin, the pain. My head is screeching with the shouts of Blakey as he slams the boot into the mess tin, splitting my lip; my brain singing with the crunching of teeth.

I drop like a stone, curl up in a ball on the floor, punching out as the girl approaches me, and I don't fucking believe this – I'm blubbing like a fucking baby. She crouches down and cradles me for a second, and I think, *What a love, what a love!* But oh, bollocks, here comes the blood again. It splatters, a snowflake of bright red on her cheap white plastic shoe.

She shakes me off. Spits on me.

'*Fich dich, scheiss Kerl,*' she spits out.

The clatter of heels echoes through the car park as she totters off, and I'm left alone, spastic and shivering.

You little prick, I think. *You worthless little prick*.

Too right, glad you've finally seen sense, comes the reply from the voices in my head.

Voices which – if you lot are interested – seem to be getting louder and angrier by the day.

Fallingbostel Base – Medical Reception Station

Manny

'In accordance with the Queen's Regulations for the Army, 1975, I would like to hand myself in for drug addiction.'

'Which drugs would that be, Private Manning?'

'Cocaine and Ecstasy, sir.'

'And you've been addicted for how long? What is the nature of your addiction?'

'I just can't take it no more, sir. I'm craving cocaine all the time. Wake up first thing wanting a line, same again last thing at night. It's ruining me life, sir. It's like there's some sort of beast inside overpowering me, forcing me to – '

Oh, fucking hell, I interrupt myself – does that sound too bloody OTT?

I go over the lines I've thought up again, as if I was rehearsing for a play. Yeah, you lot are right. A fucking tragedy at that.

Fuck about! This plastic chair's doing my back in! I fidget. Stretch my legs. Stand up and sit back down again. Do they deliberately make them uncomfortable or what? The connecting door to the senior MO's office is closed but I can hear him clear as day barking down the phone. Meanwhile, his secretary carries on typing on the word processor, oblivious, not stopping to look at me once.

Ignoring the increasing lack of air in the room, I practise them lines again, thinking, *Come on, Manny, think of it – hand yourself in, four weeks of rippers, but then out – dishonourable discharge or not – and freedom.*

Freedom from orders. Freedom from fucking rules and regulations. A sudden waft of beeswax floor polish drifts up then – and I think, *Yeah too right, freedom from polishing floors in the guardroom when I've been put on ROPs.* I mean, if there's one smell that's gonna remind me of the Army it's this, the pong of sickly yellow beeswax which first wafts up your nose on day one of the basic training.

'Right you are, speak to you next week,' I hear the MO thunder from the other side of the wall.

My palms sweat; my fingers break out in pins and needles; my legs go...

Am I really gonna go through with this?

A sudden thought of Emma lags in the back of my throat with my saliva as I gulp. Fucking miss that dozy mare. I know what would she say. 'Have a bit of self-respect. No need to go this far. Just sort yourself out. Don't ruin your Army career all because of some stupid drug.'

And I think, *Yeah, Em, you're right – not just yet.*

I won't give them the satisfaction.

Won't give Iain the chance to say I owe him something; need to settle my debts with him before I bang out back to Blighty. Besides, six more months and my five years are up and I get out of here, legit, like.

For once in my life I'm gonna do what's right.

I hear the MO's voice shouting, 'Come in!' and I bolt up out my chair.

'I'm – um – feeling much better, thanks,' I say to his weasel-faced secretary, and he waves his hand dramatically to beckon me back as I dash out of there quicker than a greyhound out of a trap.

Yeah, just one more trip to the Dam and I can pay Iain off, I decide, as I race down the corridor. Simple as – finish with the drugs; knock them on the head as of today. Army career's not completely finished just yet.

Only, as I wander back in a daze to the lines, a familiar urge scratches at me. Well, might as well finish what I've got left of my stash first. What harm can it do?

Fallingbostel British Army Base

Cal

I try and focus on the TV screen. Arsenal v Parma – the European Cup Final.

If ye looked in on us, ye'd think it was just another night in the lines: lads moping about bare-footed and bare-chested, wearing baggy summer shorts; fitba on the box; Jonesy yapping his usual high-pitched bullshit, moaning that he cannae even beat 'that cunt Chun-Li' on Street Fighter II; Manny monged out tae fuck on hash yoghurts, trying tae cope as the walls bend in around him; Davie knocking us up, planking his arse on my pit, taking the urine out of Jonesy fur his crap video game skills.

Except it isnae just any other night in the lines. It's my last night before I head down Paderborn tae fly out on Ops tae cook fur the 2RA, at Žepče. Didnae believe it a hundred per cent till I got the letter through with the notice of my tour and my flight details.

Private Calum Wilson, 231042189,
07.50, 7 May 1994, Paderborn to Split.

Whoah, goal! A real beauty fae Arsenal. Hoofed right in the back of the net.

Davie leaps up in the air, cursing, stumbling intae my green canvas travel bag. He fuckin hates Gooners.

'Watch out!' I say. 'It's taken me hours tae get my shite thegither.'

'Sorry, chum,' he says, sheepish. Then, as if to make up fur it, 'Got everything, then?'

'Aye, think so.'

'Combats?'

'Aye'

'Norgie?'

'Aye.'

'Helmet?'

'Och, c'moan, leave it out, man!' I say tae Davie. I mean, I know it's my first time on Ops, but telling me the basics in front of the other lads? It's just embarrassing!

Then Jonesy in all his ginger-haired glory pipes up, 'Yeah, but you better make sure you take yer Walkman – you can spend hours waiting for them UN flights.'

'Yes, Mum,' I say, even mair scunnered. I mean, it's bad enough Davie telling me what's what, but Jonesy?

Even so, when his back's turned, I dive in the bag tae check.

'What about your wash bag? You might wanna nip to the NAAFI, get yer soap, deodorant and that – you never know what'll be available over there,' Jonesy continues, eyes flicking fae his Super NES tae me again – wanting tae remind everyone he was the first chef in wur unit who went out tae Bos.

'Alright, alright; I know, I know,' I say, mair scunnered by the minute.

'And a book? Have you got a book?' Davie pipes up again.

Now there's one thing I didnae think of.

Manny roots around in his locker, and chucks over that *Trainspotting* that he's finally finished. 'Get a load of that. Closest you'll get to the dirties out there, that's for sure.'

And surely that's it?

Yeah, no mair suggestions, thankfully; the lads are now fully focused on the game again.

The rest of my stuff's already been put in MFO boxes – either tae be sent out ahead, or the big stuff like my hi-fi an that tae be kept fur my return. Jesus: my entire life packed in a fuckin box. Anyway. In Paderborn the storeman will gie me the UN beret I huv tae wear before I step on the plane.

Gulp.

Four and a bit years of running about stupit, of drills and runs, the PT and the weapons-handling, it's been leading up tae this…

'So you shitting the Big One then, Happy?' Jonesy goes. Trust him tae pick up on the panic trampling across my coupon.

I puff out my chest, and bellow, 'Away and shite,' across the room.

But Davie – who's a Tankie, don't forget – makes a joke of it. 'Nah, slop jockeys ain't in any danger – it's the other lads who want to be afraid.' He pauses fur effect. 'Of the slops' meat-mangling, I mean.'

'Oh, yeah, what about the danger from landmines and snipers, then? He's got to get from A to B, don't he?' That's Manny, sticking up for us, but – typical Manny – making us feel worse.

'Cheers, lads,' I say, chucking a pair of boxers that've fallen out my bag in their general direction. 'I feel much better now.'

It's funny. Before, when Bos come on the telly, I closed my ears tae it. It was like, if I didnae think about it, it didnae exist. Or, when some of the infantry lads spoke about it, discussed their experiences of seeing active service in Iraq, it was like they were storytelling, that it was a fantasy, that didnae relate tae me.

Now it's like I'm taking in everything I can on the subject, wi my five senses; or mair, even – that there's another new sense where I absorb all I can about the war. Aye, yous are right. What a selfish fuck! I'm no the only wan, though, am I? I mean, what is it wi us humans where we're only bothered by things that affect us personally? I mean, c'moan! You might think ye give a fuck about folk in other countries, but huv ye ever bothered yer arse tae really get tae the truth, tae care enough tae do anything about other folk's suffering?

It's funny how things can suddenly open yer eyes tae stuff.

It's like when I met Steffi, I hud never thought about religion fae a non-believer's side of things. She's taken me towards brand new ways of thinking. I mean, do I even believe any –

Fuck me, I am gonnae do that Davie! He's only knocked my stuff flying again, miffed 'cause Parma huvnae equalised yet.

I cannae help smiling, but.

He's been a real pal, and ye cannae help being carried along wi him when he's on wan. Och, they've all been good pals – all except one, that is.

I blink back tears, pretending tae sneeze when Davie notices. He slaps me on the back, pulls me out of earshot of the others and whispers, 'Good soldier like you, you'll be alright, mate.'

His touch reminds me of the happy hugs of ravers I've known through the years, and – as a blast of fresh summer air comes in through the windae – I realise those times are over. Sure, I'm no stupit, I knew they hud tae end at some point, but I never knew they would be over, like that, in a gust of summer wind and a sudden feeling that life goes on.

That ye huv tae do yer growing up at some point.

That ye huv tae dry yer eyes. Pick up yer teddy. Move on.

Hold on, what's up? Manny's rushing past us, his coupon a pucey lime-green.

'Gonna puke,' he says, steaming towards the bogs. Worried about that lad. Davie will look after him, right enough, but, still, we've been back tae wur usual double act these past couple weeks. What is he gonnae do without me?

Dutch/German Border

Manny

My heart's pumping all the way down to the soles of my feet. *Biddy-boom, biddy-boom, biddy-boom.* I check the mirror, change gear slickly, the control of my driving at odds with the shit-storm of worries blowing through my mind.

Iain's acting all 'give a fuck', as if he wasn't bricking it and all, getting me to crank up the radio when that 'Age of Love' tune comes on. He sings along, waving his arms in the air, as the sounds of the techno ricochet around the motor. 'Ah, ah, ah, ah, ah, ah, ahhhhhhhhhhhhhhhhhh.'

Talk about tone deaf! I'm like, 'Pipe down, will ya mate?' I mean, the last thing we need's to bring attention to ourselves, what with fifty grand of pills nestling in the boot of my car, hidden in the lining of an old parka.

Not felt this car-sick since I was a boy and my mum used to drive us down to Brighton on bank holiday weekends. From one depressing seaside town to another – what was the fucking point? I wind down the window, despite Iain's warblings and insistence at having the radio at full volume. I want to let my arm dangle free and easy, catch some rays, make the most of the sunny day, despite being cooped up in a metal box. Another fifty km to the border, then about another hundred to Hamburg after that. Fuckin nause. I put my foot on the pedal and accelerate, swerving to overtake a lorry.

'Easy, tiger!' Iain goes as we cut back into lane.

I push it that bit more. The sound of horns blasting across the motorway mixes with the music on the radio. Ha! The look of panic on Iain's grid is priceless.

'So, matey, you really gonna hand yourself in for drugs, then, do your time, then fuck off back to Blighty?'

My hands grip the steering wheel tighter, and I flare out my nostrils. Typical Iain: you wind him up, he'll skewer you with a one-liner.

'You what?' I say. 'Who told you that little nugget?'

'Well, Paddy mentioned – ' he starts.

'Yeah, Paddy can fuck right – '

'Let me finish! Paddy told me that Cal told him just before he left for Bos that you was thinking of it. Don't have an eppy!'

'Oh, right,' I go, well unimpressed by Paddy. Yeah, you lot are right – and Cal, I'm unimpressed by Cal and all. I mean, there was me thinking whatever me and Cal said was between us, off limits to big mouths like Paddy. Okay, as you know, it crossed my mind – to hand myself in, I mean. But my head's telling me not yet: tough it out for six months and I'll be out of here...

Thankfully after that little exchange only the radio blares out for a bit, Iain playing air-guitar whenever a rock track comes on – always knew he wasn't a true hardcore raver – and we zoom along the dry, dusty motorway, past the motorway service station, not stopping for food, making do with paprika crisps and old biscuits, the footwell of the passenger seat a right old mess of crumbs and empty crisp packets; and all the while thinking about telling that cunt Iain what I think of him once this little trip settles the score between us.

I drum my fingers on the steering wheel as we sit at some lights on the edge of some random Dutch town – Deventer, the 'Welcome to' sign says – and, bored as fuck, I just come right out with something Iain might not like, figuring, well, won't be seeing much of him in the near future; might as well ask.

'So boss.' The 'boss' to keep him sweet. 'Tell me something.' Keeping my eyes steady on the road ahead – no chance of eye contact.

And he's sort of like, 'Yeah, go ahead, fill yer boots.'

So I ask him something which has been bugging me, and probably you lot and all, for a while, 'Yeah, what it was...'

He picks at his fingernails and sighs impatiently while I squirm.

'... what it was is, how comes you boned Steffi, if you wasn't that into her?'

And he goes, 'Who says I wasn't into her?'

I glance sideways for a sec and see that he's looking moodily out the window, still picking at his nails.

'Oh,' is all I can think of to answer back.

He turns his body completely away from me then, and he mumbles, so I can only just make it out, 'Bloody wish I had told Steffi I was into her, what with Kelly walking out...'

You have to practically scrape my jaw off the floor at that one.

'... yeah,' he goes on, 'and there was me worried I was a jaffa, but turns out the bloody little bitch has been taking the Pill all along.'

More than just my jaw scraping the floor now!

But there's no time to brood over it all: why Iain went with Tamara straight away that time if he was into Steffi; why he put it about that Steffi was a slapper after they did it; how come Kelly's seen sense and finally left him, how she's got her own back in the end – good girl! – 'cause up ahead I spot the police check for the German border.

My pulse races... *biddy-boom*... my blood nearly bursts out my veins... *biddy-boom*... my breathing is heavy and quick... *biddy-boom*. If I didn't know better, I'd think I'd bombed a wrap of speed, the way I'm sweating and grinding my teeth to dust.

And relax! Needn't have worried – the border crossing's deserted; you can almost see the tumbleweed blowing by.

There's only one bloke sat on his tod at the window of the tin border check hut, chuntering away on the telephone. He don't even barely seem to notice us, apart from looking at our passports, which he checks, nodding to himself slowly.

'Welcome to Germany,' he says, a fake smile plastered across his mush.

His words act like temazepam on me, and I flop, well knackered all of a sudden.

Thank fucking Christ.

We've done it, we're nearly home and dry.

Iain puts this into words. 'See, told ya you was being a big girl's blouse. Done this more times than you've had hot dinners.' Cheesy grin. 'Come on, mate, pull over, will ya? I need a slash,' he continues, as the sign tells us we're on German soil.

Bloody hell. Wants to prolong my agony, does he? I'm all for caning it back to Hamburg, dumping the shit at Taff's – job done; game over. I won't owe Iain nothing any more, and that'll be me and him finished. All the same, I'm thirsty as fuck. Maybe having a break for five minutes, getting myself together for the next leg of the journey's not such a bad idea.

So I pull up in a lay-by just on from the border crossing hut, thinking, Christ, it must be well hot in there for that border guard. Speaking of which, I need some shagging air and all; I'm suffocating. Nothing for it but to step out of the car and lean against the bonnet for a sec. Ouch! The metal's burning hot. Then, shielding my eyes from the sun, I look down at the white lines on the asphalt, which are wibbling in its rays; the heat's making me trip out slightly. It's weird: the road markings are different on each side of the border – on the German side they're freshly painted; on the Dutch, the paint's chipping away with shavings of old paint. Yeah, weird to think, ain't it? You cross the line, and that's you in a different country, different language, different customs. You cross the line and that's you –

Hold up! Iain's tearing out the bushes from the lay-by. What's that? He's shouting, waving his arms wildly. I walk towards him, cock an eyebrow, as if to ask, *What you on about?* when... what the? Fucking hell!

Out of nowhere – sirens... dogs barking... men shouting... the flash of an ID card glints in the sun... the smell of a dog's breath... the stale green of the German police uniforms... and – what the? – English voices...

The fucking Monkeys, the RMPs are here and all. Is this some kind of fit-up?

Iain's face is blank as he stands stiffly by the motor. One of the German coppers opens up the boot while the dogs bark furiously.

And that's it for me, I think – end of story.

The silence in the car closes in on me, my mind racing whether they're taking us to Army or civvy nick. My temples throb, my throat tightens, and I can't think of nothing but my mum and dad, Emma, and Cal. Them four who done nothing but big me up, and I threw it back in their faces. How could I look any of them in the eye now?

And do you know what? I know my emotions should be stewing up, that I should be angry with myself for getting in this deep, for letting them down; that I should be terrified about what's gonna happen; that I should go ape-shit at Iain, maybe, for getting me into this so easy, as if it was a trip to fucking Lidl.

But I don't feel any of them things.

Instead, I've only got one feeling, prodding and poking at me, like a bully – embarrassment. Can't believe we got caught; that I'm gonna have to fess up to my mum and dad about this; that Emma will find out what a lame prick I am, that I can't even do the bad things in life right.

And it's sort of like, it's one of them self-fulfilling prophecies, innit? Yeah, yeah, you lot can sit there with your cup of tea, in your comfy armchair, on the train to your nice job, sat up in bed – or whatever – and give it all the finger-wagging bollocks. Think about it, though. Bet you weren't one of them who was always told you was shit – by yer mum and dad, by your teachers, by some Army cunt.

I glance sideways at Iain, sat with his fists clenched, his face a closed book, and I think of the words on the Army career leaflet when you join up: *Be the best you can*. I chuckle. Quietly at first, but then, as the senior RMP sat between me and Iain looks me up and down as if I was shit on his shoe, it comes up louder, and I crack up laughing.

'Be the best you can,' I say out loud, between sniggers.

Which for a loser like you, the senior RMP's eyes seem to say, as he continues to look dead ahead, *is nothing more than a dirty crim. And a fucking hopeless one, at that.*

And all of a sudden my laughter's cut short, when I realise that he's bang on the money.

Chapter Nine

Cal

The rising heat fae the hot plates is intense, overpowering the hot dryness of the dusty summer air. No point trying tae wipe away the sweat that pours fae underneath my beret – it's like Glesga rain: it doesnae stop tipping down.

The Master Chef tellt me I'm lucky I didnae come down here in winter, fur all that. 'Colder than a witch's titty at night,' was the way he put it. And that's him sleeping indoors, no in these fuckin metal Portakabins us junior ranks are kipping in, by the way. Which are hardly five-star accommodation now, in June, either. I mean, you wouldnae huv tae be a polar bear tae overheat maist nights.

Sounds as if cooking fur the lads was a cake-and-arse party during winter an aw. Apparently, sometimes supplies didnae make it through, 'cause of bad weather; other times the equipment froze up, so the cooks hud tae go tae plan B – sanger-bashing.

Think about it. The lads come back fae a day or night's patrolling in sub-zero temps, avoiding the so-called 'celebratory fire' of the drunken Serbs, and all wur lot could offer was a round of soggy sandwiches. Not that we're getting much fresh or goodies through fae the airport at Sarajevo now, even.

Shepherd's pie fae a powdered mix, or curry, cooked by yours truly, the day.

'Oy, Wilson, *blar blar blar.*'

That's Sergeant Weeks, shouting over fae the other side of the cookhouse, a makeshift kitchen sandwiched between the officers' quarters and the quartermaster's store in this auld abandoned factory. I can barely make him out, though; the doors and windaes are wide open so wur conversations are up against the rumble of vehicles, the stomping of boots and the general clatter of life on camp.

I cup my hand tae my ear and yell back, 'Eh?'

He ambles across the flair of the cookhouse, stopping tae huv a word wi other of the slop jockeys along the way. Then when he's finally in my earshot he goes, 'I said you're on the lag, mate: first sitting's in five.'

'Four minutes tops,' I reply, panicking, 'cause I've been rambling about in my own mind for a while.

And by the time I've said this he's right on top of us, elbowing us aside fae the stove. The other lads stop what they're doing and snicker. Och, no, he's never? He is. He's gonnae taste my effort – I mop my brow wi my apron as he picks up a spoon, leans over the madras and slurps up a teaspoonful of curry. 'Mmm, top madras,' he says, raising his eyebrows. 'Just the right amount of heat.'

And I say, 'Thank you, sarn't,' but at the same time thinking, *Is he fuckin kidding me wi that 'heat'?*

I'm minded then of wan a my da's sayings: 'Madras in the evening, mad arse in the morning.' Ha! Always the fuckin comedian, my da, even when the cancer was flooding his lungs. I chuckle out loud, and Rudie – the other private come over here fae Fally, a quiet lad I barely know – knits his eyebrows in a question. I wave as if tae say 'private joke', my hand drooping like a wilted flower in the heat.

It's funny, but. Since being here in Bos, I can think about my da without aw that blame and anger choking me up. In fact, I can think about most things in a positive way, back tae my auld 'Happy' self, mair or less. The 'less' being when Iain slithers intae my box, evidently.

Och, forget about him, I tell masel – beg masel actually – as I transfer the huge metal pot over tae the serving area. Why worry? I mean, I'm pleased as punch that the sarge tellt me I done a good job, the day.

And here he's again, bellowing at the top of his lungs, 'Okay lads – and lady,' acknowledging the one female soldier in wur unit, 'showtime!'

We group behind the hot plates, and immediately a plague of hungry lads swarms over us.

'Oy,' Rudie whispers, as I turn out plate after plate of curry and shepherd's pie tae nods and grunts of thanks. 'Got a couple of cans of lager from the bar – fancy a beer after shift?' He says it shyly, his voice rising at the end of the sentence as if he was afraid of letting the words out.

'Aye, you're on.'

Beer's the wan thing we can get hold of here tae take the edge off; the wan distraction tae look forward tae at the end of shift. Well, unless ye can get hold of some of the local plum brandy, Slivovitz – or, as we call it, 'sleep in the ditch'. But somehow I'm no that bothered. Funny, isn't it? I mean, back in Fally, as soon as ye finished work, yer first thought was, *Right, how soon can I get battered? And how badly?*

Here, though, we're forced tae be healthy, tae think straight, what wi the Operations 'two-can maximum' rule. Och, okay, some of the lads choose tae ignore that. It's like speeding, isn't it? Some folk keep tae the limit; others… well. I'm no wan a them. I'm sticking tae the rules out here, so I'm no permanently feeling – as Withnail said – like a pig shat in my heid. Even been doing weights I've borrowed fae some health nazi. It's given me time tae think, so it has, tae take on a mair positive outlook on life again. Aye, I know it's crazy tae feel positive among this human suffering… but it's like – well, it's like the confused sludge of wan E'd-up night after another has been vacuumed out my brain.

And this clearness, this sharpness in my mind has me thinking I did the right thing tae get revenge on Iain, tae...

Och, what's that? My rosary beads are clagging tae my chest. What fur? Guilt? Cannae be. I mean, no way, man – what I did was right. Even so, there's just the germ of a doubt, a niggle of something black and dark and fearful that's slowly growing inside my heart. I fiddle wi the beads. Screw up my forehead in concentration. Try and conjure up the image of Christ. I mean, we're taught that when He's present, there's no need tae be afraid. But is He? Present, I mean?

But this question soon drifts out my mind, 'cause Rudie's saying, 'C'mon, let's sneak a fag before the next sitting,' and we nick behind the cookhouse fur a crafty wan.

Would yous believe I'm smoking twenty Lambert and Butler a day now? Aye, I know I said we were being healthy – and I've always said I'm pure dead against smoking, right enough – but, well, there's fuck aw else tae do here sometimes but scratch yer baws and huv a smoke as you listen tae the mortars pounding in the distance. And, I mean, we've got tae do *something* tae combat wur stress levels.

Which as yous can imagine are through the roof, working an eighteen-hour shift, seven days a week, in a smoky, oily, burny-hot cookhouse. Insult tae injury, it's no like there's any let-up fae the heat of the cookhouse when wur shifts end. Sleeping in they Portakabins, I mean. It's nae wonder we don't usually hit the hay right after shift but lie outside in wur maggot bags till stupid o'clock, blethering about the war, wur families, or what huv ye. Boots on, mind, in case the shit hits the fan and we huv tae leg it tae the shelter.

Ceasefire?

That's a fuckin joke.

Never mind. It might not even matter if the fighting continues, 'cause we heard reports that auld Douglas Hurd says we British troops will pull out if the arms embargo against Bos is lifted by the UN. Could be out of here in weeks, then! Mibbe I'll ask the lads if I can go out on foot patrol wi them before we bang out, or ask tae do some cooking in the field, break the – what's it? Monotony.

KABOOM!

On the other hand, I think, as another mortar detonates, sticking two fingers up at the peacefulness of the hills behind the solid brick walls and barbed wire of camp, *mibbe I'll stick here, thank you very much.*

I smoke the fag in fast wee puffs, still no inhaling deep inside, in the hope it willnae be so bad on my lungs. Only soon the comforting smoky smell is overpowered by a honk of sweat and perfume rising above the heavy, sticky air.

'Skip-licker,' Rudie says, the first words that've been spoken since we came outside.

I stick my heid around the corner and, right enough, it's the unmistakable smell of a woman wi her nose in the slop-bins, fishing fur leftovers. Some of the locals huv been deployed tae the camp by the UN tae do odd clerical and menial jobs. Ye sometimes see – and smell – them like this, looking fur food. This wan, a Bosnian Muslim, by the looks of the headscarf, is – uh-oh. She's clocked me. I duck back around the corner.

'You not gonna say something?' Rudie asks, stubbing out his fag on the brick wall behind us.

'No way, pal, didn't auld Weeksie tell ye? We're tae turn a blind eye tae they women, let them get on wi it.'

'Fair dos.'

'C'moan,' I say. 'Next sitting will be coming in.'

But I stumble as I try tae stand, and Rudie has tae grab my wrist and hoik me up, a look passing between us acknowledging the bone-aching work that still faces us, the day. And, as I dish up fur the second sitting, I think about they women, trying tae fend fur their families, make the best of things as the world explodes like diarrhoea in a toilet bowl about them.

All because of religion, an aw.

Makes ye think, doesn't it? I mean, what is God up tae when ye've neighbours slitting each other's throats in a deadly game of 'my God's better than your God'?

C'moan tae fuck!

My eyes well up, no fur the first time since I've come down here. Mibbe Steffi was right: mibbe we are worm food when we die; I mean, mibbe there's no Big Guy in charge, deciding everything we do, or else why would He have created this fuckin mess?

That's a heid-fuck, don't yous think? But let's not mull it over any further, 'cause a ladleful of curry is heading fur the flair instead of some corporal's mess tin.

Six-thirty pm. The last of the second dinner sitting drift off – downtime fur them after a hard day's weapons-handling, vehicle-servicing, patrols and other duties. No such downtime fur us slop jockeys yet. I crack my knuckles. Stretch my arms above my heid. Yawn.

I turn tae the others, ready tae get on wi the pan-bashing, only tae see Rudie's back at the stove, frying up a round of egg sandwiches, or egg banjos as they're affectionately known – the secret staple of the British Army.

'What the – ?' I begin.

He looks sheepish, wipes away a dollop of egg yolk fae his T-shirt. 'Hungry after dishing out all that scoff!'

I laugh at his explanation, and think of Manny. Back in the day, when we first got tae Fally, he made a plate of banjos thinking some of the lads were coming back fur a scoff after exercise, only to realise they'd ducked off intae town fur a swally. 'Waste not, want not,' he said, and arsed the whole lot, so he did. Fuckin grease monkey!

Manny, Manny, Manny.

Mibbe he'll sort himself out. Huvnae heard a fuckin word fae him since coming down here…

I think of him back there at Fally, probably ignoring all they promises he made tae take it easy, no doubt still losing it mind, body and soul tae the dirties.

And as I look out over the green, smoky hills behind us, my thoughts turn tae me and my future, thinking that – even with the chaos, even with the guilt that lies like a brick at the bottom of my stomach – I'm glad I'm here, taking things in, moving on wi my life. If only, though, I gulp, I didnae huv tae make a decision about signing up fur another four years or going back tae civvy street after this six-month tour's up. But mibbe something, or should I say someone, will make my mind up fur me...

What's that?

Aye, too right – it's a heid-fuck. My five years are up soon, could be out of here in a few months – or I could be back in Fally. Who knows?

Up tae me really.

A surprise sharp twinge of homesickness hits me then – fur Fally, I mean; a desperate longing tae see how Manny and the rest of the crew are getting on.

I know! The communications lad in the Rebro's got a phone line going tae the UK. Offered me a phone call 'cause I sorted him out wi some stuff fur his mess tin while he was in theatre. Mibbe he can get a line going tae Germany an aw... I could phone the kitchens down Fally – let Manny know I was thinking of him... check that he's staying away fae that cunt Iain...

Aye, that's it. I'll hunt down the Rebro guy, call him. But fur some reason my heart somersaults in anxiety at the thought. Mibbe later, I think, as I look up at the clear blue sky, which fur once isnae hidden by billowing mortar smoke.

Mibbe the ceasefire's in full effect after all?

Fallingbostel British Army Base – Regimental Jail

Manny

'Mark time!'

Twenty lads in single file march on the spot at double time, waiting for the duty RP – who's marching at regulation pace – to catch us up. I turn to Iain and hold his glare. Don't know what's worse. The fact we're probably going to be banged up for a long stretch, or that I'll have to do the time with him. We wait for the next order. Here it comes.

'Forward!'

My legs are two giant sea slugs; I ain't got the energy to fart these days, never mind this physical exertion… but we're off again.

'EFT 'ITE 'EFT 'ITE 'EFT 'ITE! 'EFT 'ITE 'EFT 'ITE 'EFT 'ITE!

'Mark time!

'Get your fucking knees up!

'Up!

'Up! Up! Up!

'Get your fucking knees up you idle cunts.

'Mark time!

'Oy, you sloppy! Manning! Get your slop jockey knees up!

'Forward!'

Same routine every day. Mornings, after breakfast, we're cunted about with all the crappy jobs on camp, and if there's none, we're put in the prisoners' area in the guardroom. Then time somehow passes till five o'clock – till now, that is – and over to the cookhouse for dinner. It's alright for the lads who get visitors to break the nut-numbing repetitiveness. Me, I've had one visit from Davie – that's it.

And who's fault's that, eh?

Do what, you lot? You agree with the old voices, do you? That I've only got myself to blame; that we're masters of our own destiny? Yeah, right. Think that, would you, if you'd been hanging about with a shit-magnet like Iain? Fucking slimy-faced, two-timing, drug-pushing cunt.

What's that? What about a visit from my parents? Well, haven't even told them what's gone down yet, if you want the truth. How could I, my dad being a copper and that? And Emma. I'm sure she must have heard on the rave-vine by now. Not a peep from her either, though.

'Halt!'

201

Hold up, here we are, come to a stop outside the cookhouse, me and the other prisoners jostling, elbows out, as we're chivvied along to, 'Get the fuck in line.' I make an O with my lips and push through a few quick breaths of air; let my fists unclench; bring my back up straight. Basically, try and look all 'give a fuck?' I mean, it's undignified, don't you think, to be paraded with the other scum from the guardroom in front of my old workmates?

Still, at least we get to the cookhouse early, have the luxury of eating before the rest of camp. And hopefully I can ponce some fags off Jonesy. I mean, the last few times I was in the nick the guards went easy on me, handed out fags willy-nilly. Now I'm being done for something serious – for drugs – I'm taken for a junkie, the lowest of the fucking low, forced to stick to the two-fags-a-day rule. Hold up, though. Is Jonesy trying to avoid me or what? I try to catch his eye, holding two fingers in a sideways V to my lips to make the international 'smoker in need of fags' sign. I reach the front of the queue and he says simply, 'Pie or fish?' same as to the others, but gives me a thumbs-up – to the fag request, I suppose. I nod to the pie and, after he's dolloped me out a serving, I scan the room to find a pew as far away from Iain and the others as possible. There – one by the window, that'll do.

Only, I've just sat down when a scraping of the chair next to me is accompanied by a gruff Geordie accent whispering in my ear, 'Sharesies, yeah?'

'Eh?' I answer the thin-faced lad who's sat down next to us. Ah, I see. Jonesy's come good – dropped a handful of fags on my meal tray. Fair play to him. I square them away in my pocket, nodding to the lad who didn't dob me in to confirm that yes, I'd share.

Then, before you know it, the duty RP's hollering at us again. 'Clean up your diggers, you fucking throbbers!'

'Ckin hell! I don't chuffing believe it. I'm not even halfway through my main. I exchange a look of disgust with the Geordie.

'I'm not joking,' the RP continues, 'get a fucking wiggle on, you lazy gob-shites!'

Throbber.

Cunt.

Gob-shite.

Knob-gobbler.

Shitbag.

Shit-magnet.

Waste of oxygen.

Shit for brains.

Ain't been larded with this many insults since the basic training. The basic training… Sergeant Blake. Fuck about. Why did my brain do that? Make me think about him again. More to the point, why didn't I do it – just bang out of the training as soon as he started giving me grief. Get out while I had the chance? I mean, not end up… like this.

Still, at least there's one thing from the basic training that's come in handy in the punt: 'Skive to survive,' we was told during our first week by one of the nicer PTs when he found out Blakey was in charge of our troop. That is, don't use up all your energy for one task, 'cause the next thing you know yer gonna be cunted about again double. A lesson which is useful right now, I'm thinking, 'cause exactly twenty minutes after we started eating, here we go again.

'Mark time!'

And with that we're marched back to the jail before most of us have finished our scoff. I flick my eyes over the line of twenty reprobates being marched back to the guardroom. A ragbag of laggers, losers and liars. No wonder the usual crowd of Army Barmy lads eyeball us as we're marched across the parade square. I spot that cunt who nicked my Walkman, Dozzer, and anger (or is it shame?) catches in my throat; my mouth goes dry. Fucking Blakey! If it wasn't for him…

And then *It* starts up again: the banging temples; the sickness in the pit of my stomach; the ticking time bomb in my skull.

Them eyes on me, I can't take it!

I want the ground to swallow me whole, want to stare down at my feet. But of course I've got to march across the parade square: chin raised, knees up, as proudly as if it was the trooping of the shagging colour.

'Alright lads, fifteen-minute recreation break,' the duty RP says as we arrive back at the guardroom, out of breath and sweating, and we all line up in the 'at ease' position, one hand behind our backs. Yeah, would you believe it? Even on our fag-breaks in the nick we have to be 'soldiers'. And if we make any step out of line, that's it, 'recreation break' over. Might as well shoot us on the spot and be done with it.

Still, where would be the fun in that for the brass?

Anyway. At least we're all in this together, I think, as I get off on the nicotine buzz, and I'm even comforted a little by the waxy stink and metal bars of the guardroom. Rather here than out there getting evils from every fucker that goes past.

'Right, break's over. Prisoners' area, now, on the double!'

And that's that. Fifteen minutes' 'recreation' and me and the nineteen other losers are marched off at double time to jostle for oxygen in the prisoners' area, while we wait for our last dirty job of the day before lock-up. A few minutes later and we're herded in, the others lads grouped in a circle, nattering. Me, I ignore them, lie on a bench, hoping to catch forty winks. But their voices are raised so I've no choice – I'll have to listen to their conversation.

'Simon Mayo,' one lad's saying.

What they on about?

'Mike Reid,' says the nearly-dead-looking Geordie.

'Bruno Brooks,' says a chubby-faced older guy.

Oh, right – it's a bust-up over who's been the best Radio One breakfast DJ. And then Iain forces his way into the conversation, starts giving it large. 'Dave Lee Travis,' he says, more forcefully than the others. 'It's got to be DLT.'

There you go – as if you needed any more proof of what a tasteless, ignorant, woeful sack of shit that fucker is. Dave

Lee Travis? I mean, weren't he, like, on that show in the '70s, anyway?

Man, I'm on a short fucking fuse today. A line. That would sort me right out. It don't help that every time I look at Iain's grid, it's like looking at a reflection of my need for coke. Yeah, you lot have got me bang to rights. I can't look at much without thinking about sniff.

Fuck about. Now they're on to which was the best Saturday morning kids' show, *Swap Shop* or *Tiswas*?

Me, I couldn't care less. Radio, telly, work, school, breakfast, lunch, dinner. Bollocks, bollocks, bollocks, bollocks, bollocks, bollocks, bollocks.

I pull a scratchy blanket over my head and try again for sleep; try and put a stop to the constant march of the drums throbbing through my brain.

I know. I'm a walking, taking, sleeping cliché.

Like I give a fuck. I mean, you've been against me since the start, so it's no surprise you're sticking the boot in now. I mean, fuck me, I don't even like myself. I huddle in the corner, trying to shut out the light and the noise of the lads chuntering on.

'Manning, you little twat, wakey, wakey. Parade square. On the fucking double, you lazy little cabbage mechanic.'

Brilliant. Just brilliant. In the simple act of lying down I've managed to wind the duty RP up. Hounds me from dusk till dawn 'cause he thinks slop jockeys are the lowest of the low.

Oh, yeah, very funny. Now he's telling me to get into my chest rig and webbing; to go out and sweep the parade square – which is the size of a football pitch, incidentally – with a fucking dustpan and brush. The more ridiculous the job for a beasting, the better, as far as the RPs are concerned.

Fine by me. Get me away from Iain. From the guardroom. From the misery of my fucking existence.

If only, I think, if only...

Cal

The smell of oil and sweat hums about the Land Rover. I pull at my helmet. Should huv asked the store man fur a new wan – mine wouldnae be lost on the peak of Ben Nevis. Nae chance of me taking it off, but. I've a white-knuckle grip on my weapon an aw, an SA80 assault rifle. Not cocked and ready tae fire – the UN don't allow that. Just as well. The lads tell me the issue weapons are forever jamming, and mine is covered in black sticky tape.

Besides, I'm about as useful tae the Poachers as a concrete parachute – they're hard as a bag of fuckin spanners.

It's quiet as a nun's fart in the Land Rover, till out of nowhere this wan lance jack, Lance Corporal Graham, 'the Scouser', starts blethering on about his time in Northern Ireland, taking a ride in a Warrior through PIRA territory.

'... never felt so close to meeting my maker, like. And so next time out we kept a closer eye out for missiles, made sure we had more than the usual thirty rounds... still, worse here, what with chance of sniper fire at any – '

My stomach goes fae hiccups tae full-on acrobatics.

'Alright, that's enough of yer walting for one day,' the lieutenant in charge of the convoy says, and everyone giggles nervously.

We're headed fur the Maglaj Finger right in the middle of the shit-storm, by the way. The Poachers huv been given orders tae set up observation posts, OPs, tae monitor the supposed cease-fire and ensure all the aid gets through. And tae make sure the warring factions – the BiH (the Muslims) and the HVO (the Croats) – play nicely wi wan another; all the while making sure the nutters fae the Serb Army don't go off like hornets in a sock. Aye, I know I said I'd rather rub my arse wi a brick than get sent out in the thick of it. Wur RSM hud other ideas, but...

And so here I am wi the Poachers, 3 Platoon, several guys in two Warriors – the infantry's fighting vehicles – out in front of the convoy, the rest of the platoon in four-tonners, wan a which is towing the cook set behind, and us lot in a crappy Land Rover. The road is bumpy, which is the second factor huvin a – what's it? laxative – effect on my bowels – if yous remember, I'm nae good on they show rides, and this journey could be mistaken fur a fuckin rollercoaster, right enough.

That is, wan where the terror of being fuckin bushwhacked adds tae the bone-shaking thrill of the ride.

Wish we could wind down the windaes, get some air in; that I could peel off the second skin of sweat between me and my body armour.

I bite my cheek tae take my mind off the sickness cooking up in my stomach.

Hold on. What now? We've been rattling along slowly waiting fur the vehicles in front tae search fur booby traps, but now the convoy comes tae a stop. I look out the windaes, wishing they were bullet-proofed, and fur the first time see the scabs and wounds on the landscape close up. I mean, just think, this used tae be a rich and beautiful country, and now it's filled wi mair craters than a teenager's coupon: pot holes destroying the roads, walls pock-marked wi bullet holes. And, hold up, what's that racket? A group of weans are stood at the roadside, shouting. I crane my neck fur a better look. They seem tae be selling petrol fae auld lemonade bottles and – what's that? – toys and other household stuff.

I nudge the corporal sat next tae us, a long-faced Welsh lad who looks like a fuckin horse. 'Hoy, mate, can I chuck they weans some crisps fae the compo?'

His eyes follow mine towards the kids, who are now waving their hands wildly at the convoy. He turns his heid away. 'Nice thought, but no, sorry – UN orders. Apparently some kids died before, got their legs caught under the wheels of a Saxon as they scrambled for goodies handed out by the infantry.'

I let out a small gasp, then look down, embarrassed.

'We got a rap on the knuckles from the UN for that.' He glances back at the kids. 'Blessed shame though, isn't it?'

But it's too late tae sort them wi some crisps, anyway, 'cause the convoy's started rattling along again.

I think back tae a month ago and the journey fae Split tae Žepče. Three days in the coach fae Croatia tae Bos wi a kamikaze driver, watching as the landscape changed fae holiday-ville tae a fuckin war zone. Still, the view was nothing on this. We've passed one town that was fuck-all but rubble: collapsed buildings, burnt-out cars lining the streets, not even the whisker of a stray dog or cat. Then, in the next village, one house hudnae been touched, gleaming in the sun like a white tooth in a mouthful of rotten pegs. Not that it was occupied, either; in fact, the whole place was fuckin deserted.

But in some towns, like this yin we're passing, folk are still trying to get on wi life... now that's weird. A group of women are stood gossiping a bit further down the road, huddled outside a bombed-out building. Nothing weird about that, yous might think, but they're wearing winter coats and shawls... in this fuckin heat?

'Oy, lieutenant,' I go. 'What's wi they women? They must be cooking up.'

'Think about it – it's cold in the mountains.' I shrug my shoulders and he shoots me a baleful look. 'They have to be prepared to leg it up there and hide – with as many of their possessions as possible – in case of an attack.'

If they were giving out prizes for numtpiness the day, I'd be the winner – no contest.

But the lieutenant doesnae seem tae mind and, anyway, he's distracted 'cause the Land Rover's come tae a sudden halt at an isolated house on the edge of town, not bombed, but deserted-seeming; seems like the lads up front must huv found a suitable building fur the OP.

And now he's in full professional mode, saying, 'Fall out, lads,' and – tae the other chef sent up here with us, CJ – 'Two hands on your fucking weapon.' The lad jumps, grabs his rifle wi both hands, and the lieutenant continues, 'We're looking for booby traps, trip wires, anything dodgy really.'

I jump out the vehicle, my weapon, despite its compactness, heavy at my side, my boots weighing me down an aw. Man, this heat; think it will be in my bones forever. We pair off, my legs jellying as I approach the front door wi the Scouser, sandwiched between two sets of infantry lads. There's a small yard outside, hoaching wi bricks and glass. We pick wur way across it, and the Scouser whispers in my ear, 'House must have been cleansed.'

Cleansed? Ye've got tae be kidding me, I think, as I gingerly tread across the gap where the front door used tae hang. Inside, the stench is unbearable; the walls are mudded wi blood, and the place must huv been used as a toilet. *C'moan, Cal, deep breaths*, I tell masel as my boots crunch heavily on a carpet of broken glass and debris and we edge forward tae take in the rest of the room.

It's a fuckin car crash, so it is.

I bite at my cheek again. Harder this time.

'Oy, Scouse,' I go, minding that I probably sound like a stupit wee fanny. 'Why we staying here? It's a fuckin toilet. I mean, where are we gonnae set up the cook set? It isnae hygienic.'

'See those Warriors out there?'

'Aye.'

'We need enough room for them to manoeuvre outside, as well as at least two evacuation routes.'

I look at him dumbly.

'You know – in case we need to withdraw under fire.'

Under fire? My body tenses but my coupon is a mask of bravery and professionalism as I say, 'Och, aye, of course.'

And then we inch forward slowly. Breathe in, breathe out. Minds on one thing – booby traps. The first room, what must huv been the living room, is a fuckin horror show – stuffing from the sofa bursting out like a scarecrow's... a kid's dolly sitting lonely in one corner… family photos lying shot-up on a battered auld wooden table.

Och, no, this is too much, man!

I swallow as I look at the smiley faces in the photos. A wee boy and girl. A sunny day on the beach. And what's that on the dolly in the corner? A dark stain spreads like a birthmark on its face. Blood. It's only blood, isn't it? I breathe through my mouth trying tae avoid the smell of pish which is stronger here than in the hallway. *C'moan, Cal. Pull yersel thegither!* The Scouser blinks at me. A single blink of encouragement, tae say, *C'mon, you can do it.* I blink back, willing the bad scene tae huv changed in the flick of opening my eyes. Some chance.

But, thank the Lord, we don't find anything dodgy, and soon enough the place is deemed safe wi shouts of:

'Living room clear,' fae the Scouser.

'Bedrooms clear,' fae upstairs.

'Kitchen clear,' the lieutenant shouts. 'Okay, lads, let's get to it!'

And so we get on wi the job of making the place fit tae live in, no fucker speaking apart fae the most basic orders and what huv ye. I try tae put a wall between me and what's gone on. Wish, like yous, I could put the book down, no think about it. Aye. Yous are lucky, right enough. Picking and choosing when ye think about war, spewing yer opinions down the pub, probably some anti-Army folk among ye. I mean, c'moan tae fuck! We're trying tae help these folk. And what's the alternative? Let they Muslims, Serbs and Croats maul the fuck out of wan another like fuckin wildlife? Neighbour against neighbour, friend against friend…

Och, I'm sorry. It's no yous I'm huvin a pop at. It's just… it's just I didnae know how proud I'd feel tae be serving till I come down here.

Anyway. An hour of cleaning, rinsing and clearing passes before me and the other chef, CJ, can head out tae the Bedford and heave in the No. 4 cook set fae the trailer. Equipment that husnae changed much since World War Two, by the way – two gas rings on a trailer, just, steel boxes on top fur ovens. First things first, we need tae get the tea urn going and put on a brew fur the lads. Then I go at unpacking the rations like a mad yin, pulling off my body armour and webbing now that we're safely indoors, my combats and a T-shirt mair suited tae the strangling heat of the day. CJ goes further, pulling off his T-shirt tae reveal the ugliest tattoo I've ever seen in my puff.

I push images of bullet holes and blood intae a different department of my box. I'm thinking instead of canned beef stew, bread and potatoes... of putting on yet another brew fur the lads... of whether we've enough powdered milk tae last...

'Mork calling Orson.' CJ pulls me out of my trance, putting two potatoes on his heid, like antennae.

'Car spanner, doctor,' I go back, getting masel intae gear. He hands us the tin-opener, puts his T-shirt over his mouth like a surgery mask.

Here we go: the banter, the fuckwittery. Surprised it took us this shagging long tae get down tae it. I mean, what else is there tae do but crack on in the face of aw this fuckin carnage?

And so me and CJ get to it: wur main job will be tae cook fur the lads who stay behind, but we'll also huv tae organise the compo fur the mess tins of the Poachers, who'll be away fur a day or two at a time. So, as I unpack the rations, I try and bring tae mind the rules on compo that are drilled intae ye in basic training. They should:

a. Be substantial.
b. Contain popular food.
c. Be satisfying.
d. Be attractively presented.

Aye, right, I think as I get tae the tins of canned meat and loaves of stale bread, *ye'd huv tae be the Great fuckin Soprendo tae manage that little list wi these rations.*

I say this out loud and CJ laughs and slaps his thigh as if it was the funniest thing he'd ever heard anybody say.

Cal

Travelling back tae the Eko Factory after two weeks in the field is no different tae the journey down here. Same scorched houses, same fucked-up landscape, same clenched bum-cheeks in the back of the Land Rover.

I huvnae hud a proper wash in that time neither. I am fuckin humming.

Ah, here we are, at last!

I breathe a sigh of relief as the Land Rover pulls around the final bend towards the base camp, spying the UN flag hanging limply over the gates. The French Army are stagging on, the day, noses in the air, weapons limply at their sides – typical French! We salute them and then the driver revs up, tears across camp tae park, and we jump out the vehicle in a bundle of excitement, stretching wur legs, the first time we've been free and easy wi wur bodies in days.

'Nice one, soft lad. Laters,' the Scouser says, slapping me on the back. Aye, too right! Would yous believe me and him have bezzied up over the last two weeks? That's what sleeping in a maggot bag in a state of constant fear will do fur ye, eh?

I say the required goodbyes and nice to work wi yous, etc. and then head straight tae the SQMS, 1) 'cause I've run out of buckshee and need tae pick up my laundry and 2) tae see if I've any post fae the real world.

Three letters. *Result!* I think, grabbing the envelopes fae the sarge wi a mumbled, 'Cheers, sarn't.'

I look at the senders. Private David Shepherd, one from my ma and one in a girl's handwriting. Could it be...? And mair tae the point, still nae word fae Manny, then?

Anyway. Can read them later. Needs must, first: that is, a shower evidently. Besides, I cannae face mair tales of fuckin raves and dirties or my ma's fuckin mindless shite.

What? Yous think I'm jealous of Davie and the crew back at Fally? The truth is I cannae even think about that world, it's

212

like a fuckin alien planet tae me now, so it is. Anyway. They two weeks in the field huv decided things fur me. Think I'll forget the four mair years of this, of blood, sweat and tears, and try my luck on civvy street; get a job in wan a they hotels up Glasgow town centre. I mean, life has turned out pretty good fur me so far. Why would I think the future'll be anything different? You expect a shit-bomb fae life and that's exactly what it'll lob at you, if yous want my opinion.

I turn this over in my mind as I cross the dusty camp tae the shower block, past grimy mud-slicked vehicles and lads who're no much cleaner themselves, past techie guys bored out their skulls lying in the first sunshine we've hud fur days, past a pair of lads who look shit-faced – the jammy dodgers – probably got hold of some of that 'sleep in the ditch' stuff…

Ah, here we are at last – the shower block. My body's pure screaming out fur a proper wash. And even though the flair of the shower block's swamped wi mud and it stinks way up to high heaven, I cannae ignore the lure of the magical sound of hot running water, of huvin the chance tae get cleansed. I mean, cleaned.

I shudder. *Cleansed.*

And that word flicks a switch in my mind, makes it turn tae a picture of they family snaps and the bloody room, and I'm weighed down like a sack of tatties wi the thought of the family, of us leaving their place this morning as clean and as liveable as possible in case they return. *Oh, aye – return. Who am I kidding?* I scold masel, as I turn down the dial and the water jets down my back in powerful, freezing cold gushes. And would yous believe the iciness isnae unpleasant? In fact, it's – what's it? Exhilarating.

I feel crazy, happy, alive, like I drapt a fuckin tablet, despite the brain-numbing tiredness in my limbs. I slip intae my clean combats, feeling smugger by the minute, and mosey, whistling, obsessed wi catching up on my kip, back across camp. I imagine a pure white room, freshly laundered sheets, the window ajar, white curtains blowing in a light breeze. Och, okay, I know,

I've come over all Laura Ashley. That's sleep deprivation fur ye, eh?

Doesnae take me long tae make it back to wur tin hut – the chefs' accommodation being near the main building. Probably 'cause of aw the fuckin hours we spend in there. I fling masel on the bed and open the bluey fae Davie. Huv a peek at that, and then I'll be in the land of the Big Zeds. My ma and that other letter can wait fur morning.

Pte D. Shepherd
231076453
BFPO 179
30 May 1994

Cal,

Thought I'd better write 'cause things have gone majorly tits-up down here. Manny and Iain are in the Army jail awaiting trial in Colchester. They were caught with a shitload of stuff coming back from Holland. They're not sure whether they're going to get Army or civvy nick yet. I've managed to see Manny once and he's been asking for you. He's not in a good way, mate. Thought you'd want to know. Oh, and another thing which should cheer you up. Kelly's left Iain. Found out about his wandering cock and that was him, dumped. Never rains but it pours, eh?

Anyway. Take it easy, mate. Let us know what's going down with you.

Davie

I don't
I cannae
I can hardly
  Breathe
I am wide, fucking, awake.

Manny

The MO's eyeballing me as if he was inspecting a slick of shit on his boxers. Thinks I'm on the wind-up, don't he? That I'm spinning him a line so that I can spend the rest of my jail time in Germany in the cushiness of the med centre.

I explain again, sitting up on the examination bed.

'Come on, doc, I ain't joking. These headaches have been going on for months, my temples are throbbing. I'm like a fucking Gremlin – can't look at lights. I ain't fucking about.'

He takes off his glasses, blows on them, polishes them with his tie.

'I mean,' I say, my voice lowering, 'I think it might be serious.'

Come on, don't you think, you lot? Could be one of them brain tumours, couldn't it? Or a delayed reaction to all the pills, and the rest that I've done?

But the doc's looking at me with that 'wouldn't wipe my arse with yours' look on his grid again as he pushes some papers around his desk and says, 'Serious, you stupid little toe-rag? You've been getting migraines. Headaches for hypochondriacs, old ladies and sensitive little flowers.'

Oh. Right.

And I haul myself off the examination bed, pulling back on my formal number two dress kit while he writes out a prescription, tells me that I'm gonna have to jump through hoops to get more medication, that I'll have to come and see him each time I need some more pills, 'cause little shit-heads like me can't be trusted not to put an end to our miserable existences.

Then he's like, as he hands over the prescription, looking at me over the top of his glasses, 'Get out of my surgery, you stupid little twat.'

And that minute's breather I had lying on the examination table, the five minutes sat in the waiting room, they was like a smack in the face, a reminder of life without the duty RP breathing down yer fucking neck from dusk till dawn. There he is, grid like a fishwife with PMT, collecting my tablets from the nurse, waiting to escort me back to the jail with a 'Soldier and escort, by the right, quick march!'

I tell ya, they say drugs are bad for you, but since going without I feel more like a bag of tripe than ever. The Ecstasy's not a problem – not that I'd say no if somebody wanged a couple of tablets my way. But the sniff. Fuck. About. Headaches. Cravings. I would literally kill for a line. Okay, so you lot might think that's what got me into this world of shit in the first place, and okay, you might be right. And yeah, I could have considered going straight if things had worked out with Emma or whatever.

But in here – the boredom, the routine, the discipline. They make the longing worse – and then some.

'Alright, Manny. Doc says you can lie down in the cells for a bit. That you need peace and quiet.'

That's the duty RP, his grid screwed up like a crushed paper bag, giving away what he really thinks, i.e. *You jammy little shit*.

BANG! He slams the cell door shut. The cunt.

But, soon after, the medication begins to kick in. It's bliss.

How many of them would I have to do to get into lost-it land, I wonder? And do you know what I'm also wondering? If it was wishful thinking, as it happens. That I've got a tumour eating away at me, I mean. First my muscles and my bones, then my vital organs, then my brain. No less than I deserve, a loser like me. No wonder Emma binned me. Probably she was waiting for some excuse. The Iain thing was perfect. And Amy. Me being in the Army, that made it easy for her, didn't it? And why shouldn't they get rid of me?

I am fucking nothing.

A useless scrote.

A waste of fucking oxygen.

'Manning! Visitor!'

216

Hold up. I raise myself up on one elbow. It's Davie. He enters the room, his mouth half-grinning, half-grimacing as he extends his hand. My fingers are floppy as I shake it under the watchful eyes of the lads on guard duty.

'Ten minutes, max!' one of them says.

Davie raises his hand in a half-arsed thumbs-up, then turns to me. 'Easy, guy.'

'Alright, mate,' I say. But I don't get up. Just stay like I was, raised on my elbow, laid out on one side.

'So, uh,' he says, 'how are you?' Nervous laugh. 'I mean, in spite of – um – everything,' he adds quickly.

'Yeah, yeah, alright, geez,' I say, yawning as if to indicate how fucking relaxed I am.

Davie yawns and all; tugs on his lower lip. 'So, I told Emma what's happened like you asked. You heard from her?'

'Nah, mate.'

'Mum and dad?'

'Ditto. Wrote to them finally but not a peep.'

Neither of us can seem to think of anything to say then – the sound of the lads in the prisoners' area next door drifting in for a while, me lying down with my eyes shut – till Davie breaks the silence, pushes me to say something, to tell him what's what with the trial and that.

'Well,' I say, after a pause, 'the lawyer reckons the head bean-counters won't want to pay for our bed and board for Army nick. She's gonna try for dishonourable discharge and civvy jail. Worst she reckons is a short time in the Army nick down Colly while we wait for the court martial.'

'Small mercies,' he says, biting at his fingernail. 'Small mercies.'

Too right, I think. I've heard about Colchester – 'Colly'. Beastings from the minute you wake up. No TV or radio unless you've been a good boy. Give me a fucking civvies' nick any day – telly, no beastings or PT, no cleaning your own cell.

'Iain,' Davie's asking me, after I've chuntered on about that for a bit. 'How you two getting on?'

So I tell him about that little head-fuck and all. That Iain's banging on about being grassed up, otherwise how else did the RMP know when and where to come get him? Tell Davie that, now he comes to mention it, Iain's doing my nut; that I think I'm gonna lose it big time if I'm banged up with him for a long stretch.

I open my heart up to Davie, basically.

But not quite. Don't tell him something else on my mind. Something the doctor said. *Put an end to my existence.*

And I'm sort of, like, how easy would that be? I mean, what fucker would fucking give a fuck, if I put an end to things? World would be better off without me, wouldn't it? Oh, come on, you lot, you've thought I was a yob from the offset, don't give it the 'no need to go that far, life is precious' and all that.

So I think, if I did do it, how could I get it done?

Hang myself with my belt? Nah – knowing my luck it wouldn't work and I'd be left dangling there like a twat. Do a Kurt Cobain and get hold of one of the guns from the guardroom? No way, too messy! Try and stock up on the tablets? Take as many of them as poss. No again. Same as method one – too much chance of failing. Failing, ha! Least there's one thing I'm good at...

'Oy, Manny, mate, we ain't got long. Come on, mate, talk to me,' Davie says, practically eyeball to eyeball with me now.

But I close my eyes, and realise that the migraine's wearing off as I think of my options, only to reject them one by one. Poison. No, couldn't get hold of it. Slitting my throat. Gassing myself. Jumping off a fucking cliff.

No! No! No!

And then there's a stomp of boots in the corridor, a rattle at the door, and Davie's like, 'Gotta go, mate.'

And I think, *Thank fuck, 'cause I've got nothing left to say.*

So I go, 'Thanks for visiting.' Then, just as he's at the door, but still in earshot, I repeat, 'Honest: thanks for coming.'

Pause. 'But I ain't being funny, man... not much point in you visiting again.'

'What – really?'

I nod quickly, as that prick corporal shows him out the cell. 'Be off to Colly in a few days, anyway.'

And Davie turns back, looking well confused, as he says simply, 'Well, okay, if that's what you want, of course. No dramas.'

Probably he'd be one of the first to celebrate if I was out of the way. No doubt them lot think the Monkeys are gonna get out of me who else is into the dirties in the regiment. Fuck about! Might as well give them a list of who *isn't* into the dirties.

Well, apart from the one guy. The one who pretends to be into them, but isn't. 'Cause even though it kills me to say it, Iain's probably right. That we was grassed up, that is.

Who, though? Well, Jonesy, obviously. But somehow it don't add up. I mean, did he know we were going to the Dam that day? And anyway, one person has it in for Iain for sure. Cal...

Oh, come on, Manny, have a word with yourself! Stuck in by your best mate? Not likely!

I bang my fist against the cell wall in frustration and think of my options again. Or option, more like.

Oh really, the voices sneer, *go on, then, like to see you try.*

They're right, of course. Topping myself's not gonna happen, is it? Haven't got the guts to do it, have I? I'm that much of a pointless urine stain on life that I couldn't even organise my own... suicide.

There, I've said it.

I curl up on the pit, pulling the blanket back over me, rolling the word over my tongue for a bit, and it's weirdly soothing, like ice cream. And so I send myself to sleep as the migraine fades completely with a one-word lullaby: suicide, suicide, suicide, suicide, suicide, suicide, suicide, suicide, suicide, suicide, suicide, suicide, suicide, suicide...

Cal

The ice cream van stands on the grassy island in the middle of the scheme. *No Ball Games Here.* The children smile as they play, dressed in bright shorts and sunny T-shirts. A dog cocks its leg and pisses up a lamppost. Teenagers mooch about, thinking they look the biz in their '80s Sergio Tacchini.

I'm observing the scene fae a distance, watching the kids pile out of every block, rushing the ice cream van in a rainbow of movement; the song of the van haunting the concrete walls of the scheme, kids and grown-ups alike both craning their necks tae listen in.

My auntie Edie's stood on the grass in an evening gown, tapping her foot along tae the music fae the van – the musical score tae her favourite film. What's it again? *Silk Stockings*, that's it. Happy feelings wash over me at the memory, till the spell of the song is broken when the giant Mr Whippy on top of the van lights up. It twists and turns in time tae the music, drawing the children like moths. Then, all of a sudden, the driver appears at the windae, wearing a white chef's hat, his face brightly made-up. He waves slowly, wi menace. What's he? Looks like… um… cannae put my finger on it. I know! He's wan a they… aye, wan a they ventriloquist's dummies, but evil, like a baddie in a horror film…

And the kids, they've turned. They're no laughing and smiling now. They're fuckin street rats, chucking stones at the van. Aiming fur the driver. No fur the lance jack. The driver's a lance jack now in his regimental gear! And the glorious Technicolor of the song is being swamped wi drab Army olive green.

'Sno a ice cream van. It's a fuckin four-tonner!

The lance jack's in wan a they recruitment vans, trying to get the kids fae the scheme tae join up. I try and run towards it – tae warn they kids no tae give their lives away tae the Army, that it's not all about abseiling and kayaking and fuckin adventure sports like they recruitment films make out – but my legs are zombied tae the spot...

... then, somehow, in a flash I'm there, in front of the van, tearing at the Army issue webbing which now smothers it. I want tae get at that fucking hauf-screw tae tear at his fuckin...

... I'm standing behind the hot plates. The recruitment/ ice cream van driver is next in line, his face illuminated by the lights of the counter. He's holding out his plate.

Please, sir, can I have some more?

In the brightness I can see his face clearly now. It's Iain. It's only fuckin Iain. I plate him up the scoff fae the metal trays, each wan containing a different kiddie's toy. Plastic Action Men and Barbies in wan, their limbs broken and twisted; baby dollies in another, decapitated.

Iain reaches out fur two Barbies. I smack him across the knuckles wi my spatula.

Only wan. Naughty, naughty.

Then, suddenly Steffi's beside me, naked, and she's grinning, saying, *Do you want sauce with that?*

And we all three look down at once intae the vat of sauce, as if we were puppets on a string, controlled by the same hand. It's dark and red and reminds me of something. A feeling, just. If I could only put my finger on it...

Iain's looking at me, horrified.

It ain't sauce, mate. It's blood. I glance down again and there in the heated steel display are two children, their little bodies shot tae bits. I open my mouth tae...

'Huunnng!'

I cry out, the hauf-scream escaping fae way back in my imagination and I bolt up, wide awake now, in a pond of sweat. I kick wildly at my sheets... watch them fly through the air... land on the flair.

Rudie's mattress squeaks as he groans and turns over, his snores breaking up the silence of the room. I whip the sheets back up tae the bottom bunk, panting, wiping the dregs of the nightmare fae my coupon and my back wi wan a them.

Deep breath in, deep breath out, and I leap tae look under the bed, hauf expecting that driver tae be hiding under there. Iain tae be hiding under there, that is, desperate to gie me a doing.

And I now recognise that the feeling that has been haunting my dreams, that has been gnawing at me night and day, that the black, dark feeling biting intae my heart was the Devil playing his tricks, persuading me I was right tae do what I done.

The Devil has lost now though 'cause I can see clearly things fur what they are; I can't sugar-coat it any mair.

It wasnae right, wasnae justified.

I done it out of anger. Betrayal. Hurt.

It was – I gulp, make the sign of the cross – a sin.

I fiddle wi my rosary beads, cursing the Devil's wiles, kicking masel for not visiting the padre tae be reunited wi the Lord of the Church before we come out here.

And yet... and yet there's the weeniest germ inside me, wondering, even if I hud've gone tae confession, would I feel – what's it? Liberated.

Bee bee bee beep.

Och, c'moan, man, no way! The alarm. 5.55 a.m.

Rudie's cheesy feet soon dangle fae the top bunk and I sit brooding as he gets dressed on automatic pilot.

'Come on, chum,' he says, jumping down fae the bunk, while I continue tae nestle in bed in my boxers, 'five minutes to get to the cookhouse as per usual.'

I turn over on my pit, slowly, like a pig on a spit, and as I come face to face wi my locker I spy the other letters I received yesterday. I pick up the wan fae my ma first. Get that wan over with and then treat masel wi...

Could write my ma's letter masel, mind you... I tear open the blue envelope wi her distinct spider scrawl on it... aye, right enough. *Missing you, son, blar blar blar. Proud of you, son. Blar blar blar.* But what's this? *Yer auntie Edie isn't well.* I scan forward tae the end of the letter. *The doctors are giving her no moor than a few months.*

Fuckin what? That's me. Done.

I tumble off my pit, somehow dragging on some trousers and a T-shirt and I run, all I want tae do is run...

'Oy, oy!' Rudie shouts as I stumble past him. 'Wait up!' but I'm out the door, dragging my heels across camp.

God. Ha! The Army. Ha! Family. Ha!

Auntie Edie – the way she's looked after me. She's the wan who brung me up. No that fuckin alky. She's the wan who tried tae talk me out of it when that recruitment van come on the scheme; the wan who signed my permission letter when I joined up. The wan who waved me off when I headed down on the train fur Aldershot tae start the fuckin training.

And I run until I'm just outside the padre's tent. Only then something weird happens. A sudden thought. A strange and sudden question that asks, *What use is the Lord of the Church when your world's falling apart? What, in fact, does God huv tae do wi any of this, at all?*

Chapter Ten

Manny

What the fuck? Endless explosions barge in on the killer quiet of another night in the cells. Three months I've been here now. Three months of cleaning duties, kit inspections and breaking wind just to pass the time. I crick my neck to try and sneak a peek beyond the bars, knocked for six as another colourful cluster of fireworks breaks out.

Look at us, they're boasting, laying it on thick as a sprinkling of diamonds showers over the rooftops, *see what you're missing on the outside*.

Someone's having a right old knees-up: bonfire night ain't for a while, surely? Reminds me of that time at the fireworks display down the Alster with Emma. Could have been any of the times we spent together, to be fair – her trying to sweet-talk me into 'going straight', me going straight as a Curly Wurly.

Fucked that one right up, didn't I?

Lost the chance to get with a diamond bird who cared about me, even if she was out to improve me, change me, get me to wear hair gel – the usual female bollocks.

Didn't care that much though, eh, readers?

Still no word from her, no visits, no phone calls. Jack shit, in fact.

Course, I could get the ball rolling, write and tell her how I'm sick as a parrot about what I done, tell her she was right all along about the coke being a leech on life. Bog-all difference it would make to me now, though, banged up in the fucking Army nick for about the longest stretch any cunt's ever heard of, awaiting trial. Yeah, too right. Write to Emma, have her come visit – what would that achieve?

Sweet FA, that's what.

Remember that our lawyer said we'd only be at the Army nick for a week or so? Sorry, not nick, 'Military Correction and Training Centre'. How wrong could she have been? Got to wait here six months before our case even gets to court martial. The brass's way of punishing us by delaying it, keeping us in Colly for as long as they're allowed. Turns out the CO wants to make an example of us before this new policy for compulsory drug testing, 'CDT', comes into play in the spring. Show the other lads that there's no place for drugs in the Army. Yeah, right. And there's no place for Pauline Fowler in *EastEnders*.

Anyway, looks like a long sentence in civvy nick, even after we spend months banged up in here. Six years, the lawyer reckons now. I was sick to my fucking stomach when she told me.

A sickness which has only got worse in the months we've been here. I turn over on my pit, putting my hands to my ears as more explosions sound in the distance.

Anyway, I was right about Colly being a nightmare, if you lot want to know the truth; even from day one we knew we was in for six months of being cunted about. Me and Iain was flown over to Brize Norton, handed over to the staff from Colly and flung like old rubbish in the back of a van. Felt like we was sat in that effing van for days, driving to the arse end of everywhere to pick up other detainees; noses pressed to the windows till we got shouted down by the driver to 'Keep still and look straight ahead, you revolting little shit-bags.'

Then we had to use our ears, listen out for clues where we was, or clock the occasional reminder out the window by chance that, yes, we was back in Blighty: Radio One blasting from a car stereo at a traffic lights; the flash of orange of a Sainsbury's sign when we was stuck in a jam during rush hour. I had to jump out for a slash in a petrol station at one point. Sight of them Ginsters, the Sunday papers, Walkers Crisps. Don't know about Iain, but these markers that we was back in the UK nearly did for me.

Close, they was leering at me, *but no cigar, matey. You ain't going home any time soon. And just think, you're only down the road from yer mum's place*, they jeered, as we drove into Essex.

Iain and me were the only ones to be handcuffed, being as we were 'the worst offenders and most likely to abscond', so the platoon sergeant escorting us said. Most of the other detainees were headed into A Company for a few days or weeks – lads who'd gone off the rails or AWOL and would get a short, sharp shock in the nick before heading back to their units. Some lads in the van had even heard that it would be a bonus to spend time here; that it could help them get promoted faster when returned to their units.

Not for the likes of me and Iain.

We was headed here, for D Company, lumped in with the serious offenders: the thieves, the wife-beaters, the pervs. Told right away that we couldn't mix with the A Company lads, that even though there's no ranks in the Glasshouse we were shit on the shoes of the others. 'Druggies', 'no-marks', we was labelled right from the start. 'Make no mistake,' we was told, 'you're in for it now, lads.'

The first night weren't as bad as expected, for all that. We was made to sit in this huge reception area, knackered from the journey, antsy 'cause we didn't know what to expect, 'cause no brass will tell you what's gonna happen in Colly; your expectations are based on hype and rumours from previous Soldiers Under Sentence – SUS for short.

Looked like it was gonna be okay at the start. Right away they brought us a brew and sandwiches, let us make a phone call to say we'd arrived. One or two of us found something interesting to look at on the floor at that point, no fucker on the outside being interested in *our* weasel words. Then, one by one, the other lads were interviewed at the work station, handing over their medical papers, personal references and other paperwork from their units.

Me and Iain was kept shitting it till last. I went after him, my hands trembling as I handed over my papers to the platoon sergeant, his grid patchy red like ink on a blotter. And then it was a shocker, 'cause he was like, 'You need to be psychologically assessed. It might be C Block for you, mate. C Block,' he added with a fangy grin, 'being where they send the really evil little shits and the pansies at risk of suicide.'

So I was sort of like thinking, *Fuck about!* But then I remembered the pissy-faced welfare officer back at Fally who'd wheedled my darkest thoughts out of me in my exit interview.

As it turned out I wasn't a fully blown fruit loop – not then anyway – and I was beasted to the Med Centre the next day to be passed fit for detention in D Block. Then, what do you know? The 'rehabilitation' began: 7 a.m. starts in nearby woods. Tripping over our feet, doing a daily mile-and-a-half run, each of us weighed down by an artillery shell on our shoulders. Who'd've thought I'd ever be thankful to Sergeant Blake? Remember him? It's sort of like I owe him for being the evillest cunt I ever come across, 'cause now there's not much they can do that fazes me.

Do you lot also remember that thing I told ya? 'Skive to survive', from the basic training? It don't work in here. Here you learn to keep pushing it, to work like a Trojan, so you can improve your basic fitness. Otherwise they get back at you with niggly little punishments: fag breaks taken away, last in the line for scoff, that sort of twisted bollocks.

Talking of twisted, I ain't seen much of that scum-bag, drug-pushing, girlfriend-stealing arse-wipe Iain. He's forever exercising in the yard or in the gym, flexing his muscles in front of the other detainees. Getting all pumped up for when he gets out, no doubt, for all them ladies he's gonna bang. The ladies loves an ex-con. Or so I've heard him saying to his new hangers-on. The tool. And when we do see each other face to face, we dance around one another as if we was doing the opposite of some sort of mating ritual – not sure which of us wants to break the face of the other more. Thank fuck I'm in a different dorm to him, or who knows what would happen.

In the distance, the firework display climaxes in a crescendo of machine gun fire. What I wouldn't give for a gun. *Rat-a-tat-tat*, three rounds in Iain, leaving enough ammo to finish myself off, of course. Yeah, that thought, suicide, it's with me like a second skin now. '*Bock*,' Steffi used to call it, a sort of lust for life, I suppose. My *Bock* is slowly but surely fizzling out like a Catherine wheel.

Embarrassing, ain't it? A twenty-one-year-old bloke with all to play for, crying for his teddy and for his future. Suppose I could contact the welfare officer, talk it through. What's that expression? *A problem shared is a problem halved.*

Like fuck it is.

Glasgow

Cal

Coming 'home'. It's a major disappointment, if yous want tae know the truth. Like going back tae a favourite film and finding out it wasnae as good as you remembered. *Caddyshack*, fur instance. Only tae be rediscovered wi a lungful of skunk.

Och, I know, it must sound bad and wrong tae be thinking of such matters when it's my auntie Edie's funeral, the day (aye, she passed away last week) but, well, if the Army teaches you anything it's tae deal wi the hate bombs life chucks at ye wi a sense of humour. Probably why I'm dealing wi it so much better than my cousins Malcy and Gordon.

Mind you, the brass would claim the Army teaches ye mair than that. *If you've got it in you, we'll bring it out,* wan a they

228

Army training videos went. Aye, right. Sick gallows humour, drinking ten pints of lager without boaking, cracking wan off in a ten-man dorm unnoticed: that's what they bring out of yer typical squaddie.

But seriously. What about Manny and me? What did they bring out of us? I don't know. Me personally, I think mibbe it's done me good. My time in Bos, I don't know, mibbe it's tellt me what I'm capable of. Capable of? Huh! I shiver as I think what else I've discovered I'm capable of… and I hauf-heartedly make the sign of the Cross. Breathe out. Try and reason wi masel tae move on.

As fur Manny, the Army brung something out of him, that's fur definite. His self-destruct button, I mean.

I've wrote tae him, of course. Tellt him how sorry I was what happened wi Iain, and tae gie me a heids-up when he's wanting a visit. I mean, it wouldnae be me tae let him fester down there, let him worry that no fucker was thinking of him. But since Bos, and my auntie Edie, well, there just husnae been the time.

I lock my fingers thegither in a bridge, fling my arms over my heid, lie back on my pit and stare at the ceiling, thinking; hoping the poor fucker's bezzied up wi somebody, that mibbe his parents huv paid him a visit.

Rat-a-tat-tat!

Hang on. Somebody's at the door.

'Cal, my darlin', will you be wanting any breakfast? We've got tae leave in a hauf-hour.'

My ma. Clucking after me like a mother hen. Wes're both staying here wi my uncle Bob till after the funeral. After her letter – that one I received in Bos – I was returned tae my unit, then when Edie died that was me – on compassionate leave. I never made it back in time fur the 'death-bed' scene. A fuckin car crash, so my cousins tellt me. My ma plus too much emotion plus a bottle of whisky equals a cluster fuck of epic – what's it? Proportions.

'Cal!'

'Aye, I'll be down in five minutes,' I go, lying my heid off. A snail's got mair chance of making it down the stairs in five minutes. My body's fucked, so it is, every last burst of energy pure eaten up by the stresses of the last three months. I mean, since I've arrived, it's all I can do tae make it tae breakfast in the morning, never mind talking to my family. Or what's left of it.

Me and this bedroom ceiling huv got tae know each other pretty well the last few days. In fact, I've got tae know every line, every crack, every bit of chipped paint. I'm also bezzie pals wi my auntie Edie's flowery wallpaper. I squint, reach out and touch the wall. I swear all they tablets down the years have fucked up my eyesight. Ah, there it's. A darker patch of brown where I flung a cup of tea at the wall after another dead-end conversation wi my mother last night, after the vigil. Wanted tae confront her about the drinking, but of course the only drinking we talked about was huvin another brew: avoiding the subject, sitting glued tae late-night telly – typical fuckin family, sweeping wur problems under the carpet.

'Cal!'

There she is again, my ma, her muffled voice rising above the sound of some daytime TV show up the stairs.

I burrow further under the duvet.

'Callum Brodie Wilson! The funeral cars have arrived early. We've got tae go, son.'

The *In Paradisum* sounds out as we lift the coffin, marking the end of the funeral Mass: time tae take the body tae the grave. I'm holding my breath as the others form a procession behind the coffin; the faces of me and the other pallbearers sweaty, grey and grave; the pace of wur steps at odds wi the banging tempo of my heart; my mouth staying tight shut until we reach the great open double doors of the church when I can finally – *foooooooo* – blow out some air through pursed lips.

A few steps intae the churchyard and we stand stock still again fur a minute but, hang on… urgh… what's happening?

I mean, we're just stood here but it's as if I'm still moving... hands shaking... eyelids twitching; as if the Earth has turned up the speed of its axis, and everything's dizzying and flying about me. I stumble over the thoughts whizzing through my brain, try tae recognise the emotion.

What am I? Sad? Aye, greetin like a wean in there, so I was. But, no, that's not it.

Jealous of my ma fussing over my cousins? Nope. Not likely.

The priest comes out, offers his consolations tae my cousins, puts his hand on my shoulder. I flinch and the red mist descends.

Aye, that's it.

I'm angry: beelin over wi anger, so I am.

That fuckin garbage spewing out the priest's mouth at the vigil yesterday and just now at the Mass. Nothing about my auntie Edie. How she took me in when I was a wean. Looked after her fuckin baw-bag of a husband wi his gammy leg. How she put up wi her fuckin alky sister (that's my mother, in case yous huvnae been paying attention). Nothing about how she loved country music, was obsessed wi Dolly Parton, put a pound aside every week so she could visit that Dollywood. I snort back a sneer of disgust. Nothing about *her*, in fact. Nope. Instead we heard what a good Catholic she'd been, that she'd been baptised, not 'fallen out of favour with the Church'. Add tae this the fuckin endless stream of patter about the resurrection of Christ and aw they Hail Marys...

C'moan tae fuck! Show her some respect, I think. Could have spoken about her life! No some guy who's been deid fur two thousand years.

C'moan Cal, concentrate, I think; cannae get het-up about that now, 'cause we've started marching again. And it takes a humungous effort and I'm crunching my feet slowly... slowly... wan after the other... down the gravel path... try tae pick up my right foot... Earth's gravity pulling me down... air round about me thick and heavy, and I –

No way, man! Think I blanked out fur a sec.

I tug at the tie squeezing at my neck. Steady the arms holding up the casket.

'Cal, c'moan,' Malcy, my aulder cousin says, taking me by the arm, directing me towards the cemetery fur the burial.

And I look him in the eye, whisper, 'How can you no say something?'

He's like, 'What? Say what?'

'Wasn't bloody Jesus who fuckin died, it was my auntie! Your mother.'

And he hisses, 'Fur fuck's sake. Not here, not now,' and, louder, 'C'moan, not much further.'

'Aye, c'moan son, pull yersel thegither,' my mother says, reaching out fur my arm, unsteady on her feet.

The whisky off her breath could fuel a fuckin bonfire.

And the sight of her face, the smell of her breath, they words fae the priest – they're doing my fuckin brain in.

I beckon over wan a my uncles.

'Gonnae – ' I falter. 'Gonnae help us out? Cannae breathe,' I say, and he gives me evils as he takes my place at the back of the casket.

I fall back behind the others, pull at my tie again. That's no better! I pull it right off and sink ontae the flower beds, crushing a row of perfect orange – what are they? Chrysanthemums? And by the time I've steadied masel back up, my mother's swaggering towards us… no… lunging towards us.

Slap! She wallops me on my left cheek.

'You cannae behave like that at yer auntie's funeral.'

The cheek, the fuckin cheek!

'You… you… fuckin hypocrite,' I yell as I sook up the rancid smell of her whisky breath. And as I feel the whole lot of them's eyes on me, I turn around and say the first thing I can think of. 'Yous… yous… are all fuckin hypocrites.'

Which doesnae even make any sense but at the same time there is a sense in me, a sense of something – what's it? Relief? Aye, relief, as I realise it's not only my auntie Edie who's deid and was buried the day, but that my family ties are broke fur once and fur all – that even... aye, that even my love fur God, that's over an aw.

A crowd of rubberneckers gather while a row starts up between my cousins and my mother. My mother lashing out, the priest's arms going round like a windmill as he reaches out tae try and keep the peace; nae fucker looking at me, nae fucker bothered how I am, so I leg it down the drive, my legs and feet light and carefree, flying me out the big gates of the church; the driver of the hearse's jaw smacking the flair as I turn around and stick two fingers up back at my family... running down the hill... tearing off my suit jaiket... the lights of Glasgow twinkling below us – the city of my birth that should be a close friend and feels mair like a distant relation.

But who cares? Who cares if this isnae haim? 'Cause I'm suddenly aware that there's a family waiting fur me back in Fally, on they dance flairs across north Germany, the lads in the cookhouse... mibbe something even better if I play my cards right... and as the tears roll down my face I know that's what my auntie Edie would have wanted – fur me tae take a fair crack at my Army career, tae be 'the best I can'. Tae be me; that's tae say, tae to be 'Happy'.

'The Glasshouse', Colchester – D Company

Manny

Six p.m. No sooner have we downed our diggers than the staff and platoon sergeants whip off their berets. *Time to take it easier, lads*, they're saying, *even we can't keep up the cunting British bulldog act all day long*.

Could have fooled me.

Hold up: one of them, the patchy-faced Jock who did my entry interview, is coming over, holding something in his fleshy, liver-spotted hands. There you go again – another reminder that booze in the Army gets a big tick, while drugs score a big fat zero. He's probably got my migraine tablets. I have to apply for them in advance, and they'll only give me one at a time; write down in a little book when I take them so that I can't build up a decent supply for you know what.

'Got that pen and paper you applied for,' he says, waving it in my direction.

It's only taken about two weeks. The cunts.

'Go on, mate, fill yer boots, you've an hour of free time,' he goes, smiling as if he's handed me a winning coupon for the Pools.

Big wows, I'm thinking.

But I say, 'Cheers, staff,' as I stuff the loot in my pocket, 'cause I'm trying to build up my recommends, so that they go a bit easier on me, for reasons you'll find out soon enough.

Now I've been here a bit, I spend less time cooped up in a cell. The dorms are unlocked at 7 a.m. and we're not locked up again till 5.15. Later, in the evening, we get another hour of unlock, where we're free to do whatever. Well, depending on what level you're at in their fucked-up staging system, that is.

For a stage one lad like me the endless free time is filled with radio, pointless banter with other stage one lads, trips to the library for a day-old newspaper. Sure to be followed by an argument with the librarian that all the papers have gone to the stage two and three lads, as per usual. To get to stage two you need three recommends for your kit or fitness from the platoon sergeant. At this level, as well as level three, you step up to the hot plates first, and you get to watch telly and play games and that in the rec room. Anyway. Who cares about free time? There ain't that much of it; most of the day we're worked like dogs – getting our kits ready for inspection, doing PT or on cleaning duties.

Oh, and you lot won't guess who's managed to smarm his way to stage two? Yeah, only Iain. Even though we done the same crime, waiting for the same trial, for some reason his face seems to fit around here. Probably something to with his makeover as Rocky Balboa, a shagging fitness freak, I mean.

Thank fuck he has, though, 'cause stage two lads get smaller four-man dorms and I won't have to cosy up with him. In fact, almost tempted to be a bad boy, so they fling me down C Block, and I won't have to clock his cuntish grid at all.

Almost tempted, that is – don't want to scupper my plans.

I skulk back to the cell, hoping the other lads will be making the most of the free time outdoors or in the library or wherever.

Result! Empty.

There's one shabby chair at the shared writing desk in the middle of the room, and I perch on it, looking dead ahead at the bleached green wall, gripping the biro which feels weird and unfamiliar in my hand. I jab at my palm absent-mindedly with its nib, dark thoughts rushing like heavy water through my box – it's impossible to think clearly and get stuff down. Maybe the radio would help? A nice background noise to soothe me along. I stick it on. *The Sunday Chart Show.*

Wicked. Not.

Yet another reminder of what I'm missing. Nights back home when my mum and dad and I used to bounce around the room to Blondie and the like on a Sunday afternoon. I'm trying to write a letter to them, as it happens.

How do I get it across, though?

Will they even give a fuck?

Not like we've even spoken since – what was it? July? After they didn't write back to me I tried calling them one day. After a few – you know, a bit of chit chat – that was it: they made it clear they've sent me to Coventry. Bet Dad was stood behind Mum, though, hurrying her along. It'll be that old bastard stirring things up. I've thought of calling my aunt instead, get to Mum through her. You know, the one that works in a bookshop, 'cause she's a hippy and is all peace and love, love and peace. That kind of bollocks. Sure, she'd probably forgive, might even help get Mum on side. But it's too late for that now.

The heavy synth of Olive, 'You're Not Alone', blares out the radio, disrupting my train of thought.

That's a fucking laugh, the pen mocks me. *You of all people – course you're alone. Such a loser that you don't even fit in with this bunch of fucking misfits.*

I lash out at the radio in anger, and I'm sort of like gob-smacked as it tips off the edge of the table, lunging for the floor. I make an embarrassing leap, flying through the air to catch it. Result! I just manage to snatch it before it hits the floor, and snap the button to 'off'. Last thing I need is to get done for breaking it.

That tune always fucking pissed me off. In fact, I hate every fucking tune I can think of now. Don't miss my music. Don't miss my drugs no more, neither. Yeah, I know I've not mentioned them for a long while.

But I'm dead to the heartache I had when I was coming off the coke. Dead to the heartache I had over Emma, to the same I had over Amy. It's as if someone's put a brick in that place where you're meant to feel stuff, leaded my feelings to nothing. And would you believe it: now all that's sorted in my bonce, my headaches have gone?

What's that? You lot don't believe I've had it with the drugs? Well, believe. I wasn't even tempted when some prick told me you can get hold of the dirties if you manage to sneak over to A Company. Apparently them lot are allowed into town weekends, and the brass are a bit lax on the old searches when they come back on camp. I couldn't care less. I've had it with the old dirty rugs. Hate them, in fact.

Yeah, you've got me bang to rights, I hate everything. I'm bubbling over with hate now, as it goes.

I hate that spider scurrying across the writing desk. I hate this fucking leaky pen. I hate a world where the accident of where you're born gets you started down a crappy or a good road in life… and don't get me started on the Army. Wish I could boil the whole fucking lot in acid; dissolve it into oblivion.

But it's not just things I'm dead against. Did I also mention that I hate you?

Yeah, you.

I hate you for your freedom, for your life out there, however crappy it may be. Don't worry, though, mate – not like I hate you especially. I hate everyone. I hate the cunts who get up to do the nine-to-five, the loadsamoney twats who suck the corporate cock, the family men with their trophy wives. I hate everyone from John Major to the next lad who kisses Emma. I hate Cal.

No, no, no, the voices say, *even you're not that dead from the neck up to see that, if anything, Cal was the one lad who tried to help you.*

Tried to help me? Yeah, right! Tried to stick me in, more like. Now I'm sure it's him: he's the reason me and Iain got caught so easy. He's threatening to visit but I mean what's the point? Even if he didn't grass us up, why would he want to visit a loser like me?

'Cause, yeah, I think, rabid with hatred now, letting out a babyish sob, *most of all, I hate my fucking self.*

'Ughhhhhhhhhhh.' I wail as I take my pen, gouging into my arm with its knife-like point, going at the surface till the skin unzips, ripping away at years of stupidity and wrong choices and not fulfilling my potential and blue ink and flecks of red blood collect in a puddle of viciousness and hatred and everything that's wrong with the fucking world, and I'm seeing red again: the red of Blakey and the training, the red of that prossie, the red that reminds me that I'm an out-and-out colossal loser.

'The Glasshouse', Colchester – C Block

Manny

The walls are having a right laugh at my expense today.

Look at you, they're smirking, *fucked it up for yourself big-time, haven't ya?*

Pick on someone yer own size, I feel like saying, till I realise they're the biggest thing in here, hulking over the room in giant slabs of grim, grey slate. And, to be fair, there's naff-all else for them to take the piss out of. The only other things in the room are a mattress, the bog and a blanket for bedtimes. A special kind of blanket, it is, one that can't be ripped up, 'cause the brass have got it in their boxes that I'm a kamikaze prisoner after a few of them pen incidents went down. Lucky they haven't found the letter yet, or I'd be up to my grid in excrement. Makes me wonder if they'll find it when the time comes.

That time ain't now.

On special observation in an unfurnished cell, I am, checked every fifteen minutes. Like that time I had a hernia operation when I was a teenager – doctors and nurses pestering you with medicines and taking your temperature, driving you up the wall. Only, in hospital you get to watch telly, you're pitied, looked after, wrapped in cotton wool.

Here you're wrapped in shagging barbed wire.

This special suit I have to wear when I'm locked up in the cell is like a hospital gown and all. Strip clothing, they call it, made out of the same fabric as the blanket. Cold as a witch's tit in here at night. But still they won't let me have no more blankets or clothing.

And what's all this about? you lot are wondering. Well, I can't be trusted with myself, apparently; they reckon I might do myself an injury.

The walls have a right good laugh at that one.

I reckon Cal would come down just as hard on me.

'How did ye end up in here, ye great tube,' he'd go. 'I always tellt ye the coke would do fur ye.'

The platoon sergeant's footsteps tell me he's approaching for the second – or is it third? – fifteen-minute check of the evening. What would I know? I've been dead to the world these last three nights, as soon as my head hits the mattress. In any case, I give a thumbs-up when I sense he's right outside with his eyeball on the spy hole and then I flop back down on my pit.

238

As a boy, my mum used to tuck me up at night, and my dad would come in for a last kiss, right up to when I left home for the Army, would you lot believe? 'Such a good sleeper, he was, as a baby,' Mum would tell her friends, after she'd had a few. 'Such a good boy,' she'd chunter on. Then to me, 'Pour us another drink, will you, love?'

'Look at him now,' my dad, half-pissed on Southern Comfort, would then pipe up, 'fucking yob, who can't get off his backside to get a job.'

What's that poem? Something about your Mum and Dad fucking you up?

Yeah, them, the Army, mates. They fuck you up.

Oh, they do, do they? And you don't lay any of the blame at your own door, then?

Them walls again, having a good old sneer.

Funny that, 'cause lately I'm wondering if I've laid it on a bit thick about Iain being to blame. I mean. I've never made the right choices in life, have I? Fucked up that chance to become a joiner on the YTS. Bigged myself up thinking I could be the A-levels type instead, so I hardly never even turned up for it – thought I could retake my maths CSE and go to college. Course I never did. After that I fully embraced my dad's label for me, 'daft cunt'. Didn't make any effort on the Army entry test, thinking I'd sail through it, I was such an arrogant little shit.

And what about the choices I've made in my private life? Biggest mistake I ever made, choosing Iain over a future with Emma. If only I'd have told him where to get off, me and her would be together now, have some long, skinny red-haired baby, after we'd enjoyed each other for a few years.

Yeah, you can jog on with them thoughts, the walls jeer.

Yeah, too right, she'd have only binned me anyway eventually…

Besides them kind of 'should've, could've' thoughts, the dead space in my brain is well clogged up with random shit now. 'Cause night-times here there's nothing but the walls and the blackness and the night to keep you going. The thing is, it's not silent. Not by a long chalk. I clap my hands over my ears to shut out the slow, rhythmic drip of time passing and snatches of rave tunes getting louder by the minute. Here we go again.

Drip, drip, drip. *Feel the melody that's in the air.* Drip, drip, drip. *I need your lovin'.* Drip, drip, drip. *Like the sunshine.* Drip, drip, drip. *Just close your eyes and dream with me.* Drip, drip, drip. *You'll hear the sound of music.* Drip, drip, drip. *This is hell below, you're all gonna go.*

This is hell below, you're all gonna go. That's more like it.

Anyway. Remember I told you lot early on that I'd rather die than give up my raving? Don't think my legs could last five minutes now. They're permanently lazy, sleepy, heavy. It's like I've got a cramp in my bones, deadening my senses and my energy. Yeah, too right, you lot, my body's a fucking wreck now, as it goes. I look like a bag of shite untied in the middle; ain't ever been so skinny, even when I was bang into the sniff. Can't stomach the food they're serving up here. I complained to the CO about it, but if anything it's been worse since then – greasy, undercooked, none of it fresh. The staff even gave me a daddy talk about it before sending me down here, to C Block.

'Just trying to understand,' he was saying. 'There must be some explanation why you've become a food-refuser and a self-harmer.'

As if he cares.

And I was like, 'Fuck about, sarge,' not minding my 'p's and 'q's, being as I'm already in seven degrees of shit, 'it ain't that I'm on hunger strike or some bollocks, I just ain't eating that slop. End of.'

Still, last time I saw myself in a mirror, I was well freaked out. My arms were the spit of a road map – B-roads of veins and scratches joining up at the wrists and elbows; the deepest cut of all sticking out like the shagging M1 tearing up the middle. My skin's spotty and greasy and all. Probably 'cause of the lack of fresh fruit and veg, like I mentioned.

Hmm, no hot dates for you this Christmas, then, the walls butt in.

Cheers for that. Like I need reminding of all them cunts out there, living life to the full as the holidays approach. Mince pies and jumpers, mulled wine and fairies on the tree. All them little extras you get at Christmas: the sneaky kisses, the pigging out, the glitter.

That bollocks flies in the face of life on the inside.

In here, it's the opposite of Christmas, 'cause your life is scraped away to nothing. I mean, it's sort of like you're boiled down to what's inside you, or what's left of what's inside you.

In my case, fuck all.

Drip drip drip. *Let's spread our wings.*

Fuck about, them noises again!

Drip drip drip. *And fly away.*

Yeah, I'm stripped away to nothing now. Just the drip of memories and tunes filling my box – the very least of being human.

Might as well be a slab of grey slate.

I jump up all of a sudden from my pit, taking the night and the walls aback.

'Come on, then, you lot!' I'm shouting at the top of my lungs. 'Try and find something funny to say about that!'

And as the stomp of boots and rattle of keys come down the corridor, I notice that, for once, the walls don't answer back.

Fallingbostel British Army Base

Cal

I'm standing next in line tae Jonesy, ready fur the chefs' parade in the cookhouse. Shoulders brace, heels come thegither as in walks Sergeant Clarke. Aye, Sergeant, no Corporal. Would yous believe the bastard's been promoted? And so the parade wi the RSM in tow...

Still the same nit-picking arse-wipe, Clarkey though. Here he comes. Stalking down the line like a hunter after his prey –

241

eyes narrowed, hands like talons, ready tae pounce. Och, no, he's stopped in front of us.

'Morning, Jock. Good to have you back,' he beams.

I jump back in amazement.

Don't think I've ever seen Clarkey smile. 'Sno a pretty sight. I mean, ye wouldnae huv tae be a dentist tae see that his teeth are smeggin rotten.

And so I fluster a 'Morning, um, sergeant,' as he continues down the line, leaping on the new boy, Ratty, scunnering over each item of his kit one by one: his hat's crooked; his apron's got a speck of dirt on it. It isnae, and it doesnae, as far as I can see. But still I can't help watching in amusement as Ratty's face becomes a pressure cooker, pure busting tae explode. And still Clarkey keeps on at him, till he finds the chink in his kitchen armour – the hands.

He always gets them wi the hands.

'Have you scrubbed those?' Clarkey turns the terrified lad's palms over as if they were a pair of freshly laid turds.

'Well, sergeant,' newbie stammers, 'I, uh, I uh, yes – '

'And the nails? Have you cleaned under your fingernails?'

A look of fear darkens Ratty's coupon and the rest of us in the line purse wur lips as we try not tae snigger.

'No. Um. Sarn't. NO, SERGEANT,' he yells loudly, as if volume is his best line of defence.

'SINK NOW, HOT WATER AND ANTI-BAC, YOU REVOLTING SOAP-DODGER,' Clarkey retaliates wi enough force tae near blow the young lad's chef's hat off.

The line breaks down intae chaos as the lad scurries off fur the sinks.

'And what're you lot doing standing around gawping? Get to fucking work!'

And tae think I could be out of this – be out of the discipline, the slaggings and the routine. But no, I chose to sign up for another four, didn't I?

What was the alternative? Stay at my auntie Edie's place wi my ma and my uncle and cousins fighting like cats and dogs?

Och, yous are right, I could huv mibbe made a go of things on civvy *strasse*, but it's no like I didnae consider my options.

After the funeral I stayed in a hotel for a couple of days, deciding my future. Even went up the Job Centre in Argyle Street in Glasgow centre one afternoon. Hung out in the queue wi the schembos in caps and minging trainers, wi the single mothers and their mucky-faced bairns. Got as far as chatting wi the woman behind the desk, a baw-faced auld witch stinking of fags who tellt me, aye, there would be plenty of work fur me labouring, or cheffing in auld folks' homes; that I could even start work right away without my P45 if I signed this special form. And that was me decided. 'No, thanks, missus,' I said. I mean, form-filling, aw that real-life stuff. Why would I do that when I could sign up fur another four years?

'Cause in a way – and I know this'll sound mental as fuck – Army life's easy when yous think about it. No stresses of bills and forms and what huv ye, BAOR allowance making me richer than most cunts I know back haim. I mean, ye've just got tae keep yer heid down, put up wi the mental scars and the bullying.

And if ye can do that, well, ye've a job fur life.

Besides, there was something else pulling me back here. Or should I say someone else?

Ow! Hold on. Jonesy's dead-armed me. 'Come on, then, Happy, chop chop... get to the... chopping.' Then, as he makes sure I see the stripe on the silver rank slide on his beret, 'See what I did there?'

Aye, another promotion in the cookhouse, would yous believe? 'Cause he kissed the brown ring after his tour in Bos, Jonesy was put forward fur the JNCO Cadre course. And he only shagging passed wi flying colours, didn't he?

The thing is, I'm no being funny, but me and the others – Davie, Tommo an that – huv another idea as tae why he was promoted. I mean, it was obvious the little ginger grass was gonnae rise up the ranks after what he done.

Oh, aye, yous don't know. I've been that distracted wi the funeral an that, that I never let on. What he done, I mean. Well, it was obvious tae the rest of us that Iain and Manny were stuck in, that it must've been someone fae wur crew who done it. A few nights of serious drinking and talking after I got back fae Bos and me, Davie, and Tommo finally put two and two thegither and come up wi Jonesy.

I mean, that we guessed it was likely Jonesy who hud a word wi wur RSM, tellt them about Iain and Manny. Way we see it, he probably suggested that if the CO was wanting tae catch out the lads who'd been dealing on camp, how come they'd no searched the pad houses – that, in particular, how come they'd no searched the house of a certain lance jack? Then mibbe they'd find what they were looking fur. Fur the drugs, I mean.

What? Yous… yous never?

Yous thought it was me?

C'moan tae fuck!

Hang on a sec, what's Ratty up tae? He's going off like a frog in a sock, so he is – ripping off his chef's hat, stomping on it on the flair.

I walk over, say calmly, peering over his work space, 'Cool the beans, man, what's up?'

His coupon flushes scarlet. 'I've fucked up the pan, let it boil dry.'

Now, what's he up tae? Taking a water bottle, shaking it over the baked beans, the side dish fur the morning fry-up.

'What ye doing, ye nutter?' I ask, grabbing the saucepan handle.

Now his face is a picture of pure exasperation, and he's like, 'You told me to cool the beans.'

The numpty.

'Cool the beans, chill out, calm down – it's an expression!'

Lucky he sees the funny side, and together we sort out the mess.

Huv been helping young Ratty a fair bit since returning fae Glesga, in fact. He's just got that kind of face crying out tae be looked after – looks about twelve, so he does. In fact, it's this attitude, a 'can-do positive' attitude, Clarkey calls it, that has hud me put forward fur the lance corporal course an aw. I know, can yous believe it? Me? Mr happy-go-shagging-lucky wi a stripe in his sights.

But back tae mair important things.

Tae Iain and Manny and them ending up in the jail – yous've got it all wrong.

I mean, I can see why, 'cause I tellt yous I was in bits over Iain, but I never shopped him tae the Monkeys if that's what yous were thinking. Mind I tellt yous way back at the beginning – I'm no what ye'd call educated, but I'm no exactly stupit neither. Aye, it crossed my mind, that one way tae get him back would be tae stick him in tae the RMP. But I knew they Monkeys' eyes would be everywhere afterwards; knew that there was as much chance of Manny giving up the sniff as me giving up Irn Bru – so he'd've been caught out at the same time as Iain.

So no, my act of revenge hud a mair personal edge. Well. It was when Iain started slagging Steffi after he went wi her, tellt everyone that she was a 'groundsheet', an 'easy-lay'; that she was putting it about all over camp. First he fucks her, then he fucks her over? That was me, pure aching tae burst his face, tae get revenge. So I decided on the tube train that day that I'd stick Iain in tae somebody.

But no the RSM.

No, it was Kelly.

It was Kelly I went tae see before I left fur Bos. Tellt her how Iain couldnae keep his cock in his trousers; about the tarts, the one-night stands… the drugs. But when I found out she'd left him, I was gob-smacked. I mean, I thought she loved him tae pieces. Hud tae ask forgiveness fae the Lord of the Church if it was a sin… hud tae ask masel if I'd done right.

But I've put all that guilt behind me now. Now that I'm over the Church… and now that I know Kelly's gonnae be okay. On the way tae see her after work, as it goes. She couldnae stay at her and Iain's bit on camp, of course, but she's found a wee place in Fally so she can carry on wi her job at the gift shop – she's been allowed tae do that at least. I've been around there a few times recently. Aye, yous've got me. Me and her… something's happening between us… something, ye know, romantic.

Remember how it was wi Steffi? Being in love wi her was like huvin a bee buzzing around that I couldnae swat away. Or, tae put it another way, it was like my heid was in a contest wi my heart, but the heid was losing 'cause the heart was a fuckin bully, playing tricks on me, telling me that even if Steffi was cool, even if she didnae seem keen – that she'd come around in the end.

But now, it's different: it's like something special has grown between me and Kel, that we both discovered how bad Steffi and Iain hud made us feel, and how we'd become slaves tae they feelings. 'It's the ones that make you feel good, not bad, that you should be with,' is the way Kelly puts it.

And she does make me feel good. Buys me wee pressies – a Wispa or a copy of *Mixmag* or whatever. Just tae show me that she was thinking of me. And I make her feel good an aw. She's putting on weight, looks better than ever. Can yous believe stressing over Iain was making her waste away?

'Oy, Happy! Have you even started on them veg?'

Och, here he comes, Clarkey, his coupon puckering in random annoyance. Some things never change, eh? Best get on wi it in case he keeps me back late. Off out in Hamburg, the night, so we are. What? First yous think I'm a grass, now yous think I've gone straight, knocked the raving on the heid? No way! Thought yous would know me by now. Hardcore till I die. Or at least till they bring in CDT in the spring…

What's that? No. That's it. Clarkey's about tae burst my backside. Besides, yous must be sick of my voice – that's enough about me.

Postscript

Colchester
14th October 1994

Dear mum and dad

If you get this, it means I've done 'it'. They havent' made it easy for me though. Hopefully you'll forgive me. I mean. I've done a lot of really shitty things that have upset you in the past. 1. Being born a boy. I know you always wanted a girl. 2. Not getting in the grammar school. 3. Joining up. 4. Getting nicked, of course. Still, at least this latest FUCK UP will be the last one.

It's a shame you didn't come down to visit me here. Don't worry. Not blameing you. I mean it would have been nice to say goodbye though. Talking of which make sure you say goodbye to nana for me. The old dear. Who'd have thought she'd last longer than me?!!!!

I guess I owe you some kind of explination being as your the ones that brought me into the world. It's hard to say but I'll try. I owe you that much I guess. For ages now I've felt I like I'm looking over a cliff and below there is nothing. Blackness and nothingness. And it's like even though there's nothing I want to step over the edge. Do you see what I mean? I mean it's like with the trial coming up, wev'e no chance of being let off.

Life is a pain in the arse really when you think about. Most of all it's unfair. Like where you was born and all that makes a difference to how the whole rest of it turns out. Again. Not blameing you. Just saying. I suppose it's bad luck. Mainly.

I've got to be quick so only a couple more things.

Since I don't beleive in anything out there afterwards this is easy for me. So don't worry.

For the same reason. No funeral or grave or nothing like that.

I don't know how I'm going to do it yet cause you never know whether they're going to C Block me or D Block me or what have you. That's why I'm writing this now in case I get in one of my black moods and they don't want me to have a pen or even a toothbrush. Anyway. I guess they'll tell you what happened. Whatever I done I hope it was quick.

Got to go. Don't be angry.

Manny

Acknowledgements

A couple of books proved very useful for background information: *Picking up the Brass* by 'Eddy Nugent', a very funny look at basic training in the British Army in the 1980s; and Les Howard's *Winter Warriors*, a fascinating account of his tour of duty in Bosnia during the winter of 1995–96. I am also hugely grateful to Les for answering my further questions with such patience and in such great detail.

I owe huge thanks to several others who helped me colour in detail about life in the military in the 1990s. On technical and procedural maters regarding the 'cookhouse' I very much appreciate the input of 'Duty Cook' aka Mark, and Rex Shafee. I am also enormously indebted to Jude Williams, who so entertainingly told me about his life in the British Army in the 1990s, and who did not seem to get bored answering my endless questions on the subject.

Further help came from DJ Marc Riley for kindly confirming when the phrase 'it's all gone Pete Tong' came into existence, although Marc does not credit himself with coining it. Big up as well to Sound of Eden and DJ Nookie who gave permission to use lyrics in the novel from their massive rave tunes from the 1990s.

The Book of Glasgow Patter was a great source of inspiration for the Glasgow slang included in this book, as were my mother (Irene McKinnon), my aunty, uncle and cousin (George, Marion and Emma Wilson), as well as my late grandad (Bill McKinnon).

Massive and particular thanks to Vicky Blunden and Candida Lacey and all at Myriad Editions for their enthusiasm, guidance and insights. Also to Linda McQueen for her eagle-eyed copy-editing skills and support, and to Dawn Sackett for spot-on proofreading. The excellent cover was designed by Ed Bettison, for which I'd also like to say thank you.

I was very grateful to those who read early drafts and encouraged me to keep going: Debbie James, Dan Bouquet, Daniel Whiston, Ben Bristow, my mother again, and, last but not least, my husband Roly Allen without whose support, love and tremendous patience this book could not have been written.

AFTERWORD :

ABOUT THE BOOK :

How did you begin writing the book?
In its first incarnation the book was a series of letters, as I thought this would be an appropriate form to evoke the era just before the proliferation of mobile phones, email and the like. After a while, I came to find that form too limiting and decided that Cal and Manny's voices might work better as two narratives side by side. But I did keep one or two of those original letters in the novel, thinking it would be interesting for any twenty-something readers to take a peek into a world without the instant communication methods they now take for granted.

What encouraged you along the way?
Simply put, I just felt this was a story that had to be told, so I was determined to finish telling it. After completing the second draft I entered it into the Myriad West Dean Writing Competition and was over the moon when it was shortlisted. This gave me the confidence to finish my third and final draft, and was also the novel's route to publication.

How did you develop your characters?
I felt I had got into Cal and Manny's heads fairly soon after I started writing them. It's a cliché, but then the characters seemed to take on a life of their own: it was easy from that point on to know how they'd react in any situations I threw at them.

How did you find writing two male voices as your lead characters?
It was liberating to write as men, as I could be completely removed from the realm of my own experience. Although I find the term a bit sexist, I've always been a bit of a tomboy, anyway – getting my knees dirty climbing trees as a child, drinking cider in the park with my male school friends... and later on, during the time the novel is set, I suppose I would have been called a 'ladette'. In short, channelling my inner male was really not difficult. I did find myself pulled up by my husband on certain, shall we say, anatomical issues, though, so I'm grateful for his help on that!

Did you know how the novel would end when you began it?
Manny's fate was always set in stone; in fact the final letter in the book was part of the epistolary first draft of the novel. Cal was to have a different fate originally, but as I went on it just didn't seem fitting for the hero of the book. So in the end 'Happy' got the ending that I felt he deserved.

How important was research to the writing of the book?
Hugely! I wanted to do the characters justice by getting my facts straight about life in the British Army in the early 1990s, so I interviewed soldiers who served at that time, read a few useful books and regularly visited the Army social networking site, ARRSE. That said, my main aim was to tell an engaging story, so I wouldn't claim *4 a.m.* as some sort of historical document; it's safe to say I cherry-picked the information from those sources which I felt would add most to the story.

Did you visit the locations you were writing about?
The book is triggered by events I witnessed at first hand when living in Hamburg in the early '90s, at the time the book is set. It was such an eventful year that I had snapshots in my mind of all the locations mentioned there. Les Howard's brilliant *Winter Warriors*, an account of his time in an infantry battalion in Bosnia, provided inspiration for the locations of Cal's tour in the Balkans. The base at Fallingbostel is a real place, although I've never been there; the Fallingbostel of the book is a creation based on a mixture of research and my experience of similar bases.

What did you enjoy most about revisiting the 1990s in the novel?
I had mixed feelings about revisiting the '90s – thinking back to a time when I had so few responsibilities brought more than the occasional nostalgic tear to the eye – but on the other hand I enjoyed reliving the newness and excitement of the music and drugs of those times. I do worry that 21st-century youth culture is caught up in a vortex of homogeneity and derivativeness. Of course the latest cultural revolution might be happening 'underground' right now – possibly literally, in a sweaty cavernous club. I do hope so, but I don't get out enough to know!

253

In what ways did you draw on your own experiences?
Without the experience of having raved with friends from the British Army based in Germany in the early '90s, the book could not have been written. Having said that, the action of the plot and the emotional journey of the characters are pure fiction.

Are any of the characters based on people you have known?
Some of the events in the book are loosely based on real life, but the actual characterisation of each protagonist is an amalgam of traits of different people I've known, with a healthy dose of imagination and invention thrown in.

Did you have concerns about fictionalising real people?
Yes, massively. That's why I tried hard to maintain a certain detachment from the people who inspired the story. Cal's character does have certain things in common with an old friend of mine, but I hope this would be taken as a compliment since Cal is (to my mind, at least) the book's hero, and is certainly intended to be the most sympathetic character in it.

Which of your characters did you most enjoy writing?
Cal and Iain were the most fun to write. Dreaming up Iain's next dodgy move or nasty little trick gave me a kick. As for Cal, I guess with my being Scottish but having lived in England for most of my life, it gave me the chance to feel close to my Scottish heritage. Glasgow slang is a language all of its own, and as a languages graduate I enjoyed 'translating' Cal's speech into Glaswegian, as well as recalling the slang and funny phrases used by my uncle and my late grandad in my childhood.

Do you think the novel is political?
I did have political motivations in writing the book, yes. In terms of the politics of British fiction, if there is such a thing, I wanted to represent characters whose lives don't often make it above the cacophony of middle-class voices so prevalent on the bookshelves nowadays. In that sense I hope the book has a social conscience beating away at its core. It's also interesting, and very depressing, to see a parallel between the youth unemployment which saw Cal and Manny join the Army in the late '80s, and the huge rise in youth unemployment right now.

What about drugs? Did the novel intend to make any political comment on those?

I'd say the novel definitely argues throughout that there are double standards, in the Army, in the government and from the establishment in general, towards recreational drugs and alcohol. Manny points out the hypocrisy of an Army that seems to encourage squaddies to drown themselves in vodka or wifebeater, but which comes down like a ton of bricks on recreational drugs. It was my intention to illustrate the destructive effects of alcohol, while at the same time showing that Ecstasy can be a force for good. I believe MDMA should be legalised, and consider it infinitely less socially and physically harmful than alcohol or tobacco.

Did any object, visual image, or piece of music inspire you as you wrote?

The classic rave track '4 a.m.' by Orca was the soundtrack (in my mind only – I write in silence!) when writing the book, as well as tunes by Sound of Eden, Nookie and Baby D. But '4 a.m.' is the most significant, as the mood and lyrics of the track are central to the sense of transition I tried to evoke in the story. And of course it also gave me the book's title.

Is there a moral of the story?

My aim was to present, through Manny and Cal, two very different outlooks on life. Through Manny I wanted to evoke the sense that there is a kind of self-fulfilling prophecy to being a pessimist, while 'glass half-full' folk like Cal do often seem to come good. The moral being: try to stay positive and you will more easily negotiate the bumpy path of life. Unfortunately, as a doom-and-gloom merchant who spends much of my life pissing and moaning, I have more in common with Manny than I'd care to admit...

A WRITING LIFE:

When do you write?
Boringly for the author of a book about all night-raves, I'm a 9-to-5 person; I just don't have the stamina for midnight oil and whisky/coffee sessions long into the night.

Where do you write?
Brighton Jubilee Library provides a quiet, studious environment when I find myself losing focus. Otherwise I write at home at whichever free tabletop I can find.

Why do you write?
A desire to create characters who I don't think make much of an appearance in contemporary fiction, as well as a compulsion to tell a good story, and finally with the hare-brained fantasy of some day making a living from doing what I love best.

How do you start?
Tea-drinking, internet-surfing, out-of-window-staring, then panicking and finally getting into gear.

Do you have any writing rituals?
Not really, but I have got into a bit of a habit with the above.

Who or what inspires you?
Interesting people whom I've met in my life, and for this book the soldiers I spoke to as part of my research. Also, my favourite writers: mainly those from the 1940s and '50s British 'bleak chic' period: Patrick Hamilton, Julian Maclaren-Ross, James Curtis, as well as contemporary Scottish writers: Louise Welsh in particular is a brilliant storyteller.

What do you read if you need a prompt?
Anything and everything. I think reading is as important as the actual writing of a book itself.

Do you revise and edit your work as you go?
Probably too much. I can't bring myself to 'just get stuff down' as all the writing manuals advise.

What single thing would improve your writing life?
Huge wads of cash to pay for childcare.

What distracts you from writing?
It's more the case that writing distracts me from everything else.

Are you working on a new novel?
Trying to… it's not coming as easily as *4 a.m.* My aim is to write a story set over a short time-frame with a strong female lead. Thematically there will be some things in common with *4 a.m* – lost souls, drugs and misspent youth – but the voice, narrative style and structure will be completely different.

What novel do you wish you'd written?
For its perfect reasons why and why not to write, Knut Hamsun's early modernist classic *Hunger*. Why to write: the book's forensic investigation into the mind of an impoverished writer is a masterclass in interior monologue. Why not to write: in a cautionary tale for all wannabe authors, Hamsun's autobiographical writer becomes so destitute that he is forced to eat wood shavings and chew his own buttons.

What tips would you give aspiring writers?
I don't think there is a magic formula, but the usual tips of reading your own material aloud, getting 'readers' to provide feedback, entering competitions and reading widely are all very useful. I'd also advise learning to listen to the self-critic who sits nagging on your shoulder. Unless of course they are telling you everything you do is crap. In which case, tell them to shove off, because my final tip would be to keep going, no matter what.

MORE FROM MYRIAD EDITIONS

When Julia Rosenthal
returns to the suburban estate
of her childhood, the unspoken
tensions that permeated her
seemingly conventional family
life come flooding back. Trying
to make sense of the secrets
and half-truths, she is forced to
question how she has raised
her own daughter – with an
openness and honesty that
Susanna has just rejected in a
very public betrayal of trust.
Meanwhile her brother, Max, is
happy to forge an alternative path
through life, leaving the
past undisturbed.

But in a different place and
time, another woman struggles
to tell the story of her early years
in wartime Germany, gradually
revealing the secrets she has
carried through the century,
until past and present collide
with unexpected and
haunting results.

ISBN: 978-0-9565599-6-8

'Isabel Ashdown's storytelling
skills are formidable;
her human insights
highly perceptive.'
Mail on Sunday

It's more than twenty years
since Sarah Ribbons last set
foot inside her old high school,
a crumbling Victorian-built
comprehensive on the south
coast of England. Now, as she
prepares for her school reunion,
39-year-old Sarah has to
face up to the truth of
what really happened back
in the summer of 1986.

In her eagerly anticipated
second novel, *Mail on Sunday*
Novel Competition winner
Isabel Ashdown explores
the treacherous territory of
adolescent friendships, and
traces across the decades
the repercussions of a
dangerous relationship.

ISBN: 978-0-9562515-5-8

MORE FROM MYRIAD EDITIONS

'The most surprising fact about this story of identity is that it is a début novel. Brimming with lush descriptions of the colour, tastes and sounds of Brazil, this is a satisfying and engaging story about the reality of one man's childhood memories. A fantastic read.'
Leicester Mercury

'Full of surprises, crackling with energy, and with characters bristling with life.'
Kathryn Heyman

'*Invisibles* is so well plotted and put together that it has almost no signs of this being a first time effort, and looks more like the work of a highly experienced writer. For the ultimate reading of this book, turn up the central heating, pour yourself a 'caipirinha' and put on some background samba music.'
The Bookbag

SELECTED FOR AMAZON'S RISING STARS

'Haynes's powerful account of domestic violence is disquieting, yet unsensationalist. This is a gripping book on a topic which can never be highlighted enough.'
Guardian

'A very impressive first novel. The pain and frustration of OCD is brilliantly evoked and I winced every time Cathy embarked on yet another ritual. The contrast between Cathy's two lives is cleverly draw. This is a fantastic personal read with plenty for a reading group to discuss.'
NewBooks Magazine

'A tense and thought-provoking début novel with dark moments. Its portrayal of obsession will send a shiver down your spine and you'll hope that you are never in that position.'
Shotsmag

ISBN: 978-0-9565599-1-3

ISBN: 978-0-9562515-7-2

MORE FROM MYRIAD EDITIONS

**WINNER OF THE AUTHORS'
CLUB BEST FIRST NOVEL
AWARD AND SHORTLISTED
FOR THE GREEN
CARNATION PRIZE**

'Fast-moving and
sharply written.'
Guardian

'There is a deceptively relaxed
quality to Kemp's writing that is
disarming, bewitching and, to be
honest, more than a little sexy.'
Polari Magazine

'London itself, in its relentless
indifference, is as powerful a
presence here as the three gay men
whose lives it absorbs.'
Times Literary Supplement

'Drawing inspiration from the life
and work of Oscar Wilde, just as
Michael Cunningham's *The Hours*
drew from Virginia Woolf,
London Triptych is a touching
and engrossing read.'
Attitude

ISBN: 978-0-9562515-3-4

'An intense study of grief and
mental disintegration, a lexical
celebration and a psychological
conundrum. Royle explores loss
and alienation perceptively
and inventively.'
Guardian

'An experimental and studied
look at mourning. Playful, clever
and perceptive.'
Big Issue

'Royle's meandering prose –
which seems at once anarchic
and meticulously arranged – is
appropriate to the subject matter:
the disarray and isolation a man
experiences when his father
dies. There are moments of
delightfully eccentric humour
and impressive linguistic
experimentalism.' *Observer*

'Nicholas Royle's first novel
is a story of loss and love. He
captures the absolute dislocating
strangeness of bereavement.'
New Statesman

ISBN: 978-0-9562515-4-1

MORE FROM MYRIAD EDITIONS

**SELECTED FOR
WATERSTONE'S
NEW VOICES**

'This reads like an author on
their fourth or fifth book
rather than their début novel.
The prose is masterly, the
characters are fully drawn.'
Savidge Reads

'Every single page is full to
bursting. Yet every single word
earns its place. The whole novel
is breathtaking in its scope and
originality. This is a multi-layered
read. Thoroughly recommended.'
The Bookbag

'Hillyer's meticulous research
and gift for atmosphere brings
London and its rich history to
life; his handling of Brippoki's
hallucinogenic episodes is skilfully
done and his use of Dreaming is
sensitive and understated.
The result is a charming, unusual
and poignant book.'
All About Cricket

ISBN: 978-0-9562515-0-3

**SHORTLISTED FOR THE
WRITERS' GUILD AWARD FOR
BEST FICTION BOOK**

'A beautiful début about a son
trying to break free from his father.'
Financial Times

'Lyrical, warm and moving,
this impressive début
is reminiscent of Laurie Lee.'
Meera Syal

'Passages in this novel made me
laugh out loud and others were
extremely moving. I silently gave
three cheers for Ellis when I reached
the end of this book. A poetic,
moving and evocative read.'
The Bookbag

'A warm coming-of-age story that
tackles family relationships, secrets,
belonging and self-acceptance.'
Coventry Telegraph

'A very fine, funny and
moving read.'
David Baddiel

ISBN: 978-0-9562515-2-7

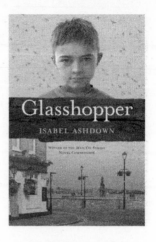

'Imagine Brighton in chaos. Communities are divided – socially, economically and physically. The council is all-powerful, inconvenient people are "dealt with", children are controlled and tolls strangle the transport system. Dickinson creates a world that only vaguely resembles our own. This intriguing story brings the issues of political influence, red tape and corruption to the fore – if only by making us relieved that it seems improbable it could come to this.'
Liverpool Daily Post

'As a satire, it works well, and is completely believable as a "nightmare present" scenario.'
The Bookbag

'I was pleased to find myself rapidly becoming engrossed in the strange world which Robert Dickinson has created.'
A Common Reader

ISBN: 978-0-9562515-1-0

SHORTLISTED FOR THE WAVERTON GOOD READ AWARD

'Tender and subtle, it explores difficult issues in deceptively easy prose. Across the decades, Ashdown tiptoes carefully through explosive family secrets. This is a wonderful début – intelligent, understated and sensitive.'
Observer

'An intelligent, beautifully observed coming-of-age story, packed with vivid characters and inch-perfect dialogue.'
Mail on Sunday

'A disturbing, thought-provoking tale of family dysfunction that guarantees laughter at the uncomfortable familiarity of it all.'
London Evening Standard

'An immaculately written novel with plenty of dark family secrets and gentle wit within. Recommended for book groups.'
Waterstone's Books Quarterly

ISBN: 978-0-9549309-7-4

**DRAMATISED FOR RADIO 4
WOMAN'S HOUR**

**WINNER OF THE PEOPLE'S
BOOK PRIZE FOR FICTION**

'*The Cloths of Heaven* is a wry,
dust-dry, character-observation-
rich gem of a book with one of
the most refreshing comic voices
I've read for a long while.
This book is a bright, witty
companion – values and attitudes in
the right place – acute,
observant but also tolerant and
understanding and not afraid
of a sharp jibe or two.'
Vulpes Libris

'Lesley Thomson is a class above,
and *A Kind of Vanishing*
is a novel to treasure.'
Ian Rankin

'Thomson skilfully evokes
the era and the slow-moving
quality of childhood summers,
suggesting the menace lurking just
beyond the vision of her young
protagonists. A study of memory
and guilt with several twists.'
Guardian

'Graham Greene with a bit of
Alexander McCall Smith thrown in.
Very readable, very humorous –
a charming first novel.'
Radio 5 Live

'This emotionally charged thriller
grips from the first paragraph,
and a nail-biting level of suspense
is maintained throughout.'
She

'Populated by a cast of
miscreants and misfits, this début
novel by playwright Eckstein is
a darkly comic delight.'
Choice

'A thoughtful, well-observed
story about families and
relationships and what happens
to both when a tragedy occurs.
It reminded me of
Kate Atkinson.'
Scott Pack

'Fabulous... fictional gold.'
Argus

ISBN: 978-0-9549309-8-1

ISBN: 978-0-9565599-3-7

'Imaginative, clever and darkly claustrophobic.'
The Big Issue

'An exquisitely crafted début novel set in a post-apocalyptic landscape. I'm rationing myself to five pages per day in order to make it last.'
Guardian Unlimited

'Martine McDonagh writes with a cool, clear confidence about a world brought to its knees. Her protagonist is utterly believable, as are her observations of the sodden landscape she finds herself inhabiting. This book certainly got under my skin – if you like your books dark and more than a little disturbing, this is one for you.'
Mick Jackson

'This is a troubling, beautifully composed novel, rich in its brevity and complex in the psychological portrait it paints.'
Booksquawk

This celebration of Brighton and Brightonians – resident, itinerant and visiting – is a feast of words and pictures specially commissioned from established artists and emerging talents.

'I loved writing a piece with crazy wonderful Brighton as the theme... a great mix of energy and ideas.'
Jeanette Winterson

'Give a man a fish and you'll feed him for a day. Give him *The Brighton Book* and you will feed him for a lifetime.'
Argus

Contributors: Melissa Benn, Louis de Bernières, Piers Gough, Roy Greenslade, Bonnie Greer, Lee Harwood, Mick Jackson, Lenny Kaye, Nigella Lawson, Martine McDonagh, Boris Mikhailov, Woodrow Phoenix, John Riddy, Meg Rosoff, Miranda Sawyer, Posy Simmonds, Ali Smith, Catherine Smith, Diana Souhami, Lesley Thomson, Jeanette Winterson

ISBN: 978-0-9549309-2-9

ISBN: 978-0-9549309-0-5